## SPOTTING A SPY

Finn crept up behind her, then, without warning, pinned her to the ground with one arm twisted behind her back. The girl did not shriek out, as Finn had expected, but struggled to be free. Finn had to press her face firmly into the dust, her knees clamped hard into the girl's side.

"What do ye think ye're doing, spying on us like that?" she hissed in the girl's ear.

"I be an outrider," the girl panted.

"An outrider for whom?"

The girl said nothing. Finn dragged her to her feet and began to force her down the slope towards the camp, keeping her arm twisted up her back. The girl moved abruptly and Finn found herself sailing over her shoulder, landing with a thump in the grass. Then she was on her feet, throwing herself at the girl. Finn was surprised to find herself well-matched and exerted herself more fiercely.

Finn threw her to the ground and pinned her there with the girl's head locked within her elbow.

The girl gave a breathless whistle. Finn heard the thunder of hooves and then the bay was rearing over them, his black mane tossing. . . .

# The
# Forbidden Land

### Book Four of *The Witches of Eileanan*

---

# KATE FORSYTH

A ROC BOOK

ROC
Published by New American Library, a division of
Penguin Putnam Inc., 375 Hudson Street,
New York, New York 10014, U.S.A.
Penguin Books Ltd, 80 Strand,
London WC2R 0RL, England
Penguin Books Australia Ltd, 250 Camberwell Road,
Camberwell, Victoria 3124, Australia
Penguin Books Canada Ltd, 10 Alcorn Avenue,
Toronto, Ontario, Canada M4V 3B2
Penguin Books (N.Z.) Ltd, 182–190 Wairau Road,
Auckland 10, New Zealand

Penguin Books Ltd, Registered Offices:
Harmondsworth, Middlesex, England

Published by Roc, an imprint of New American Library,
a division of Penguin Putnam Inc. Previously published in
an Arrow Book edition by Random House
Australia Pty Ltd.

First Roc Printing, May 2001
10  9  8  7  6  5  4

Cover art by Judy York
Cover design by Ray Lundgren

![ROC] REGISTERED TRADEMARK—MARCA REGISTRADA

Printed in the United States of America

*for Binny and Nick—*
blood-kin and soul-kin
in memory of all the imaginary worlds
we created and lived in,
and with thanks for a lifetime of
love and support.
Write on!

*She can overcast the night and cloud the moon,*
*and make the Devil obedient to her croon.*
*At midnight hours over the kirkyard she raves,*
*Digging unchristened weans out of their graves;*
*Boils up their livers in a warlock's pow,*
*Runs widdershins about the hemlocks low;*
*And seven times does her prayers backwards pray.*
*Then, mixed with venom of black toads and snakes,*
*Of this unsousy pictures oft she makes*
*Of anyone she hates—and makes them expire*
*With cruel and racking pains afore a fire:*
*Stuck full of pins the devilish pictures melt;*
*The pain by folk they represent is felt*
*Whilst she and her cat sit howling in her yard.*

—Allan Ramsay,
      Seventeenth-century Scottish poet

# THE LOOM
# IS STRUNG

# CASTLE RURACH

Finn brushed away the crust of snow and sat in the embrasure of the battlement, her legs hanging out. Carefully she packed her pipe with tobacco and, shielding the sparks from the wind with her hand, lit it with her flint. With a sigh of pleasure, she drew in a lungful of sharp-scented smoke. For a long moment she held it in her lungs, then breathed it out in a long plume that was dragged away by the frosty breeze.

She inhaled again, leant back her head and puffed out a series of perfect blue smoke-rings. As far as she could see there was no sign of life, only the sharp spears of snow-laden pines crowding close about the feet of towering grey mountains. "Does anything ever happen in Rurach?" she said to the elven cat curled on her lap. "Flaming dragon balls, I'm as bored as a eunuch in a brothel!"

Goblin yawned, showing a mouthful of tiny but very sharply pointed fangs. "I canna help agreeing," Finn said. "Do ye think we should run away and join the pirates? At least then we'd see some adventure."

The cat arched its back and hissed.

"No? Ye do no' like that idea? No, o' course, ye dislike water. Ye would no' have to swim in it though.

I believe the pirate ships are quite snug and there'd be fish to eat every day."

Goblin tidied up her whiskers, not deigning to reply. Finn sighed again and stared up at the sharp silhouette of the Fang. For once, it was not wreathed in clouds but cut into the sky like a sabre leopard's tooth, dominating the horizon.

When Finn had first seen the sleeping volcano, she had been troubled by an odd sense of recognition. It had woken all sorts of half-memories in her, a longing or homesickness that she had not then understood. She had then been travelling through the mountains of upper Rionnagan, on the far side of the Fang, and to her knowledge had never seen the tall, symmetrically shaped mountain before. As far as she knew, Finn had never before left the city of Lucescere where she had lived on the streets, picking pockets and begging for scraps of old food in order to survive.

Finn had been one of a gang of beggar children who had had to flee Lucescere after helping Jorge the Seer and his young acolyte Tòmas the Healer escape from the cruel seekers of the Awl, the Anti-Witchcraft League. That had been in the days when suspected witches were burnt to death. In company with the old, blind man and the little boy, Finn and her gang had taken refuge from the Awl in a hidden valley at the very foot of the Fang. There they had formed the League of the Healing Hand, a fellowship sworn to protect the two witches who, despite having such potent magical abilities, were in themselves frail and rather helpless. The League had ended up being very important in the overthrow of the Awl and the restoration of the Coven, and had earned the heartfelt gratitude of the new Rìgh, Lachlan MacCuinn.

Remembering, Finn thought rather wistfully that

those years had been the happiest of her life. Although there was always the danger of losing a hand as a pickpocket or being captured as a rebel, there had been the close comradeship of the gang and the constant thrill of pitting one's wits against the world and winning. Although Finn was never cold or hungry anymore, she was lonely now and sullen with misery. The constraints of court life chafed her unbearably and she felt all the court ladies, including her own mother, disapproved of her greatly.

It had been five years since Finn had discovered she was not an orphan of the streets, as she had thought, but the daughter of the prionnsa of Rurach. She had been kidnapped by the Awl as a mere child of six in order to force her father to their will. She had only discovered the truth during the Samhain rebellion which had put Lachlan MacCuinn on the throne and returned the Coven to power. Her father had then brought her back to Rurach, to meet a mother she had not remembered, and to learn to be a banprionnsa. Although Finn had felt a wrench at leaving her friends, she had been eager to see her home and her mother and to enjoy a life of ease.

But although Castle Rurach was as luxurious and comfortable as she had imagined, it was also boring. Built high in the mountains, it was a long way from the crowded streets of Lucescere, with its merchants, artisans, street performers, thieves and idle nobility. A young lady of Rurach was expected to spend her time with the other ladies of the court, plying her needle in exquisite embroidery and discussing the newest way to cut a sleeve. Finn had no interest in fashion, refused to learn how to sew, and thought of her mother's retinue as a gaggle of fussy old hens.

The towering range of mountains that culminated

in the crooked spire of the Fang was no longer a source of wistful longings but instead a prison wall which kept her locked away from the world with no chance of escape. If Finn had known the secret way over the mountains, she would have run away long ago, searching out her old friends in Lucescere. She did not know it, however, and so she took what pleasure she could in defying her mother and shocking the castle.

Goblin had curled up to sleep but suddenly the little cat raised her head, ears pricked forward. Finn tensed. She heard a step on the stair. She knocked out her pipe with one hand and thrust the other into her pocket, drawing out a small square of tightly folded black material. With a shake it billowed out into a cloak which she wrapped around her swiftly. Wherever the silky stuff brushed against her skin, it tingled and stung, and all the little hairs rose. She pulled the hood up to cover her face, and sat very still.

A gangly young man came out on to the battlements and stood hesitantly. Her father's piper, he was dressed in the castle livery, a black and green kilt with a white woollen shirt and black jerkin. Although he had wrapped his plaid around his thin shoulders, it was bitterly cold out on the tower heights and he shivered and rubbed his arms.

"My lady Fionnghal?" Ashlin the Piper called. "Are ye here? Your mother desires your presence. My lady?"

Finn said nothing. Ashlin stared about with a troubled expression and called her again. When there was no response he turned and clattered back downstairs. Finn stuck out her tongue at his retreating back and shrugged off the cloak, which somehow always made her feel even colder. She huddled her furs closer around her neck and brought out her precious hoard of tobacco. "Why canna they ever leave me alone?" she said resentfully to the cat, who was still curled up on her lap. "Always following me about, spying on me, tittle-tattling. Anyone would think they had naught else to do."

She puffed on her pipe angrily, kicking her legs against the stone. "I wish my *dai-dein* would get better," she burst out in a sudden wail, then bit the stem of her pipe hard and said no more. Her father Anghus MacRuraich had been injured fighting ogres in the mountains and had lain near death for a week. Although the castle healer had told them his fever had broken and he would now recover, Finn could not help fearing he might suffer a relapse.

She was knocking out the ashes from her pipe when she suddenly felt a prickling at the back of her neck. She glanced over her shoulder and saw an old man step quietly out of the doorway. He was a short, stocky figure with a flowing grey beard, round pink cheeks and blue eyes twinkling between deep creases. He was her father's gillie and had served Anghus ever since the laird had been a mere lad himself. Finn did not know him very well since he rarely left her father's side and so had been absent from the castle most of the time since she had come to Rurach. His kilt was so faded it was a comfortable blur of grey and olive, and he wore his beard thrust through the wide belt that held his kilt together. A thin dagger, black as jet, was stuck through the disreputable scrap of ribbon holding up one stocking. The other stocking was tied up with twine.

"Och, there ye are, my lady," Donald said placidly. "Bonny afternoon for a smoke." Finn said nothing. He came to lean on the battlement beside her, looking up at the mountains and feeling inside his sporran for his pipe and tobacco pouch. Swiftly, without a glance downwards, he packed his pipe and stuck it in the corner of his mouth. "Smells like Fair Isles smoke-weed ye've got there," he said conversationally. "True tobacco is rare these days, wha' wi' pirates and the blaygird Fairgean on the rise. Most have to smoke herbs or seaweed these days."

"Here, have some o' mine," Finn said sweetly, offering him her own leather pouch.

"Och, no need," Donald replied. "I won a pouch full from Casey Hawkeye just last night. He be the lucky one, his uncle being the harbour master at Dùn Gorm and taking his taxes in tobacco. I should have enough to last me a wee while longer."

There was silence while Donald lit his pipe and drew up the flame. When the tobacco was burning merrily, he pulled the pipe from his mouth and said placidly, "The question is, lassie, where it is ye got your smokeweed."

"I do no' see what business that is o' yours." Finn's voice was honey-sweet. "And I do no' think my dear mother would approve o' ye being so familiar as to call me 'lassie'."

"Och, I have kent your mother since she was a wee bit o' a lassie herself. She'll no' mind," he replied equably. "It's more likely that she'll be disapproving o' ye smoking a pipe, that I can promise ye."

"Oh, ye think so? If only I had kent."

"And even more o' ye stealing, lassie," he said softly.

Finn flushed and fidgeted with the tassels of her coat. She forced herself to raise her eyes and meet his gaze with a look of outrage. "Are ye accusing me o' theft?"

"Lassie, do no' be lying to me on top o' it all. I ken ye must have stolen the smokeweed from Casey Hawkeye and he kens it as well. No' that he has said aught and naught is what he will say. We do no' wish to be getting ye into any more strife than ye're already in. But I am sore ashamed o' ye, lassie. It is one thing to be picking pockets when ye're starving on the streets and do no' ken any better, but to be diddling your father's own loyal men, that is no' worthy o' ye."

Finn was silent. She held the elven cat up to her face and rubbed her hot cheek against Goblin's cool fur. Donald smoked in silence for a while, leaning on his elbows. His wrinkled brown face was peaceful.

"It does no' matter what I do, she disapproves o' everything anyway," Finn suddenly burst out. "Ye're right, she does no' approve o' me smoking or having a wee dram o' whiskey every now and again, or wanting to play curling wi' the lads . . ."

"Och, well, curling do be a right rough game now," Donald said. She threw him a look of exasperation and saw his blue eyes were twinkling. "Ye mun remember that our mam was raised in the auld ways, when lassies did no' have so much freedom and were expected to mind their manners and do wha' they were told. Your grandfather was a very strict, starched-up sort o' fellow, and proud o' his name and his clan. Your mam was never allowed to forget she was a banprionnsa and direct descendant o' Sian the Storm-Rider herself."

Finn screwed up her face and he patted her shoulder. "She's gone and worrit herself into a fret over ye, lassie. Should ye no' go down and let her ken ye're safe?"

Finn's jaw set firmly. "What has she got to worry about so? It's no' as if I'm ever allowed to do anything or go anywhere. What can I do to hurt myself? Prick myself with a needle? Stub my toe kicking my mealy-mouthed cousin in the arse?"

"Fall over the battlements?" Donald said with a slight edge to his voice. He glanced down at Finn, still sitting in the embrasure with nothing between her and the ground but three hundred feet of air. "That is no' the safest place to perch, lassie."

Finn glanced down. "Do ye no' ken they call me 'the Cat'?" she said mockingly. "A wee drop like that does no' worry me."

"It worries all o' us who care about ye though," Donald said, the edge in his voice slightly sharper.

"Are ye trying to tell me my dear mother would really care if I fell off?" Finn tried to make her voice hard and sarcastic. "She'd probably heave a big sigh o' relief to be rid o' me and another o' happiness that her precious Aindrew would then inherit the throne. Ye canna tell me she does no' wish he was the first-born."

"I can and I do." For the first time since Finn had met her father's gillie, there was no kindly twinkle in his eyes. "When the blaygird Awl took ye away, I thought your mam would die o' grief. Her eyes hung out o' her head wi' weeping and she was naught but a shadow o' herself all the time ye were gone. I was there when your father brought ye back to Castle Rurach. Ye canna tell me ye did no' see how full o' joy she was to have ye home!"

Finn dropped her eyes, feeling a little niggle of shame. Her mother had run across the drawbridge to greet them, her hair all unbound and her feet still shod in soft slippers. Finn had not even had a chance to dismount. Her mother had pulled her from the saddle, weeping and holding her so closely Finn had thought her ribs would break. Enveloped in a golden cloud of sweetly perfumed hair, listening to her mother's choked endearments, Finn had been filled with happiness. She had hugged her mother back as hard as she could and then felt her father's arms embracing them both as he had cried, "See, my Gwyneth, I promised ye I would find our lassie and bring her home to ye! Now we can be a family again."

But her father had spent only enough time at home to get his wife with child, before riding out to deal with the civil unrest wrenching Siantan and Rurach apart. The two countries had been joined into one with the marriage of Anghus's parents. Ostensibly his mother had been meant to rule as an equal with his father, but Duncan MacRuraich had been an autocratic man. It was his will which had directed the actions of the Double Throne and the people of Siantan had suffered as a result, causing much dissatisfaction.

Although Anghus had reluctantly agreed to dissolve the Double Throne, with Finn's cousin Brangaine Nic-Sian named as banprionnsa of Siantan, Anghus had then had to contend with the problems caused by the rising of the Fairgean. Each autumn and spring, as the migrating hordes of sea-faeries swept up and down the cost, the attacks of their warriors grew ever more vicious. Consquently, Anghus had spent only short periods of time at home in the past five years, leaving Gwyneth to struggle with her foul-mouthed, light-fingered daughter, her baby son Aindrew, and her unfailingly polite yet distant niece, Brangaine. It had not been a happy time and the initial affection between mother and daughter had cooled into misunderstanding.

"It's just I do no' feel like I belong here," Finn muttered as she allowed Donald to help her down from the wall.

"O' course ye belong here, lassie," Donald said
warmly. "Are ye no' a NicRuraich? Can ye no' tell
where anyone is merely by thinking o' them? The
bluid o' Rùraich the Searcher runs strong in ye, as
anyone could tell simply by looking at ye. Do no' be
such a porridge-head!"

Finn laughed reluctantly and followed the old gillie
down the tower stairs, the elven cat tucked in the
crook of her arm. "If only she did no' *fuss* so," she
said. "I feel like I'm being *stifled*."

"Wha' ye need is a guid day's hunting," Donald
said encouragingly. "We've all been cooped up for
weeks wi' the snowstorms; it's enough to make anyone
cranky. A day out on the hills will make ye feel a wee
bit better."

Finn's hazel eyes lit with green lights. "Och, if only
I could!"

"It's a clear, frosty day," Donald said thoughtfully.
"Happen we'll bag ourselves a crested pheasant which
ye can have for your supper."

Finn was so pleased with this idea that she came
into the great drawing room with a light step and a
happy face. Her mother was sitting on a chaise lounge,
her embroidery frame before her. Brangaine sat at a
stool at Gwyneth's feet, a selection of silk threads
spread over her skirt, while Finn's brother Aindrew
leant against her knee, playing contentedly with a pile
of brightly coloured toys. Unlike Finn, he had taken
after his mother, sharing the same pale silken hair,
fine skin and green eyes. Brangaine had also inherited
the MacSian fairness, both women having long, pale
hair bound into a plait that hung over their shoulders
and down past their knees. The firelight played over
the three corn-silk heads, bent close together, and

over the blue and grey plaids that both the women wore about their shoulders.

Finn's step faltered and she scowled. The handful of middle-aged women gathered around the drawing room looked up and silence fell over the room. Gwyneth rose with a welcoming smile, holding out her hands to Finn. "Where have ye been, dearling? It's been hours and no-one has been able to find ye anywhere!"

Finn gave a clumsy bob and said, rather gruffly, "I'm sorry, mam. I did no' mean to worry ye. The sun is out for the first time in days and I just needed a breath o' fresh air . . ."

"But it is after noon and ye've been gone since we broke our fast."

"I went down to the stables to see Cinders. I knew she would be restless after being cooped up for so long and thought I would take her out for a ride but Casey said none o' the grooms were free to go out with me. He would no' let me take Cinders out by myself—he bade two o' his men escort me from the mews. When I refused to go and ordered them to unhand me, he told me no' to be such a foolish bairn." Her voice rose with indignation.

"Ye ken ye must always be accompanied if ye wish to ride out," Gwyneth said with some exasperation. She took Finn's hand and drew her down to sit next to her. "I do no' make these rules to vex ye, dearling. These mountains are dangerous, ye ken that. What if ye were to be thrown and break an ankle?"

"Cinders would no' throw me! I have no' lost my seat in years."

"What if she was threatened by a woolly bear?"

"We're no' afraid o' a stupid bear!"

"Och, ye should be. Ye ken they are surly, unpredictable creatures, and certainly no' the only danger in these parts. What if a troll came down from the mountains, or a pack o' goblins?"

"I wish some would, at least then there'd be some excitement!" Finn burst out.

Gwyneth sighed in annoyance. "Finn, a pack o' marauding goblins is no' something to wish for! We may be safe here in the castle, but what about the crofters? Goblins have no respect for life or property—they hurt for the pleasure o' it. Ye will be the NicRuraich one day; it is your duty to guard and protect your people. Wishing harm to come to them for your own childish pleasure is no way to behave."

Finn bit back rebellious words, but her eyes smouldered and her jaw was set firmly.

Gwyneth took a deep breath to contain her exasperation, then said affectionately, "Dearling, I ken ye find our life here rather tedious but indeed, peacefulness means happiness. There has been so much strife here for so long we auld ones are all rather glad to have some peace and quiet for a change. Your father is home now, thank Eà. As soon as his wounds are fully healed, he'll take ye out riding the boundaries and teach ye more about the laird's duties. Until then, ye must bide here in patience."

"Yes, mam," Finn said dutifully and let her mother kiss her cheek.

Donald had been waiting quietly just within the door. He had taken off his tam o'shanter and his shining bald dome was rosy in the firelight, fringed all round with grey curls. "I beg your pardon, my lady, but I ken how cooped up the young ones must be feeling wi' the snowstorms keeping them so much inside. I was thinking I could be taking them out for a ride and maybe beat up some pheasants for your dinner, seeing as how we are all sick o' eating mutton-and-taties."

Gwyneth smiled, looking out at the blue sky. "It does seem to have cleared up. If ye take Casey with ye and some o' the men, I do no' see any reason why Fionnghal and Brangaine should no' go out . . ."

"Excuse me, my lady, but I fear a storm is brewing," Brangaine said respectfully.

Finn stared at her with hatred. "But the sky is clear! There are no clouds . . ."

"The clear sky is deceptive, I'm afraid, Fionnghal," her cousin replied sweetly. "A storm front is coming and heavy with snow. By mid-afternoon the blue sky will be gone."

"Well, in that case there be no question o' ye riding out," Gwyneth said decisively. "The storms do come very quickly here, ye ken that, Fionnghal. I do no' wish for ye to be caught out in a snowstorm." She saw the look of bitter disappointment and dislike on Finn's face and said comfortingly, "Never mind, dearling. The next clear day ye can ride out, I promise ye."

"It's fine today!"

"Aye, for the moment, but ye ken Brangaine has the Talent. If she says a storm is coming, ye can be sure that it is."

"She'll probably whistle up a storm just to make sure I canna go out!" Finn cried and leapt to her feet, knocking over her mother's embroidery frame. The court ladies threw up their hands and several cried aloud in condemnation. The elven cat hissed at them from Finn's shoulder. Finn turned and ran out of the room, knocking over a little gilded table on her way and smashing the heirloom jug that stood upon it. Dashing tears from her eyes, she did not stop, slamming the door shut behind her.

Distressed, her mother ran after her but although the corridor stretched both ways as far as the eye could see, there was no sign of her wayward daughter.

That afternoon a blizzard engulfed the castle in a tumult of snow and wind that had everyone huddled up in their plaids. It did not make Finn feel any better knowing that Brangaine had been right and that any expedition into the forest could well have ended in disaster. She moped around the castle, staring out the windows at the whirling snow and blaming her cousin for ruining her life. Although her mother reprimanded her gently, Finn was unable to shake a deep sense of injury and cast Brangaine many a smouldering glance.

That evening she was allowed to see Anghus for the first time, the castle healer having pronounced him strong enough to survive a visit by his tempestuous daughter. Finn's sulky expression cleared as if by magic, and she eagerly followed Donald into the prionnsa's bedroom and threw himself upon her father.

He embraced her with his one good arm, though he winced with pain, saying "Careful, lassie, those ribs are still a wee bit tender."

She lifted herself away a little, saying urgently, "How are ye yourself, Dai? Ye look awful!"

The prionnsa smiled ruefully. "Thank ye, dearling."

She examined his face closely. He was pale and haggard, with dark shadows under his hazel eyes. The bones of his face and hands seemed more prominent, and she thought with some distress that there was more grey than chestnut now in his long, curly hair. Two white streaks were clawing down into his magnificent red beard, which flowed down over his chest.

"Are ye sure ye be feeling better?" she asked anxiously, settling herself by his side with Goblin curled up on her lap.

He nodded, smiling a little. "Much better, lassie. Though I could wish ogres did no' have such filthy personal habits. The healer says his claws were so dirty it was as if he had dipped them in poison."

"Was it exciting?" Finn asked rather wistfully. "Fighting an ogre, I mean? I wish I'd been there."

"I canna tell ye how glad I am that ye were no'," Anghus replied, all traces of humour vanishing from his face. "Finn, I was lucky to escape the ogre alive! Three o' my men were no' so lucky. Do ye think their widows and orphans do no' wish with all their hearts that that blaygird ogre had no' stayed deep in the mountains? It was no' exciting, Finn, it was tragic."

Finn nodded her head, though her mouth once again had resumed its sullen droop. Anghus looked at her carefully. "Your mam tells me ye have been most restless and unhappy," he said gently. "What is wrong, lass?"

She kicked the leg of the bedside table, turning her face away. "Och, naught."

"It does no' sound like naught," her father said, pulling her a little closer so he could see her face. She glanced at him, then away, her brown cheek colouring, her hands pulling at the elven cat's tufted ears.

"It's just there's naught to do here," she burst out. "Dai, could I no' go to the Theurgia in the spring?"

Anghus frowned. "But ye have excellent teachers here. We have spared no expense in bringing the very best to Castle Rurach. There's a witch who trained at the Tower o' Two Moons itself, no' to mention the dancing-master, the music teacher to teach ye the lute and spinet, the scribe to teach ye how to write with a courtly hand . . ."

"I ken, I ken," Finn said dispiritedly. "My hours are very well provided for."

"Then what is the problem?"

She met his gaze squarely for the first time. "I'm bored."

"Oh, Finn, everyone finds the winter very long and boring. The days are short and the weather too inclement for many excursions outside the castle walls. But what canna be changed must be endured. Ye must find something to do to keep yourself busy. Brangaine is much your age; what does she do with her time?"

"Och, bluidy Brangaine!" Finn's hazel eyes hardened. "She's naught but a stuck-up corn-dolly, content to sit and sew a fine seam and smirk at herself in a mirror."

"That doesna sound very fair, Finn," Anghus frowned. "Your mother tells me Brangaine works hard at her lessons and . . ."

"Och, for sure," Finn said bitterly. "Everything Brangaine does is perfect. She's just perfect in every way, the toad."

"Fionnghal, it troubles me to hear ye speak this way. Ye must remember that this is your home and Brangaine an honoured guest. She has had an unhappy life, poor lass, losing both her parents so young and so tragically. And she has a heavy load on her shoulders, inheriting the throne o' Siantan when she is still just a young lass, and the land in such trouble. Do ye no' think ye could try a wee bit harder to be friends with her? She is your cousin after all."

Finn said nothing, lifting Goblin so her face was hidden by the elven cat's sinuous black shape.

"Come, lassie, do no' look so cross. I tell ye what, next fine day we'll take the horses out for a whole day, just the two o' us. What do ye say?"

"If we ever have a fine day," Finn muttered, then said, with a rather unconvincing smile, "Och, aye, that would be grand, Dai."

The next fine day brought news that changed everything, however. A messenger struggled up to the drawbridge, cold, exhausted and frightened, his horse ridden close to death. The messenger's shirt was half-torn from his back, the skin scored with three deep lines caused by a Fairgean trident.

"The sea demons have come, my laird," the messenger cried, falling to his knees before the MacRuraich. "More o' them than ever, my laird. We couldna keep them back. Already we've retreated to the third loch and still they keep on coming!"

Every year, the rising of the spring tides brought a bloodthirsty horde of Fairgean swimming down the coast of Rurach in pursuit of the blue whales, who migrated south each spring to mate in the warm, shallow waters of the southern seas. Over the past ten years, the sea-dwelling faeries had been growing in strength and numbers, causing great havoc as they swam up every river and stream, killing every human and beast they could find.

Ten years of constant raids on coastal towns and villages had armed the Fairgean with swords, daggers, and spears forged with iron, rather than their traditional weapons of coral and sea jewels, and honed their fighting skills so that each year it grew increasingly difficult to drive them back into the sea. With their steel weapons, the Fairgean were able to cut through the nets strung across the river to entangle them, and were able to fight on an equal footing with the laird's soldiers.

Every year saw a flood of refugees fleeing the coast and river as the Fairgean transformed into their land-shape to rampage across the rich, rolling farmlands that filled the hinterland. The spring crops were trampled, herds of goats and sheep had their throats cut, and many crofters, stubbornly staying to defend their land, were murdered. Trade between the towns and the countryside was impossible without the freedom to boat up and down the river, and so lumber sat rotting in the yards, the furriers were unable to sell their winter cache of furs, the stonemasons and metalsmiths sat idle, and shipwrights starved. Every spring and autumn, the highland towns were crowded with refugees from the lowlands and each year, fewer and fewer returned to their farms in the lowlands. For the past few years, the MacRuraich had been struggling to fend off famine and disease, for the highlands simply did not have the resources to support so many people.

The news that the Fairgean had struck again, so early in the year and with such force, made everyone anxious and afraid. Almost immediately Anghus was calling for his sword and his horse, though a white-faced Gwyneth was begging him to remember how weak he still was. He only caught her to him and kissed her, telling her to be brave and to keep the castle gates locked tightly. "If they have swum as high as the third loch already, we canna be sure they will no' swim higher," he said grimly. "Start preparing for a siege, dearling, and keep those gates shut!"

The MacRuraich and his men rode out that very afternoon, leaving Castle Rurach defended by only a few scant men. Over the next few weeks Gwyneth was kept busy, sending out messengers to the nearby towns and villages and stocking up with food and weaponry. She had little time to pay any attention to Finn, who could not help feeling neglected. Her father had ridden out with no more than a ruffle of her hair and an injunction to be good, while her mother was so preoccupied days could pass with her saying no more than, "Please, no' now, Finn!"

To make matters worse, the blizzard had blown over and the weather was clear and fine. Every day the loch sparkled, the wind was fresh with the smell of sun on pine needles, and the far blue distances beckoned Finn with the promise of adventure. Not all her pleading or sulking convinced Gwyneth to allow her out of the castle walls, however. The news from the south was very bad. For the first time in four hundred years, the Fairgean had penetrated Loch Finavon, the fourth loch from the sea. Anghus and his men had been driven back with terrible losses of life, and were now making one last valiant stand before retreating to the castle. Many of the Fairgean had transformed into their land-shape, climbed the river banks and were now hiding in the forest along the river's edge. There had been a surprise attack on a village less than a day's ride away from the castle. Since no Fairgean had ever invaded so deep into the highlands, the village was not well guarded and most of its inhabitants had been slaughtered. With the Fairgean threat closing in upon the castle, Gwyneth had no intention in allowing Finn to ride out, no matter how defiant her daughter grew.

The more tense and anxious the atmosphere in the castle, the more difficult Finn found it to contain her restless energy. All the squires had gone to attend the MacRuraich and his officers so there was no-one to practice swordplay with. She had ridden her horse Cinders round the outer bailey so many times she knew every crack in the wall and every tuft of grass. Most of the potboys and stable lads had been con-

scripted into the army so there was no-one to play
football with, and the castle guards were all too busy
to spend time telling her stories or teaching her to
wrestle. She practised shooting with her little crossbow
until she could hit the bulls' eye more often than not,
then amused herself by exploring the secret passages
and spying on the servants through the peepholes clev-
erly concealed in the carved panelling. This proved to
be such a fascinating pastime that Finn lost track of
time, only realising how late it was with a little squeak
of dismay when she saw a procession of lackeys carrying heavily loaded trays up the back stairs to the
dining hall. Nothing was more likely to anger her
mother than Finn being late for her dinner again.

Finn scrambled up the secret stairway, through the
dark, labyrinthine passageways and out the hidden
doorway closest to the dining hall. It had been hours
since she had eaten and she was very hungry indeed.

The secret doorway was concealed within the huge
fireplace that took up most of one wall of the landing.
Given the warmth of the day, the fire had luckily not
yet been lit so that Finn was able to scramble out
without too much trouble.

Unfortunately she was just crawling out of the fireplace, the elven cat at her heels, when her cousin
Brangaine came demurely down the stairs, dressed in
leaf-green silk which brought out the colour of her
eyes, her long blonde hair shining in the candlelight.
She looked Finn up and down, then said sweetly, "Has
my lady sent all the chimneysweeps out to fight the
sea demons, that ye must be sweeping up the cinders
yourself, Fionnghal?"

The daughter of Gwyneth's younger sister, Brangaine had been brought to Castle Rurach after being
named laird of the MacSian clan. Although Gwyneth

said Brangaine needed to be taught her duties and responsibilities as banprionnsa of Siantan, Finn knew her mother hoped some of Brangaine's poise and civility would rub off on her. Nineteen years old, Brangaine had been brought up in seclusion at her family's country estate by three maiden aunts who had instilled in her every rule of courtly deportment. Brangaine knew what fork to use when eating quail, when to say "your honour," the exact degree of curtsey required for every rank of society, and how to be civil to the servants without bring too familiar. Brangaine never spilled food down her clothes, or tore her skirt playing chase-and-hide with the servant lads, or was caught stealing honey cakes from the kitchen. Her hair was always smooth and shiny, her boots were always well-polished, and she always had a clean handkerchief. The very sight of her was enough to put Finn's teeth on edge.

At first Brangaine had been polite to her cousin but Finn had been uncomfortable in her newfound place in life and had been quick to take offence at what she saw as Brangaine's smirk of superiority. Brangaine's comments and suggestions had gradually become edged with mockery, though always delivered with such sweetness of demeanour that only Finn had heard the derision beneath.

At her cousin's words, Finn glanced down at herself in some dismay, only then realising how very dirty she was. Her skirt was covered in dust and ashes, and the hem was dangling where she had caught it on some nail. Her knees were black and her brown curls all in a tangle. She eyed Brangaine with dislike, saying loftily, "No' at all. I just dropped something and had some trouble finding it."

Brangaine smiled her superior smile. "Happen ye'd best brush the cobwebs out o' your hair and change your clothes afore your mother sees ye. That is, if ye have a dress that's not all torn and grubby, which I doubt."

"At least I'm no' some muffin-faced prig, scared to lift a finger in case I break a nail," Finn flashed back.

Brangaine's eyes lingered on Finn's hands, the nails all broken and black as a blacksmith's. "No, no-one could accuse ye o' that," she said coldly. "Though I'm sure we all wish ye'd wash your hands occasionally. It's disgraceful the way ye run about looking ye're the daughter o' a swineherd instead o' the MacRuraich . . ."

Finn's temper snapped. With an inarticulate cry, she sprang forward, punching Brangaine in the jaw. Her cousin fell back with a shriek, falling over a little gilded table and smashing the vase of flowers that stood upon it.

At the sound of the scream and the crashing porcelain, the door to the dining hall swung open and the court ladies looked out. When they saw Brangaine sprawling amongst the flowers and the shards of broken vase, Finn standing over her with clenched fists, they cried aloud in consternation, fluttering forward with raised hands and mouths open in dismay. "Oh, my lady, how are ye yourself? Are ye hurt? Gracious alive, you be bleeding, poor lassie!" they cried.

Gwyneth came out after them, her beautiful face tense with anger. "Fionnghal, what in Eà's name have ye done?"

"I punched her in the gob," Finn replied inelegantly. "And she deserved it too, the polecat!"

"Ye did what?" Gwyneth cried. "I canna stand any more o' this wild behaviour, Fionnghal! Is this the way a lady behaves? Look at ye! Ye look like ye've been dragged through a hedge backwards. What am I to do with you?"

Finn glowered back at her, the elven cat crouched at her feet, tail lashing. Across the room Brangaine was being helped to her feet, her eyes bright with tears, her lip split and bleeding.

Brangaine pulled her lace-edged handkerchief from her reticule and daintily patted her lip, glancing down at the bright stains with consternation. She said, rather breathlessly, "Och, please do no' be too angry with Fionnghal, my lady. Indeed it was my fault; I was teasing her."

Finn flashed Brangaine a look of surprise and resentment. *That's right, make me look even worse, ye sly-faced prig,* she thought. The elven cat hissed, her tufted ears laid back along her skull.

"No matter the provocation, a lady should never lose her temper," Gwyneth said, trying to control her own. "There is no excuse for striking ye like that. Look at your mouth, ye poor wee lassie. Nan, will ye ring for some ice and a cloth? Fionnghal, I want you to apologise to your cousin at once."

"I shall no'!" Finn cried passionately. "She deserved to be thumped, the slimy sneaking toad!"

"That's enough!" Gwyneth cried. "Fionnghal, ye are no' a street-bairn anymore. Such conduct is absolutely unacceptable! Ye shall stay in your room until ye have the grace to apologise to your cousin and beg forgiveness for your rude, uncivilised behaviour."

"I'd rather eat roasted rats!" Finn cried. "She does naught but needle me and sneer at me and make me look a gowk."

"Ye mistake her," Gwyneth said icily. "Brangaine is a lady born and raised, and has far too much courtesy ever to speak or act unkindly. Ye are too quick to take offence."

Finn protested passionately but Gwyneth would not listen. When her daughter still refused to go to her room, she called in the guards and bid them escort her away. Eyes flashing, Finn drew her little eating dagger but they disarmed her and marched her away with hard hands clamped around her arms. She stared back at her cousin with hostile eyes, not believing the look of guilty apology which Brangaine cast her way.

The heavy oaken door slammed shut behind her and she heard the key turn in the lock. Finn turned and pummelled it with her fists, then flung herself down on her bed, burying her hot face in her pillow. *It's no' fair,* she said to herself, reliving Brangaine's superior smile as she had called Finn a pig-girl, her contemptuous glance from Finn's cobwebbed curls to her dirty, scuffed boots.

The sting in Finn's eyes subsided as she remembered with satisfaction the moment when her fist had met Brangaine's jaw. Finn had spent much of her life fighting for survival on the streets of Lucescere. Her punch packed some power. Finn grinned, then rolled over and stared up at the ornate ceiling, *I must get out o' here afore I go stark raving mad!*

Goblin was sitting at the end of the bed, delicately washing one paw. She watched as Finn leapt to her feet and rushed over to one of the tall, narrow windows that lined the wall, then began to wash her hind leg. Finn flung open the window and leant out.

The castle was built on a high rocky crag overlooking Loch Kintyre, which lay dark and shadowy some three hundred feet below. The castle was virtually surrounded by water, with the swift, turbulent rush of the Wulfrum River curving round the base of the crag on the northern flank. The walls of the crag were as steep and straight as any sea-cliff, broken at the base by sharp rocks that glistened black with slime.

The road to the castle ran up through thick forest to the edge of a deep, shadowy ravine, carved out of the rock by a fast-running burn that tumbled its way down to the loch in a series of white rapids and waterfalls. The only way to traverse the ravine was across the castle drawbridge, which remained closed at all times. Of all the strongholds that Finn had seen, Castle Rurach was surely the most impregnable.

Although Finn was confident of her ability to climb in and out of any tower or castle, the height of the walls and the wicked rocks below made her reluctant to brave the drop unless she really had to. She had no rope and even if she tied every curtain and sheet in her room together, they would not be long enough to help her even a quarter of the way down. Most important of all, the valley below was sunk in shadows as the sun sidled down behind the mountains. It would soon be night and Finn had no desire to attempt that descent in darkness.

Finn gave another little sigh of frustration and crossed the room to kneel down before the arched doorway and peer through the keyhole. All she could see was the bulk of the manservant set to guard her door. She wished she had something sharp to poke him with but they had not given back her little jewelled knife. If only she had allowed her mother's ladies-in-waiting to teach her how to knit! A long, sharp knitting needle thrust into his posterior would really make that block-headed, stone-faced footman yowl.

"Just ye wait," she muttered at the footman's rear end. "I hope she has ye whipped for dereliction o' duty once I'm gone. I hope she has ye sent to fight goblins in the mountains.''

She kicked the door but that only served to bruise her foot. Finn cursed and began to stride along the length of her suite, staring out the tall windows at the star-pricked sky. Her skirts swished as she paced. Impatiently she swept them up in one hand so they did not hinder her steps. *I shall no' apologise to that lamb-brained, mealy-mouthed corn-dolly! There mun be some other way out o' here!*

As Finn reached the end of the room and flung herself round to pace its length again, Goblin raised her black triangular head and observed the pacing girl through slitted aquamarine eyes. The elven cat then yawned, showing a long pink tongue and put her head down again, eyes closed.

*Nay, I shall no' be calm,* Finn hissed. *I wish my daidein was home, he'd take my part. He wouldna believe that muffin-faced prig!*

She rummaged around in one of the chests in her dressing-room until at last she found a little bundle shoved right down the bottom. Wrapped up in a square of yellow-embossed blue cloth were a pair of gloves tipped with steel claws and two odd contraptions of leather and steel that were designed to be strapped on over a pair of boots. Tangled up with them was a handful of long spikes and some pulleys and rope. All this was Finn's climbing equipment, which had been made for her on the orders of Iseult of the Snows, Lachlan's wife, in the days when they had been rebels together, plotting to overthrow Maya the Ensorcellor, the fairge princess who had bewitched the former Rìgh Jaspar into marriage and had ruled the land so cruelly.

Finn gave a little hiss of satisfaction as the tools

clattered on to the floor, but almost immediately she bit her lip in consternation. The gloves and boot racks were now far too small. Finn had been only twelve when she had climbed the two hundred foot rampart behind Lucescere to let Lachlan and his rebel troops into the city. She was now almost seventeen and her limbs were much longer than they had been five years earlier. In addition, the rope had decayed in the damp atmosphere of the old castle and was rotten in parts.

She sat back on her heels, and smoothed the cloth out over her knees. A rather odd-looking yellow hand was sewn clumsily on to the sky-blue cloth, with broad yellow stripes angling out from it, meant to signify rays. It was the original flag of the League of the Healing Hand and it brought a sting of tears to Finn's eyes. After a long moment, she folded it up again and thrust it into the pillowcase with the spikes and pulleys and her little hammer.

Eventually Finn's temper died and she was left feeling very low and dispirited. She sat in her chair in front of the fire, moodily jabbing the logs with the poker. The sound of a key in the door brought her flying upright but it was only her maid-in-waiting, Raina, with a tray of food. Accompanying her were two stern-faced guards. Finn stood silently, her chin up, her hands clenched before her, as Raina put the tray on the table before the fire and retreated with a mocking glance that said, more clearly than words, "Serve ye right, ye muffin-faced brat."

At first Finn decided she would not touch any of the food but after a while the smell of the mutton stew broke down her defenses and she ate hungrily, telling herself she needed to keep her strength up if she was to escape the castle. She wrapped up the bread, cheese and fruit in one of her pillowcases, and wished that she had not been so hasty in drawing her knife, since she would surely need one on her travels. Despite her isolation all afternoon, Finn had not lost her resolve to quit the home of her forebears.

# THE JONGLEURS COME

T he next morning dawned bright and clear. Finn hung out the window, smelling the wind and cursing fluently. Here it was, as still and warm as summer, and she was locked up like a criminal in her own castle!

Suddenly her eyes lit with excitement. A procession of caravans was winding up the steep road to the castle, their parrot-bright colours vivid in the sunshine.

"Jongleurs!" she cried. "Happen they'll have news o' the court!"

The little cat perched on her shoulder gave a plaintive miaow. Only then did Finn remember her incarceration and her smile faded. "Surely mam will let me out to see the jongleurs?" she said to the elven cat, who only slitted her aquamarine eyes in response. With a sinking heart, Finn watched the jongleurs' brightly painted caravans cross the drawbridge and disappear within the thick walls of the castle.

All day Finn paced her rooms, waiting for her mother to relent and send someone to let her out. When Raina brought her a tray of black bread and cheese, she begged the maid to tell her when she would be set free. Raina shrugged, lifted an eyebrow, and went away without a word, and Finn suddenly wished she had been nicer to her maid. She had thought of her maid as the frontline of her gaolers, however, and had often spied on her to gain information that she could use as leverage to stop Raina reporting her movements to her mother. Now Finn was paying for her underhand ways—and the debt was high.

She watched the guards shut her bedroom door with mingled fury, frustration and misery choking her throat. It seemed Gwyneth's determination was as great as her own. Unable to help feeling a new sense of respect for her mother, Finn sat and toyed with her meagre rations, making and discarding one plan after another.

Without a reliable rope or climbing equipment, Finn was loath to attempt the perilous descent from her window. She was more determined than ever not to apologise for thumping Brangaine, yet she longed to escape the confines of her room and enjoy the rare entertainment the jongleurs offered. There had been six caravans in the procession, which promised a wide variety of performers. There would be music and singing, without a doubt, and juggling and acrobatics, and maybe even a performing bear, like Finn had seen in Lucescere. The jongleurs would bring news as well, which Finn was hungry to hear. She could escape her rooms by trickery but that would only make her mother angry and she would be locked up again as soon as she was found—and how could she watch the jongleurs and listen to their tales of the court and the countryside if she was being chased all over the castle? Unless, of course, they could not see her . . .

Finn whiled away the long, dreary afternoon as best she could, waiting until it was time for Raina to bring her dinner. At last the sun sank down behind the mountains and darkness fell over the rank upon rank

of serried pine trees. Finn flung open the window so
that the evening breeze swept into the room, sending
the heavy curtains swaying and riffling the pages of
her books upon the table. She knotted the rope about
the post of her bed and threw it out the window, then
drew out the little square of silk she always carried
with her in her pocket. Finn shook it out into the long,
black cloak and wrapped it about her, pulling the hood
over her head. A little snap of static, a shudder of
cold, ran over her. She rubbed her arms, moving her
shoulders uneasily. Goblin miaowed, and she bent and
picked up the little cat, sliding her into the cloak's
deep pocket.

At last Finn heard the bolt sliding back and the
grate of the key in the lock. She stood silently in the
shadows, trying to breathe as shallowly as she could.
Then the door swung open and a ray of light struck
into the dark, cold room. Raina's portly form was silhouetted against the lantern flare. She stepped forward hesitantly, a tray in her hands. "My lady?" she
called. When there was no response, she called again.
At the note of alarm in Raina's voice the guards
stepped forward, one holding up the lamp. Its flame
leapt and guttered in the wind.

As Raina and the guards searched her rooms, Finn
slipped silently out the door and down the corridor.
A deep thrill of gratification ran through her veins.
*They thought to keep Finn the Cat locked up but I've
shown them now,* she thought.

As she hurried down the back staircase, Finn could
hear the sound of music and laughter from the grand
hall. She slipped soundlessly along one of the side
passages and in through the servants' door at the back.
She hid herself behind the heavy velvet curtains hang-

ing down from the gallery and peeped out through
the crack.

Down three sides of the great, vaulted room ran
long tables where the men and women of the castle
sat, the boards before them loaded with platters of
meat and bread and roasted vegetables and jugs of ale
and spiced wine.

Gwyneth sat at the high table with her niece and son
and the principal gentlemen and ladies-in-waiting, while
at the two long side tables sat the bard and the harper,
the seneschal, the sennachie, the purse-bearer and cup-
bearer, and the other men and ladies-in-waiting, all
sitting according to their rank and position. Behind
most of the nobility stood their personal servants, all
wearing their master's livery and expressions of the
utmost superciliousness. As the kitchen staff brought
in the heavy trays and dumped them on a side table,
the squires would all leap forward and squabble over
the choicest pieces of meat or game, which they would
then present to their master or mistress with bent
knee.

At the tables at the far end of the room sat the
highest-ranking servants. They did not usually eat in
the grand hall but had been admitted so they too
could watch the jongleurs. They did not eat from gilt-
edged porcelain plates like those at the high tables,
but used trenchers of black bread instead, piling them
high with mutton and potato stew and any scraps of
roast stag or pheasant or honeyed pork that the nobility scorned to eat or throw to the dogs squabbling
under the tables. When the juices of the stew had
soaked the bread so it was too soft to use as a plate,
they ate it or threw it down to the dogs, seizing another from the wooden platter in the centre of their
table.

While the crowd feasted, they were entertained by the jongleurs who performed in the centre of the room. Finn craned her neck to see, but her view was obscured by the castle cook's massive form. All she could see was a juggler's swiftly rising circle of golden balls, then a sudden whirl of colour as an acrobat somersaulted high into the rafters.

The hall was bright with firelight and candlelight so that even the lofty vaulted ceiling was clearly illuminated. Finn hesitated, then bit her lip, pulled the hood even closer about her face, and slipped out from the shelter of the curtains. Having to dodge and sidestep to avoid the hurrying servants, she made her way up the length of the hall until she could step up onto the dais where the high table was set.

Many of the tall, ornately carved chairs at the high table were empty, since Finn's father Anghus and most of his men were still absent. Finn slowly eased out one of the chairs, wincing a little as the wooden foot scraped on the floor. Waiting until everyone's attention was transfixed by the fire-eater swallowing a flaming torch, Finn slipped into the chair and sat down on the soft leather seat, leaning her elbows on the table.

She watched in delight as the fire-eater bent backwards till his long ponytail was brushing the floor, then thrust the flaming torch down his throat, closing his mouth over the blaze so his cheeks glowed red. Slowly, theatrically, he withdrew the torch, now black and smoking, then pulled himself upright, his cheeks still bulging and glowing with that weird red light. From his pursed lips curled a tendril of smoke, then he spat out a long blast of flame that scorched her face. Finn leant back instinctively, trying not to scream with the others.

The fire-eater juggled six blazing torches, swallowed them one by one, then used his fiery breath to ignite a hoop of paper. A black-eyed girl around Finn's age somersaulted through the ring of flame, then cart-wheeled away down the hall as the fire-eater began to juggle daggers and swords back and forth with a young man in a sky-blue jerkin and a crimson velvet cap with a bhanais bird's feather. A cluricaun in a green satin doublet skipped in to dance a jig between them, the bells on his toes and around his neck chiming as he whirled and pranced amidst the vortex of spinning knives.

Further down the hall Finn could see two boys stalking about on high stilts, their ridiculous hats brushing against the rafters. A man with a forked beard the colour of flax was entertaining the servants' table with card tricks and a fast-paced patter of jokes, while a woman leant nearby, strumming a guitar. Other musicians wandered about, playing fiddles or flutes, or rattling tambourines tied up with many-coloured ribbons.

The black-eyed girl was now doing a series of elegant back flips that took her right across the hall, then did a handspring that took her up into the rafters where she swung upside down like a brightly coloured arak. Then she somersaulted down, landing on the shoulders of the crimson-capped man, who had the same bright eyes as she did, black as pools of ink. She leapt down lightly and they bowed to tumultuous applause.

Wishing that she was an acrobat instead of a banpri-onnsa, Finn waited until everyone was watching the young jongleur, who was demonstrating her incredible flexibility. Finn then slowly reached out her hand and slid a slice of roast pheasant from the platter in front of her. Glancing about to make sure no-one was watching, she slipped it into the shelter of the cloak and shared it with the elven cat. Both of them had had nothing but prisoner's rations to eat for two days now and they were starving. Finn was glad to eat, for the comfort as well as the sustenance. Somehow the cloak of invisibility always made her feel uncomfortable, as if it were made of some prickly material rather than the silkiest of fabrics. It rubbed her up the wrong way, causing her hair to snap with static and her flesh to rise in goosebumps. It was like wrapping herself in the cold and deadness of a winter night, rather than in something to keep her warm. She was always rather glad to hide it away in her pocket once more, though she was never able to leave it in her chest of drawers or in her cupboard, always needing to have it where her fingers could brush it at a whim.

Finn was just stealing a little meat pie from the plate of the man next to her when she felt a little prickle of unease. She glanced about and saw her brother Aindrew was staring her way with an open mouth and an expression of the utmost bewilderment. She looked down and realised it must look as if the meat pie was floating through the air. With a chuckle she concealed it within her sleeve then ate it quickly, trying not to let any flakes of pastry fall out of her mouth. She was tempted to pour wine into a goblet just so he could see a jug lift and pour out a stream of red liquid all by itself. She resisted the temptation and was glad she had when she saw Brangaine was also gazing at her apparently empty chair with some amazement. A meat pie falling from the edge of a plate could be put down to natural causes; a pouring jug could not.

The next time Finn took one of the delicious meat

pies she was careful to drop a fold of the cloak over
it before lifting it so it too would be concealed by the
magic of the garment. After a while Aindrew stopped
glancing her way every few minutes, too entranced
by the jongleurs to bother about a floating meat pie.
Brangaine was not so easily distracted. Finn felt her
gaze often and was careful not to draw any more attention to herself, invisible or not.

No-one at the castle knew about the magical cloak.
Finn had guarded its secret carefully.

She had first found the cloak in the relics room at
the Tower of Two Moons during the Samhain rebellion that had overthrown Maya the Ensorcellor and
given Lachlan the throne. In gratitude for their help,
he had allowed each of the eight members of the
League of the Healing Hand to choose one treasure
to have for their own. Finn had chosen an ancient
hunting horn embossed with the shape of a running
wolf, because the same emblem was on the medallion
she wore around her neck. She had not then known
that the wolf was the badge of the MacRuraich clan
and that the horn had the power to call up the ghosts
of the clan's long-dead warriors. She had only discovered the horn's magic later, when she had blown the
horn in a desperate call for help and had received
assistance of the most unexpected kind.

The older boys had chosen swords or daggers, except for Jay the Fiddler who had taken a beautiful old
viola and Parlan, who had chosen a silver goblet with
a crystal in the stem. Johanna the Mild had chosen a
jewelled bracelet while her baby brother Connor had
wanted a music box.

Chance had caused Finn to pick up the cloak as
well. At the time she had told herself that since she
had been the one to face all the danger in climbing

the wall, she should have something more than the others. She had kept the cloak secret, without really knowing why.

Like the horn, the cloak had proved to be magical, hiding anyone who wore it under a guise of invisibility that not even the most powerful sorcerer could penetrate. Finn had used it to escape the Awl, then Lachlan had hidden himself in it while he confronted his dying brother. Later, Maya the Ensorcellor had stolen the cloak to escape Lachlan's wrath. Most thought she must have the magical cloak still, for it had not been found during the clean-up after the Samhain victory. Only Finn knew that she had used her own clairvoyant talents to search for it through the maze, finding it at last under a hedge near the Pool of Two Moons where Maya and Lachlan had had their last confrontation. She had folded it up and hidden it in her pocket and told no-one, not even when Meghan had instigated a frantic search for it during the ensuing days. She had brought the cloak of invisibility back with her to Castle Rurach and used it often to escape the scrutiny of her attendants or to eavesdrop on the conversations of the servants.

Just then Finn saw her maid Raina speaking in a low voice to her mother's chief lady-in-waiting, Lady Anne Montgomery. Her fat old face was distressed. Finn tensed. She watched as Lady Anne allowed Raina to approach the high table. She curtsied respectfully, then bent down low to speak to the banprionnsa. Gwyneth's face whitened until she looked as though she might faint. She gave a few quick orders then leant back in her chair, sipping at her wine, trying to hide her distress. Raina hurried away and Finn watched as various officers were called away from the tables. They went with worried faces and Finn could not help feeling a certain satisfaction. She sat back to enjoy the show, knowing that half the castle guard would now be searching for her. Not one could possibly guess that she sat in their very midst, under the blaze of the chandelier, and only a few chairs down from her mother.

The platters of roast meats and vegetables had been taken away and now the servants were carrying in plates of honey cakes, sweetmeats and dried fruits. The jongleurs had gathered around the frail form of an old woman, who had been carried into the centre of the room on a chair all carved and painted with leaves, flowers and birds. Her hair was white, her olive-skinned face a mass of wrinkles. The hands which rested on the carved arms of her chair were bent and twisted as birds' claws. On her wizened breast hung many necklaces of amber stones, some as big as eggs, others as small as teeth.

Finn's eyes widened a little in surprise. She recognised the old woman. She was Enit Silverthroat, a great friend of the Keybearer Meghan NicCuinn. Finn had last seen her at Lucescere five years earlier, singing for the Rìgh and Banrìgh. It was said she could sing birds to her hand and people to their death. It was a rare privilege indeed to hear Enit Silverthroat sing.

Softly the musicians strummed their guitars and clàrsachan, the fiddler raised his bow and the cluricaun lifted his silver flute to his mouth. As music spilled melodiously across the grand hall, the loud hum of conversation died away. Then Enit began to sing and an awed silence fell upon the audience.

Although her voice quavered in places, and once cracked mid-syllable, it was so poignant with longing and sorrow, so rich in cadence and experience, so pure and melodic that involuntary tears rose in the eyes of many. Finn heard a stifled sob and saw that her mother had raised one hand to shield her eyes, and that Brangaine was bending close over her, comforting her with a gentle hand. Finn herself felt a pang of regret that she had to struggle to repress.

At last her voice trailed into silence and the crowd applauded wildly. There were tears on Enit's face and the black-eyed girl bent to kiss her withered cheek. The old woman smiled a little and lifted her crippled hand to pat the girl's smooth brown cheek. The jongleurs began to play a much-loved ballad and the young man with the crimson cap again led the singing.

> "Lassie wi' the yellow coatie,
> Will ye wed a moorland Jockie?
> Lassie wi' the yellow coatie,
> Will ye come an' live with me?
> I have meal and milk in plenty,
> I have kale and cakes full dainty,
> I've a but and ben most gentry,
> But I want a bonny wife like thee."

He was very handsome, with tousled dark curls, dusky olive checks and an impudent smile. Finn could feel his attraction herself and noticed how all the court ladies were smiling and fluttering as he wooed them with his words of love. Even Brangaine was blushing a little, somewhat to Finn's surprise. Her cousin's face was usually very pale and serene, her mouth set in a rather melancholy droop. No anger or passion ever seemed to ruffle that calm exterior. To see her responding to the amorous glances of a jongleur made Finn grin.

"Although my measure be but small,
An' little gold I have to show,
I have a heart without a flaw,
And I will give it all to thee.
Lassie wi' the yellow coatie,
Ah! Take pity on your Jockie;
Lassie wi' the yellow coatie,
Come be my love an' live wi' me."

Everyone clapped and cheered as he finished with a
flourish and there were calls for more. Only Gwyneth
seemed immune to his charm and Finn felt troubled
as she saw how pale and unhappy her mother looked.
For a moment she wanted to fling off the cloak of
invisibility, reassure her mother that she was alive and
well, and beg her forgiveness for being so stubborn.
She fought back the urge and let herself enjoy the
music.

It had been some years since she had heard such
skilled musicians. In Lucescere her best friend had
been a fiddler who had played with just the same
verve and passion as this young fiddler, though without his polish and poise. They even looked rather the
same, though Jay had been thin and pale and under-
nourished, while this young violinist was tall and
brown and laughing. Dressed in a forest-green doublet
and satin crimson breeches with a feather of the same
colour stuck in his cap, he was playing his fiddle with
immense skill and animation, so that many in the audience began to beat time with the handles of their
eating knives.

Then the cook got up and began to dance a jig with
the butler, showing all her petticoats and her thick,
blue-veined legs. With shouts of glee, many others
among the audience began to dance also, some leaping

up on to the tables. The fiddler played faster and faster, and the dancers whirled round giddily. Laughing, the young juggler led a dancing procession round and round the grand hall until everyone was on their feet, everyone but Gwyneth, alone and pale in her great chair and the crippled old singer, alone and swarthy in hers. Even Finn was dancing, although she knew any misstep could cause her unmasking. The black cloak swirled around her as she spun and hopped, and one hot, sweaty body after another cannoned into her, much to their confusion. As Finn danced she thought to herself, *this fiddler's got magic in his fingers, just like Jay . . .*

A suspicion stole over her. She remembered that Jay had been apprenticed to Enit at the Tower of Two Moons, to learn what she knew about the songs of sorcery. She twirled her way towards the fiddler, who bowed and scraped in the centre of the jostling crowd as if he stood in the eye of a storm. At last she was able to come close to his side and look up into his hazel eyes. Just then his bow faltered and he looked about, saying hesitantly, "Finn?"

Jay gratefully accepted a goblet of mulled wine from one of the serving maids and stood back against the wall to watch Nina dancing. With her orange velvet skirts swirling up to reveal slim, brown legs, she spun and swayed around the room, holding the audience spellbound. Jay sipped his wine and examined the crowd closely, looking for Finn. He had seen no sight of her, even though he could have sworn he had felt her close.

Suddenly he felt fingers tugging at his sleeve. He glanced down and saw a hand reaching out from behind the tapestry hanging down the wall. It was small and finely made, but rather grubby. He bent a little, trying to see who it was attracting his attention in such a surreptitious manner. Finn frowned at him, her finger to her lips, then beckoned him closer.

"Meet ye in the hall outside," she whispered.

Jay swallowed down his wine thoughtfully, then made his slow, unobtrusive way round to the door and out into the corridor.

Finn was waiting for him, hopping up and down on one foot in impatience. She was dressed in a beautifully made riding dress of green velvet, its divided skirt splattered with dried mud. The white frill at her throat and wrists was also rather dirty and dangled from one sleeve where she had caught it on a nail and torn the lace. Her long brown boots were scuffed and muddy.

"Ye do no' look much cleaner than ye did in the auld days," he said critically. "Though at least your clothes fit ye properly now."

"Och, dinna ye start!" Finn cried. "Who cares about clothes? We've much more important things to talk about!" She looked him over critically, then said, "Though look at ye, fine as a proud laird's bastard!" She flipped his crimson feather with one finger.

Jay pushed her hand away, colouring hotly under his tan. "I was disappointed indeed when I did no' see ye at the high table with your mam. What are ye doing skulking about behind tapestries?"

"I dinna want anyone to see me, o' course. Why else?" Suddenly she threw her arm about his shoulder, reaching up to kiss his lean cheek. "Och, Jay, it is glad indeed I am to be seeing ye! It has been so long syne I last saw ye! What are ye doing here? Did ye come to see me?"

"Aye, o' course," he replied, though his cheeks burnt even hotter. "We came here on purpose, to ask ye . . . But, Finn, this is something Enit will be telling your mam about later. Ye will hear it all then. I shouldna be out here talking to ye now, we're in the middle o' a performance! They'll all be wondering where I am . . ."

"Canna they do without ye a while?" Finn cried. "I have no' seen ye for so long—can ye no' bide here wi' me a wee and tell me what ye've been doing all this time?"

"But we shall have audience wi' ye after the performance," Jay said, a little bemused. "We can talk then."

"I may no' be able to," Finn said with a theatrical groan. "I have escaped my prison to see ye—if they catch me they'll lock me up again and I may no' be able to escape again."

"Whatever can ye mean?" Jay cried, considerably startled.

Finn sighed. "I'm a prisoner in my own home," she said sadly. "Ye wonder why I must sneak around and hide behind tapestries, but if anyone saw me they'd drag me away and lock me up and put such heavy guards upon me that I'd never be free again."

"Ye canna be serious! Do ye mean ye're kept locked up in a dungeon?"

"Well, it's no' exactly a dungeon . . . but I have been locked up—and fed nothing but black bread and cheese—wi' the meanest set o' guards ye could imagine, as stiff as if they'd had pokers shoved up their arses."

"But why? What have ye done?"

"Naught! Well, no' much. I punched my cousin right in her smirking mouth, but she deserved it. The slyest, sickliest, most double-faced sow ye've ever met! Ye should've seen it, Jay. She went head over heels and smashed a vase and all the court ladies screeched like hens in a whirlwind. It was grand!"

"And they locked ye up for that?"

"Aye, is it no' unjust?"

"Well, happen banprionnsachan are no' supposed to punch each other," Jay said rather uncertainly.

"As if I care a jot for that! I've never met anyone who more deserved a good pummelling than Brangaine. They should be thanking me instead o' locking me up and trying to make me apologise. Jay, I hate it here. Naught ever happens and they want me to learn to sew seams and sit with my hands folded and listen to the hens quack . . ."

"I think it's ducks that quack, no' hens."

"Who cares? I just want to get away from here and have adventures. Can I no' go away with ye? I'd love to travel about with the jongleurs and perform and sing songs. I bet ye have adventures all the time!"

"We've had a few," Jay agreed with a smile in his voice. "But that's why we're here, Finn—to ask if we can take ye wi' us . . ."

Just then they heard the door behind them open. Music and laughter spilled out with the blaze of light. Finn looked about frantically, then opened the lid of a chest and leapt inside. Jay turned as the handsome young jongleur looked out, his guitar in his hand.

"Jay, what do ye do? Why are ye out here all alone?"

"Sorry, Dide—I'm just coming."

"Are ye no' well?"

"Nay, I be grand. I'll be along in a wee bit."

Dide nodded his head, though he looked puzzled still. He shut the door again and Jay looked round for Finn, who was peering out from the chest, which she had opened just a crack. "We'll talk again later," he whispered, and went back into the great hall.

Finn chambered out of the chest, her cheeks burning hot with excitement. Jay had come to take her away!

Anxiety suddenly chilled her. If only she had not angered her mother! Gwyneth might well forbid her to go. *Happen I'd best apologise to Brangaine now and get it over and done with,* she thought.

She walked back into the noisy hall with her heart pounding and her palms prickling with sweat, making her way through the crowd towards the high table. Her appearance caused the court to murmur in surprise, but her mother did not notice, leaning her cheek on her hand and staring without seeing into the depths of her wine glass.

Finn was struck by how wan her mother looked, with shadows under her beautiful green eyes and in the hollows of her cheeks. She knelt by her side and seized her limply hanging hand in hers, saying sincerely, "I be sorry, mam! I do no' mean to trouble ye so!"

Gwyneth started upright, knocking over her glass. "Fionnghal! How ye startled me! Where have ye been? We've been searching for ye everywhere. I was sure ye must've fallen to your death."

"Nay, I would no' fall," Finn said indignantly, then tried to soften her tone, saying, "I'm just grand, mam, as ye can see. I'm sorry to have worried ye and I'm sorry I punched Brangaine, though indeed she deserved it!"

Gwyneth was mopping up the spilt wine with her napkin. She said distractedly, "What am I to do with ye, so wild and reckless ye are?"

Finn opened her mouth to cry, "Let me go with the

jongleurs," then swallowed her words. After a moment's hesitation she said meekly, "I do no' ken, mam. I'm sorry ye think me wild; I do no' mean to be. Happen it's because I'm used to having to look out for myself and being able to do whatever I want to do. I never kent I was a banprionnsa, ye must ken."

"Aye," her mother replied wearily, looking down at her stained napkin. "And I must admit ye were impetuous as a wee lassie too, always getting into mischief." She sighed and crumpled the napkin up. "Still, ye shall rule Rurach one day and ye must learn some sense. Ye canna be hitting out at anyone ye dislike, or sitting down to judgement in a torn and stained kirtle. Ye shall be lady o' the MacRuraich clan, ye ken."

Finn again had to bite back rebellious words. She bowed her head and said nothing.

Her mother said, "Well, if ye are willing to make a formal apology to your cousin and promise me to try and mind your manners in the future, I suppose ye can stay and watch the rest o' the show. It was a shame ye had to miss so much. I ken ye find Castle Rurach very dull."

Finn knew her mother was hoping she would deny this but she could not, since it was true. So she simply nodded and sat down next to her mother. They sat in silence for a long while, watching the antics of the cluricaun, who pranced about before them, turning head over heels and kicking his furry legs in a high-spirited jig.

Then Enit sang again, accompanied this time only by Jay and his viola. The candles were sinking low and shadows gathered in the corners, twisting and flowing like dancing ghosts.

"I wish, I wish, I wish in vain,
I wish I were a maid again;

A maid again I never will be,
Till apples grow on an orange tree,
Aye, till apples grow on an orange tree.
Now there's a tavern in the town
Where my love sits himself down;
He calls another lassie to his knee
And tells her the tale he once told me,
Aye, tells her the tale he once told me.
I wish, I wish my babe was born
An' smiling on yon nurse's knee;
An' I myself were dead and gone,
Wi' green, green grass growing over me,
Aye, wi' green, green grass growing over me."

The viola caught up the melancholy refrain and swept down in a cascade of low, thrilling notes. The hairs rose on Finn's arms and a little shiver ran down her spine. She glanced at her mother, wanting to share her pleasure in the beauty of the music. To her dismay she saw tears sliding down her mother's cheeks. She touched her sleeve awkwardly, saying, "What is it, mam?"

"It's naught," Gwyneth said abruptly, trying to wipe away her tears without anyone noticing. "I miss your father. I wish he were here and safe. I wish there was peace."

"Happen there will be peace soon," Finn said. "Lachlan the Winged will prevail!"

"Peace?" Gwyneth said harshly. "There has never been peace, as long as I can remember. If it is no' rebellion in the provinces it is the blaygird murdering Fairgean. There will never be peace, as long as a sea-faery still lives."

Finn was troubled. "Lachlan and Iseult will sweep

them away again," she replied stoutly. "No-one can fight like they can."

"We thought there would be peace forever after Jaspar the Ensorcelled won the Battle o' the Strand. Look what happened to him, enchanted by a Fairge witch and sucked dry o' his life till he was naught but a dry husk o' a man. Ye forget I was born in Siantan, my bairn. My people have fought the Fairgean for hundreds o' years. They never forget and they never forgive. As long as there are Fairgean in the seas, we shall never be at peace."

"Lachlan and Iseult will sweep them away again," Finn said stoutly. "He will raise the Lodestar and they'll be sucked down into a whirlpool and drowned, and we can all be comfortable again."

"Comfortable wi' the deaths' o' a thousand sea-faeries on our conscience?" a melodious voice rang out. Finn and Gwyneth looked up, startled. The hunched figure of Enit Silverthroat sat before them in her chair, supported on one side by Dide and on the other by Jay, both looking uncomfortable. The little cluricaun was pressed close against her knee, his ears swivelling anxiously, his wizened little face miserable.

"The Rìgh has repealed the Decree against the Faeries, remember?" Enit said softly. "It is against the law o' the land to talk o' destroying those o' faerykind."

"Surely that does no' include the Fairgean?" Gwyneth was astonished. "Ye canna mean the Rìgh does no' intend to take action against those black-bluided sea-demons? For the past ten years they have laid waste to my country, killing any living thing that fell into their slimy, webbed hands. They have caused such pain and heartbreak . . ." Her voice cracked.

"Wha' do ye think we have caused the Fairgean?"

Enit said, the quiver of absolute conviction in her voice. "The Carraigean made it a fashion to wear their scaled skins, for Eà's sake! The cliffs o' Siantan and Carraig had been their homes for thousands o' years and yet when our ancestors came here, they drove them off, causing their children to drown or freeze to death in the icy seas."

Gwyneth stood up, her face frozen into an expression of distant politeness. "I see ye canna have spent much time in my country. If ye had, ye would have seen the terrible toll the Fairgean raids have had on the Siantans."

"We have just come from Siantan," Enit replied softly, her hands trembling on the arms of her chair. "Indeed, there is much trouble there: many people homeless and going hungry. I do no' mean to sound as if I do no' understand how ye must feel. I ken your mother was killed by marauding Fairgean. All I am saying is that . . ."

"The Fairgean raped and murdered my mother and my elder sister," Gwyneth said in a cold voice. "They cut off my brother's hands and feet, and made him watch. They are the cruellest, most savage and disgusting creatures on the face o' the earth!"

"Yet did your father no' launch the most merciless o' reprisals? Did he no' have hundreds o' the seafaeries captured and put to death in a horrible fashion?"

"They made my brother watch as they gutted my mother and threw her entrails to their blaygird sea serpents!"

"There has been much evil done on all sides," Enit replied gently. "I ken your childhood was tragic indeed and I understand why ye hate the Fairgean . . ."

"Yet ye defend them!" Gwyneth's voice rang out

and many in the riotous crowd heard her voice and turned to glance at her, surprised. She subdued her agitation, gathering up her skirt and inclining her head to the old woman. "I am weary and wish to retire. I am sorry ye think me implacable in my hatred for the sea demons. All I can say is that ye obviously do no' come from near the sea. If ye had seen the years o' terror and grief that I had seen, ye would agree wi' me that the only hope for peace in this land is to wipe out the Fairgean once and for all."

Enit leant forward as if wishing to say something else.

Gwyneth held up her hand forbiddingly. "I understand ye have messages for me from the Rìgh. I shall take audience with ye in the morning. Goodnight." She waited for the old woman to duck her white head in an awkward curtsey before sweeping from the room, her head with its crown of fair plaits held high.

Finn lowered her eyes, embarrassed. She had never seen her mother so impassioned. Normally Gwyneth was the most gentle and considerate of women, prone to mercy in the judgement hall and kindness to the lowliest of the castle folk. It was like seeing a lamb with two heads to hear her mother talk with such ruthlessness. She heard Jay murmur something to the old woman, then he and Dide lifted the chair and carried her away, the cluricaun following close behind, his tail dragging on the floor.

Rising to follow her mother, Finn saw her cousin standing against the wall, her blue-grey plaid held close about her, her hand clenched around the Mac-Sian badge pinned to her breast. Conscious of Finn's gaze, Brangaine bit her lip and dropped her hand, colour rising in her cheeks. For the first time Finn wondered how her cousin felt about inheriting a land in thrall to the Fairgean threat. Siantan was surrounded on three sides by the sea. Its economy relied on trade, ship-building and fishing, all of which industries had been destroyed by the rise of the Fairgean over the past ten years. Finn wondered whether Brangaine hated the Fairgean as much as Gwyneth did and wished to annihilate them too. There was no clue in her cousin's closed face. Finn stroked the soft fur of the elven cat crouched on her shoulder and went thoughtfully to bed.

The next morning dawned grey and blustery. The servants went about their work with pale faces and wincing eyes. The cook was indisposed and many of the lairds snored still in their rooms, so that the company at the breakfast table was rather thin. When Gwyneth came down from her suite, she too was pale and drawn, with reddened eyelids. Brangaine came with her, and at the sight of her cousin Finn coloured hotly and bit her lip. She came forward swiftly, though, and made her apology in a gruff voice, her cheeks burning. Brangaine brought her hand to her swollen lip self-consciously but accepted the apology with gentle thanks. Gwyneth's look of approbation was enough to drown out the little sting of resentment Brangaine's forbearance gave her and Finn gave herself over to daydreams of travelling with the jongleurs and having adventures.

At last her mother pushed aside her barely touched plate and rose to leave. Finn bounded after her, barely able to contain her excitement, the elven cat at her heels like an ink-black shadow. Brangaine followed at a more decorous pace, her downcast face as usual rather distant, her hands folded before her.

The jongleurs were already waiting in the drawing room. In their bright shabby clothes, they looked like a flock of storm-tattered exotic birds. They rose as Gwyneth and her retinue came in, bowing with a flourish of their feathered caps. A murmur rose as the court complimented their jongleurs on their performance and exclaimed at some of their tricks and songs.

"I hope ye enjoyed the show, my lady?" the fire-eater said with a grin, resplendent in a worn crimson doublet and striped hose.

"Indeed I did," Gwyneth replied politely. "It is rare that we have much entertainment at Castle Rurach these days." She sat straight-backed in her velvet-upholstered chair, her pale hair combed into a plait that hung down to her knees. The blue-grey MacSian plaid was draped around her shoulder and pinned with a large, translucent blue jewel. "I found the music particularly affecting and only wish my husband could have been here to listen to your songs as well."

"We caught up wi' the MacRuraich at Loch Finavon," the fire-eater replied, bending his black head so none but those nearest to Gwyneth could hear what he said. "I be feared there was no' much time nor mood for singing."

Her green eyes flashed up to meet his. "What news o' my husband?"

"He sends his dearest greetings, my lady, and says they have managed to hold back the Fairgean, though wi' a very high cost in men. They are sore tested, my lady. The Fairgean do no' seem to weary and attack at any time o' day and night. Again and again they have broken through the palisade across the river. The MacRuraich would be glad o' some reinforcements."

Gwyneth frowned and twisted her fingers together. "I have already sent most o' the castle guard," she murmured. "Indeed, there is barely a man o' fighting age left in the entire country. We shall have to see if we can raise some hardy lads from the refugees from the coast."

The fire-eater, a rather heavy man with a gold ring in his ear, then brought Gwyneth up to date with many happenings around Eileanan. He told of weddings, births and deaths, lovers' quarrels and reconciliations, fortunes won and gambled away, estates inherited and dowries given, shipwrecks, bankruptcies and scandals, the killing of ogres and sightings of dragons. Since news was always hard to come by, Gwyneth and her ladies listened eagerly. At last he got up to demonstrate the latest dance step from the royal court at Lucescere, whirling Lady Anne Montgomery around until she was breathless and laughing.

Under cover of the chatter and music, Enit was carried by her grandson and granddaughter to sit by Gwyneth's side. Imperious green eyes met unfathomable black ones.

"I have news from the Rìgh," the old woman said softly. Gwyneth nodded her back stiff. "There has been much unrest in Tìrsoilleir since they lost the war," the jongleur said, with a quick glance round to ensure none were listening. "The Keybearer thinks it is time to take a hand in the weaving. They have a plan which they hope will help in the unravelling o' the Kirk's rule."

"What is that to do wi' me?" Gwyneth asked, hostility barely concealed in her voice. "As ye have heard, we have our hands full here, with the Fairgean invading the rivers and lochan, and the people rioting for grain in the highlands."

"Aye, I ken," Enit said, her expressive voice warm with sympathy. "As I said to ye last night, we have been travelling all through Siantan. We have only just come through the Sgàilean Mountains into Rurach . . ."

"And what was your business in Siantan?"

"We're jongleurs, my lady. We've been travelling the country, singing the auld songs and telling tales o' the Bright Wars and the young Rìgh. It seemed a guid time to remind the countryfolk o' the grand auld days, when the dragons were our allies and witches were loved. Lachlan the Winged is well aware there are many who still mistrust the Coven and who shelter Seekers o' the Awl."

Gwyneth nodded. "We have done what we can to stamp out the Seekers," she replied defensively. "There were many in Siantan, and much unrest."

"Aye, I ken. That is why we were there. The singing o' auld songs and the telling o' auld tales can sometimes do what force canna do."

Gwyneth brought the plaid closer about her neck as if she was cold. After a moment the old woman went on in a low voice: "It is always guid to hear what the countryfolk are muttering about in the corners. We are the ears and the eyes o' the Rìgh and have always travelled the most dangerous roads for him."

"I have heard that it was ye who found the Rìgh when he was trapped still in the shape o' a blackbird, and ye sheltered him and helped him find himself as a man again," Finn burst out, her eyes shining. "And I heard tell that ye were the true Cripple, the one who masterminded the rebellion against the Ensorcellor!"

Enit flashed her a look and said very softly, "And that is a true tale but no' one for the common telling, lassie."

Quenched, Finn subsided. The old woman leant forward, her amber beads clinking. "We were called back to Lucescere in early spring. It seems the Rìgh has a

new task for us. We are on our way back to Rionnagan now."

"So what brings ye to Castle Rurach?" Gwyneth
asked warily. "Ye have lost some weeks coming this
far north. Ye could have crossed the Wulfrum above
Loch Finavon and headed across the Tireichan
plains."

Finn held her breath, looking from her mother's
pale determined face to the dark, inscrutable face of
the old woman. Goblin's small, triangular head turned
at exactly the same rate and angle, as if the elven cat's
mind and body was fully attuned to Finn's.

"We have come because His Highness Lachlan
MacCuinn has requested the help o' your daughter,"
Enit replied quietly.

"Fionnghal! But she is naught but a lass. What
could the Rìgh be wanting with her?"

"They want me to break into a castle and steal
something?" Finn suggested hopefully. She sensed her
mother's horror and wished she had held her tongue,
particularly as Enit smiled in amusement and said,
"Aye. Well, at least, *someone*."

Very coldly, Gwyneth said: "Fionnghal is heir to
the MacRuraich, Enit Silverthroat, no' some common
thief. It is absolutely out o' the question!"

"But mam . . ."

"That is enough, Fionnghal! Ye are only a child still
and heir to the throne o' Rurach . . ."

"I'm seventeen, no' some snotty-nosed bairn! Ye
were near married at my age . . ."

"Mind your tongue, lassie, else ye'll be sent back to
your room until ye learn some manners!" Gwyneth
then turned to Enit and said icily, "I am sorry, but I
canna be allowing my daughter to play the part o'
some sneak-thief. It is absolutely out o' the question."

"Ye canna stop me!" Finn cried, leaping to her feet, the elven cat flying from her lap and landing gracefully with a twist of her body. The chatter subsided as everyone turned to look at Finn. Colour flooded her cheeks. Her mother folded her hands and looked at Finn coldly until she was squirming with shame and embarrassment. Then deliberately Gwyneth turned back to Enit. "As ye can see, Fionnghal has much to learn about the dignity and demeanour required o' someone o' her breeding and position. If her father was to be killed in the consummation o' his duty, she would be laird o' the MacRuraich clan and banprionnsa o' Rurach. She needs to be here, to learn how to fulfill her obligations to her people."

"The prionnsachan have a sworn duty to the Rìgh o' the land as well," Enit said gently, a subtle lift of her finger keeping angry words from spilling from Finn's lips. "The MacRuraich clan have sworn fealty to the MacCuinns and are obliged to answer his call. I'm afraid there is no-one else who can do what Finn can do. Her peculiar combination o' talents is rare indeed, as ye must ken."

Spots of hectic colour burned in Gwyneth's cheeks. "And what o' the Rìgh's obligations to his vassals?" she replied quietly, her hands clenched together. "We sent troops to the aid o' the MacCuinn and the MacFóghnan in the winning back o' Arran, yet still we have received little aid in the repelling o' the Fairgean from our shores. When is the Rìgh going to wipe out the sea-faeries once and for all?"

Enit's dark face was troubled. "The human population o' Eileanan needs to be united and at peace afore the Rìgh can be dealing with the problem o' the Fairgean," she answered. "Ye ken we canna be fighting two wars at once."

"Yet we have been beset on all sides ever since my husband helped Lachlan the Winged to the throne," Gwyneth said bitterly. "We have had the Fairgean swarming in the seas, Seekers hiding in the villages, the uprising of Siantan against our rule and the dissolution o' the Double Throne, riots for bread in the countryside, famine and pestilence and the need to feed thousands o' refugees from the coast and rivers. When is the MacCuinn going to come to our aid?"

"His Highness has sent ye men and arms . . ."

"A scant five hundred, and all o' them hungry!"

"Indeed the Rìgh kens ye have had a hard struggle the past few years. He has no' been idle, ye must ken that. There has been much to do since the Tirsoilleirean were driven from southern Eileanan. I shall tell him your concerns and ask that more relief soldiers and supplies be sent."

Gwyneth was silent, though the colour in her face had drained away, leaving her white and haggard. Enit played with her amber beads, which glowed like trapped firelight. "Your daughter has particular skills that the Rìgh is in dire need o'."

"Aye, thieving and deceiving and sneaking about like that wicked cat o' hers," Gwyneth said with bitter shame in her voice. "Very well, take her. She does no' wish to be here anyway."

Gwyneth rose, clutching the plaid about her shoulders. Finn stared at her in dismay but her mother did not meet her eyes, sweeping out of the drawing room with her head held high. After a moment Brangaine rose and followed, and a murmur of speculation rose. Finn bent and picked up the cat winding about her ankles, and cuddled her under her chin, staring round at the whispering crowd with fierce, defiant eyes.

*        *        *

The jongleurs left the very next day.

Finn was left behind, though secret arrangements were made for her to join Enit Silverthroat's caravan a week later at the border with Tìreich. Enit had insisted that none must know that Finn was to travel in the jongleurs' company. "Too many o' our Rìgh's plans have unravelled at the seams," the old jongleur had told Gwyneth. "There are enemy spies everywhere. Even the son o' one o' the Rionnagan dukes has been tried as a traitor, Eà curse his black heart. The MacCuinn has insisted that as few as possible ken your daughter has left Rurach. Tales o' the banprionnsa who can climb like a cat have travelled far and wide."

"Tales o' the banprionnsa trained as a thief," Gwyneth had said.

"We canna risk anyone wondering why the Rìgh has need o' Finn's particular talents. No-one must ken, and I mean no-one. Ye mun make up some excuse. Say ye are sending her away for safekeeping, or to punish her for her wildness. Whatever ye say, make sure it rings true. Tell no-one the truth."

"But how can I? I would no' send Fionnghal away without her maid and some men-at-arms to guard her, at the very least. What tale can I tell that would be believed?"

"Ye are better able to judge that than me," Enit had replied.

"We could pretend I'd run away," Finn piped up. "I could tie together all my blankets and hang them out the window, then leave some scraps o' cloth on a tree in the forest . . ."

Her mother had looked at her coldly. "Aye, so I would have to send out search parties to *pretend* to look for ye, when your father needs every man he can get to help him drive off the Fairgean. Do no' be foolish, Fionnghal. The idea is to draw as little attention to yourself as possible. That way the whole countryside would be buzzing with rumours and every eye on the lookout for ye."

"Tell them ye're sending me to the auld witches' tower in the mountains," Finn had suggested with a grin. "So all the ghosts will frighten the foolishness out o' me."

"That's enough, Fionnghal. Take that evil-eyed cat o' yours and go look over your history book, for I am sure ye will no' do any studying once ye've gone."

Finn had picked up Goblin, stroking her triangular head lovingly. "She doesna have evil eyes," she protested. "They're bonny!"

Gwyneth had sighed. "Please, Fionnghal, do as I bid for once."

"Aye, mam," Finn had answered meekly, too excited about her impending escape to protest. She gave a little curtsey and left the room, Goblin riding in the crook of her arm as usual.

Two days after the jongleurs had left, a foam-flecked horse galloped up the steep, winding road to the castle, bearing a messenger from the army. He carried frightening news. The MacRuraich's troops had been driven back and the Fairgean had swarmed up the river and into Loch Crossmaglen, the fifth loch from the sea. Not once since Castle Rurach had been built had the Fairgean penetrated so deep into the countryside. They were little more than a day's ride away from Loch Kintyre and the castle itself.

That night Finn was shaken awake in the dark of the night by her mother. Gwyneth's face was haggard in the light of the lantern she held in one hand. "Pack quickly, my bairn," she said, her voice shaky with repressed tears. "It is time for ye to go. Take only what is most necessary. I shall see ye downstairs."

When Finn came bounding down the stairs a few minutes later, she carried only a small bag, her crossbow and a quiver of arrows slung over her shoulder. The elven cat leapt along behind her like a living shadow.

She came to an abrupt halt at the sight of her mother standing in the great hall, little Aindrew clinging close to her side. Next to her stood Brangaine in travelling clothes—a riding dress of blue serge with a long matching coat over the top and her plaid pinned round her shoulders. By her feet was a small trunk. Behind her stood Ashlin the Piper, his beloved bagpipes in the cradle of his arm, and Donald the Gillie, beaming at Finn, his unlit pipe in his hand.

"What is Brangaine doing all dressed up?" Finn cried, undisguised hostility in her voice. "Look at her, fine as a proud laird's bastard!"

"I have decided what is the best thing to do," Gwyneth replied curtly, her hands gripping each other. "I am going to send ye all to safety to your father's hunting lodge, high in the mountains."

She held up a hand to still Finn's protest. "Your father's auld nurse lives up there with her son and his wife. If the Fairgean win through to Lock Kintyre we shall be in a state o' siege. It is quite reasonable o' me to want to keep ye and my wee laddie safe. Ye shall ride out with a small number o' guards and once ye are clear o' the castle, ye and Brangaine shall leave them and make your way down through the forest to meet up with the jongleurs on the far side o' the river."

"Brangaine!" Finn cried. "Why her?"

"Your cousin has offered to accompany ye on your journey," Gwyneth said coolly. "She will be able to watch over ye and make sure ye mind your manners."

"Nay!" her daughter cried hotly. "I do no' want her! She'll ruin everything."

"If Brangaine stays, so do ye," Gwyneth replied. "I have had a message from your father, and he agrees with me that she should go to watch over ye. He has sent Ashlin and Donald back to accompany ye also. They will serve ye both and guard ye. I would have liked to send more but your father needs every man he can to hold back the Fairgean. Besides, Enit says it is imperative that none but the most trusted ken ye travel in the Rìgh's service. It seems the tales of Finn the Cat-Thief have spread." Her voice was bitter.

"But Lachlan doesna want Brangaine!" Finn cried. "What use will she be on an adventure? She'd be worried about getting her hair mussed, for Eà's sake!"

Colour rose in Brangaine's cheeks. "I have the Nic-Sian Talent," she said with a tremor of anger in her voice. "A talent with weather is always o' use."

"Brangaine has offered to keep up your lessons in courtly demeanour," Gwyneth said coolly, "and make sure ye do naught to disgrace your name. It is very thoughtful o' her to offer to go when she must be made uncomfortable."

"What a dray-load o' dragon dung!" Finn cried. "She just wants to go so she can ruin it all for me . . ."

"If ye do no' like it, go to the hunting-lodge with Aindrew," her mother said tersely. "Though I ken ye will do anything to shake the dust o' Rurach from your shoes."

Finn flushed crimson. She had to press her lips together to stop angry words from spilling out. The little cat hissed and arched her back.

Suddenly Gwyneth softened. "Och, Fionnghal, have a care for yourself and come home safe to me!" she cried and pulled Finn to her. Finn stood stiffly within her mother's sweet-scented embrace until at last Gwyneth let her go.

The banprionnsa said rather shakily to Donald, "I put my wee lassie's safety in your care, Donald. I ken I can rely on ye to keep her safe."

"That ye can," he replied cheerfully. "Do no' fear for us, my lady, Eà shall shine her bright face upon us."

"I hope so," Gwyneth said, her voice thick with tears. She stood alone in the huge, shadowy hall, her plaid pulled close about her, watching as Brangaine, Aindrew and Finn followed Donald and Ashlin out into the inner bailey, where horses and men waited. Aindrew pulled back against Brangaine's hand, crying for his mother, but Finn did not look back.

# CARAVANS

～∽

Finn sat on the step of the caravan, eating her porridge and staring out over the plains, which undulated away as far as the eye could see. The long grass swayed, waves of silvery colour rippling away as the wind swept past. The only feature in all the wide landscape was a great tree on the far horizon, its shape silhouetted against a brilliant blue sky.

It was hot. Finn wore only a thin linen shirt and a pair of shabby breeches which tied under the knee, leaving her calves and feet bare and caked with dust. Her hair was dragged back into a bunch at the back of her neck, and her sleeves were rolled up past the elbow. She could smell a tang of wood-smoke in the air but otherwise there was only the clean, strong wind and the sharp scent of the herbs growing in the grass. Finn scraped her bowl clean and put it down with a sigh. She was happy.

The four caravans were drawn up in a semi-circle around the fire, the horses hobbled near by. Dide sat on the step of his caravan, strumming his guitar and talking to Jay and Ashlin, who were eating bannocks with honey. Brun the cluricaun was fussing around the fire, making a fresh pot of tea for Donald as he fletched his arrows. Nina was sewing up a rent in her skirt and Enit was talking with some birds that had fluttered down to perch on her knees. Despite the warmth, the old woman wore a crimson shawl wrapped close about her thin form. Lying back in the grass was Dide's father Morrell, smoking his pipe and blowing perfect smoke-rings up into the sky, where they were torn apart by the wind.

Finn groped around in the pocket of her breeches and pulled out her own pipe and pouch of tobacco. Nimbly her fingers went about their work while her eyes roamed about the camp, enjoying the colour and activity. She stuck the pipe in the corner of her mouth and tried to catch a spark from her flint, but the breeze was too strong. She wandered down to the fire to drag out a burning twig with which to light her pipe. Morrell saw her and beckoned to her lazily.

"Come amuse me, lassie, an' I'll light it for ye."

Finn sat down next to him and he conjured flame with a snap of his fingers and held it to the bowl of her pipe. Fragrant smoke billowed up and he said with a wink, "By the stink o' that, it's Fair Isles smokeweed ye're puffing on. Could ye be sparing a man a pinch o' that, by any chance? Sick to death I am o' smoking dried grass, which is all they'll sell a man in the marketplace these days."

Rather reluctantly Finn gave him a pinch of her tobacco, conscious of how thin her pouch was growing. Morrell knocked out his pipe, packed it again cheerfully, lit it with his thumb and drew back greedily. "Aye, that's the stuff!" he sighed and drew out a battered silver flask from his pocket which he unscrewed and drank from deeply. "Och, naught like a wee dram and a lungful o' smokeweed!"

He amused her by breathing out his smoke from his nostrils in two long streams like a dragon, then showed her how to send one smoke ring drifting through the centre of another, until six blue hazy hoops hung above them in ever-widening concentric circles. Finn lay back in the grass to practice, Goblin curling up on her stomach. She suddenly became aware of a long blue skirt towering over her. She shaded her eyes with her hand and peered up through the smoke. Brangaine stood over her, her face stern with disapproval. As always, she was clean and neat, her fair hair tied back in a plait, her boots shiny.

"I do no' think your mother would approve o' ye smoking a pipe," Brangaine said.

"Well, mam is no' here, is she?" Finn replied mockingly.

Her cousin's lips thinned. "Ye look like naught but a beggar lass."

"Why, thank ye, my dear," Finn replied. "That was exactly the look I was going for."

Brangaine breathed through her nose in exasperation, the sound far too genteel to be described as a snort. She turned on her well-polished heel and marched over to the fire, where she helped Brun wash up the breakfast plates, the griddle and the porridge pot.

"Och, a braw lassie," Morrell said admiringly. "And wi' such bonny manners."

"There be too much o' the stink o' sanctity about her for my taste," Finn replied morosely.

"Aye, well, happen if ye were a laddie ye'd sing a different tune," Morrell replied with a wink, before settling down in the grass again, his cap pulled over his eyes.

Finn smoked the rest of her pipe in silence, then got up and went down to the fire, the elven cat at her heels. Not looking at Brangaine, she said to the cluricaun, "Is there aught I can do to help?"

"Nay, thank ye kindly," he replied in his gruff voice, looking up at her with bright brown eyes set in a furry, triangular face. His ears were exceptionally large and pricked forward with eagerness. Dressed in the rough clothes of a farm lad, he had cut a hole in the trousers for the long tail which he used rather like another hand, picking up spoons to be polished or some kindling to fling on the fire. "Bonny Brangaine has done it all."

Brangaine smiled at him.

"Is she no' the sweetest thing?" Finn showed her cousin her teeth.

Brangaine's smile faltered for a moment then she answered as sweetly, "Aren't I?"

"Indeed ye are," Brun assured her with absolutely no trace of sarcasm. Brangaine laughed and said, "Thank ye," and Finn walked away, shoving her hands in her pockets.

To her surprise Enit looked up as she passed, saying softly, "Why do ye beat each other wi' nettles, ye two? Are there no' stings enough in this world?"

Finn did not answer. The old woman stroked the head of the bird perched on her knee. "Jealousy cuts both ways, lassie."

Finn flushed scarlet. Her pace quickened, Goblin protesting, as she bounded along at her heels. Soon the camp was left behind and the strong, sweet-smelling wind was blowing through her. The heat in her cheeks subsided and with it her embarrassment and anger. She climbed up the hill to stand in the shade of the tree, Goblin leaping up her body to crouch on her shoulder. Together they looked out over the rolling plains. Far away was a thin wavering line of purple mountains, with nothing between but smooth, silver-green hills. Finn smiled and stroked the elven cat's soft fur, the last of her resentment vanishing. Indeed, Brangaine had not been nearly as bad as Finn had imagined she would be these last few weeks. Finn could almost imagine she had been trying her hardest to be conciliatory.

Despite the slow pace of the caravans, Finn had been very content these past few weeks. She spent her days riding her pony Cinders across the plains, hunting birds and coneys with Donald for their evening meal, or sitting up on the driver's seat with Jay or Dide as they taught her how to drive the caravan. Every night they sat around the campfire, singing and cracking jokes and playing cards. Despite all Finn's attempts to find out more about the purpose of her journey, none of the jongleurs would tell her a thing.

"Dinna keep asking me, Finn! Ye'll be told when the time is right," Dide had answered one evening.

"But why will ye no' tell me?" Finn had demanded. "What harm could it do to tell me now?"

"Ye never ken when a spy may be listening," Dide answered, his voice very soft. Finn stared round at the empty plains scornfully, saying "But there's no' a soul for miles!"

"That ye can see," Dide answered. "These plains are deceiving. They look flat but really they undulate like a sea serpent's back. A whole train o' caravans could be concealed just beyond the next rise and one o' their outriders lying in the grass watching right now. The Tīreichan outriders are trained to creep through these grasses without anyone seeing."

Finn stared around. "I dinna believe it! No-one could creep up on the Cat without me kenning!"

Dide grinned at her. "And what about a bird or a mouse? See that raven sitting on the roof o' my caravan? Who is to say that it is no' the familiar of some witch, listening to every word we say? Meghan o' the Beasts is no' the only witch who can talk to birds and animals."

Finn had stared at the raven uneasily and it had stared back with its round yellow-ringed eye. "But can ravens understand our language? When Isabeau talks to animals, she talks in their language." Unconsciously she lowered her voice to a whisper.

"No' always, if the animal has lived among humans for a long time. And I notice ye talk to your wee elven cat in human language and she seems to understand every word ye say."

Finn had stroked Goblin's silky head complacently, saying, "Aye, that be true."

"So will ye stop asking me questions all the time that I canna answer and that may give the game away if someone overheard?" Dide said sternly, no trace of laughter in his face or voice. "I canna tell ye how important it is that none ken o' your mission, Finn. Whoever the spy in the Rìgh's camp is, he or she has already cost us the lives o' many hundreds o' good men. I do no' want to add yours to them."

So Finn had given up trying to learn the purpose of her journey and thrown herself into the role of a jongleur lass with enthusiasm. Nina had begun teaching her how to walk on her hands, a skill Finn had always longed to learn, and the young banprionnsa revelled in running barefoot and having her hair in a tangle with no-one to care or reprimand her.

Sudden movement caught Finn's eye. She shaded her face with her hand, staring out at the plains. A bay horse was cantering along the shallow valley on the far side of the hill, a rider crouched low on its back. Finn watched until it swerved down the curve of the slope and out of sight. It had been a beautiful beast and the first sign of human life since they had left the last village in Rurach.

Her curiosity sparked, Finn put down the elven cat and quietly followed the curve of the hill down, Goblin silent as ever at her heels.

The horse was cropping grass at the bottom of the valley. It wore no bridle or saddle and its luxuriant mane and tail had never been trimmed. Finn crouched in the grass and scanned the hills closely. At last she saw a slight break in the flowing ripples of grass at the crest of the bank overlooking the jongleurs' camp. Stealthily she crept along the slope, then wriggled up through the grass.

A girl was lying on the hill crest, watching the camp below. She wore dusty leather breeches and long boots, and her vigorous brown hair was tied back in a thick plait.

Finn crept up behind her, then, without warning, pinned her to the ground with one arm twisted behind her back. The girl did not shriek out, as Finn had expected, but struggled to be free. Finn had to press her face firmly into the dust, her knees clamped hard into the girl's side.

"What do ye think ye're doing, spying on us like that?" she hissed in the girl's ear. The stranger did not reply, just tried to heave Finn's weight off her back. Finn twisted her arm harder.

"I be an outrider," the girl panted. "It's my job! Get off me, ye great lump!"

"An outrider for whom?" Finn snapped.

The girl said nothing. Finn dragged her to her feet and began to force her down the slope towards the camp, keeping her arm twisted up her back. The girl moved abruptly and Finn found herself sailing over her shoulder, landing with a thump in the grass. She

lay still for a second, more dazed by the unexpect-
edness of the manouevre than by the fall. Then she
was on her feet, throwing herself at the girl. They hit
the ground hard, rolling down the slope as they wres-
tled. Finn was surprised to find herself well-matched
and exerted herself more fiercely. An elbow in her
ribcage winded her and she grunted, seizing the girl
around the neck and grinding her face in the ground.
The girl managed to twist over and then it was Finn
who was tasting dirt. Goblin leapt at the girl's face,
claws raking, and she started back, swearing, so that
Finn was able to wrest herself free.

Over and over they tumbled, panting and swearing.
Finn threw her to the ground with a cross-buttock,
then pinned her there with the girl's head locked
within her elbow.

The girl gave a breathless whistle. Finn heard the
thunder of hooves and then the bay was rearing over
them, his black mane tossing. Finn had to spring aside
to avoid being struck by the unshod hooves. In that
instant the girl had rolled over and leapt on the
horse's back. She gave a mocking cry, then the horse
wheeled and galloped away, his tail held up proudly.

Finn swore and dusted herself off. Her shirt was
torn and grass-stained, her hair was in a tangle, and
she was conscious of aches and pains where she had
been pummelled. "Some lassie," she said admiringly,
watching as the racing horse and rider disappeared
over the horizon.

She limped back down to the camp, Goblin marching
before her, tail erect.

Donald was filling a bucket with water from the
stream and looked up at her without his usual twinkle.
"Wha' be the matter, lassie? Ye look like ye've been
wrestling wi' a woolly bear!"

"Some strange lass was spying on us!" Finn said with heat. "She was watching from yon hill. I tried to make her tell what she was doing but she got away, the bluidy bullying beast!"

Donald was frowning. "Happen we'd best tell Enit," he said. "It probably means naught but we do no' wish anyone spying on us and carrying tales about what we do."

Finn nodded. "That's what I thought."

She helped him carry the dripping bucket back to the camp and then told Enit what had happened with some excitement. The others gathered round her and she demonstrated the holds she had used and how the girl had got free of them, her audience exclaiming and laughing. Brangaine stood at the edge of the group, a slight frown of disapproval on her face.

"An outrider," Dide said. "I wonder which caravan?"

"Get your chores finished, my bairns," Enit called. "We shall be having guests soon, by the sound o' it."

"Guests?" Finn asked, rather disappointed at the old woman's placidity.

"Aye," Enit replied. "Your spy would have been an outrider for one o' the horse-caravans, wondering who it was that travelled through their lands. No' all travellers are friends, ye ken, in these troubled times. The jongleurs are always welcome, though, so we have naught to fear, although they may be annoyed at one o' their outriders being beaten up."

Finn was a little crestfallen. "How was I to ken?" she demanded. "All I saw was some strange lassie sneaking up on the camp. It could've been anyone."

"That it could," Enit agreed. She beckoned to Nina and Dide, who seized the arms of her chair and carried her back to her caravan. Dide then bent and gathered the frail form of the old woman in his arms and carried her in through the door, leaving the chair at the foot of the steps. Nina waited till Dide had emerged, then bounded up the stairs to assist her grandmother, shutting the door behind her.

Finn sighed. Seeing a little smile on Brangaine's face she scowled, shoved her fists into her pocket and slouched off to help Morrell polish the horses' tack.

"Ye could groom the horses for me, lassie," he said with a grin. "It's been a while since they've had a guid spit and polish, and we want them looking their best for the thigearns, that we do."

"What's a thigearn?" Finn asked curiously, seizing a currycomb and beginning to worry out the burrs from the brown mare's mane.

"An' ye a banprionnsa wi' your own governess," Morrell mocked. Finn scowled and said nothing. He grinned at her. "The thigearns are the horse-lairds," he said. "They tame and ride flying horses, which is something no ordinary man can do. For one thing, the flying horse is hard indeed to catch and for another thing, they do no' submit easily to a man's will. A thigearn must ride his flying horse for a year and day without ever dismounting afore the flying horse will accept him as master."

"A year and a day?" Finn's eyes rounded in amazement.

"Aye, a year and a day without ever putting foot to ground."

"How do they sleep?"

"Lightly," Morrell grinned. "As soon as an untamed flying horse feels its rider's control relax, it does its best to buck him off. When ye think the beast can fly high into the sky, this is no' something ye want to have happen to ye, men no' having wings. They say a

thigearn learns to sleep for mere seconds at a time
and with his legs always clamped tight."

"How do they go to the privy?" Finn demanded.

"With great difficulty," Morrell chortled. Finn
laughed too and the fire-eater leant close and said,
"Ye should always watch where ye put your foot near
a thigearn."

"Yuk!" Finn cried and instinctively glanced at the
sole of her boot. Morrell laughed out loud and tossed
her a soft brush to sweep out the sweat and grime
from the mare's coat. Finn caught it deftly and worked
with a will, sweeping the brush down over the
mare's withers.

"Are there no' any lassies who ride flying horses?"
she demanded after a while.

"No' that I've ever seen," Morrell answered. "It
takes much strength o' will and body to be taming a
flying horse."

Finn gritted her jaw, immediately imagining herself
soaring into the sky on the back of a winged horse.
"I wouldna delude yourself, lassie," Morrell jeered.

"Ye never ken," Finn said loftily. "Casey Hawkeye
says I'm a bonny rider considering I dinna learn to
ride till I was thirteen."

"And I'm sure that ye are," Morrell replied with
mock-seriousness. "The lassies in Tìreich are riding
afore they can walk, though, my bonny banprionnsa."

"I thought we were meant to be keeping all that a
secret," Finn said rudely. "I'm naught but a jongleur
now."

"No naught about it," Morrell protested. "There be
no higher calling than that o' a jongleur, my proud
lassie. Travelling the land, free as a bird, bringing song
and laughter into people's miserable drab lives. Och,
it's a grand life."

"Better fun than being a banprionnsa, that I can testify to," Finn replied rather morosely.

"Aye, I'd wager it is," he answered. "Och, well, lass, ye're a jongleur now and ye're right, we'd better no' be forgetting it. Ye never ken who may be listening."

Finn had just finished grooming Morrell's mare when a wild calvacade of riders suddenly careened over the hill, galloping down towards the camp. Neighing and tossing their manes, the horses swept round the half-circle of caravans, the riders on their backs shouting and waving their hats. They all rode without saddle or bridle, though some of the horses wore halters with one long rein. They came to a snorting, sweating halt and one of the riders called, "By my beard and the beard o' the Centaur, if it be no' the fire-eater himself. How are ye yourself, Morrell, my lad?"

"Balfour, ye auld rogue! Guid it is indeed to see ye. I be just grand, though sorry I am to be seeing ye looking so grey. Your new wife riding ye hard?"

"Och, indeed, canna ye tell by the grin on my face? I think ye're in need o' a young wife yourself, Morrell, so fat and lazy ye've grown. Look at that paunch! Too much o' the water o' life and no' enough exercise, that be your trouble."

"Obh obh! I get enough nagging from my mam and my daughter to be needing more from a wife. Will ye no' stand down? All this talk o' the water o' life has made me thirsty. Come share a wee dram wi' me and tell me all the news."

"Whiskey afore noon? Och and why no'?" Balfour dismounted gracefully. As soon as his foot had touched the ground, the rest of the riders sprang down. They made no attempt to bind the horses, who put their heads down and began to crop the grass contentedly. They all sat down near the fire, shouting greetings to Dide and Nina, and drinking from pewter mugs which Morrell filled up from the barrel slung to the underside of his caravan. Finn sat down with them, staring at the riders in fascination. They were all tall and brown-faced, wearing leather boots that reached above their knees and wide-brimmed hats decorated with plumy feathers. Their clothes were drab in comparison to the jongleurs, being the same dusty colour as the plains, and both men and women wore breeches, a fashion Finn heartily approved of. All had long hair tied in plaits and many of the men wore their beards split into braids or bunches.

"Where is Himself?" Morrell asked, replenishing Balfour's mug. "Ye still ride wi' the MacAhern, do ye no'?"

"O' course," Balfour replied. "He'll be here soon." He shaded his eyes with his hand, looking out to the far distance. "Here comes the rest o' the caravan. Himself will no' be too far behind. His wife is close to her birthing time and he does no' wish to fly too far from her."

Finn followed his pointing finger and saw a long procession of caravans winding their way down the slope towards them. She jumped to her feet and went to stand at the edge of the camp, staring at the procession with curious eyes. Unlike the carts of the jongleurs, these were not decorated with fancily carved wood and brightly painted pictures, but low and long with curved roofs. Painted in varying shades of pale grey-green and yellow-brown, they were almost invisible against the blowing grass. As they came closer, Finn saw with surprise that they were pulled by teams of two huge dogs.

"Look at the size o' those dogs, my lady!" Ashlin said shyly, coming up to stand by her side. "They're as big as ponies."

"Aindrew could ride on their backs," Finn replied with a little pang as she thought of her young brother. She hoped he was safe in the hunting lodge and that her father had driven away the Fairgean. She pushed the thought away from her, not liking to think of the alternative. "Ye shouldna call me that, though, Ashlin. I be just Finn now."

He nodded his head, abashed. "Aye, I be sorry, my . . . I mean, Finn." He blushed, blurting out again, "I be sorry, it just sounds so . . ." He came to a stop, unable to express his feelings.

She grinned at him. "Say it over and over to yourself, ye ken, like, 'Finn, Finn, Finn.' Ye'll soon remember." She laughed at the wave of hot colour that scorched his face. "I did no' ken ye blushed like a lassie," she teased. "Nay, nay, do no' look so mortified. I like it. I think it's sweet."

He struggled to find some answer but could think of nothing and so stood back, blushing harder than ever. Finn gave his arm a little pat. "Now I be sorry," she said. "I was only teasing." She smiled reassuringly and looked back at the caravans, giving Ashlin a chance to recover his composure.

Riding near the caravans were a number of outriders, and horses of all colours and sizes ran loose on either side. Suddenly one of the horses spread a pair of rainbow-coloured wings and soared up into the sky. Both Finn and Ashlin cried aloud in amazement and even Brangaine gave a little gasp of wonder.

It was a huge creature, as tall and powerful as a carthorse, with a thick honey-coloured coat. Its mane and tail were pale gold and very long and luxuriant,

and from its noble brow sprouted two widely spreading antlers. As it flew it tucked its legs up under its
body. Its feathered wings were very broad, tinted
honey-yellow and crimson near its body and darkening
through shades of green and violet to an iridescent
blue at the wingtips. On its back a man was crouched,
dwarfed by the flying horse's immense size.

Those on the ground watched in awe and envy as
the magical creature frolicked through the air, folding
its wings and plunging at a terrifying speed, stretching
them out to soar up again. At last it came gliding
down to land near the caravans, the great beat of its
rainbow wings causing dust and leaves to blow about
madly, stinging their eyes.

Morrell had leapt to his feet to watch, just like everyone else in the camp, and now he bowed low to
the winged horse's rider. "Ye honour us, my laird,"
he said. "Will ye no' stand down?"

The man inclined his head and leapt lightly down,
caressing the warm, honey-coloured flank before
allowing Morrell to bend over his hand. "Welcome to
the land o' the horse-lairds once more, Morrell the
Fire-eater," he said. "Where is your sweet-voiced
mother?"

As if she had heard him, the caravan door opened
and Nina looked out. Dide came at her call and carried the crippled old woman down the stairs, depos-
iting her gently on her cushioned chair. Enit had
changed her skirt to one of orange velvet and in her
snowy white hair she wore a jewelled comb. Nina and
Dide carried the chair over to the fire, and set her
down rather heavily. Enit inclined her head as far as
she was able. "My laird," she said.

"Enit," he replied, with a courteous inclination of

his head. "I look forward indeed to hearing ye sing once more."

"I thank ye, my laird," she answered and he came forward to bow over her hand.

"Who is he?" Finn whispered to Ashlin, who gave a little shrug.

Brangaine rolled her eyes. "Did ye no' hear them call him the MacAhern? Can ye no' see his plaid and brooch?"

"But surely the prionnsa o' Tìreich would no' live in a caravan," Ashlin said, keeping his voice low.

"Everyone in Tìreich lives in a caravan," Brangaine sighed in exasperation. "There are no towns or villages here."

Ashlin and Finn made a face at each other and Finn whispered, "Ken-it-all."

The MacAhern had joined the others around the fire, accepting a swig of whiskey. The Tìreichan caravans pulled up in a loose circle around the jongleurs, completely surrounding them. The drivers leapt down from the driving-seats and unharnessed the big dogs, who lay down in the shade of their caravan, panting. Short-haired, with coats of grey-brown or reddish-brown, the dogs had a ridge of hair that ran down their spines, giving them an aggressive look. Their brown eyes were mild and friendly, however, and they seemed to grin as they panted, salivating heavily. The herd of horses cropped the grass all about, with no attempt made to confine them.

Children leapt down from the backs of their ponies, while those few too old or ill to ride climbed out of the caravans. The MacAhern leapt to his feet and went forward to help down his wife, who was heavily pregnant. She was near as tall as he, with a thick brown plait that fell down to her bare feet. She was dressed in a loose yellow smock and looked more like a crofter's wife than the wife of the prionnsa of Tìreich.

"Whiskey at this time o' the morning!" she exclaimed in disapproval, glancing at Morrell who was refilling a handful of mugs at the barrel.

"Och, a thirsty man can drink a wee dram at any time o' day or night," Morrell answered, bowing extravagantly without spilling a drop. "How are ye yourself, my lady? Bonny and blooming, that I can see!"

She smiled and thanked him and he offered her one of the pewter mugs. "Thank ye, but I think I'd rather share a cup o' dancey with your mother," she replied with a rather tired smile. The MacAhern helped lower her to the ground and Morrell gave her his own saddle for her to lean against.

The peaceful little camp had in an instant been transformed into a bustling village, with women shaking out straw-coloured mats from the caravan steps and asking their menfolk to fetch water for the washing. The children clustered close about Dide and Nina, asking questions and begging them to perform. Obligingly Dide began to juggle with his flashing silver knives and his sister walked round the camp on her hands, much to the children's delight.

"What do ye do?" a little girl with four long plaits demanded of Finn and Ashlin. "Can ye walk on your hands?"

Questions were fired from all sides.

"Can ye eat fire?"

"Can ye put your foot behind your ear?"

"Can ye ride astride three horses?"

"I play the bagpipes," Ashlin replied diffidently. The children were impressed, for the bagpipes were rare in Tìreich, and so obligingly he played a martial pibroch for them. They clapped enthusiastically, then demanded Finn show them what she could do.

"I can climb," she said but received only blank looks, most of these children never having seen a castle wall or towering cliff. "I can steal that bracelet off your wrist without ye even realising," she said then. They jeered at her. So Finn amused them by pulling coins from their ears and pebbles from their boots, then amazed them by pulling out something that she had stolen from each of the children without them being aware of it.

Dide cartwheeled over to them, did a high twisting somersault, then began to juggle twelve golden balls in intricate wheels that spun high into the air. The children gasped in wonder. Catching and casting them up again with one hand behind him, then with his feet, then with his head and shoulders, then with the sharp tip of his dagger, Dide kept them in a continual state of amazement. At last he caught all the glittering balls, and bowed with a flourish. The children went running off to tell their mothers and Dide said, very low, "I would no' be making a spectacle o' your pickpocketing, Finn."

"Why no'?" she said with a flush. "They liked it just as much as your juggling."

He tossed up his dagger and balanced it on the tip of his nose. "Firstly," he replied, his head bent back, his voice rather muffled, "we do no' want ye drawing attention to yourself. In many o' the villages that we pass through the jongleurs are the biggest, brightest thing to happen all year. People talk about what they see. Even here in Tìreich, where there are no villages, the caravans often cross each other's paths and what else is there to talk about but the jongleurs?"

He caught the dagger by its hilt, tossed it in the air

and then sheathed it without again catching it in his hands. "Secondly," he said, "we jongleurs already have a reputation for thievery. It's no' a view we want to encourage."

Finn's colour darkened. "Well, what am I meant to do?" she replied rather sulkily. "Surely a jongleur lassie would have some show to put on. Will it no' be more suspicious if we do naught at all?"

Dide smiled. "True speaking indeed. We'll have to think o' some routine for ye and Brangaine and Ashlin to perform. No' pickpocketing, though, Finn."

"Oh, fine," she answered, shoving her hands in her pockets. "I only did it so they wouldna think it was odd o' me no' to have some trick like ye and Nina."

He laughed at her and she could not help but laugh back. "Happen we can set up a rope for ye to dance on," he suggested. "I saw a jongleur do that at the Summer Fair a few years back."

Finn's imagination was fired. "I wager ye I could!" she cried. Talking animatedly, she followed Dide back to the fire, where Brangaine was helping Brun to knead bread dough and Morrell was entertaining the riders with tales of the court.

Finn's voice faltered when she saw a tall, brown-haired girl sitting beside the MacAhern. She was both pleased and sorry to see the scratch marks marring the smooth brown of her cheek.

The girl scowled at her and Finn scowled back.

"So this is the lassie who caught ye unawares," the MacAhern said humorously. The girl did not answer, just frowned more heavily.

"Aye, ye mun forgive her," Morrell said easily. "This is Finn's first time in Tìreich and she does no' ken much about your ways."

"Is she new to your caravan?" the prionnsa asked,

eyeing Finn curiously. "Were ye no' travelling with Iven Yellowbeard and Eileen the Snake when ye last came through Tìreich?"

"Aye, but they were keen to stay in Rurach and we thought we'd head to Dùn Gorm for the Summer Fair, so we parted ways," Morrell replied comfortably.

"Ye'll need to make haste if ye wish to reach Dùn Gorm by Midsummer's Eve," the MacAhern answered, raising his eyebrow.

"Och, we thought we'd cut through the Whitelock Mountains, save some time there."

"Hard work for your horses," the prionnsa answered with a frown.

"Aye, but they've done it afore and are sturdy wee beasties. I've heard tell Ogre Pass through Cairncross is safe enough these days now the Rìgh has repaired the highway."

"Aye, he's been a busy man by all accounts," the MacAhern said and their talk veered to politics.

Finn glanced at the girl next to her once or twice, then said, rather abruptly, "I'm sorry about jumping ye. I dinna ken ye were an outrider for the MacAhern's caravan. I thought ye were spying on us."

"Why ye thought anyone would want to spy on a jongleurs' camp is beyond me," the girl answered, just as abruptly.

"Ye might have been a bandit," Finn snapped.

"True enough," she answered, her voice slightly more conciliatory. She hesitated, twisting the cup in her hand round and round, then said, rather arrogantly, "I be the Banprionnsa Madeline Maire NicAhern."

Finn opened her mouth to give her name and titles just as arrogantly, then bit her lip, saying brusquely, "I'm Finn."

"What do they call ye?"

Finn shrugged. "Just Finn," she answered after a moment, wishing she could say "Finn the Cat," as she would have liked.

"They mainly call me Madeline the Swift," the banprionnsa answered proudly.

"Madlin the Mad!" a boy interjected cheekily from the other side of the fire.

"Ignore him," Madeline replied loftily. "He's naught but a laddiekin. He's my brother Aiken but we mainly call him 'the babe'."

"No' for long," her mother interjected with a smile, one hand smoothing the curve of her pregnant stomach. "It willna be long and we'll have a new babe."

Madeline did not look too happy about this. She prodded the dirt with the toe of her boot.

"Would ye like some dancey?" her mother asked, lifting a little silver pot out of the fire. It was bubbling madly, its lid jumping up and down with the steam, while a strong aroma drifted through the air.

"Some what?"

"Some dancey. It's made from the berries o' the dancing-goat bush. Much better to start the day off with than a dram o' whiskey."

"I'll have a taste," Finn said, curious as ever, and accepted a mug of a hot, bitter brew, cooled with a dash of mare's milk. As first she screwed up her face at the taste but after a few sips she grew accustomed to it. A warm glow spread through her and she felt a little buzz of energy.

"It makes ye want to dance," Madeline said. "That's why we call it dancey. They say it was first discovered when a goatherd noticed his herd leaping and dancing about after eating the berries. That's why the bush is called the dancing-goat bush."

Finn accepted another cup and was soon so restless

she had to get up and move about. She and Madeline
wandered around the bustling village of caravans, talking. Finn found she had little she could say about life
as a jongleur, having only been one for a scant few
weeks, so she avoided the subject, questioning Madeline about life on the plains instead. Madeline introduced her to the two huge grey dogs that pulled the
MacAhern's caravan. Although Goblin hissed and dug
her claws into Finn's shoulder at the sight of them,
the massive dogs did not even bare their teeth at the
tiny cat. Called *zimbaras,* the dogs were known for
their placid nature as much as for their loyalty and
strength, Madeline said, and lifted the lip of one to
thrust her hand into its cavernous mouth. The dog
only panted and slobbered on her, so that she had to
wipe her hand dry on her breeches.

The afternoon was spent eating, drinking, singing
and talking. Jay and Morrell played their fiddles, Brun
blew upon his little flute, and Nina banged her tam-
bourine and sang with Dide, who strummed his guitar.
Balfour demonstrated amazing tricks with a rope,
which Finn decided she had to learn how to do, then
many of the horse-riders leapt up to dance around the
fire. With the women wearing breeches like the men
the reels and strathspeys looked rather odd, for Finn
was used to seeing the swing of skirts. Their dancing
had a fierce energy to it, however, that more than
made up for its lack of grace.

When all were too breathless to dance any more
they listened to Ashlin, who solemnly played a lament
on his bagpipes. He was much cheered and praised,
so that he flushed and grew shy and would play no
more. Then Enit sang, her only accompaniment the
larks high in the sky. Little shivers ran over Finn's

skin and she watched how the old woman held her audience spellbound with her voice.

By now the sun was sinking and fires were being built all round the camp for the cooking of the evening meal. Kindling was rare on these grassy plans and so the fires were fed with dried horse manure, making the smoke rather pungent. The jongleurs' audience dwindled as children were called home to help prepare the dinner and the riders went out to feed and water the herds.

Only the MacAhern and his family stayed at the jongleurs' fire, for Enit had asked them to join the jongleurs' evening meal. While they had played and sung, Donald had gone out hunting with his bow and arrow and now had a brace of coneys hanging by the step. He skinned them expertly and spitted them on long steel rods which he set up over the fire. Brun scrubbed handfuls of potatoes and carrots and Finn helped him peel them with a glow of virtue.

As the younger ones worked to get dinner ready, Morrell and Enit sat by the fire, talking in low voices to the MacAhern and his wife. Finn listened as she peeled and found they were talking seriously about the state of affairs in Eileanan. The MacAhern was most interested in all the young Rìgh had been doing and asked many questions, which Enit did her best to answer.

It was soon clear to Finn that Lachlan and Iseult had paid a high price for their victory in the Bright Wars. Many concessions had been made to the lairds and merchants for their support and the young Rìgh was now having to fulfill those promises. Lachlan's armed forces had been greatly depleted by the struggle to win the war and, despite the signing of the Pact of Peace, there were still many pockets of civil unrest.

Seekers of the Awl were still being sheltered in some villages, bandits infested the forests and pirates infested the seas.

However, order was slowly being restored to the countryside. Trade was once again flourishing, despite the dangers of sailing the seas. The highways had all been repaired after years of neglect so merchant caravans again travelled from highland to lowland, and from country to country. Industries in the major cities were slowly recovering their strength and the pastures had all been replanted. Of the countries sworn to the Pact of Peace, only Siantan still suffered unrest and famine, and Enit assured the MacAhern that the Rìgh was taking steps to assist them.

"What o' Tìrsoilleir?" the prionnsa asked. "I have heard that the Greycloaks have had hard fighting to win only a few leagues o' land."

"Och, there is no doubt the taking o' Tìrsoilleir shall cost the Rìgh dear but he shall prevail in the end."

Something about Morrell's voice made Finn glance at him curiously. He was smiling as good-humouredly as ever but Finn noticed Dide was frowning slightly as he carved the coneys into portions.

The MacAhern then asked for news of Isabeau the Red, the twin sister of the Banrìgh, Iseult of the Snows. He had first met the red-haired apprentice-witch in the days when Maya the Ensorcellor had still ruled, before Isabeau had discovered she was a banprionnsa and the direct descendant of Faodhagan the Red, one of the First Coven of Witches. Isabeau had stopped his entourage in the forest in order to return to him the Saddle of Ahearn, a sacred family relic of the MacAhern clan, thereby earning the prisonnsa's undying gratitude and friendship.

"Och, I am no' the one to ask," Morrell answered

with a grin. "I'd be asking Dide if ye be wanting news
o' that lassie."

"Last I heard Isabeau was in Tìrlethan," Dide answered rather curtly. "She spends half her time wi'
her mother and father at the Towers o' Roses and
Thorns and the other half wi' the tribe o' horned
snow-faeries that raised the Banrìgh."

"Och, aye, I met one o' them at the signing o' the
Pact o' Peace a few years back. A very grim looking
man with his face all scarred."

"That would've been Khan'gharad, Isabeau and
Iseult's father. He was ratified as the prionnsa o'
Tìrlethan that day, if ye remember."

"Och, how could I forget? Such a dramatic entrance
they made, flying in on the back o' a dragon!"

Dide made no reply, staring down at the coney leg
held untasted in his hand.

"I always kent she was one o' the blood," the Mac-
Ahern said with satisfaction. "Though she was dressed
as a serving lass the first time I met her. Och, I'll
never forget my surprise when I was first introduced
to the Banrìgh after the victory at Rhyssmadill! She
was the living image o' the serving lass I'd met that
day on the road."

"Except for her scars," Morrell said. "It be such a
shame a bonny lass like the Banrìgh let herself be
slashed up like that."

"She be a Scarred Warrior," Finn said impatiently.
"The scars show how cannily she can fight. They are
marks o' great honour."

At her words the MacAhern turned haughtily to
look her up and down, obviously offended that a dirty
jongleur lass should have the temerity to interrupt
their conversation.

Finn did not notice, continuing with a laugh, "I remember the first time I met Isabeau! She dinna even ken she had a twin sister! We were as muddled as hens in a whirlwind afore we managed to work it out. I was there when they met for the first time, ye ken. They might as well have been looking into a mirror, except for Beau's hand, o' course . . ."

"Another wee dram, my laird?" Dide asked, bending in front of Finn to offer the MacAhern the whisky flask, surreptitiously elbowing her as he did so. Finn fell silent and, though the MacAhern regarded her coldly for a few minutes, he accepted the whiskey and turned his attention back to Morrell, who had begun recounting a tale of Iseult's incredible prowess at hand-to-hand combat.

"What o' the Coven?" the MacAhern asked then.

"The witches have been scouting in the countryside for anyone o' Talent to join their Theurgia but indeed the Keybearer Meghan is finding it difficult. There are so few fully trained witches to help teach the younger ones and so much to do, what with the infirmary she's set up in Lucescere and the blessing o' the orchards and the fields." Enit sighed. "So much knowledge was lost with the burning o' the towers. Ye ken I speak with Meghan often. Well, it's downhearted she's been the last few months and sorry I am to see it, Meghan never having been one to lose heart."

"She is auld," the MacAhern said.

"Aye, auld indeed and showing it now," Morrell replied.

"We're all auld now, my laird," Enit replied with a sigh. With the firelight dancing over her hunched back and seamed face, she looked ancient indeed and Finn, in the midst of all her ardent youth and vitality, felt sorry for her.

The MacAhern was sunk in thought. He barely noticed when Morrell topped up his mug with whiskey or Nina offered him the platter of roast coney. "Ye may tell Meghan NicCuinn they may send acolytes to *Tùr na Thigearnean* as they did in the auld days, if she so desires. Our wisdom is no' what is taught in *Tùr na Gealaich dhà* but it is witches' lore, nonetheless."

Enit stared at him. "Was the Tower o' Horse-lairds no' destroyed by the Ensorcellor like all the other towers, my laird?" she asked in a whisper, so Finn had to strain to hear.

The MacAhern laughed. "We o' the plains do no' feel the need to build towers and palaces o' stone," he answered mockingly. "We have few possessions and do no' want more to weigh us down and make us slow. The Ensorcellor sent soldiers against us but we hid in the grass and they could no' find us. They tried to burn us out but the Loremaster brought rain in from the sea and doused the flames. They tried to starve us out but in a battle against the coneys, the coneys will always win. They tried to ambush us but one by one we picked them off with our bows and arrows. Eventually they left. What they told the Ensorcellor I do no' ken, but as long as we kept ourselves to ourselves, she did no' bother us."

"So *Tùr na Thigearnean* still stands?"

"Indeed, ye saw him dance this afternoon," the MacAhern answered, smiling. All stared at him, bewildered. He looked round at them all, saw everyone was listening, and frowned.

"Do no' fear," Enit said. "All here are loyal to the MacCuinn and the Coven."

He accepted a coney leg from the platter Nina was holding. "Ah, but are they loyal to the MacAhern?" he asked, an edge to his smile.

"If the MacAhern is loyal to his Rìgh," Enit replied.

The MacAhern bit into the roast meat thoughtfully, his wife and daughter watching rather warily.

"We do no' have much paper here in Tìreich," he said at last, once he had finished the coney leg and tossed it down for his dog, who lay beside him. Everyone wondered at this strange divergence in the conversation but he went on, "Paper is expensive to buy and books are heavy to carry around. So we tend to learn our lore off by heart, in songs and poems and stories. All our children are taught this way. I myself can read and write and so can my children, but to most o' the bairns, words are naught but squiggles on the paper."

Enit nodded, saying, "Aye, I canna read nor write myself. We jongleurs have no need o' such things."

"Since we do no' have books, we do no' need a tower to keep them in," the MacAhern continued softly. "Our tower o' learning is a man, the Loremaster. He carries all our history and wisdom in his head and his heart. Ye ken what our motto is?" As Enit nodded her head he said softly, *"Nunquam obliviscar."*

Both Finn and Ashlin looked involuntarily at Brangaine and she smiled rather smugly and whispered, "It means 'I shall never forget'."

"Is this no' dangerous?" Dide asked. "Wha' if he should die?"

"We do our best to keep him safe. If it came to a choice, my people would choose his life over mine, have no doubt. He teaches what he kens to the Lorekeepers and in time, will choose one to succeed him. The best o' the Lorekeepers ken as much as he does."

"So there is no tower," Enit breathed.

"A living tower," the MacAhern answered. He pointed away across the camp to a small, dark-skinned man with a forked beard and grey hair tied in bunches that hung down to below his belt. Although he was far too far away to hear what the prionnsa said, the Loremaster lifted his head and gazed at them, then raised his hand in greeting. Finn recognised him as the man who had danced a stirring jig over crossed swords that afternoon.

"In the auld days many young acolytes used to come and travel with us and learn our ways, and we sent many o' our young to the Tower o' Ravens or the Tower o' Two Moons, wherever they wanted to go. Then the Coven grew rather arrogant and scorned our lore, which is all to do with horses and the way o' the plains. Fewer came then. I can remember only one or two strangers travelling with us in my childhood. Since then, none, no' for many years." The Mac-Ahern rubbed his forehead with his hand then glanced at Enit again. "So tell Meghan NicCuinn what I have said and if she is willing, well then, I will allow strangers to sit at the feet o' my Lorekeepers again."

She nodded and thanked him, and talk veered to other matters. Eating hungrily, Finn noticed that Brangaine glanced often over to the caravan of the Loremaster, her face very thoughtful. Finn teased her about it, saying, "Ye wish to sit at his feet, Brangaine? Ye'll be getting your dress dirty."

For once her cousin did not rise to the bait, but just looked at Finn rather sadly and walked away.

After they had all eaten, a crowd gathered again, to watch Dide juggling and Morrell swallowing swords and flaming torches. Finn caused rather a stir when Goblin came stalking out from underneath the caravan, where she had been sleeping, to leap up Finn's body to her shoulder. All knew that elven cats were among the fiercest of all animals, although tiny. It was said an elven cat could never be tamed, yet here was a mere girl with one riding on her shoulder. Many of the children wanted to pat Goblin but the elven cat hissed and arched her back and would let none near her, much to Finn's satisfaction.

It had been a long day and Finn was tired and as jittery as a hen on a hot griddle after drinking too much dancey. She took the little spade and went off into the darkness to find somewhere private where she could relieve herself before going to bed. Overhead the starry sky seemed to stretch forever, the ring of scattered fires small against that immeasurable darkness. It was cool and quiet away from the camp and Finn took her time wandering back, staring at the stars and letting her jangled nerves slowly relax.

Horses were wandering loose beyond the camp and Finn skirted them warily, then came through the low brown caravans towards the inner circle of tall, ornate, parrot-bright ones. A flicker of blue caught her eye and she glanced across to the Loremaster's cart, as low and brown as the others. He sat on the step, fondling the ears of his two big dogs, and listening to Brangaine who stood before him, talking earnestly. Finn watched for a moment, then made her silent way through the caravans until she stood hidden behind the one closest to the Loremaster's.

". . . there are none left in Siantan who ken the secrets," Brangaine was saying. "Canna ye be showing me the trick o' it? I ken I could do it, if only someone could show me how!"

"Riding the storm is no' something that can be learnt in an evening," the Loremaster answered. His voice was very deep yet very gentle. "And I am no weather witch, no' like the sorcerers ye speak o'."

"Yet the MacAhern said ye brought rain . . ."

He nodded and looked up from the contemplation

of his dog's head, straight across to where Finn crouched, hidden in shadows. His gaze seemed to pierce the darkness and strike straight into Finn's eyes. She flinched back. It felt like she had been struck across the face, a whiplash of mortification and shame. Brangaine had turned too and was staring where the Loremaster stared. Not wanting her cousin to know she had been spying on her, Finn turned and slipped away.

She crawled under their caravan, the cat curling against her side. She tried to sleep but the laughter and music were too loud. Spinning wheels of fire sent light darting against her closed eyelids and Finn pulled her blanket over her head, wondering why she felt like crying. Some time later she felt Brangaine creep in beside her and turned over so she would have more room. She could hear Donald's snores as he slept rolled in his plaid at the outside edge of the caravan and knew Ashlin slept on the other side, so that she and Brangaine were protected from any of the drunken revellers who staggered about outside. Finn did not feel safe, though. It was as if the Loremaster's gaze had flayed away some hard, protective covering that Finn had grown over her inner self, vulnerable as a snail's soft horns shrinking away from the light. She cuddled the elven cat up close to her cheek and let the thick fur soak up the dampness on her lashes.

In the cool grey of the morning the horse-riders packed up and went on their way, giving the jongleurs a sack of dried dancey berries and several bushels of native grain as payment for the entertainment. Within minutes there was only a few patches of flattened grass and a few charred circles to show where they had been. The jongleurs packed up camp as well, almost as efficiently as the horse-riders, and by the time the sun was up they were on their way, heading towards the purple line of mountains that rose and sank on the far horizon.

That evening Morrell set up a rope between two stakes for Finn to try walking on. Everyone's laughter at her awkward attempts only made Finn more determined and she practised until she could manage to walk the entire length of the rope without falling off.

"At the very least we can dress ye up as a jester and ye can amuse the crowds with your tomfoolery," Morrell grinned. "Ye're like a windmill, your arms flailing about like that."

"Just ye wait!" Finn cried. "I'll be dancing and cartwheeling on the rope afore ye have time to scratch yourself!"

"Ye canna cartwheel on the ground; what makes ye think ye'll learn to do it on a rope?" Brangaine said sweetly and Finn tossed her head in response, unable to think of a stinging retort.

She found some consolation for her lacerated pride after dinner, when Dide began to teach them the words of the most popular ballads. After listening to Brangaine sing no more than a few bars, Dide suggested as tactfully as he could that it might be better if she busied herself collecting coins from the audience during the performances.

"Ye be such a bonny lass, ye'll coax many a gold coin from those who'd only offer me a mere copper," he said.

"While if they heard ye sing they'd offer us naught but rotten tomatoes," Finn interjected joyously. "Och, it's a voice to beg bacon with!"

Dide rolled his eyes. "Thanks for that, Finn!"

Brangaine flushed deeply and said nothing. After a while she rose and went to watch Nina, who was doing stretching exercises beside the caravan. Finn was able to relax and enjoy the music, taking pleasure in having Jay, Ashlin and Dide all to herself. As always, Dide was full of jokes and puns and clever witticisms, his nimble brown fingers flying over the strings of his battered guitar as he sang ballad after ballad. Although her merriment was genuine, Finn could not help laughing just a little bit louder and longer than was natural, casting the occasional glance at Brangaine to make sure she was feeling properly left out. Nina was too kind a girl to allow Brangaine to mope, however. Soon the two girls were giggling themselves as Nina taught Brangaine the steps to a dance that the NicSian's three maiden aunts would never have approved of her knowing.

After they had sung and laughed themselves hoarse, Finn and Ashlin lay back to watch the fire and listen to Jay and Dide as they played for their own pleasure. Everyone drew close then, for the two friends wove a spell of enchantment with their music that caused Finn's eyes to prickle with an unidentifiable longing. Dide had put away his guitar and played a small clàrsach, held on his lap as he sat on a fallen log. Jay stood, a tall, lean shadow in the night, his viola lifted to his chin, bending and swaying as he swept his bow across the strings.

When they had at last finished and all were preparing for bed, Finn said to Jay in rather a small voice, "Ye always had the magic in your fingers, Jay, but I swear ye played better tonight than I have ever heard anyone play."

"Thank ye," he said in a low, humble voice. "It is my *viola d'amore*. She has a haunting voice, does she no'? Ye ken she was made by Gwenevyre NicSeinn herself? Enit says she is one o' the great treasures o' the MacSeinn clan and never should have been given to me. But what was once given canna be taken away, and so now she is mine. I thank Eà for her every day."

He cradled the beautiful viola in his arms, running his fingers lightly over its scrolled neck, which had been carved into the shapely form of a woman, her eyes blindfolded. Finn felt a stab of jealousy, but she said with genuine feeling, "Aye, her voice is bonny indeed. But it is no' just her, Jay. It is ye. Ye truly are marvellous."

"Thank ye kindly," he replied with a trace of embarrassment in his voice. "I am lucky to have been taught by Enit, for she is truly the greatest musician I have ever kent. Even if she is naught but an auld gypsy woman, as Dillon once said." There was a trace of bitterness in his voice.

"Och, what did Scruffy ever ken except giving orders?" Finn said breezily. "I think Enit is wonderful."

For the next few days the wavering blue line of the hills stayed far in the distance, for the troupe could travel little more than twenty miles a day. There were few roads in Tìreich and the horses were pulling a heavy load so needed to be rested often. Finn spent much of the days out hunting with Donald, until she grew both fast and accurate with her little crossbow and arrow, while the evenings were spent singing around the campfire and practising her tightrope walking. They were happy days for Finn, who revelled in her freedom.

Gradually the hills on the horizon grew steeper and darker, and their way grew slower as the undulating plains gave way to low foothills. They entertained another caravan of horse-riders, and had many of their stores replenished in payment. The very next morning they reached the highway and began the climb into the Whitelock Mountains.

The highway wound up, switchbacking back and forth to avoid growing too steep. There were many signs of fresh repairs and several way-stations had been built to give travellers a place to rest for the night. Here Morrell was able to wheedle payment in whiskey and bacon, much to his satisfaction.

The road was busy and they passed many merchants with convoys of wagons loaded with timber, cloth, spices, precious glassware or sacks of grain. All those heading west were eager for news of Rurach and Siantan and shook their heads when they heard the Fairgean had penetrated as deep as the fifth loch. Some wondered whether to turn back, but in the end pressed on, reluctant to lose their profit. The jongleurs entertained them all, and were paid with goods ranging from a hutch of live chickens to a new embossed sheath for Morrell's claymore.

For several days it rained and they walked with their heads hunched in misery and water running down their necks. The girls slept inside the caravan, trying to find space to stretch out amidst the barrels of whiskey and ale, the jars of tea and honey and dried fruit, the cases of musical instruments, the sacks of oats and flour, the carcasses of cured ham and mutton, the bunches of dried herbs and the patched costumes hanging off hooks. Finn began to think life as a banprionnsa was not so bad after all; at least she had a castle in which to shelter from the rain.

Then Cairncross Peak reared its ugly head out of the clouds. The road grew so steep they led the horses rather than make them carry the extra weight of a driver. At times the road was so narrow no-one could have walked beside the caravans without falling into the abyss that yawned on one side, its bottom hidden in mist. On the other side a great cliff rose, straight as a wall. They could not stop and so they pushed on into the darkness, everyone carrying a flaming torch, the sharp-eyed cluricaun leading the way. At last the road widened out into a plateau. They made camp hastily, eating bread and cold bacon as they wrapped the shivering, sweating horses in their blankets and secured the caravans with rocks behind the wheels to make sure they did not roll down the cliff in the night.

During the night the rain stopped. They woke to a clear, sharp morning, the bulbous shape of Cairncross Peak looming directly above them. At one edge of the plateau was a tall stone pillar, all covered over with moss. At its apex was a tall stone pillar surmounted by a crossed circle, sacred sign of the Coven. Engraved on the body of the pillar were a long list of names under the words, "Here died many followers of the MacCuinn, Hartley the Explorer, at the Battle of Ogre Pass, in the Year 106. May Eà embrace her children."

The words had only recently been re-cut, so they were easily read. Finn gave a little shiver and looked up at the narrow pass cutting its way beneath the looming peak. "Do ye think there are any ogres left?" she asked rather anxiously.

"I heard tell the Rìgh's road-team had to kill a few when they were repairing the highway," Morrell said, for once nor smiling. "None o' the merchants we spoke to on the road had seen any, though, Finn, so I would no' fret."

"I've never seen an ogre," Jay said. "Are they as fearsome as the stories say?"

Dide nodded brusquely, harnessing his sturdy grey mare to his caravan. They did not stop to cook, eating hard bannocks and honey as they walked. The walls of the pass rose up all around them, cold and dark as a prison. Far above the sky was white, bleached of all warmth and colour, the cliffs black and glistening. Then the darkness faltered, and they walked out into a fair prospect, all sharp-pointed peaks and green valleys, strung with winding rivers like gleaming quicksilver. Far above a dragon flew, and Brangaine exclaimed aloud in awe and terror, having never seen a dragon before. Finn was able yet again to brag of her friendship with Isabeau and Iseult NicFaghan, who flew on dragon-back, and Dide told the story of how he had first met Isabeau and how she had changed the outcome of a dice game in an inn with a point of her finger.

Morrell laughed. "I would have lost a pretty penny if it had no' been for her, the bright bonny lass that she was."

"I had never seen a witch afore," Dide said. "I was fascinated by the idea o' someone being able to turn over a pair o' dice with naught but the power o' their own mind. I knew my granddam could sing a bird to her knee and that Da could whisper the horses but I'd grown up wi' that, it did no' seem like magic to me. It was when I met Isabeau that I began to want to do such things myself and try my hand at it, and then we were hiding my master and he taught me as much as he himself remembered."

"Which was no' much, since he was naught but a laddickin himself," Morrell said rather sarcastically.

"Do ye mean Lachlan, I mean, His Highness?" Finn asked, hazel-green eyes bright with curiosity. Dide nodded and she said, "Why do ye call him 'master'?"

"Because that's wha' he is," Dide answered serenely. "I pledged myself to his service when I was but nine years auld and swore I'd help him throw down the Ensorcellor and get back his rightful place. It took another nine years but we did it in the end."

"And now he is Rìgh," Brangaine said. Dide nodded. He pulled down his guitar from the caravan and sang her "Three Blackbirds," the ballad he had composed describing Maya's ensorcellment of Lachlan and his brothers.

Enit and Nina sang the sorrowful refrain with him, pure-voiced as larks:

"O where have ye flown, my black-winged birds,
Leaving me all alone?
O where have ye flown, my black-winged brothers?
Where have ye flown, my brothers?"

Brangaine had to clear her throat and surreptitiously wipe away a tear from the corner of her eye and Dide was silent for a long time afterwards.

They saw no ogres, to everyone's relief, but the dragon flew with them for some days, keeping everyone's nerves on edge. Donald was careful to kill nothing larger than a bird or a coney for their supper and a close watch was kept over the horses, who were hobbled within the circle of caravans at night. At last they passed out of the dragon's territory and everyone relaxed.

The next day, the land gentled down into hills and the road began to run along the white, roaring rush of the Ban-Bharrach River. The sun shone dappled through fresh green leaves and birds sang on all sides, quite a few perched along the rim of Enit's caravan. Suddenly the birds clapped their wings and flew up into the branches. Finn was sitting up with Jay on the driving-seat of his caravan and saw his brown hands tighten on the reins. Dide swung back his plaid so that his daggers were in easy reach and Morrell kept his hand near his claymore. Everyone scanned the forest with keen eyes but there was no sign of any movement. After a while the birds sang again and Jay relaxed.

"Bandits," he replied in answer to Finn's question. "They rarely rob jongleurs for they ken we have naught o' any value and are prepared to fight for the little we do have. I pity a fat merchant wi' a wagon full o' grain, though; he'd no' be so lucky."

Although all were conscious of being watched several times over the next few hours, they were never challenged. The very next day they met a squad of soldiers on the road, all wearing the blue cloaks that showed them to be in the Rìgh's service. They were riding the roads in search of bandits and were pleased to hear the jongleurs had sensed some only a day ahead. They stopped only long enough to tell the jongleurs news of the Rìgh and to hear how matters stood in Rurach and Tìreich, then they trotted on down the road, their cloaks swinging.

Soon the troupe of jongleurs was driving through a great, dark forest where the trees arched high overhead. They came to a tall pair of iron gates set in a massive wall. There were guards there dressed in kilts and long blue cloaks, with claymores strapped to their backs. They opened the gates straightaway with a salute to the heart, and the troupe of jongleurs drove on into a park with green, sunlit vistas between trees whose bark was much scarred and blackened with the marks of battle.

"All this belongs to the MacBrann. He and my master are close, however, and the MacBrann lets him stay whenever he wishes. Lachlan does no' often come

here, though. There are too many black memories
here." Dide glanced about him with a grim mouth.

"So why is he here now?" Finn asked curiously but
the jongleur shrugged and would not answer.

The trees thinned. Ashlin suddenly cried out in
amazement and pointed. Ahead, tall, delicately pointed
towers soared into the sky, sharp and blue as daggers.

"Rhyssmadill?" Brangaine asked rather breathlessly
and Dide nodded.

The horses quickened their pace a little, responding
to the unspoken excitement of the drivers. Finn leant
forward, eager to see as much as she could of the blue
palace, about which she had heard so much. Then she
saw a bright glimmer and gripped her hands together.

"The sea? Is that the sea?" she cried.

Brangaine shrank back in sudden fear. "No' the
sea?"

"Aye," Enit said, twisting round in her seat so she
could see Brangaine's face. "Do ye fear the sea,
lassie?"

"Who does no'?" Brangaine replied rather shakily.

Enit rattled her amber beads. "I'm sorry, my lass,
but ye'll have to get over that particular dread, for
we'll be spending a great deal o' time on it! We sail
out o' Dùn Gorm just as soon as the winds are fair."

Brangaine could only stare at the old jongleur in
dismay.

# RHYSSMADILL

"No' quite what ye expected when ye heard we're to stay at the blue palace, hey, Brangaine?" Finn sat up in the straw, her arms wrapped around her knees, grinning at her cousin.

Brangaine looked around at the piles of straw, spread out her plaid and sat down. "Why should I have expected anything else?" she replied with a faint edge of mockery. "Most o' the jongleurs are camped out down in the city square, with barely enough room to scratch themselves. At least we've room to spread out here." And she lay back in the straw, her arms stretched above her head. "Ah, that be good," she said mendaciously. "Far softer than the stones o' the road, which is all I've slept on for more months than I can remember."

Finn gave a little snort but said nothing more, conscious that the loft was just above the main stables. She could clearly hear the gentle sighs of the horses, the clatter of buckets and the murmur of the stablehands' voices, the distant cry of a groom as he exercised one of the mares in the yards. Enit had reminded them forcibly of the importance of maintaining their disguise as jongleurs while in the palace and Finn was determined that if anyone let the elven cat out of the bag, it was not going to be her.

Despite Enit's warning, Finn had been rather surprised that the jongleurs had been directed to the stables, having subconsciously expected to be taken straight to the royal court. Enit and Dide were, after all, Lachlan's oldest friends and most loyal supporters. Finn had felt rather indignant when they had had to unharness their horses themselves and then were shown their sleeping quarters in a dusty, straw-filled loft. Dide had guessed her thoughts and thrown her one of his flashing grins, thanking the servant who had directed them with such heartfelt gratitude that Finn was left with no illusions that this treatment was considered most generous for a troupe of travelling players.

"Are ye hungry?" Nina said, her chestnut-red head popping above the straw as she climbed up the ladder. "Dide says ye may come across to the kitchen and eat if ye'd like. The scullery maids are always happy to give us a few scraps in return for a love song."

Brangaine and Finn looked at each other, then scrambled to their feet. Apart from an overwhelming desire to see more of the fabled palace than its high grey walls, they were sick to death of rabbit and potatoes.

The kitchen was a huge, hot room lined with black pits of fireplaces where whole carcases of sheep and deer were turned on spits. A scarred table ran the entire length of the room, crowded with servants cutting up vegetables, plucking goose feathers and pounding dough. A place was found for the troupe and they were brought a platter of meat off-cuts, some black and crunchy, others pink and bleeding. A pot of thick vegetable soup was swung off the fire and on to the table, accompanied by a basket of bread, so hard with grain the trenchers had to be soaked in the soup before they could be chewed and swallowed. Despite the simplicity of the fare, the food was delicious and Finn ate hungrily, looking about her with interest. The kitchen was as busy as an ants' nest stirred with a stick, people rushing back and forth with platters and bowls and jugs, all streaming and smelling delicious. At the far end of the kitchen a thin, scrawny-looking man was carefully creating a fantastical erection of spun toffee that Finn realised was meant to be a dragon in full flight. She watched in fascination as the dragon took shape under his skilful fingers, its wings spread.

"That is the head cook, Fergus the Cross," one of the scullery maids said, serving Finn another ladle of soup. "He is well named, the biggest crosspatch ye'd ever meet. He can cook, though, having trained under Latifa."

"But he's so skinny. I thought cooks were always fat," Finn replied, swallowing her soup hungrily.

The scullery maid laughed, her blue eyes dancing. "Latifa was; as fat as a Midwinter goose she was. No' Fergus though. Naught any o' us prepares is ever guid enough for him and he spits it out in the hearth. The Rìgh's own cook will be dying o' starvation if he do no' watch himself."

She moved away to top up Dide's bowl, smiling at him and tossing back her plait of honey-coloured hair flirtatiously. He smiled back, saying admiringly, "Ye grow bonnier each time I see, Elsie my sweet. Are ye planning to jump the fire tonight?"

"Only if it is ye I am jumping wi'," she said boldly.

He laughed. "Do no' tempt me, my bonny. I dinna think ye'd be liking the life o' a jongleur and indeed I'd be a bad husband to ye."

"The reward may be worth the cost," she replied, smoothing her hand down over her hip.

"Obh obh!" he laughed. "Ye have grown up, Elsie my sweet. Do ye speak so bold to all who come to eat your soup?"

She blushed. "Nay, only to ye," she answered, rather low. He pushed her away gently. "Your cross cook is glaring at me," he whispered in mock terror. "Ye had best be getting back to your work, lass, else he'll be cracking me over the head with a griddle."

"Happen I'll see ye later tonight," she said, lingering.

"Aye, we'll be playing in the palace square. Come and I'll dance a reel wi' ye."

"I'd like that," she replied, blushing.

Once the jongleurs had all eaten their fill, Dide cradled his guitar on his lap and sang them all a love ballad, his voice sweet and true and full of ardour.

"One morning in the month o' May, down by a
   rolling river,
A young shepherd did wander, and there beheld
   a lover.
She carelessly along did stray, a-viewing o' the
   daisies stray.
She sweetly sang her roundelay, just as the tide
   was flowing.
Her dress it was as white as milk and flowers
   adorned her skin.
It was soft as any silk, just like a lady o' honour,
Her cheeks were red, her eyes were brown, her
   hair in ringlets hanging down,
Her lovely brow without a frown, just as the tide
   was flowing.

O it's there we walked and there we talked and
    there we lay together;
The wee lambs did skip and play, and pleasant
    was the weather,
By the rolling river we did lie, underneath a blos-
    soming tree,
And what was done I'll never tell, just when the
    tide was flowing."

He looked so handsome in his shabby crimson jerkin,
with his black hair tied back in a long ponytail and a
gold ring gleaming in his ear, that Finn was not surprised at the languishing looks the scullery maids cast
him. He made it seem as if he sang for each one alone,
so that Finn whispered to Jay, "I'd wager he'll have
a few assignations later tonight, the flirt!"

"Done!" Jay whispered back. "Though ye'd be losing your bet, lassie. Dide sings to them all but he toys
with none. He's no rakehell."

"I find that hard to believe," she said and then, at
the quick, hot glance Jay sent her, continued, "No'
that he's a rake, I ken that! I mean that he never
dallies with any o' these lassies always hanging off
his sleeve. They be ripe for the plucking, anyone can
see that."

"Maybe so," Jay answered rather unwillingly, "but
Dide is no' interested in *them*."

"No?" One of Finn's eyebrows rose. "Meaning he's
interested in someone else? And who, pray tell, might
that be?"

Colour rose in Jay's cheeks. He said nothing.

"No' that blonde bit teasing him afore?" Finn said
in some dismay.

"Elsie?" Jay's voice was incredulous. "Ea's green

blood, no! Dide canna bear her, though she's always after him, that one."

"Aye, ye can tell she's as good a maid as her mother," Finn said with enough spitefulness in her tone for Jay to look at her in troubled surprise. "I hate those giggly girls that always think they're so fine," she explained, colour rising in her cheeks.

Dide was now amusing the crowd by juggling the pots and pans back and forth with Nina, reeling off a constant stream of lively chatter and jokes as he did so. The scullery maids laughed and sighed, whispering to each other behind their hands. The lackeys and pot-boys were all beginning to cast black looks at Dide, and the thin, sour-faced cook was looking more cross than ever.

"That's enough!" Fergus the Cook suddenly exclaimed. "We have a feast to prepare tonight and I canna have ye idle wastrels distracting my staff with your tomfoolery. Out, out!"

Laughing, the jongleurs all fled, Dide catching up a hot pie from the table as he went.

"Och, ye've broken a few more hearts tonight, my lad," Nina teased. "What shall ye do when they all come looking for ye later?"

"Run!" Dide cried. "Brangaine, will ye hide me under your skirts if they come hunting me down?"

Brangaine flushed crimson, for she had been as riveted by the jongleur's performance as any of the other maids. "No' I!" she answered. "Ye must reap what ye sow."

"Then I be in trouble indeed," Dide answered. "That Elsie will be jumping the fire wi' me if she has to crack me over the head wi' a jug first! Promise me ye'll protect me, Finn."

They spent the next few hours preparing themselves

for the night's performance. Nina shook out her purple satin skirt, sewn with knots of red and gold ribbon to cover the worst of the darns, and polished her red dancing shoes. Enit arranged her sparse white hair on top of her head, securing it with her jewelled combs. She draped her gold-thread shawl about her hunched shoulders, then began to sing scales, her voice rippling up and then down the register. Dide washed out a few gravy spots on his sky-blue doublet and combed the bhanais feather in his crimson cap, then tuned his guitar, strumming along to Enit's melodious voice. Jay lifted his bow and joined the music, the rich coloratura of his viola filling the stables with beauty. Morrell turned over his torches, checked the button on his vanishing sword, and polished his gold earring. Brun fastened bells to his hairy toes and hung them around his neck, jangling along with his usual odd collection of brightly polished keys, rings, buttons, bottle tops and one small christening spoon.

Finn and Brangaine had borrowed some of Nina's clothes as soon as they had begun joining in the jongleurs' performances. Finn was wearing an orange skirt, yellow petticoats and a blue and orange bodice, with blue and orange ribbons woven through her hair. Since her feet were larger than Nina's she went barefoot, with an anklet of bells on her right ankle. Brangaine had reluctantly allowed the jongleur lass to dress her in a green velvet gown, trimmed with gold lace and ribbons, and worn over a silk scarlet petticoat. Her fair hair was worn loose, tied here and there with red velvet ribbons. Freed from her plait, it hung down to her knees, as straight and shining as a silk curtain. Her eyes picked up the colour of the green velvet bodice, giving them the bright hue of a new spring leaf.

"Ye'll be fighting off the lads with a barge pole tonight, my bonny," Morrell said. Brangaine gave him her coldest look and turned her shoulder against him.

Finn made a little face, getting tired of always hearing how pretty and perfect Brangaine was. Seeing her expression, Ashlin leant close and said eagerly, "Ye look bonny too, my lady . . . I mean, Finn."

"Thank ye, kind sir," Finn said with a sweeping curtsey. "I must admit I thought I looked rather fine. I like your outfit too: very handsome."

Ashlin had dressed rather shyly in Dide's second-best outfit, a velvet doublet of a rich orange colour with green ribbons and embroidery, and green-patterned orange hose. On his head he wore a rather absurd cap of orange velvet with a long green feather. He blushed and smiled his thanks, his long, bony hands fidgeting with the long wooden flute that Brun had whittled for him.

Donald looked him over with a satirical eye but said rather kindly, "Well, handsome is as handsome does, but ye'll do well enough, my lad. Take care o' Finn and do no' be drinking too much o' the Midsummer ale."

"Are ye no' coming to the party?" Finn asked, noticing for the first time that Donald still wore his shabby old kilt and tam o'shanter.

He shook his head, smiling beatifically. "I be too auld," he said, "to be learning new tricks. I be happy indeed to rest my weary bones in the straw and mind all our stuff. Come the morning, I'll be fresh as a daisy while all ye young folks will be feeling mighty worn, I'll wager more than a penny."

"But do ye no' want to see all the mummery and watch the jumping o' the fire?" Finn demanded.

"I've managed to avoid the jumping o' the Midsummer fires all my life. I dare no' watch it now in case some doughty auld maid takes it into her head to jump it wi' me," the gillie replied with a twinkle in his eye. "Nay, nay, off ye go, lassie. I'll be just grand here with my pipe and the horses to keep me company. Have fun now."

Outside the stables, a late dusk was lingering, warm and still. In the inner gardens, lanterns had been strung from tree to tree, and long trestle tables were set up with cakes and sweetmeats. Crowds of people were dancing and laughing, dressed in their finest. Garlands of flowers had been hung round the neck of every statue and adorned the heads of the women so that the dance floor looked as if the garden had come alive and was waltzing. A round yellow moon hung between the dark spires of the palace, casting a bright radiance over the garden.

Jongleurs roamed through the garden, delighting the crowd with their songs and acrobatics. Some walked on stilts so it seemed they were giants. Others juggled oranges or swords, danced energetic reels over crossed swords, or built high pyramids by kneeling on each other's backs. One told wicked stories by the ale-barrel, his audience gasping with laughter.

Dide and Morrell set up a high rope for Finn. Carrying a beribboned pole to help aid her balance, Finn slowly walked across it, much to the amazement of the crowd below. She did a slow pirouette, then stood on her hands and swung her legs over her head until she stood again. Emboldened by the applause of the crowd, Finn then walked across the rope on her hands, and then did a few simple cartwheels and handsprings that sent the crowd wild. Her heart hammering with fear and excitement, Finn swung from the rope by her knees, and then her hands, dismounting with a rather wild somersault that nonetheless had the crowd cheering and clapping. As she landed on Dide's shoulders, she heard the clatter of coins on the pavement as the audience threw her a golden reward.

Dide sang a seductive love song after that, while Nina danced a slow, sensuous dance, gathering up her skirt to one side and swaying from side to side, showing off her slim, brown legs and high-heeled red shoes. Ashlin and Brun played their flutes, Morrell played his fiddle and Jay the viola, while Enit sang the lovely, wordless refrain.

Alternating music with juggling and fire-eating, acrobatics and dancing, the jongleurs had soon gathered a large crowd that was generous indeed with its coins, much to Morrell's satisfaction. "We're paid double tonight," he whispered to Finn, "for the Rìgh pays for our entertainment for his guests and the guests pay for their own. Och, Midsummer's Eve is always a happy time for jongleurs!"

It was long past midnight when Dide caught Finn by the elbow and whispered in her ear. "Come, it is time for us to meet wi' my master. Follow me when I beckon and draw no attention to yourself, do ye hear me?" Finn nodded and he said, "Tell Brangaine and Ashlin to stay close on my heels." Then he was gone, strumming his guitar and calling out jokes to the crowd.

A thrill ran down Finn's spine. She had almost forgotten they were here on the Rìgh's secret business. As she whispered the news to Brangaine her heart was hammering, her palms growing sticky. Would they find out tonight what Enit had meant, when she had said they planned to set sail from Dùn Gorm just as soon as the winds were fair? Would Finn at last find out what, or who, she was meant to steal?

They heard Dide's merry voice ringing out over the garden. They turned and saw him leaping and cavorting at the head of a long procession of dancers, spinning wheels of fire in his hands. Nina danced past, grinning at Finn, Ashlin dancing behind her, one hand grasping her waist, the other clinging to the hand of a fat, laughing matron. Then Brun cartwheeled past, his bells ringing. Finn spun, trying to keep her eyes on them all. Suddenly a large warm hand grasped hers and she was dragged into the dancing by Jay, his hazel eyes laughing down at her, his viola case strapped to his back. She laughed back and let herself be led through the gardens, in and out of yew trees and hedges, through a fountain, trying to keep her skirts out of the water, trampling over a flower bed, everyone shrieking with laughter. Then the procession danced up the steps and into the palace, Dide twirling the two flaming torches, up, down, round and round.

"There be a thorn bush in our garden,
  white with flowers be our thorn bush,
  and at the back o' the thorn lean a laddie
  and lass,
And they're busy, busy herryin' at the cuckoo's
  nest.
And it's hey the cuck and ho the cuck and hey
  the cuckoo's nest,
And it's hey the cuck and ho the cuck and hey
  the cuckoo's nest,
I'll give anybody a shilling and a bottle o' the
  best,
If they'll rumple up the feathers o' the cuckoo's
  nest," Dide sang and everyone joined in
breathlessly.

The dancers wound their way into the great hall, where the court lairds and ladies danced and flirted. Lachlan and Iseult were sitting in their tall, carved

chairs at the head table, black head bent close over
the red. For once, Iseult had not covered her hair and
her curls hung down her back like writhing snakes of
fire, bound here and there with black velvet ribbons.
She was as usual dressed in white but in honour of
the occasion her gown was of the richest satin damask,
with long bell sleeves trimmed with black velvet and
black scalloping at neck and hem. She looked every
inch a banrìgh, cool, proud and regal.

The Rìgh looked up at the sound of the singing and
laughter, and a grin flashed over his dark face. He
leapt to his feet and offered his hand to Iseult, who
smiled and let him pull her upright. They came down
the steps and onto the dance floor, the Rìgh's arm
close about her slim waist. Lachlan seized Nina's hand
and they were swung into the procession, the Rìgh's
kilt swirling up as he danced. Then Lachlan joined the
singing, his beautiful deep voice ringing out.

> "She said: 'my lad, you're plundering;' he said it
>     was no' true.
> But he left her with the makings o' a young
>     cuckoo.
> And it's hey the cuck and ho the cuck and hey
>     the cuckoo's nest,
> And it's hey the cuck and ho the cuck and hey
>     the cuckoo's nest."

Three times the riotous procession circled the room,
knocking over tables and sending goblets of wine flying. Then Dide tossed the flaming torches high in the
air, caught them with a flourish, and whirled out the
door and into the palace beyond. Screaming with glee,
the procession followed him, along the wide corridor,
up the stairs and into the heart of the palace.

Finn ran along behind, her hand held fast by Jay, her heart pounding with excitement. The Banrìgh's tall figure danced ahead of her, the red light of the torches kindling in her hair. Ahead of them many couples dropped out of the procession, throwing themselves into chairs, panting, hands to their hearts. Some withdrew into shadowy recesses to kiss and laugh. Others went in search of liquid refreshment to soothe their parched throats. Slowly the procession dwindled.

Through long galleries they danced, into the oldest part of the palace. Here the halls were narrow and of grey stone, not gleaming blue marble. Old paintings glared down from the walls, and there were stone ravens mounted at the foot of the stairs, their beaks curved cruelly. Many more of the dancers stopped, to wander through the galleries, examining the ancient tapestries with their pictures of dark forests and ancient battles. Finn and Jay ran on, eyes fixed on the twirling torches ahead of them. There were only a few candles kindled here and it was hard to see much more than jostling bodies and laughing faces. Finn suddenly realised she could no longer see Iseult's flaming red hair and paused, trying to catch her breath, straining to see through the shadows.

Suddenly a hand reached out from behind a tapestry and caught her arm. Finn had to bite back a shriek. She was dragged unceremoniously behind the curtain, Jay close behind her. She only had time to see that the curtain concealed a deep recess with a oaken door set within, half ajar. Standing within the door was Dide. He raised his finger to his lips, made a frantic signal with his hand, then silently shut the door. To her amazement Finn felt Jay slide his arm about her waist, then he had bent his head and kissed her. The first kiss only grazed her cheek, then he had caught her mouth. For a moment Finn was frozen in surprise then instinctively she responded.

A light dazzled against her closed eyelids. A merry voice cried, "Caught ye in the act! Look at ye, the sly bairns that ye are."

Bemused, Finn opened her eyes. The pretty scullery maid Elsie was leaning in, laughing, a lamp in her hand.

"I wondered what ye two were doing, disappearing like that," she said, smiling. "But it's midsummer madness tonight; people are disappearing all over the place. Come nine months, there'll be a passel o' babes being born, that I'll warrant."

Finn blushed, opened her mouth to deny that she and Jay were lovers; closed it again, blushing even harder. Elsie laughed again, said, "How can I blame ye, when I be searching for Dide the Juggler for just such a purpose? Have ye seen him?"

"He was leading the procession," Jay said, rather huskily. "Look for the spinning torches."

"I did, but it seems he has passed them on to his father, the fire-eater," Elsie said, pouting a little. "I could have sworn he was here a moment ago."

"Well, look for him in the gardens," Jay said shortly. "Canna ye see we're all alone here—or at least, we were."

Elsie laughed and put up her hands in mock-surrender. "Obh obh! Sorry indeed I am to be interrupting ye." She withdrew her head and let the tapestry drop down again. Jay and Finn were alone in the warm darkness.

There was silence between them. Finn was very aware of how close Jay was standing to her. She drew breath to say something, anything, to break the awkwardness between them. Just then the door behind them opened a crack, a draught of cool air raising the hairs on Finn's bare arms. It smelt old and musty, as if it had lain still and undisturbed for many years. Dide stood beyond, a small flame held cupped in his hands. "Is all clear?" he whispered.

"Aye," Jay whispered back. "That bonny maid ye were flirting with came in search o' ye but we fobbed her off."

"Thank Eà," Dide replied with exaggerated relief. "Who kens what could have happened if she'd found me? I could have found myself jumping the fire wi' her and handfast for all the world to see."

Jay replied teasingly, gesturing with his hand for Finn to precede him through the tall, arched doorway. Finn moved forward stiffly, aware of a stinging humiliation. It was clear to her that Jay's kiss had been merely a diversion, to throw anyone watching off the scent. She wished she had not responded so ardently. She wished she had not responded at all.

Beyond was a hallway, that ran along inside the thick stone walls. It was dark and cramped, and smelt of mice. Ashlin and Brangaine were waiting there for them, standing very close together, looking a little unnerved from being left alone in the confined darkness. They pressed themselves against the wall so Dide could squeeze past them, bringing the flame in his palm leaping to life so shadows swayed ahead of them like a procession of dark ghosts.

The passageway brought them to a steep spiralling stairwell, each step so high it was almost like climbing a ladder. At each turn of the stair was a tall lancet window on one side, with a little landing outside a thick oaken door on the other. Each door was shrouded in a veil of filthy cobwebs, proving they had not been opened in a very long time indeed.

At length they climbed out into a small round room
at the very height of the tower. Four thick candles
had been lit, their flames dancing in the warm, sea-
scented breeze that blew steadily through the tall,
arched embrasures. In their uncertain light Finn saw
Lachlan and Iseult leaning together out one of the
windows, the Rìgh pointing out landmarks to another
young couple who stood close together in the next
embrasure. Finn recognised them as Iain MacFóghnan, the prionnsa of Arran, and his wife Elfrida Nic-
Hilde, the deposed banprionnsa of Tìrsoilleir. A tall,
spare man with a gentle face, the MacFóghnan was
dressed in the heather-purple plaid of his clan, fastened with a silver brooch forged in the shape of a
flowering thistle. Elfrida NicHilde wore a charcoal
grey dress cut on austere lines, with her pale blonde
hair scraped back into a bun at the back of her head.
She looked more like a governess than a banprionnsa.

The Rìgh's squire stood stiffly nearby with a tray of
silver goblets and a jug of wine, a huge dog with a black-
patched face lying at his feet. A few other men were
grouped by another window, drinking wine and talking
in undertones. As Finn and Jay came forward eagerly,
the dog lifted its head and thumped its shaggy white
tail but Finn had eyes only for her old comrades-in-
arms, the Rìgh and Banrìgh.

"Iseult!" Finn cried. The Banrìgh turned and held
out her hands and the two embraced affectionately.

"Well met, Finn! Look how tall ye have grown!"

"So our wee cat-thief has finally arrived!" Lachlan
said. "How are ye yourself, Finn?"

"Very well indeed, your Highness," Finn said rather
shyly. She had not seen Lachlan since his coronation
and was rather abashed to find he had grown into a
kingly man, with lines of serious thought engraved on

his face. He had grown heavier during his years as Rìgh, and carried such an aura of authority and strength that she had trouble remembering him as the sullen, impetuous young man she had first met seven years ago. His magnificent wings were folded behind him, framing his body with their dark gloss, and he carried the Lodestar sceptre at his waist as always.

At the sight of Dide his face lit up and he reached forward and drew the young jongleur into a hard embrace. "Dide! So glad I am to see ye! It's too much time ye are spending on the road and no' enough time by my side, where ye should be. Are ye no' one o' my Yeomen, sworn to protect and serve me?"

Released from Lachlan's strong arms, Dide rubbed his ribs ruefully, pretending to gasp for breath. "Ye should be more careful, my master! Ye almost cracked a rib that time. Ye mun try and remember that most o' us are made o' frailer stuff." As Lachlan snorted in amusement, he went on, more seriously, "But do I no' serve ye well, my master, travelling the roads and listening to the tales o' the country folk and singing your praises?"

"Indeed ye do," Lachlan responded warmly.

"Each to their own road," Dide replied. "I should be getting myself into trouble if I did naught but follow your royal court around and sing love songs to silly maids. Nay, far better that I do what I have always done. Besides, what need o' me do ye have when young Dillon is always at your back, serving and protecting ye? He does a far better job, I promise ye!"

The squire smiled briefly, his hand dropping to caress the hilt of the sword that hung at his side. Both Jay and Finn gave a little cry of surprise and stared at him more closely. Only then did they recognise him, for the stocky, freckle-faced lad they had known had grown into a tall, powerfully built young man with a stern mouth and heavily hooded eyes. Only the thick thatch of light brown hair remained of the boy that had once been the general of the League of the Healing Hand.

"Scruffy!" Finn cried. "Flaming dragon balls, I would never have recognised ye!"

Dillon bowed stiffly. "My lady."

"Och, please do no' 'my lady' me!" she cried, troubled. "I be Finn, just like I always was."

He said nothing, merely inclined his head and resumed looking straight ahead. His dog Jed rose, however, and came to greet Finn with a wagging tail. She rubbed his rough head affectionately, ignoring Goblin, who arched her back and hissed from her shoulder. Jed whined a little, well remembering Goblin's wicked claws, and the elven cat narrowed her eyes and hissed again.

"It be grand indeed to see ye, Dillon," Jay said, rather shyly. "It has been a long time."

"That it has," he answered gravely, "and much has happened."

Finn drew closer to him, staring at him curiously. "We heard the news o' Jorge's death," she said awkwardly. "It must have been horrible for ye."

His frown deepened, his mouth compressing. Finn would have said something more but Lachlan claimed her attention again, gesturing sternly to Brangaine and Ashlin hovering behind her.

"Who are these people?" he cried. "Dide? What are ye doing bringing strangers to our conference? After all our efforts to keep our meeting secret!"

Brangaine dropped into a deep, graceful curtsey. "I am Brangaine NicSian, the banprionnsa o' Siantan, your Highness. We met at the last Lammas Conference when ye ratified me lady o' the MacSian clan and ruler o' Siantan." There was a touch of hauteur in her voice.

"Aye, I remember ye now," he answered, his voice still angry. "Wha' do ye do here, o' all places?"

"She is my cousin," Finn said rather sulkily. "She insisted on coming too." She turned to Brangaine. "I told ye he would no' like it."

"But I do no' understand," Lachlan cried, appealing to Dide. "Did ye no' understand the utmost importance o' keeping Finn's presence here secret? What is she doing accompanied by her cousin? And who is he? Her brother?"

"Her piper," Dide replied with gloomy satisfaction.

Lachlan's wings flared wide in irritation. "I suppose ye will be telling me next that she brought her hand-maid and her lap-dog too?"

"Nay, though she did bring her gillie and her lap-cat," Dide replied, enjoyment evident in his voice.

Lachlan's face was dark with anger, his jaw set grimly. "Explain!" he snapped.

"It is no' my fault, master," Dide replied rather defensively, though there was still a quiver of laughter in his voice. "We told Lady Gwyneth that Finn's journey mun be kept mumchance! Yet when Finn came to join us she had all these others wi' her, and said her mother would no' let her come without them. Castle Rurach was under siege from the Fairgean so we could no' send them back. Besides, the damage was done. I thought it best to bring them wi' us than have them wandering around the countryside, causing talk."

"Finn, ye surprise me," Iseult said. "I had thought ye a seasoned veteran. Did Enit no' explain to ye how important it was that none kent ye came to serve us?"

"I told my mother that ye would no' like it, but she said if Brangaine did not come, neither could I!"

"Ye mun remember Gwyneth NicSian is a lady o' the auld school," Dide said soothingly. "She could no more send her daughter off unattended wi' a pack o' dirty jongleurs than she could brush her own hair. Besides, it may no' be so bad. They say the young NicSian has the Talent and ye ken that could come in useful on the high seas!"

Lachlan stared at Brangaine intently. "Is this true?" he asked abruptly. "Ye can whistle the wind?"

Brangaine coloured hotly. "I have some Skill," she answered stiffly. "Ye must remember though that the Tower o' Storm is no more. I have no' been properly trained."

"Can ye ride the storm?"

Her colour deepened, her eyes falling. "Well, no."

Lachlan paced the floor restlessly. "Look at her," he said to Iseult. "She's as bonny a lass as ye'll ever see crowned May Queen. We canna be letting her step foot on that ship. Ye ken how superstitious sailors are, and the Tìrsoilleirean sailors more than most. There'd be naught but trouble if she goes."

Finn's eyes were bright with curiosity. *Tìrsoilleirean sailors?*

"And I think the piper lad should stay as well. He's skinny as a broom and has no more hair on his chin than a newborn babe."

To Finn's surprise, Ashlin came forward in a rush to kneel at Lachlan's feet. "Nay, your Highness, I mun stay with my lady!" he cried. "My laird entrusted her to my care."

Iseult looked at him curiously then bent and offered him one of her strong, white hands. He grasped it, his face distraught, and she pulled him to his feet.

"It is a dark and dangerous journey indeed that Finn sets out on," Lachlan said sternly. "She needs witches and warriors about her to protect her, no' a boy with his hands full o' bagpipes. Would ye endanger her by going?"

Ashlin was white but he stood his ground. "My laird set me to guard her and protect her," he answered unsteadily. "I swore a sacred oath."

Jay stepped forward. "He has a talent with music," he said. "Indeed, your Highness, ye should hear him play the bagpipes. He can bring a choke to your throat and a march to your step. He plays the flute as well, as prettily as I've heard. Happen we shall need every scrap o' musical talent that we can get."

Finn looked from one face to another. Matters were growing more mysterious by the minute. What good could playing the bagpipes do?

Lachlan was frowning, one hand caressing the Lodestar which glowed softly in response. Iseult laid her hand on his arm. "Such loyalty should no' go unrewarded," she said.

"The Lodestar sings his praises," Lachlan said abruptly. "Who am I to stop a man from travelling his own road? Nay, the piper may go if he so desires, though indeed, my heart misgives me. I had wanted to keep the party as small as possible."

Finn noted wryly that Brangaine made no attempt to persuade the Rìgh that she should go also, despite her promise to Gwyneth. Indeed it was clear that Brangaine felt only relief that she would not have to face the many angers of the sea. Finn cast her a quick glance of contempt that caused colour to rise in Brangaine's pale cheeks.

"Wha' about Donald?" Dide said. "Donald the Gillie."

"No' the MacRuraich's gillie?" Lachlan cried. "I kent Donald a long time syne. A doughty auld man indeed and the finest longbowman I've ever seen. He can shoot out a sparrow's eye from two hundred paces. What do ye think, *leannan*? Would such an auld man draw suspicion upon the ship? It is no' usual for a ship to carry any but the youngest and most able o' men and though I doubt no' that Donald be as brave as any o' them, we want to do naught to draw suspicion upon them."

"Your Highness, sometimes an auld sailor that has seawater in his veins instead o' bluid is made ship's cook so he can still feel the waves beneath the boards and smell the sea air, even though he is too auld and stiff to climb the ropes or haul up the sails." The speaker was a tall, stern-looking man with close-cropped grey hair under a tricorne hat and a weather-beaten face. He and his companions had been talking on the other side of the room but had drawn closer during the discussion. He gave a brief bow as he spoke, his hand held in a fist at his heart.

"Can Donald Gillie cook?" Lachlan asked with a grin.

"Very well," Finn replied with dignity, glad in her secret heart that Ashlin and Donald were to be allowed to accompany her after all. All this talk of dark and dangerous journeys was making her feel rather anxious.

"Very well, it is decided, though I do no' ken whether to laugh or sigh. Who's ever heard o' a thief with her own piper and gillie?"

"Who's ever heard o' a thief who was also a banpri-onnsa?" Dide quipped.

Lachlan smiled, then said, "Dide, the fleet is all set

to sail in the morn. What have ye and Enit arranged to explain your disappearance after the Summer Fair?"

"We are to pretend that my grandam has taken ill," Dide replied. "All ken that she is no' strong and the crippling disease that twists all her limbs is growing more painful each year. My da will set off with the other caravans, for all ken we canna afford to lie idle for long. Nina will stay in Dùn Gorm and pretend to nurse her."

"But what o' ye?" Iseult asked. "Will none notice ye are no' here either?"

Dide shrugged. "Those that travel with my da will think I stayed in Dùn Gorm with Grandam, and those that stay in Dùn Gorm will think I have gone with Da, all while Grandam and I are on the high seas. There are so many caravans here for the Summer Fair that no-one can be sure who has done what afterwards. All will be well."

"Very well then. Och, Dide, ye have no' met our captain yet, have ye? This is Captain Tobias o' Kirkloreli, a town no' far from Bride in Tìrsoilleir. He is the one who shall see ye all safe to the Black Tower. Captain Tobias, this is my auldest and dearest friend, Dide the Juggler, the Rìgh's own jongleur."

"The Rìgh's own fool," Dide replied with a smile, bowing to the captain. "Well met. Captain."

The captain bowed back, fist to his heart, then introduced the other men briskly. "This is my first mate, Arvin the Just, and this is the navigator Alphonsus the Sure. Ye could no' get a better crew; they all ken the Skeleton Coast like the back o' their hands. If any can get us safely past Cape Wrath and through the Devil's Vortex, they can."

A thrill of fear had run down Finn's spine at the words *The Black Tower*. It now deepened into a shudder that shook her slim frame. "The Skeleton Coast?" she said in a rather high voice. "The Devil's Vortex? Flaming dragon balls, will ye no' tell me where we are going and why afore I go stark raving mad?"

For a moment all were frozen into shocked silence. Then suddenly Lachlan's stern face broke into laughter.

"Finn, ye wildcat!" he cried. "Have ye no proper respect for your Rìgh? Is that any way to be asking a question o' me? Ye should curtsey deep and beg my pardon with your eyes lowered, and say, 'I beg your forbearance, your Highness, to be so rude in interrupting but may I have the honour o' addressing a question to ye?' "

"Och, what a load o' dragon dung!" Finn giggled.

"Fionnghal!" Brangaine cried. Colour burnt in her cheeks. "Please, your Highness, forgive her, she does no' mean to . . ."

Lachlan waved a hand. "Please, no need to apologise for our wee cat-thief. We are travel companions o' auld. I well remember her colorful turn o' phrase. Indeed, it does me good to hear her. I canna tell ye how tired I get o' all the bowing and scraping and licking o' my boots. At least with Finn we ken where we are."

Brangaine bowed and stepped back, her colour still high. Finn could not help smirking at her, just a little.

"Did ye tell Finn nothing o' her task, Dide?" Iseult asked, frowning a little.

"Ye said tell no-one."

"But happen she would no' have been willing to come if she had kent," Iseult replied.

Dide nodded, his merry face unusually grim. "Aye, I ken. Happen that is why I did no' tell her."

The smirk faded from Finn's face. "So what is it ye

want me to do?" she asked anxiously. "All Enit said was that ye wanted me to break into some castle and steal someone."

Lachlan's mouth quirked upwards, but he said very seriously, "That is exactly what we want ye to do, Finn. The only problem is that castle and that someone are both behind the Great Divide."

"In Tìrsoilleir?" Finn's voice rose in a squeak. "Ye want us to go into the Forbidden Land?" The Rìgh nodded. "Are we no' at war with Tìrsoilleir?" Finn said. Again the Rìgh nodded. "And we have to sail there? Even though the seas are full o' Fairgean?" The Rìgh nodded for the third time. Finn took a deep breath. She felt as if her heart was being squeezed by two giant hands. For a moment she could not say a word, then she said rudely, " 'Tis no' me that is stark raving mad, but ye, your Highness!"

"At least she remembered to call me 'your Highness' this time," Lachlan said to Brangaine with a little inflection of irony. The candlelight flickered across his dark, saturnine face and his wings rustled restlessly. Finn, Ashlin and Brangaine were all staring at him with pale, frightened faces, everything they had ever heard about the Forbidden Land rushing upon them.

Tìrsoilleir had held itself apart from the rest of Eileanan ever since its people had scorned to sign the First Pact of Peace and acknowledge Aedan Whitelock as their overlord and rìgh. Separated from the western lands of Eileanan by a curving horseshoe of a cliff, more than three hundred feet high in places, the Forbidden Land had remained in complete isolation for more than four hundred years. It was ruled by a militant council of religious fanatics who had overthrown the MacHilde clan many years ago, rejecting all ties to the Coven or to the royal family, and enforcing their own stern patriarchal religion. Elfrida NicHilde was all that was left of that once proud clan and she had never ruled, having been born long after the overthrow of her family.

Three years earlier, the Bright Soldiers of Tìrsoilleir had invaded the western lands of Eileanan in a religious crusade, determined to force all human inhabitants of the Far Islands to worship their cruel, unforgiving sun-god. Finn had heard many stories about the Bright Soldiers' brutality and bigotry. It was said their clergy whipped themselves in punishment for their sins, refused to wash, or rest in comfort, forced men to fight and pray against their will, and tortured those who refused to submit. Their grim warrior-maids cut off their left breast when they accepted the yoke of their god, and it was even said they sacrificed beasts and babies on their altars. Even though Finn had heard Elfrida NicHilde deny such tales, she knew the Bright Soldiers were ruthless in their reprisals against anyone who did not accept their faith. Had they not burnt Jorge the Seer to death, the gentlest old man Finn had ever known?

"Ye ken we have been endeavouring to win back the NicHilde's throne for her ever since we managed to drive the Bright Soldiers from our soil?" Lachlan said. As Finn nodded, he went on, "Apart from the fact that the Tìrsoilleirean shall always be a threat to us while they brood on our borders, there is no doubt we are in great need o' money and men if we are to fulfill our promise to the MacSeinn and win back Carraig from the Fairgean. Once the NicHilde sits on the throne in Bride, she shall be able to fulfill her oath o' fealty to me and bring men and arms and coin to the cause. Now, ye may no' ken this, but we won many o' the Tìrsoilleirean to our cause during the Bright Wars."

"Many o' my people believe the MacCuinn is the angel o' death," Elfrida explained in her soft voice. "The angel o' death is the warrior angel o' God our Father, the one that passes judgement on the sinful and wreaks vengeance for wrongdoing."

"It is because o' his wings and his bonny voice and his strange golden eyes," Iseult explained. "Apparently he looks like pictures o' this angel o' death."

"And because the beasts o' the air and the field fought at his command, and because o' the lad with the healing hands," Captain Tobias said unexpectedly. "To heal by the laying on o' hands is a miraculous gift from Our God the Father, and no' a trick o' the Archfiend to tempt us into evil-doing. It must be so, despite what the pastors and the berhtildes said."

"And many times Killian the Listener prophesied the coming o' the angel o' death, to smite down those who had twisted his Word for their own ends," Alphonsus the Sure said, his dark eyes glowing with fervour. "The General Assembly has grown cruel and greedy and gluttonous."

"Aye, the Fealde has grown hungry for power, and comes to the General Assembly dressed in cloth-o'-gold and jewels as if she were some whore and no' the hand-maiden o' God Our Father," Arvin the Just said. "Indeed, the Apostle Paul spoke truly when he said 'Silence is a woman's best garment'."

Finn exchanged an incredulous glance with Iseult, who smiled very slightly and shook her head in warning.

"There are many among my people who feel the young NicHilde shows more proper humility, modesty and charity than the Fealde and her warrior-maids, or even the pastors," Captain Tobias said. "She came to us all when we were prisoners-o'-war and tended our hurts with her own hands and made sure we wanted for naught. She was dressed with proper sobriety and made no attempt to flaunt herself with jewels, furbelows or buttons."

Finn glanced from Elfrida's simple attire to her own vivid, heavily decorated clothing and suddenly realised why the three Tìrsoilleirean men were looking at them all with such an air of cold disapproval.

"As ye can see, our three friends here feel strongly that the current administration o' the Bright Land is no' as it should be," Lachlan said with that faint inflection of irony in his voice. "And the many reports we receive from beyond the Great Divide seem to show they are no' alone in their thoughts."

"Ye have spies behind the Great Divide?" Finn asked in some amazement. "I thought strangers were killed if they set foot in Tìrsoilleir."

"But ye forget, my wee cat, how many o' those who came west to fight us returned to tell the folks at home what they had seen and heard," Lachlan said, smiling. "And some o' those have changed so much in their views that they now send me any news they think may interest me, all whilst spreading the tales o' the angel with the midnight wings and flaming sword . . ."

"Who shall come and topple the cruel, corrupt elders from their gilded altars, so that the people o' the Bright Land may be free o' their terrible injustice and tyranny," Alphonsus the Sure said, his voice ringing with triumph and certainty.

"Ye hear there the words o' Killian the Listener," Captain Tobias said, his sun-hardened face creasing in a grim smile. "He is the divine prophet o' God Our Father, who was wrongly accused o' heresy and dissidence and was incarcerated in the Black Tower by the Fealde and her minions. She said it was no' the word o' God he heard but the depraved whisperings o' the Archfiend, and cut off his ears so he could hear no more."

"A prophet is no' without honour save in his own country and in his own house," Arvin the Just said in the gloomiest of tones. Elfrida and the other Tìrsoilleirean nodded in solemn agreement.

"This is the man we aim to rescue," Lachlan said grimly. "Our spies tell us that the Fealde has grown afraid o' the growing ferment in the countryside and has decided it may be better to martyr this seer, rather than risk an uprising driven by the words o' his prophecy. Until now the General Assembly had thought keeping him locked away would be enough to douse the fire his words ignited. Yet since the ignominious defeat o' their invasion attempt, the Tìrsoilleirean people have begun to mutter against the Fealde and the Kirk. There is much talk o' rescuing Killian the Listener and following him in a rebellion against the General Assembly's rule. This is why we wish to free him. If Killian the Listener speaks on our behalf, happen we can win the Tìrsoilleirean people to our cause. We shall be able to help Elfrida win back her throne, and Tìrsoilleir will at last be free o' the tyranny o' the General Assembly."

"Whoso sheddeth man's blood, by man shall his blood be shed," Arvin the Just said profoundly, and his companions nodded in agreement. Finn had to stifle a giggle.

Lachlan sipped his wine, his wings relaxing. He fixed Finn with his compelling golden eyes. "That is why we need ye, Finn. Ye alone can climb into the Black Tower and let the rescue party in."

"The Black Tower?" Finn asked.

"The Black Tower is where I was born and raised," Elfrida said with a little shiver. "It is the prison where the most dangerous o' the General Assembly's enemies are kept. Traitors and heretics and the bloodiest o' murderers are sent there, and anyone that the Fealde wants to disappear. Most are executed in the square afore the Great Kirk and their heads stuck on spikes along the city walls but some disappear inside those black walls and are never seen again. No-one has ever escaped from it. My father tried when I was but a babe and died in the attempt."

"I see," Finn said. "So I'm betting no-one has ever broken in afore either."

Elfrida shook her head. "No-one in their right mind would want to!"

"Which is why ye've called in the Cat," Finn said gloomily. "Needing someone out o' their right mind."

"No-one else could do it, Finn," Iseult said. "Believe me, we have thought o' and abandoned many plans to rescue the prophet but this is the only one that has any chance o' success. If you could climb up the walls and break in without anyone seeing . . ."

"Killian is the gentlest auld man ye could imagine," Elfrida said with a break in her voice. "He has already been punished horribly—tortured and maimed for daring to speak out against the Fealde. My people have a deep reverence for prophets and they have grown to hate the General Assembly. If he should still be alive and we could bring him out o' the Black Tower and set him to preaching again, well, happen it be the best chance I have o' winning back my throne."

"Can ye at least tell us if he is still alive?" Lachlan said urgently. "Please, Finn?"

"How?" Finn replied shortly. "I'd need something o' his to hold."

Elfrida slipped her hand within her pocket and pulled out a crude wooden cross to pass to Finn. The cross was hung from a leather thong, much knotted where it had been broken.

"Killian gave me this the last time we met," Elfrida said pleadingly. "Can ye tell anything from it, Finn? Is he still alive? Is he held in the Black Tower still?"

Finn held the wooden cross in her hands, shutting her eyes and concentrating. She saw a dark cell, lit only by the flickering light of two torches shoved into braziers. An emaciated old man hung on the wall, filthy rags hanging from his skeletal frame. Thrusting a long scroll of paper at him was an armour-clad soldier with close cropped grey hair, wrapped in a long white cloak emblazoned with a red cross. "Sign!" the soldier hissed and the old man shook his head feebly.

Surprised at the light timbre of the soldier's voice, Finn looked closer and felt a shock of surprise as she saw the cloak fell unevenly over the soldier's mail-clad chest. It was a woman with only one breast.

Standing behind the berhtilde were a row of guards in full armour, wearing white cloaks with a design of a black tower upon them. There was also a small, stout man in a long black cassock, holding a jewelled cross in his hand. Against the wall was a long table covered in peculiar tools and instruments, some heating in a brazier of white-hot coals. A huge man with a shaven head was turning the tools in the coals, his bare muscular arms shining with sweat. He lifted one out and threatened the prisoner with it, and the old man cowered away. As he pressed one cheek into the damp stone, Finn saw there was an ugly coil of red scars where his ear had once been.

"He's alive," Finn said rather faintly. "They torture him. They want him to sign some kind o' confession. They want him to say he is in league with the Archfiend. He refuses."

Elfrida gave a little sob and there was a hiss from the three Tìrsoilleirean sailors. The captain cried, "God be my witness, I swear I shall do aught I can to save your blessed prophet from their evil machinations! May your retribution fall upon the Fealde and her minions!"

"Poor Killian," Elfrida whispered. "I do no' ken how he can still live. Nine years he has been imprisoned in that hell-hole and all that time they have tried to make him recant. They starve him, they beat him, they torture him, and still he refuses to sign a false confession. He is an auld, auld man and weak as a newborn kitten. I canna think how he has survived."

Finn went to pass back the cross but Lachlan said, "Nay, keep it, Finn. Ye'll need it. The Black Tower is built within a massive compound that has many thousands o' prisoners locked up inside it. Ye will need to find where the prophet is kept afore ye can free him and there is no doubt he will be closely guarded. Ye will need to Search him out with the cross afore ye can free him."

"The Black Tower is surrounded on all sides by a massive, strong fortress," Captain Tobias said. "Its walls are two hundred feet high and it is built on an island whose cliffs stand five hundred feet out o' the sea, sheer as glass. They tell me ye can climb that but by God's teeth! I doubt it. No-one has ever climbed it afore."

"I can climb anything," Finn boasted, though she felt a little light-headed.

"Pride goest afore destruction and a haughty spirit afore a fall," Arvin the Just said sourly.

"I have drawn maps o' the tower, as well as I can remember," Elfrida said anxiously, giving Finn a sheaf of papers. "Plus anything I can think o' that may be useful to ye, like the guards' routine and what they wear and who else may be found within the tower. Ye will go, will ye no', Finn? Indeed, they tell me there is no-one else who can possibly climb that cliff or break into the fortress without anyone kenning."

Finn slipped her hand within her pocket to caress her cloak of invisibility. "For sure," she answered. "Am I no' the Cat?"

Elfrida breathed a long sigh of relief. "Thank ye! Now I ken we shall overthrow the Fealde and win back my crown!"

"Sufficient unto the day is the evil thereof," Alphonsus the Sure said gloomily. "Let all things be done in due order. We have first to brave the Skeleton Coast and Cape Wrath afore we need worry about the Black Tower. Let God be merciful upon us."

Finn felt a little sick. Images of cutting off ears, witch-fires, avenging angels and a coast littered with bones whirled in her head. She glanced rather wildly at Dillon, still standing ramrod-straight against the wall with the tray in his hands. "I think I need a slurp of that wine, Scruffy," she said. "Better make it several slurps!"

# THE WEAVER'S
# SHUTTLE FLIES

# SHIP OF FOOLS

T he Black Sheep Inn was one of many crowded
together down near the wharves. It was a narrow, dirty place, smelling of ale and tobacco
smoke, and only dimly lit by whatever sunlight could
pierce the years of accumulated grime on the windows.
Even though it was not yet midday the common room
was crammed full of people, shouting out for more
ale, arguing over the toss of a pair of dice, or singing
loud sea shanties.

Most of the jostling crowd were sailors, enjoying
their last chance to drink an inn dry before setting sail
that evening on the turn of the tide. Most were
dressed in breeches tied under the knee with string,
coarse shirts rolled to the elbow, and long boots, much
stained with salt. Many were barefoot.

Finn and Ashlin lay on their stomachs at the head
of the stairwell, looking down on the crowd below
with joyous excitement. Both were dressed in the same
sort of rough clothes, with their skins stained dark
brown with berry juice. Goblin sat between Finn's
arms, watching with the same expression of curiosity
in her slanted aquamarine eyes as her mistress.

Dide appeared in the doorway of a room down the
hall and whistled softly. When Finn and Ashlin looked
up, he beckoned them to return to the room. It struck

Finn forcibly how different Dide looked now that he was masquerading as a sailor. With the shedding of his flamboyant clothes, the jongleur had somehow shed all the impudent charm that had seemed so much of his natural personality. He now walked with the rolling gait of a man who was used to the constant movement of a ship's deck. His movements had all the economical briskness of a sailor used to cramped quarters instead of the excitable gesticulations of a jongleur used to performing to a crowd. He even spoke differently, with a rough coastal accent spiced with the oaths and expressions of a sailing man. Thoughtfully Finn thought she had much about the art of masquerade to learn from the young jongleur.

She scrambled to her feet, lifting Goblin to lie against her shoulder and casting one last, regretful glance down at the fascinating hubbub below them. Just then the door to the inn opened, a shaft of sunlight setting the smoke to swirl about. For a moment all Finn could see was the dazzle of sunlight on a mass of fair hair, then she heard ribald whistles and catcalls as the sailors near the door greeted the girl stepping within.

"Och, no," Finn breathed in dismay. "What is she doing here?"

Brangaine had paused in the doorway, taken aback by the barrage of lewd suggestions. She drew her plaid more tightly around her body, even though it was sweltering hot in the crowded room, then lifted her chin and stepped in. Amongst all those rough brown men she looked like a princess in her pretty gown and slippers, her silky blonde hair hanging down to her knees in a thick, loose plait.

"Och, the lamb-brained ninny," Finn breathed.

"She could no' have drawn more attention to herself if she'd tried!

She leant over the railing. "Dinna tell me the bawdy-house has finally sent me my whore!" she slurred in an excellent imitation of a cocky young man who had had far too much to drink. "Where have ye been, my gallimaufrey? I was beginning to be afraid I'd have to raise anchor without having got to sheathe my dirk in a ripe-and-ready lassie."

Brangaine stopped in her tracks, vivid color rushing up her throat and staining her cheeks. There was general laughter and one man slid his hand inside Brangaine's arm, saying, "Let me get her loosened up for ye, laddie."

Finn came down the stairs in a rush, drawing her dagger. "Get off her, ye frog-faced lout," she cried. "I want no buttered muffin. Me mates have paid well for this fine fancy-skirt and I do no' want to share my first bite o' giblet pie with a filthy auld goat. Get your own whore!"

Ashlin leapt down in front of her, drawing his own dagger, even though his face was white. The sailor only laughed though, and let go Brangaine's arm. She drew herself away and Finn came swaggering up to her and kissed her wetly on the side of her neck, one hand rubbing her bottom. "Aye, ye be a fine braw piece o' skirt, I warrant me mates paid highly for ye!" Finn cried, drawing Brangaine towards the stairs.

"Your first time raiding the cockpit, laddie?" one sailor cried.

Finn grinned and gave a little drunken stagger. "It may be my first, Jack Tar, but I warrant it willna be my last."

To the sound of raucous laughter they disappeared

up the stairs, Brangaine's arm stiff and unyielding beneath Finn's tight grip.

"How dare ye!" Brangaine hissed.

Finn just hauled Brangaine on up the stairs, saying through gritted teeth, "Have ye porridge for brains, ye great gowk? And us supposed to be naught but sailor lads!"

Dide was standing in the shadows at the top of the stairs, his black eyes snapping with anger. "What do ye mean, turning up here like this? Do ye wish to give the game away? Look at ye, in your silk gown and the NicSian plaid, by Eà's green bluid! Ye have as much wit as two fools and a madman!"

Tears started to Brangaine's eyes. "What else was I meant to do?" she asked as Dide pushed the three of them over the sill of the door and into the room, shutting the door smartly behind them. "Ye set sail in less than an hour. I had to see ye . . ."

"Why?" Dide replied shortly. "I thought it was agreed that ye mun stay with Nina till we were long gone and no harm could be done if ye blabbed."

"I've changed my mind," Brangaine said breathlessly. "I want to go with ye."

Finn gave a snort of derision and opened her mouth to say something rude, but Dide silenced her with a gesture. "But why, Brangaine? Ye ken this is no pleasure trip we go on. It is a dangerous journey indeed. Putting aside for a moment the fact that the Fairgean rule the seas, the coast between here and Bride is no' called the Skeleton Coast for naught. It is littered with the wrecks o' the ships that have foundered on the rocks or been sunk by sea serpents, or dragged down by a whirlpool. And even if we make it to Bride in one piece, we have to break into the most impregnable prison in Eileanan and steal away the Bright Soldiers' most closely guarded prisoner. Ye will be much safer here in Dùn Gorm with Nina.''

Brangaine was sickly pale but she swallowed and said, "I ken all that. I still want to go."

"But why?" Although there was nothing but concerned interest in Dide's voice, he was looking at Brangaine with frowning intentness, his hand resting on his belt of daggers.

"I promised Lady Gwyneth I'd have a care for Fionnghal," Brangaine replied.

"I find myself no' altogether convinced, Lady Brangaine," Dide replied softly. "Ye admitted yourself that ye hate and fear the sea. Ye ken what will happen to us if our ship is overrun by the Fairgean, better than any o' us, having lost your own parents to them. Ye'll be as out o' place on board a ship as a eunuch in a brothel. Besides, there's no love lost between ye and Finn. So, what's the true story?"

Brangaine hesitated then blurted out, "Ye'd all think I was white-livered if I stayed behind. Finn would crow over it for years . . ."

". . . If I survive," Finn muttered but Dide motioned her to silence as Brangaine went on, stumbling a little. "She's had so many adventures and I've done naught but stay at home and mind my manners and learn to sew a straight seam—I'm sick o' always being the good one. I ken I could be o' use to ye, did ye no' say so yourself? And Nina said I'd have to stay hidden away in the inn so none kent I was there. Ye could be gone for months, she said."

"Have ye looked in the mirror lately, sweet Brangaine?" Finn said charmingly. "Ye look less like a cabinboy than any primping, pampered banprionnsa I've ever seen."

"That's enough, Finn," Donald said suddenly. "Why

must ye always be biting and nipping at your cousin's heels? It is no' worthy o' ye."

Finn blushed scarlet.

"She has a point though, Brangaine," Dide said gently. "As ye can see, we have all disguised ourselves as sailors. Only my grandam has no' tried, for she canna be anything but herself. If ye were to come with us ye would have to do the same, and indeed, I do no' think ye could. Look at your soft white hands. They've never hauled rope in their life. Look at your hair."

Brangaine bit her lip, glancing involuntarily in the mirror. She stared around at the others, all dressed in cotton breeches and shirts, their faces and necks brown as berries. Finn looked as boyish as any with her hair cut short, her arms tanned and muscular under the rolled-up shirt. For a moment Brangaine hesitated then suddenly she plunged her hand into her reticule, dragged out her sewing kit and withdrew a pair of scissors with mother-of-pearl handles. She seized her long corn-silk plait in one hand and hacked at it till it came away in her hand, leaving her hair jagged just below her ears. "The hair was easy enough to fix," she said in a high, breathless voice. "Has anyone any more o' that stuff to stain the skin?"

Finn gaped at her, unable to think of anything to say. Enit held out one trembling, blue-veined hand. "Aye, I do, lassie," she said warmly. "Donald will find it for ye. Kindle a fire for the lass, Dide. She must burn every last scrap o' that hair."

Brangaine looked at the long, corn-silk plait dangling from her hand and made an instinctive move to clutch it to her. "Ye mun burn it, lass," Enit said. "We want none here to wonder who has been cutting their hair. Apart from that, it is dangerous to leave parts o' yourself just lying around. Ye have heard Dide sing the story o' how Lachlan was cursed by a feather plucked from his wing."

"Never mind, lass, it'll grow back," Dide said sympathetically and snapped his fingers so a fire leapt to life on the empty hearth. Brangaine hesitated a moment longer, then threw her plait on to the flame. It flared up, slender threads of living light, then sank away into ashes.

"Do we have any more sailors' clothes for the lass?" Enit asked. "Donald, the berry juice is in a wee pot in my bag by the door. Brangaine, ye must rub it into every part of your body. We canna risk anyone noticing a line where the colour ends. And ye must bind your breasts. Finn, help her."

"We canna be calling her "Brangaine" any more," Dide said. "Happen we'd better just call her Bran. Like 'Finn,' it's more o' a boy's name than a girl's, and that way we have less chance o' making a mistake."

"There's no' much we can do about her soft hands," Enit said. "She will have to be the son o' a landholder that's run away to sea for the fun o' it."

"What about my hands?" Finn demanded, spreading them out. Only then did she realise how rough they were in comparison to Bran's, the nails broken, the palms calloused from riding her horse, and shooting her bow.

"Och, they'll do," Dide said with a laugh. "Come now, no time to dawdle. The tide is on the turn."

Despite herself, Finn felt a stroke of cold fear down her spine. Her eyes met her cousin's and she saw Bran had shared the same instinctive chill.

The fleet left the safety of the Berhtfane with the ebbing of the evening tide. There was a grand ceremony, with many speeches and toasts of Midsummer

ale. The twenty-five ships were all decorated with
flowers and anointed with goldensloe wine, and as
they slipped their moorings and floated down the harbour towards the river-gates, the fleet was blessed by
the city sorceress, Oonagh the White.

Most of the twenty-five ships in the Rìgh's fleet had
been captured from the Tìrsoilleirean navy during the
Bright Wars. They had been wrecked during the battle
for Dùn Gorm, when the Bright Soldiers had inadver-
tently blown up the river-gates, causing the Berhtfane
to flood to the sea. The rest were the skeleton rem-
nants of Lachlan's father's navy, which had spent the
years of Jaspar's rule quietly mouldering away in the
shipwrights' yards. Quite a few of the ships had
needed to be almost completely rebuilt, with a contro-
versial Ship Tax levied by the Rìgh to pay the astro-
nomical cost. Timbers had been brought in from
Rurach and Aslinn, and men who knew the sea had
eagerly travelled from every corner of Eileanan for
the chance of earning a living from their trade.

Nonetheless, many of the seamen were Tìrsoilleirean prisoners-of-war who had sworn their allegiance to Elfrida NicHilde and through her to the
Rìgh. There were simply too few experienced sailors
from the other countries of Eileanan, thanks to the
Fairgean besieging the coast for so many years.

Ten of the ships were great galleons, each with four
masts and armed with thirty cannons and a great many
soldiers. Five were caravels, with two masts carrying
square sails and a third carrying a triangular sail, making them quick and manoeuverable, riding high out of
the water but broad enough to stay afloat in the
roughest seas. Although these too were armed with
cannon, they did not have the range or firing power
of the galleons' cannons, being designed more as mer-

chant ships than warships. The remaining ten ships were carracks: strongly built, three-masted vessels designed primarily for carrying cargo. Heavily loaded with sacks of grain, seeds and potatoes, barrels of ale and whiskey, bottles of medicines, and newly forged weapons and farming implements, they were equipped with only a limited amount of armament and so relied heavily on the galleons to protect them from marauding pirates and the Fairgean.

Luckily the admiral of the fleet was not expecting to run into too much trouble from the sea-faeries. Summer was the time when the hunters and warriors of the Fairgean were mostly much further south, following in the wake of the blue whales who mated in the warm, shallow seas of the tropics. The only Fairgean in the seas around Eileanan were those younger warriors set to guard the women who bore their young on the soft sands of southern Eileanan and the Fair Isles. With such a strong fleet, the admiral was sure the young Fairgean bloods would not attempt to attack when that meant leaving the women and their young unprotected.

The drawback to sailing in high summer was, of course, the lowness of the tides. Dragged back by the gravitational force of the two moons, the summer sea was shallow indeed and many rocks and reefs that were covered in spring and autumn were exposed. Most dangerous of all were the sandbanks which changed every year as the king tide dragged them back and forth. Rocks, reefs and islands could be mapped and avoided. Most captains only knew there was a sandbank ahead when they ran aground.

The fleet made a brave sight as they slowly glided down the calm waters of the Berhtfane towards the river-gates, their brightly coloured flags snapping in the breeze. There was much cheering from the crowd gathered on the foreshores, and the sailors all sang a light-hearted sea-shanty as they hauled up the sails. Not knowing what to do to help, Finn and Bran leant on the bulwark and waved to the crowd until the first mate yelled at them to look lively and lend them a hand. "The devil finds work for idle hands to do, so no idle hands on my watch!" he shouted. "Give them a hand raising the mizzensail, ye lazy seaslugs!"

Her fears dissolving in a great bubble of excitement, Finn ran to obey. She could hardly believe she was setting out to journey across the seas to the far end of the world, to see what no-one had seen in centuries, the forbidden city of Bride. It was as if she was the heroine of one of Dide's songs, setting out on a quest of high adventure that would save the world and bring her fame and fortune. She grinned at Dide and joined in the singing, even though she could only work out the words of the refrain:

> "Tam o' Glenvale was a sailor,
> Tam o' Glenvale stout and gay,
> Sing fala-ralla aye-do
> Sing fala-ralla aye."

The passage through the river-gates proved rather an anticlimax, for only one ship at a time could make their way through and there was much jostling for position. Captain Tobias' ship, a caravel named *Speedwell*, was one of the last to make its way down through the system of canals and locks that connected the high waters of the Berhtfane with the low waters of the sea. Since it was high summer, the sea was even lower than ever and so Finn had the peculiar experience of sailing down a narrow stretch of water, contained behind high stone walls, while sand rose high on either side, heaped with the refuse of the sea. All the ships were dragged through the canals by two teams of massive cart-horses, their coats lathered and wet.

At last the *Speedwell* slid through the last pair of gates into the firth. The sun had almost set and the water was a strange violet colour, glimmering with dusky light. Finn had little time to lean on the bulwark and watch, for the sails needed to be hoisted to catch the evening wind. With short, sharp blasts of his whistle, the bosun shouted his orders. He had been told Finn was a canny climber and so he sent her up into the rigging to help the sailors unroll the sails, warning her to keep a tight hold. Those down on the decks hauled on the ropes and one by one the white sails billowed out, catching the breeze and sending the little ship racing across the waves.

Finn clung tightly to the mainmast as the world rocked. In the last glimmer of light she could see tall rocky crags rearing up on either side, their peaks still glowing with colour. White sandbanks lifted their smooth flanks out of the bay, the water nearby a clear translucent green. In some places the water rose into odd curling ridges as different currents warred with each other over a reef, or spun into miniature whirlpools. Ahead of the *Speedwell* sailed the fleet, their sails all filled with wind as they tried to escape the dangerous waters near the seashore before the last of the light was lost.

The sudden lurch of the mast as the *Speedwell* tacked almost sent Finn crashing down to the decks. One of the sailors ordered her down, saying tersely, "The ropes be no place for a lubber, lad, no matter how canny a climber ye be. Get ye down to where ye'll be safe."

"Why does the boat change direction so suddenly?" Finn asked, as she began to slide down the ropes.

"There be rocks and reefs hereabouts that'll tear the guts out o' her should she run aground," the young sailor said. "It be tricky sailing out o' the firth. They call this the Bay o' Deception, for she looks so smooth and bonny but beneath the surface are rocks as cruel as the teeth o' a sea serpent."

Finn slid down swiftly, unable to help a feeling of relief as her feet touched the wooden deck. Goblin was curled up on a coil of rope waiting for her. As Finn bent and picked her up, the little elven cat miaowed plaintively.

"Aye, I must admit I'm peckish myself," Finn whispered in response. "What time do ye think we eat around here?"

Goblin kneaded her neck painfully as Finn went in search of her companions. A few of the sailors smiled to see her with the black cat hanging around her neck. To Finn's relief there had been no arguments about the elven cat accompanying her, for a black cat was apparently considered lucky on board a ship, unlike Enit. The presence of the old woman on board had caused many of the sailors to scowl and mutter about bad luck, even though the captain had issued stern warnings that the old jongleur was to be treated with respect.

Finn found the others in the galley, a cramped little room deep in the bow of the ship. Donald was swathed in a big white apron, stirring a pot that bubbled away on the iron stove. The room was lined with big barrels of stores, while a small wooden table was hung by ropes from the ceiling. Crowded at the table were a number of sailors, some perched on three-legged stools or barrels, the others standing. All were

waiting to be served their supper, which they would
then carry down to one of the lower decks to eat,
since there was no room in the galley for anyone to
eat in comfort. They were all drinking from pewter
mugs and Dide was telling them a tale that had them
guffawing with laughter. Perched on a stool by his
side, Bran was smiling too and Finn thought how different she looked with her short little pigtail and
rough clothes, her brown face alight with laughter.

Jay smiled a welcome at her and moved aside so
she could share his barrel, but Finn ignored him,
squeezing in between Bran and Ashlin. The piper
smiled a shy welcome and would have given up his
stool for her if Finn had not frowned at him and
shaken her head. She joined in the laughter and chatter, trying to accustom herself to the swaying of the
room and the odd rocking of the table. She noticed
how the seamen moved easily with the ship and tried
to mimic them, although her stomach was rebelling at
the smell of tobacco smoke and rum and sweaty arm-
pits and bad breath, and the heaving of the deck beneath her feet.

"Ye look a wee pale, Finn," Donald whispered as
he ladled stew on to trenchers of bread for the crew.
"How are ye yourself?"

"I be just fine," she answered faintly, cautiously cradling her stomach with one hand. "Or at least, I will
be, in a minute." She swallowed thickly, then as Donald passed her a tin plate laden with stew, got up
hurriedly. "Fresh air," she gulped and ran from the
room. She was halfway up the ladder when her stomach won out, and she was heartily sick all over her
own boots. Jay had followed her and wordlessly she
let him help her up on to the deck where she crouched
in the shelter of the mainmast, letting the night wind

cool her. Overhead the stars seemed huge, the masts and rigging like a giant black cobweb across the moon. Finn watched the masts sway back and forth, back and forth, and tried to control her nausea.

"Ye'll be fine once ye get your sea-legs," Jay said sympathetically, smoothing her hair back from her brow with his calloused hand.

Finn jerked her head away. "Why are ye no' sick?" she demanded resentfully. "Or Bran?"

"It be no sign o' weakness to be seasick," Jay said rather sternly, letting his hand drop. "The auld tales say Lachlan the Navigator was sick every time he left harbour and he was the greatest sailor Eileanan has ever kent."

Finn's only answer was to stumble for the wooden bulwark, which she clung to, gasping, as she vomited over the side. Jay held her shoulders then helped her back to her spot near the forecastle. "Try and sleep," he said, "ye'll feel better in the morn."

"Sleep here?" Finn asked, looking about her at the bare deck.

"Aye, o' course," Jay said. "Ye did no' think ye'd have a cabin like the captain, surely? We'll all sleep here. I'll get ye a blanket."

"And some water?" Finn asked in rather a faint voice, as nausea racked her again.

"Aye, and I'll see if any o' the lads ken an antidote to seasickness. Sit still and I'll be back in a moment."

Finn leant back against the mast weakly, closing her eyes. Who had ever heard of the heroine of a quest tale to be so weak and silly as to succumb to seasickness?

She had an uncomfortable night. The wooden deck was harder than rock, the blanket she had been given was scratchy and smelt of mould, the ship rolled and heaved constantly, the spars creaked, the sails flapped, the waves crashed and roared, and the bosun's shrill pipe marked the changing of the watches every four hours. Whenever she did slip into an uneasy doze, a splash of spray would jerk her awake. At last, exhausted, she did sleep, only to be woken at dawn by the bosun's call. Her watch was on duty again.

Hot porridge with a dash of rum and a quick wash in a bucket of salty seawater helped her regain some of her spirits, though her body was stiff and her eyes gritty with salt. She and Ashlin were set to washing down the decks, much to their consternation. Her arms tired quickly and Finn took advantage of the first and second mates being below deck to lean against the bulwark and rest for awhile.

To her dismay she saw the *Speedwell* was the only ship in sight. As far as she could see there was only the sea and hundreds of rocky islands, some only large enough for a bird to perch on, some crowned with ruins of walled towns. The rest of the fleet had vanished.

She whistled to Dide, who was mending a sail with a long needle. He dropped the ram's horn filled with tallow that the sailmaker's needles were stuck in, and came to her side. "Have we got ourselves lost?" she asked anxiously.

"Nay, o' course no'," he said in a low voice, casting a quick glance around to make sure none were listening. "Ye did no' think the whole fleet was to sail to Bride, did ye? Did ye no' hear they had set course for Siantan, to take supplies to relieve the famine there?"

"Aye, but I thought . . ."

"Nay, we just slipped away from the fleet under the cover o' darkness. We are headed east now, have ye no' realised? We were sailing south-west afore."

Finn stared around and only then noticed the bow was pointed almost directly into the rising sun. She also realised that quite a few of the sailors were standing huddled in groups, muttering under their breath, and staring at the position of the sun themselves.

"What be wrong with them?" she asked.

Dide sighed. "Like ye, they are troubled that we have left the fleet and even more troubled by the fact we no longer fly the Rìgh's insignia, but the red cross o' the Tìrsoilleirean instead."

He pointed one finger and Finn suddenly noticed the flags and pennants fluttering at the top of the masts and from the stern no longer carried the royal arms of the Clan of MacCuinn but were emblazoned with a red fitchè cross. "As far as most o' the common sailors are concerned, there has been a mutiny against the crown and Captain Tobias has committed treason o' the highest order. The question is, wha' shall they do about it? We mun hope that, like most sailors, they are more concerned with their own safety than wi' the Rìgh's honour, for otherwise there could be trouble."

"But do they no' ken we sail in the Rìgh's service . . ." Finn began, only to falter to a close. "Nay, o' course they do no'," she answered herself. Looking around at the small groups of muttering sailors she felt that cold finger of fear stroke down her spine again. "What will they do?"

"Time will tell," Dide answered. "Be ready for trouble, though, Finn—and remember we are on Captain Tobias' side in case o' a fight. This ship mun make it to Bride!"

Just then the door from the officers' cabins opened and the first, second and third mates appeared, Arvin the Just in the lead. A large man with beefy shoulders, cropped grey hair and a clean-shaven, prognathous jaw, Arvin had two daggers in his belt and one in his boot, and carried a pistol in one huge hand. The other two men were similarly armed, with steely glints in their eyes. They stood with their backs to the door, the pistols pointing steadily at the group of sailors rushing towards them, the guns' weight resting on their wrists. The questions dried in the seamen's throats and they came to a halt, staring at the officers incredulously.

"I see ye all recognise our pistols," Arvin said calmly. "That be good; I was afraid ye witch-loving heretics would be as ignorant as ye are foolish. Do no' think I do no' ken how to use it and that I'd be unwilling to draw bluid, for ye'd be wrong. Needs must when the devil drives."

The sailors moved uneasily, glancing at each other and then back at the steady black eye of the pistol.

"What does all this mean, sir?" one of the sailors asked then. "Why have we left the protection o' the fleet? Why do we fly the Tìrsoilleirean cross?"

"The captain has urgent business in Bride," Arvin replied curtly. There are exclamations of dismay and one sailor cried, "In Bride? Ye mean in Tìrsoilleir?"

"Aye, I mean in Tìrsoilleir," Arvin said roughly. "Where else would I be meaning?"

"But that be treason!"

"We canna sail to Bride—we be at war with the Bright Soldiers!"

"But what about the Fairgean? Without the warships to protect us, we shall be sunk by their blaygird sea serpents . . ."

In their excitement and dismay, the sailors had all lunged forward and Arvin motioned them back with his pistol. "When ye address me, ye shall call me 'sir'," he said. "Do ye be forgetting I am your superior offi-

cer? Stand back, I say, or I shall be forced to let ye
see what lead and gunpowder can do to a man!"

They stepped back smartly, even though a few were
glaring belligerently, their hands surreptitiously dropping to the daggers and cutlasses they wore in their
belts.

"We fly the Tìrsoilleirean flag so no pirates will
bother us, nor any Tìrsoilleirean warships," Arvin said
calmly. "As for the Fairgean, ye need no' fear them,
for do we no' have the Yedda on board? Do ye think
we command a ship o' fools, to set sail in the summer
seas without some way o' repelling the sea demons?
The Yedda shall sing the sea demons to death and we
shall sail on unmolested."

"Wha' do ye do, sir?" one of the sailors said. "Did
ye no' swear allegiance to the MacCuinn? Do ye have
no honour, that ye break your oath as soon as ye leave
the safety o' the MacCuinn's harbour?"

Arvin spat contemptuously. "Ye canna serve both
God and Mammon," he answered.

There was a stirring and a muttering. Then the out-
spoken sailor cried, "But this be mutiny against the
crown, sir! We canna be allowing ye to take the Mac-
Cuinn's ship and give it to his enemies!" He drew his
cutlass with an oath and leapt for the first mate.

There was a deafening bang and a black cloud of
evil-smelling smoke belched across the aftercastle.
Finn cried out and shrank back against Dide who was
standing stiffly, watching and listening intently. When
the smoke cleared they could see the sailor had fallen
back on to the deck, his cutlass fallen from his hand,
blood staining his shirt. His comrades knelt around him,
trying to staunch the flow of blood, one cradling his
head. Arvin had staggered back against his companions

with the shock of the recoil, but almost immediately recovered his balance, and was calmly reloading.

"There be no need for all this excitement," he said when the task was done and the pistol was once more pointing at the group of dismayed sailors. "We do no' want the ship, nor do we wish to turn ye landlubbers over to the General Assembly. We just need to get to Bride. I can promise ye that ye can have the ship back once our task is done. Ye can all set sail for the safety o' the Berhtfane just as fast as ye please. We'll even let ye keep the Yedda to keep your journey home safe, if ye keep your hand to the wheel now."

The sailors all looked at each other and muttered among themselves. The injured seaman moaned and clutched at his shattered shoulder with one hand.

"Ye all have two choices," Arvin said. "Ye can accept the captain's decision to change course and work to keep us all safe on this journey, or ye can take your chances in the long boat and row for shore. I'll warn ye though that the lookout has seen a sea serpent in the distance that could mean a pod o' Fairgean swim this way."

The sailors were white and frightened. "We should never have left the safety o' the fleet!" one burst out. "We do no' have the firepower to defend ourselves against a sea serpent!"

"Especially no' if ye are afloat in the wee long boat," Arvin said with a slight lifting of his lip that could have been mistaken for a smile under different circumstances. There was a long pause and then the first mate lifted the pistol slightly. "Happen I should warn ye that all the firearms on board ship are being kept in the captain's cabin for safety. I ken none o' ye will be stupid enough to try and stage a mutiny o' your own. If ye decide to throw your lot in with us, then ye may keep your own knives in case we should be attacked by pirates or by the Fairgean. It is your decision though. What canna be cured must be endured."

Dide had prised Finn's fingers from his sleeve and had unobtrusively joined the group of sailors confronting the first mate. Cowering back against the bulwark Finn saw him whispering to the sailors and wondered what he said. The muttering went on for some time, with many evil glances at Arvin, who regarded them unwaveringly. At last there was a begrudging agreement among the seamen to take their chances at the journey to Bride. They all knew they would have little chance of survival if put afloat in the longboat.

Arvin nodded, thrusting his pistol into his wide leather belt. "Glad to have ye on board, lads," he said with another lift of his granite-hard lip. "Now, let us hoist full sail, laddies, and put as much water between the *Speedwell* and that sea serpent as we can!"

The sailors ran to obey. Finn took a deep breath, the first she had taken in what seemed like ages. It seemed the crisis had passed, at least for the moment.

She swung herself up into the rigging, determined to check the truth of the sea serpent sighting herself. Up the mainmast she climbed, past the yardarm and through the rigging, past the main topcastle halfway up, heading higher still. Refusing to look down at the deck that tilted so far below, she let her body sway with the mast until she swung her leg over the side of the topmast topcastle, a tiny wooden nest at the very apex of the topgallant mast.

There she clung, looking about her, her hand shading her eyes. For as far as she could see the sea rippled away like crumpled blue satin. All about tall crags of rock thrust up through the water, some steep and bare, others round and green with high cliffs falling down to wicked-looking rocks where the water creamed.

Far below her, the deck of the ship swung to and fro as the mast swayed. The white sails billowed below her, filled with wind. Here and there a bare-chested man hung in the shrouds, tightening tackle or repairing rope. She was so high the blue line of the horizon seemed to curve.

"Wha' do ye think ye're doing, ye gowk!" The lookout turned with a shout of surprise. He was a skinny boy, not much older than Finn herself, and considerably smaller. He wore a large tricorne hat to shade his face from the sun and carried a spyglass which he had been holding to one eye as Finn climbed into his little crow's nest. He had lowered it at her sudden appearance and was glaring at her angrily. Despite the protection of the broad-brimmed hat, his face was burnt red from the sun, and his freckled nose was peeling.

"I wanted to have a look," Finn replied, grinning at him.

"There be no' enough room in here for a donbeag, let alone a great tall lad like ye!" he protested. "Do ye no' understand it be dangerous up here? They shouldna be allowing a raw recruit like ye to just climb on up."

"I dinna exactly ask permission," she answered. "Please, canna ye just let me have a squint through that spyglass o' yours? Then I promise I'll slide on down and leave ye in peace."

After a moment's hesitation he let her have it, only warning her not to drop it, "else the captain'll have ye keel-hauled, that I promise ye!"

Eagerly she lifted the farseeing glass to her eyes and peered through it. At first all she could see was blueness, but she lifted the spyglass and swung it until suddenly the steep cliff of an island sprang towards her, bare and rocky. The lookout showed her how to focus the spyglass and she was amazed to see a bird crouching on a shaggy nest of twigs on the side of the cliff. As she watched two white fluffy heads with gaping beaks suddenly thrust out from their mother's feathers, squawking for food.

She watched for some time, smiling, then swung the glass around slowly, amazed at how clearly she could see things many miles away. At last the lookout said gruffly, "Give me it back, porridge-head. It is no' a plaything. I'm meant to be on the watch for sea demons and the captain will have my hide for a floor mat if I miss their approach."

"They said ye'd seen a sea serpent. Couldna ye just show me that? Then I'll go, I swear."

"Och, I suppose so," he answered unwillingly and took the spyglass from her and focused it on the curving blue line of the horizon. "There it be," he cried in excitement. "Quick, look—do no' move the glass, for Eà's sake!"

Finn peered through the spyglass again and sucked in her breath in amazement. A great, sinuous creature was undulating through the waves, its glossy spotted scales shining in the sun. A vivid green in colour, it had a small graceful head crowned with spiny fins that ran down its curving neck. Spectacular flowing fins surrounded its gaping jaws and sprouted from its shoulders like wings. It swam with its head held high out of the waves, its immensely long body coiling behind, its finned tail creating a powerful wake behind it.

She ran the spyglass along its serpentine length, marvelling at the speed with which it coiled through the water. Suddenly she froze, the spyglass trained just above its soft orange and yellow wings. On the monster's neck rode a man. All she could see of him was a bare chest, wet flowing black hair and a raised trident, but it was enough to cause her heart to slam sickeningly, her stomach to lurch.

"A Fairge be riding it!" she gasped.

The lookout seized the spyglass from her and raised it to his eye. He stared through it frowningly, then said begrudgingly, "Aye, ye be right. Ye have guid eyes. Happen ye'd better scoot and tell the captain."

Finn slid down the ropes, landed with a thump in the main topcastle, and began the long descent down to the deck with quick and easy agility. Men sat cross-legged on the wooden boards with canvas draped over their knees, repairing a long rent in the mizzen sail. She swung down on to the deck and looked about her for someone in authority to tell. She might still be a landlubber but she knew better than to try and see the captain herself.

The fourth mate was standing by the helmsman, watching the horizon for any telltale break of water that might indicate a reef ahead. Finn told him about the Fairge she had seen and saw his sunburnt face crease with concern. He cast a quick glance up at the full-bellied sails, nodded and thanked her brusquely.

With the little elven cat riding in the crook of her arm, Finn went in search of Dide. Their watch had finished and so he was not on duty anymore. She found him up in the forecastle with his grandmother, Jay and Dillon playing trictrac at their feet.

Enit's chair had been wedged right up in the bow of the ship, so that she looked rather like another figurehead with her wood-brown face all carved with deep lines of age and her twig-like knotted fingers so stiff she could barely hold a spoon anymore. Seabirds floated around her head and perched on the bulwark before her, some sitting along the back and arms of her chair so that she was surrounded by their white feathers like a living cloak. The sound of the birds' quarrelling was deafening and Finn felt no hesitation in telling the others what she had seen, sure that none could overhear their conversation.

"Will we be able to outrun the Fairgean?" Dillon asked soberly, smoothing Jed's silky black ears between his fingers. The hound looked up at him with adoring eyes, his shaggy white tail beating the wooden boards.

Dide was frowning. "No' here amongst the islands," he answered. "I be surprised already how many sails we are carrying. It be dangerous indeed to whip the ship along at this rate in such treacherous waters."

Jay and Enit were looking very troubled indeed. "Can we no' sail out to deeper waters and leave the Bay o' Deception behind?" the fiddler asked.

Dide nodded. "That is the plan soon enough. The problem is once we lose sight o' the coastline we canna use landmarks to help us navigate and must rely on the stars and the sea, a chancy business at best. The other thing is, we have a better chance o' staying hidden among the islands, since once we're on the open sea our mast and sails can be seen for many miles."

"Still, if the Fairgean have spotted us, happen we'd best change course now and head for the open sea where we have some chance o' outrunning them," Enit staid. Her voice was heavy with dread.

"Happen ye be right," Dide answered, caressing the hilt of one of his silver daggers.

"The first mate told the sailors no' to fear the Fairgean, that the Yedda would sing them to death," Finn said. "Did he mean ye, Enit?"

Enit nodded, though her face was pinched and white. "Aye, he meant me," she answered. "Wha' do ye think I do here, an auld crippled woman like me, Finn? I am no use in fighting off pirates, like young Dillon here, or climbing into the Black Tower like ye. Do ye think the captain would ever have let me on board his ship, given how he feels about women being bad luck, if he had no' thought I'd be some use?' Her voice was bitter.

"I did no' ken ye were a Yedda." There was awe in Finn's voice. Although the sea-singers of Carraig had all died in Maya's witch-hunts long before Finn was born, she knew all about them, as any child who listened to the old tales and songs must know. The Carraigean witches had been the main line of defense against the Fairgean for centuries, for they had the power to sing the sea-faeries to death. Before they had been massacred by Maya and her Seekers, no ship had ever left harbour without a Yedda on board, no seaside town or castle had been without its sea witch, no prionnsa's retinue had been complete without a musician trained at the Tower of Sea-Singers.

"I am no Yedda," Enit replied wearily, "though I have been taught the songs o' sorcery. They would have had me, if I had been willing to submit myself to the Coven. I was never interested in being a witch, though, and I feared the power o' the songs o' sorcery. I still do."

"Yet ye've been teaching them to Jay," Finn said, staring at him with new eyes. Sudden realisation brought her gaze flying back to Enit. "And to Ashlin!"

"Aye, both the lads have talent," Enit said. "I could

no' refuse to teach them what I ken, though my heart misgives me."

"But why?" Finn asked. "Toasted toads, what I would no' give to be able to sing or play like ye do! I have seen ye bring tears to the eyes o' the roughest soldiers and why, Dide can even make Arvin the Just smile with his songs, and he be the dourest man I've ever seen."

"Aye, music has the power to move," Dide replied when his mother did not, her sombre black eyes gazing out to the tumult of waves ahead. "But like all power, it can be misused and misunderstood. The songs o' sorcery are specifically designed to compel and constrain." She heard the stress of subtle power in his voice, the lilt of enchantment. "With the songs o' sorcery ye can seduce and bring to love, ye can incite war and revolution, ye can stupefy and confuse, ye can kill. No matter how much ye wish to use your powers only for good, always ye may find ye have moved a man in ways he would no' wish for or look for. We all must choose our own path."

"But surely all art is designed to move people, to make them think and feel things they have never felt and thought afore," Jay argued. It was clear this was a discussion they had had many times before, for Dide gave a little grin in response. "Did Gwenevyre Nic-Seinn no' say that if ye can just stretch a man's mind in a new direction, it shall never return to its old dimensions? Surely that is a good thing, to make people's minds and souls greater than afore?"

"Aye, that it is," Dide responded warmly. "Why else do we sing and play and tell tales o' valour and gallantry and compassion, if we do no' want to move our listeners to high ideals and aspirations? It is just that granddam has seen the evil that can be done with such power . . ."

"But can no' all power be turned to evil ends?" Finn asked.

"Aye," Enit cried, startling them all. "And sometimes the greatest evil can be done in the name o' good. The Yedda were honoured and celebrated for what they did, yet I have seen the sea black with the bodies o' a hundred drowned Fairgean. I have seen mere babes loosen their grip on their mother's hair and sink away below the waves, their gills closed, water filling their lungs. Do ye think I wish to use my powers in such a way? My dreams are haunted by the fear that I may have to sing the song o' death, that I may cast a spell like the Yedda used to cast. Eà save me from ever having to do so again."

There was a wrought silence, then Finn whispered, "Ye have sung the song o' death afore?"

Her contorted fingers gripping the arms of her chair, Enit slowly nodded. "Aye, I have," she answered, "and I swore I should never do so again."


All that day the *Speedwell* crept through the islands, the lead-line constantly being checked to make sure deep water still lay under her hull. In some places they had to drop most of the sails, seize oars and slowly manoeuvre their way through a narrow channel of water, surrounded by wide stretches of sand on either side. Several times they saw Fairgean basking in the sun on the sand, or sporting about in the shallow lagoons formed by the retreat of the tides. They were never close enough to see more than their black heads, though once or twice male Fairgean swam after their ship, shaking their tridents and whistling mockingly.

Finn grew used to the shout of the fathoms' depth

and was taught to recognise the feel of the different
markers sewn along the lead-line's length so that even
in the blackest night she could tell how deep the water
was under the ship. No-one wanted to run aground
on a sandbank when the Fairgean were there.

Close on sunset they sailed past a tall island that
reared out of the lesser islands about it like a carthorse among ponies. Crowned with a tall, square
tower set behind a great, crenellated rampart, its steep
cliffs rose straight out of an expanse of white sand
that stretched for miles in all directions. Scattered
across the sand were a few ancient walls, encrusted
with dried seaweed and barnacles.

"That be the Tower o' First Landing," one of the
sailors told Finn and Bran as they leant over the bulwark, staring up at its stern grey height. "They say
when we first came to Eileanan, the people built down
on the shores of the island, not realising that the tides
would sweep in and drown them all. When the autumn
tides did come, it brought with it the Fairgean and
those that were no' drowned were murdered. If they
had no' built the tower they all might have died."

"Does anyone live there now?" Finn asked in curiosity, for the walls were stout still and the tower
reared up straight and tall.

"Och, I doubt it," the sailor answered. "All the
towers were torn down by the Ensorcellor, were they
no'? Besides, I've heard tell it be haunted by the ghost
o' Cuinn Lionheart. His grave is in there, ye ken, all
covered in white heather, the only place where
heather grows in all o' Eileanan. That be a flower
from the Other World, ye ken. They say he carried it
in his buttonhole and when they laid him down on
the bank after his ship was wrecked on the rocks, it
fell out o' his lapel and took root there where he lay."

"What a storm that must have been," Bran said dreamily, "to carry a ship across the entire universe. No wonder they called her Storm-Rider."

Finn made sure the sailor had stepped out of hearing before whispering crossly, "Well, your ancestor may have conjured the storm but it was mine that found Eileanan on the star-map!"

Unexpectedly, Bran smiled at her. "Aye, they all must have been amazingly powerful witches indeed," she whispered. "What a feat that First Crossing must have been! And what courage. It makes this journey seem somewhat less dangerous and foolhardy in comparison, doesn't it?"

Finn grinned. "I suppose so," she answered. "Though I still hit myself over my head sometimes, wondering what I be doing here when I could be safe in Castle Rurach."

Bran immediately sobered. "If Castle Rurach be still safe."

Finn's smile faded and her face grew troubled. "Och, I do so hope they are all safe," she whispered, stroking Goblin's silky head. "I wish . . ."

After a long pause Bran prompted her. "What?"

"Och, naught. I sure they all be fine. Come, where be the lads? I want to challenge Ashlin to another game o' trictrac. He's been winning far too many lately."

"Ye should no' say 'lads' like that," Bran reprimanded Finn as she followed her down the ladder towards the galley. "We're meant to be lads too, remember."

Finn took a breath to say something scathing, then bit the words back. "Aye, I ken. Sorry, Bran." She said the boy's name with a subtle stress.

"It's hard to remember sometimes, I ken," Bran

answered with a little giggle. "Harder for me, 'cause
I'm used to seeing ye looking all ragged and brown.
It should be easy for ye to remember, seeing me look
like *this*." She lifted the short end of her pigtail with
a grimace.

"It's odd how quickly I've got used to it," Finn
answered. "I find it hard to remember ye all pretty
and girly."

Bran gave her a little pinch in retaliation as they
came into the galley, as always crowded with the men
who were not on watch. "I'll give ye all pretty and
girly if ye do no' watch it," she hissed. "We'll see who
punches more like a lass!"

As Finn turned a surprised face towards her, Bran
chuckled and sauntered away, mimicking Finn's boyish
swagger perfectly.

Under the cover of darkness that night, the *Speedwell* changed course, setting sail for the deep unclut-
tered ocean beyond the hundreds of islands scattered
along the coastline. When Finn was roused by the bosun's whistle the next morning, it was to find the little
caravel racing along a deep swell, the coastline a mere
shadowy blur along the horizon. The sun was rising
red above an ocean the colour of tarnished silver,
turning the sails to pink. The only sign of life was the
sea birds soaring ahead of the ship, their wings stained
the same colour as the sails.

With the ship under full sail, it was hard work for
all the sailors that day. The bosun shouted himself
hoarse with the captain's orders, the deckhands were
kept busy trimming the sails as the helmsman fought
to keep the ship running as close to the wind as possible. "We'll have left that blaygird sea serpent miles
behind," Finn said to Dillon with great satisfaction

that evening as she examined her red, sore palms, rubbed raw from hauling on ropes all day.

"I hope so," he answered without conviction. "I have no wish to be drawing blade against a sea serpent."

Finn glanced up at him in puzzlement. "Once ye would have thought this a high adventure," she said, finding it hard to speak the words. This stern-faced, broad-shouldered man was so unlike the Scruffy she had known that speaking to him was worse than making conversation with a stranger.

"Would I have?" Dillon answered, gently fingering the curiously wrought hilt of the sword he wore always at his side. "I suppose I would have, when I was a bairn, with no more sense than a newly hatched chick. I ken better now."

Finn hesitated, then said with a little burst of words, "It must have been so awful for ye, Scruffy, having Jorge captured and burnt, and having Antoinn, Artair and Parlan all die like that, right in front o' ye."

He said nothing for a long time and Finn shrank back a little, sorry she had spoken. Then he said, "Ye should no' call me 'Scruffy,' Finn. Scruffy died a long time ago."

With an attempt at humour, Finn said, "O' course, ye're Dillon the Bold now, are ye no'? I keep on forgetting."

"Dillon the Bold is dead too," he answered, and his hands caressed the sword as if it were flesh. "They call me Dillon o' the Joyful Sword now."

Finn stared at him, her skin creeping. He looked up at her, a strange half-smile on his face. "This be a magical sword, did ye ken that, Finn? Do ye remember when I found her that day in the ruin o' the Tower o' Two Moons? I did no' ken then, I did no' ken that she was a magical sword." He stroked it lovingly. "She be a thirsty sword, thirsty for blood. Once ye draw her, ye canna sheathe her again until her thirst is slaked. And she will drink and drink until there is no more blood to drink, till all are dead . . ."

Jed gave a little whine and crept closer, pushing his rough black-patched head against Dillon's arm. Dillon ignored him. "Her name is *Joyeuse,* Finn. *Joyeuse,* the Joyful Sword. For she takes joy only in killing."

Finn could not look away, fascinated and horrified. He was smiling, his hands stroking the sword's coiled hilt, stroking, stroking. Then he looked up at her again and she saw his eyes were bright with tears. "So ye see why I dread battle, Finn. I never want to draw her again, though she quivers under my hand like a woman. She quivers now, scenting blood. She smells the fear o' battle."

Finn's hand crept within her pocket, where the elven cat slept curled on a small black parcel of silk. As her fingers brushed the magical cloak, her skin prickled and stung. "Happen the gifts we chose that day in the Tower o' Two Moons were no' so wisely chosen," she said.

Dillon gave a bitter laugh. "Happen no'. At least for me. Did ye no' choose the MacRuraich war-horn, that called up the ghosts o' your clan? That worked out for the best, at least, even though it's no' a horn ye'd want to be blowing every day."

Finn's fingers brushed back and forth along the silk, electricity darting up her nerves. She almost told Dillon that she still had the cloak of invisibility, that the longing to wear it sometimes almost overcame her, even though she had no need of hiding within its magical folds. She wanted to tell him how cold it made her feel, inside and out, how remote, severed from the rest of the world. If he had looked at her and smiled, or rapped out one of his orders like he used to, she would have told him. But he was stroking his sword again, that peculiar half-smile on his lips, and she said nothing.

That afternoon the sea serpent was sighted again, following their wake. Although all the sailors hung over the stern of the ship, they could see nothing and most relaxed, sure they would lose the sea serpent again. A double watch was called that night, however, the ship kept straining under a full load of sails despite the blackness of the night. In the morning all could see the sea serpent in the distance, and by noon the ship was being rocked by the great waves it threw up with the speed of its motion. Finn climbed up into the rigging again to get a better view. Even though she had seen the monster through the spyglass before, she was shocked at the size of it. It was large enough to coil around the ship three times, cracking the timbers asunder with a gentle squeeze of its coils. If it reared up out of the water it would have towered over the topgallant mast, taller by far than any tree Finn had ever seen.

By late afternoon the ship was floundering in enormous waves that broke over the bow and swept across the decks in a fury of white swirling foam. The helmsman was lashed to the wheel, and all the sailors had ropes knotted around their waists so that if they were swept overboard, they could be hauled back up to safety. All hands were on deck, fighting to keep the ship from keeling over. It was an odd experience, to have the sky so fair and blue, the breeze so warm and steady, and the ship thrown about like a leaf in a rapid. Finn was flung to her knees, unable to keep her footing on the wet deck, and only managing to keep

from being thrown down into the angry sea by her
terror-strong grip on the ropes. Ignoring the pain in
her bleeding palms, she fought her way to the forecastle where Enit sat in her chair, drenched to the skin,
her hair plastered to her skull. Dide, Jay and Ashlin
had tied themselves to the foremast, all three holding
their musical instruments high to avoid them being
ruined by the water. Dide had his battered old guitar,
all hung with ribbons, Jay had his viola with the handle carved in the shape of a blind woman, and Ashlin
had his wooden flute.

Captain Tobias and the First Mate, Arvin the Just,
were both up in the forecastle with them, shouting
angrily at Enit. Bran clung beside Finn, her white face
streaked with tears, her lip red with blood where she
had bitten it.

"Sing, for God's sake, sing!" the captain cried. "Do
ye wish us all to die?"

Finn could hear a strange, melodic whistling that
swelled on all sides, rising up to a taunting shriek,
echoing eerily all around. Then suddenly the sea serpent reared up next to the ship, its throat and belly
silvery-pale, its golden-green back spotted with purple.
A Fairgean warrior rode its neck, a long, wickedly sharp
trident in his hand, and all about the ship more Fairgean
rode astride the slimy-green shoulders of horse-eels.
Finn stared about terrified, as webbed hands reached
out to seize any dangling rope that should help them
swarm over the railing. Many of those ropes were
attached to sailors, who shouted in fear as they were
dragged towards the bulwark. They drew their daggers
and tried to fight off the sea-faeries, who were all
armed with cruel-looking tridents.

"Sing, auld woman!" the first mate shouted. "Sing,
else I'll cut your throat myself."

Enit took a deep, shuddering breath, opened her mouth and began to sing.

Pure, sweet, melodic, her voice soared over the crash of waves, the shouts and screams of the sailors, the slap of the sails and the ear-piercing whistles of the Fairgean. Crouching against the bulwark, clinging to the ropes, Finn felt a stab of pure joy. She felt rather than saw the look Dide and Jay exchanged, a look of surprise and amazed comprehension. They braced themselves against the foremast and began to play.

All over the ship sailors stopped what they were doing and turned to stare. The ship plunged on, its sails flapping wildly, no-one running to haul on the ropes or tighten the tackle. The helmsman let the wheel spin, entranced. The Fairgean paused in their climb up the ropes, turning their sleek black heads to listen. Even the sea serpent seemed to listen, swaying from side to side, while the tumult of waves slowly subsided.

Deep as the throb of the ocean, passionate as the whisper of a lover, tender as a mother's lullaby, warm as the blaze of a winter fire, the viola's contralto voice wove crimson ribbons of sound through the silver gauze of Enit's song. The fragile lilt of the flute, the warm rhythm of the guitar, Dide's strong, young voice, all gave the music depth and harmony, but it was these two voices, the haunting ethereal sound of the old woman's voice and the passionate strength of the viola's song, that cast a spell over all who heard.

Finn realised there were tears on her cheeks. She was almost overwhelmed with feelings of love and tenderness. She reached out her hand and caught Bran's, and the cousins clung to each other, sobbing and trying to speak, to explain. All over the ship men were weeping or laughing or singing, many caught up in rough embraces, or pounding each other on the back. Dillon was kneeling, both arms around his shaggy hound, tears pouring down his cheeks. The Fairgean were whistling and crooning in accompaniment, their strange alien faces alight with emotion, their slim, scaled bodies swaying in time to the music.

Hugging Bran as hard as she could, Finn rested her tear-wet face on her cousin's shoulder. Through the haze of her tears, she saw the captain and the first mate were both weeping and smiling, shaking hands as if they could not bear to let go. Enit's voice quivered with the intensity of her emotion, the music soared and swooped till it seemed the whole ship was spun in silver light. Weeping and laughing, the three musicians played as if they were possessed, and together the four wrought a spell of such power that all who listened fell to their knees, lifting up their faces in rapture. Human and Fairgean knelt together, choking with feelings too deep and powerful for words, while webbed hands met and grasped unwebbed.

At last the song quivered into silence. Enit fell forward in her chair, only the ropes keeping her from falling. Ashlin too slumped down, the flute falling from his hand, his eyes rolling back in his head. Dide dashed the tears from his face and looked triumphantly at Jay, who stood tall and proud and exultant, the viola and bow raised high.

"Ye have heard today the song o' love," Dide said, his voice still thrumming with power. "Do no' forget."

An awed silence hung over the ship and then he was answered, with shouts and whistles and bursts of song. Hats were flung up into the air, and men and Fairgean once again embraced. The sea serpent rubbed its head affectionately against the prow, coiling its golden-green length along the whole length of the ship.

One of the Fairgean strode along the deck and stood facing Dide, his hand making an elaborate obeisance as he bowed. His black hair hung down his bare back like a wet silk cloak and he wore a single black pearl on his breast. Although he had two legs like a man, his smooth, scaled skin had a sheen like that of no human, and his wrists and ankles were braceleted with flowing fins. He wore nothing but a skirt of seaweed ornately decorated with shells and twists of coral. "We . . . will . . . no' forget," he answered in halting tones. "Will . . . ye . . . be true?"

"We will be true," Dide answered, awe and amazement on his face.

The Fairgean saluted him, then gave a high whistle. All the Fairgean on board ran to the railing and dived over into the water, and the sea serpent sank away beneath the waves. The Fairgean with the black pearl looked back up to Dide.

"We . . . will . . . be true," he repeated. Then he too dived over the bulwark, his whole body curving in a perfect, graceful arc. He plunged into the sea and surfaced again some distance away, his hand raised high.

# THE BLACK TOWER

The next day dawned bright and fair. Finn leant over the rail and stared down at the Fairgean who swam along the side of the ship, whistling and crooning and cavorting through the waves for their amusement. Often they leapt high out of the water, their muscular silver tails curving gracefully beneath them, their black hair flowing liquidly behind them. The sailors threw them salted fish and the Fairgean threw fresh fish back, causing one old seaman to say, "Och, I wish they'd swim along wi' us always; it be much easier than throwing out a line in the hope o' a bite!"

By sunset most of the Fairgean had dropped behind, following the warrior with the black pearl as he rode his sea serpent back towards the islands. The *Speedwell* was alone on the open sea.

For the next twelve days the little caravel sped along the coast of Clachan, blessed with steady winds and clear skies. In all that time Enit and Ashlin lay as if dead, their breathing fast and shallow, their foreheads fevered.

"It be the sorcery sickness," Dide said, his face creased with fatigue and anxiety. "Enit be too auld for the casting o' such a spell and Ashlin too young."

"Will they get better?"

"I hope so." Dide leant his head against his hand. "I must say I feel sick and weary myself. Never have I sung such a spell."

"Nor I," Jay said, exultation still ringing through his voice though he too looked drawn and tired. "There be a deal o' power in that viola. I felt it thrumming all through me."

"We all heard it," Dide said, grasping his friend's shoulder. "And it were no' all the viola, my fiddler. Indeed your talent is bright!"

Enit woke on the twelfth day after the singing of the song of love, and Ashlin three days later. Both were thin and wasted, the old woman looking as if a breeze would snap her in two. The *Speedwell* had left the coast far behind, for they were now off the coast of Arran, a stretch treacherous with shifting sands and notorious for its resident monster, the harlequin-hydra. Many of the sailors took great delight in telling spooky tales of this *uile-bheist* to frighten the younger members of the crew. The harlequin-hydra was responsible for more shipwrecks than any other natural or magical phenomenon, they said. It was a sea snake with a thousand heads. If one was lopped off, another two would grow. It came out of nowhere, rising from the deep to strangle a ship in its rainbow-striped coils, devouring its crew and smashing the ship till nothing was left but a few stray timbers.

"Ye thought that sea serpent was a monster, but it be naught but a pussy cat compared to the harlequin-hydra," they warned.

Finn was glad they sailed far to the south of the coast of Arran.

One afternoon a few days after Ashlin had woken, Finn lay on the deck of the forecastle, playing trictrac with the young piper. It was a warm, fair day and all

the sailors not on duty were resting on the decks, playing cards or dice, or sewing up their ragged clothes.
Dide was strumming his guitar and amusing the sailors
with a song about a sailor on shore:

"Come all ye roaring lads that delight in sea-
    man's fare,
Come listen awhile to my song,
For when Jack comes on shore, wi' his gold and
    silver store,
There's none can get rid o' it so soon.
The first thing Jack demands is the fiddle in his
    hands,
a wee dram and a bonny lass wi' flashing eyes,
And Jack Tar's as happy as he can be,
Aye, Jack Tar's as happy as he can be, away from
    the rolling sea."

Dillon was eating some dried bellfruit, his spare hand
playing with Jed's silky black ears, while Jay talked
about musical theory with Enit, who sat in her chair
throwing stale bread to the seabirds. The air all about
the forecastle was white with their wings and their
raucous shrieks almost drowned out Dide's merry
voice.

Even Donald had left his galley to enjoy the warm
sunshine, dangling a fishing line over the bulwark in
the hope of catching some fish for their supper. Only
Bran did not share the general air of ease and comfort,
for she paced the forecastle, looking anxiously out to
the horizon, a heavy line between her brows.

"Got fleas in your drawers?" Finn asked lazily,
looking up from the board. "Ye're as restless as a hen
on a hot griddle."

Bran flushed and shook her head. "I smell a storm

coming," she answered. "It makes me feel very uneasy. I fear it be a bad one."

Ashlin looked about at the calm sea, the blue sky. He was thinner than ever, the knuckles of his hands very prominent. "Are ye sure?" he asked. "I canna see a cloud anywhere."

Bran moved her shoulders uncomfortably. "I canna explain it, I just ken a bad storm is coming."

The sailors nearby scoffed at her, but Finn flared up in her defense. "Bran be no porridge-head!" she cried. "He can always tell when a storm is coming!"

"Happen we'd best tell the captain," Enit said.

"Och, as if the captain'll listen to a laddiekin like Bran," one of the sailors mocked. "The lad's never even been to sea afore and has no more hair on his chin than a lass."

"I'll wager ye a week's rations o' grog that he will!" Finn said, scrambling to her feet.

"Done!" the sailor responded, though one of his friends said curiously, "Can the lad whistle the wind, then?"

Bran shook her head, flushing redder than ever. "I was born in Siantan though," she admitted. "Even the youngest goose-girl kens how to knot her apron string for a fine day there."

A few of the sailors nodded wisely, though the one who had taken up the bet folded his arms stubbornly as Finn and Bran made their way down to the captain's cabin. "Ye had best be careful he do no' have ye keel-hauled for brazen impudence," he called after them.

Ignoring him, Finn clambered down the ladder, Goblin slinking close by her heels. "Do ye think we ought?" Bran said, but Finn pulled her along, saying:

"If ye smell a storm, Bran, happen the captain should ken, do ye no' think so? Are ye no' the NicSian?"

"Sssssshhhh!" Bran hissed but Finn only laughed, rapping boldly on the cabin door.

In answer to the shout from within, she answered respectfully, "It be Finn and Bran, sir, sorry to be disturbing ye."

"Come along in then," he answered and Finn pushed the door open and stepped inside, dragging Bran in beside her.

Captain Tobias and the navigator Alphonsus the Sure was bending over a table piled high with maps and charts. Arvin and the second mate were playing chess at a smaller table drawn up between two comfortable leather chairs. There was a silver pitcher of wine and a tray of silver goblets on the table, and a finely woven carpet on the floor. If it had not been for the small, round windows and the swaying of the floor, it would have been easy to think they were in a room in a rich merchant's house, not on a ship.

Looking about the luxurious cabin with interest, Finn told the captain what Bran had said. The navigator frowned and Arvin the Just's grim mouth compressed until it was a mere crack in his granite-hard face, but the captain nodded and said rather shortly, "Thank ye for the tip, lads, we'll keep a close eye out, as always."

"But do ye no' think . . ." Finn began but he frowned and turned away from them. The second mate heaved himself to his feet and showed them the door.

"But sir!" Finn cried, only to have a large, firm hand push her none too gently out the door. It was shut in her indignant face and she turned to Bran and made a face.

"Och well," her cousin said philosophically. "Happen we should batten down the hatches ourselves."

They climbed back up on to the deck, to be met by much jeering and mockery from the sailors, which they did their best to ignore. "Just ye wait, ye lamb-brained louts! Ye'll be sorry!" was Finn's only comment, and this was met with much raucous laughter.

Above the full-bellied white sails the sky arched, pure and blue. Finn scowled at Bran, and climbed up into the rigging with Goblin, shading her eyes against the bright sun with her hand. She stayed up there for an hour, swaying in perfect rhythm with the wind. At last she came down and ate her ration of bread and salted herring in sulky silence, then took her watch with the others, refusing to answer their teasing.

Slowly, imperceptibly, the sky hazed over. The wind died, and the sea was the colour of beaten copper in the hot glare of the setting sun. The sails hung limp from the yardarm. Finn climbed up to the forecastle to join the others staring out at the sullen horizon, the colour of bruised plums. Far away they saw a sudden glare of lightning and then heard the low grumble of thunder.

"Them clouds look bad," one of the sailors said. "Happen we should tell the captain . . ."

"He willna thank ye," Finn said. "The captain doesna welcome advice."

"Och," the sailor replied, "who does?"

The fourth mate lifted the spyglass to his eye. Thunder came again, louder and more insistent. "The storm comes," Bran said with a certain amount of satisfaction, "and it's going to be a bad one!"

The fourth mate sent one of the deckhands running down to the captain's cabin and eventually both the captain and the first mate came on deck. The rising wind fluttered their coat-tails. Both stared out at the ominous sky with grim expressions. The waves were high now, smashing against the side of the little ship as she rose and fell, rose and fell. Sharp orders were snapped out and Bran and Finn exchanged glances as they ran to obey. Hauling down the sails, Finn said to the sailor beside her, "Och, well, there goes your week's grog!" and he shrugged and scowled.

Thunder growled and muttered all around them and the dark, heavy sky was lit repeatedly with lightning from horizon to horizon. The sun had set into the clouds and there was only the light of the wildly swinging lanterns to illuminate their work. Torrential rain lashed the decks, hammering upon the heads of the sailors working frantically to fasten down the hatches, secure the cannons and reef the sails.

One by one the great white sails were lashed into place against the yards. Soon only the gaunt shape of the four masts and the delicate webbing of the rigging were left, silhouetted blackly against the stark whiteness of the lightning.

Suddenly one of the sails was torn asunder by the strength of the raging wind. Ropes snapped and a sail was blown away into the darkness, torn into shreds by the force of the gale. The ship keeled sideways, dragged by its weight. Great grey waves swept over the bow of the ship, racing down the deck and sweeping many sailors off their feet. Shouts of alarm rang out. The sailors struggled to regain their footing, clinging to the ropes or grasping the hands of those still on their feet. Finn watched in horror as one was swept over the railing and into the angry sea below. For a moment his screaming face filled her vision. Then he was swallowed by the waves, rearing up for her with hungry white claws. Staggering, she clung to the railing, bitter-cold spray stinging her eyes. Then Jay was beside her, his arm about her waist.

"Hang on, Finn!" he shouted above the crashing of the waves and the roar of the wind. "We do no' want to lose ye overboard too!"

She clung to his hand and he dragged her to a safer position by the main mast. The helmsman struggled to control the spinning wheel. Another wave swept over the deck, swirling as high as Finn's waist. She fell, swallowing water. Jay hauled her to her feet, coughing, her throat raw. Rain beat against them, obscuring their vision. All was grey and furious: grey sea heaving and churning, grey wind screaming in the rigging, grey rain streaming. Every now and again Finn saw the dark figure of a man stumbling and sliding across the deck, or the twisting white shape of another sail tearing loose, but otherwise all she could see was a grey maelstrom as sea and sky spun together.

The sound of cracking wood suddenly brought all heads round with a jerk. There was a moment of horrific groaning, then suddenly the mizzenmast snapped. Down it came in a tangle of rigging and torn sails, smashing into the deck. Men screamed. The ship lurched and keeled over. The sea roared over them hungrily. Finn was dragged down into stinging, roaring, spinning darkness. She was tumbled over and over, limbs flailing helplessly. Then she slammed hard into something, so hard her ears roared and her eyes were filled with fizzing stars. She breathed water, drank fire. Then her foot met something solid and she pushed against it instinctively. Her head broke clear of the water. She coughed and choked, retching up seawater. Someone seized her hand, dragged her higher. Weak and sick, Finn crawled up the sloping deck, grasped a tangle of wood and rope, clung to it.

"How are ye yourself?" Jay's voice asked anxiously in her ear. His shoulder supported her.

"Just dandy," she answered, coughing hoarsely. "What do ye reckon?"

"Ye look as sick as a half-drowned cat," Jay answered with a half-hearted grin.

Finn immediately cried, "Goblin! Och, no! My poor wee cat!"

She was answered by a pitiful little mew, and stared wildly up into the rigging. There, far over their heads, hung the tiny elven cat, bedraggled and shivering, barely visible in the swirling rain. Sobbing, Finn held out her arms and the cat leapt into them, creeping up to tremble against her neck.

"Bran, ye must do something!" Dide shouted. "Canna ye calm this wind?"

Bran shook her head. She was clinging to the main mast, her lip crimson where she had bitten it. "I do no' ken how!" she shouted.

"Ye must be able to do something!" Dide cried. "Are ye no' the NicSian?"

She sobbed aloud. "I never had anyone to teach me the proper way o' doing it! Only my auld nurse . . ."

"I thought ye said ye had the Talent," Finn said. "Ye felt the storm rising long afore we could see it."

Bran's hair was plastered against her face, her clothes wet through. "Sensing a storm coming is nothing!" she cried. "Anyone with a pinch o' weather sense could do that. Even whistling up a wind is no' that hard, but calming a storm like this is something else again!"

"Canna ye try?" Jay said desperately. "Else we'll all drown!"

Bran clung to the mast with one hand and fumbled at her waist with the other, at last managing to undo her sash. Holding one end in her left hand, she succeeded in tying a knot in the sash with her teeth.

"Thou rushing wind that art so strong,
With this knot I bind thee," she chanted.

Still the wind roared about the ship as sailors fought to bring her upright again. Bran tied another knot, chanting:

"Thou pouring rain that art so wild,
With this knot I bind thee."

With a groan, the ship slowly regained an even keel as the sailors managed to shift the ballast in her hull. The wind still screamed into her ropes, however, and the rain lashed their faces with slivers of ice. "It's no' working," Finn whispered.

Bran tied a third knot in her sash, chanting loudly:

"Thou thunder that roars so loud,
With this knot I bind thee!"

She then lifted the knotted sash to the turbulent heavens, shouting:

"I command thee, hailstones and rain, hurricane and wind, sea waves and seafoam, lightning bolt and thunder, obey this, my will! By the powers o' air and fire and earth and water, I command thee! With these knots I have bound thee!"

They all stared out into the storm. The waves still rose high on either side, turbulent and white with foam. The wind roared in the rigging.

Bran's face was screwed up with tears of disappointment. "I told ye, I canna do it!" she cried.

"I do no' think it rains so hard," Jay said after a moment.

"I canna hear any thunder," Dide said. "And look! The ship does no' roll as far."

Bran pushed her wet hair out of her eyes. "Really?"

Slowly the waves gentled and the wind dropped till the ropes no longer screamed with the strain. Slowly the mad, headlong pace of the storm-driven ship slowed. The helmsman was able once more to control the wheel, bringing the ship back under control. Although the sea all about was still wild and white, waves no longer sought to drag the little ship down. Gradually the storm blew over, and they could see stars above the ragged clouds.

"I kent it would be useful to have the NicSian along!" Dide said with a smile, clapping Bran on the back. She blushed and smiled, dropping her lashes over her eyes so that Finn had to hiss at her, "Stop acting like a silly lass, Bran, ye're meant to be a lad, remember?"

The next morning, the *Speedwell* limped to safety in the bay of a small island. They rested there for close on a week while the ship's carpenter laboured to mend the broken mast. All were glad of the chance to rest and recover, and set foot on dry land once more. Finn was amazed to feel the sand rocking under her feet, as if the island were afloat upon the restless sea and not their storm-battered little craft.

The island had a spring of fresh water to replenish their water barrels and plenty of birds to catch and small crustaceans to gather. With nothing to do but rest and eat, Ashlin regained some of his vitality, though Enit remained frailer than ever.

Freed from her usual duties, Finn practiced her cart-wheels and tightrope walking, her rope tricks and dagger throwing, and pestered the crew with questions about every aspect of the repairs. She grew more accurate than ever with her crossbow, for the birds of the island were small and quick and very nervous, and Finn was very tired of fish.

As soon as the mizzenmast was repaired, a good number of feet shorter than it had been originally, they set sail once more. They had been blown many leagues off course and Alphonsus the Sure spent a great deal of time peering through his cross-staff, and scribbling equations on paper. Having to tack against the wind, the *Speedwell* nonetheless lived up to her name, bringing them within sight of the coast of Tìrsoilleir by the time the sun was setting the next day.

It was a stark, desolate landscape, the cliffs towering hundreds of feet above the rocky shore, and strange contorted rocks rising high out of the sea. Alphonsus the Sure was visibly relieved to have familiar landmarks once more to set his course by, and the wind swung round to the right quarter so that the *Speedwell* was able to sail confidently up that inhospitable coast.

"Hard to believe that on top o' those cliffs are some o' the best farming land ye could hope for," one sailor confided to Finn and Bran. He was a tall, brown young man called Tam, who had been kinder with the novices than many of the other sailors. He had taken the time to teach them all the different kinds of knots and to explain the use of the lead-line and the log-line.

"I was dragged up along here somewhere," he continued, "until I was pressed for the navy. One minute I was a farmer lad, thinking o' jumping the fire with the lass from the apple orchard, the next I found myself in the service o' the General Assembly, setting off to war against the witches."

"That must have been awful," Bran said.

"Aye, that it was, Bran," Tam said. "I cried like a babe when I woke, a day out o' Bride Harbour and a million miles from all I kent. I be content now, o' course, and do no' think o' Bessie o' the Apples any more, at least no' often."

"How do ye feel about us going back to Bride?" Finn asked, the elven cat on her shoulder cocking her head at exactly the same inquisitive angle.

Tam grinned. "Terrified, lad. And so should ye be. If any elder should see ye wi' that cat o' yours, they'd think ye a witch for certain."

Finn went white and shrank a little, the cat hissing and arching her back.

"I be no witch," she said, rather shakily.

"Och, lad, I'm no' accusing ye. If anyone is to burn, it will be that auld witch with her voice full o' sorcery, and those lads with their fiddles and pipes. In Bride, the playing o' tools like that would be enough to see ye charged, let alone the ensorcelling o' the sea demons, marvellous as that be." There was wonder and fear in the young sailor's voice.

Finn was suddenly aware of dangers that she had not yet worried over. She exchanged a fearful glance with Bran and made some light-hearted comment that fooled the young seaman as little as it deceived herself.

Cape Wrath was the eastern-most point of Eileanan. A great jutting peninsula, it was renowned for its ferocious storms and a dangerous passage between tall, abrupt cliffs on one side and a series of towering pinnacles of rock on the other, ominously called the Teeth of God. The only way to avoid that narrow, stormy passage was to sail weeks out of the way, for all the sea here was broken up with islands and reefs that tore the water up into contrary waves, whirlpools and rips.

With all hands on deck, the helmsman steered the little caravel through that dangerous passage. Alphonsus the Sure hunched over his maps, the sand trickling through the sand-glass by his side, the bosun shouting out the length of the log-line. As the navigator shouted out his instructions, the ship gybed from side to side, narrowly missing one cruelly sharp rock after another.

At last the *Speedwell* had sailed safely through the Teeth of God. Finn had no sooner taken what felt like her first real breath in hours when she realised they now had to circumnavigate the great spinning whirlpool called the Devil's Vortex. This was the last great obstacle between the caravel and its destination, the harbour of Bride. Again all the sailors were lashed to the ship and many calculations of time and angle were taken, Alphonsus bending to peer through his cross-staff again and again.

Finn had been frightened many times during their danger-fraught journey. When she saw the great, dark whirlpool, however, its breathtaking headlong speed, the churning of the sea all about, the terrible central vortex where the ocean was spun into a mouth of sucking air, her knees just gave way beneath her. She squeezed her eyes shut and put her head on her knees.

The ship was caught and spun like a child's whirligig. Finn's stomach flipped, the ropes cutting deep into her arms and legs as the centrifugal force dragged at her body. The elven cat struggled desperately to be free, drawing blood as she dug her claws deep into Finn's forearms. Finn held on to her tightly, though, holding her securely between her body and her bent legs. Her ears were buffeted by a deafening roar as if a thousand lions sought to tear the ship to shreds. Spray lashed her body, wetting her to the skin. She clutched Goblin closer, wishing she had kissed her mother goodbye.

Much, much later, it seemed, she heard Jay's voice in her ears, and felt his arms about her shoulders. "It be grand, Finn, I promise; we are all safe; everything is grand."

Finn opened one eye and then the other. Above her the proud spread of the *Speedwell*'s sails billowed white against the sky. The sea creamed under the caravel's bows. "Grand as a goat's turd stuck with buttercups," Finn said, releasing her clutch on the squirming cat. "I canna believe it."

"Alphonsus says he has navigated the Devil's Vortex five times now. That is more than any other living man," Jay said.

There was no sign on his face that he had faced the possibility of his own death, as Finn had. Since the singing of the song of love, Jay had been haloed by an aura of grandeur and invincibility that Finn recognised and was humbled by. She was not the only one. The sailors all gave him the deference due only to an officer, and Bran had been all shy, admiring lassie, causing Finn to frown at her more than once.

Once clear of the Devil's Vortex, the caravel made quick progress up the coast, the land gradually gentling down into smooth, green hills, a tall pointed spire marking every village.

"They be the steeples o' the kirks," Tam told Finn and Bran. "They all build them as high as they can, to give all honour to our God the Father, who dwells in the sky."

The sea rounded into a wide firth that lay blue and gentle between green headlands, each guarded by a tall lighthouse. In the mouth of the firth was a tall, peaked island, its cliffs as steep as any castle wall and more than five hundred feet high. An ugly, square fortress was built at the very pinnacle of the rock. Finn swallowed when she saw it, knowing without being told that was the prison compound frowning down upon them.

The *Speedwell* sailed past the prison into a long, wide harbour, near as well-protected as the Berhtfane. There the city of Bride nestled into a fold of the downs, tall slender spires of golden stones rising into the sunset sky. With all the towers and buildings built square, unlike the roundness of the Coven's architecture, the city had a foreign look about it that had them staring.

"Why, she be a bonny city," Ashlin said, leaning on the rail between Finn and Bran. His bony, long-fingered hands were more nervous than ever, pleating his shirt-tails together.

"Hell's bells, the city be large," Finn said, unable to help remembering the sailor's warning about witch fires. "What do we do now?"

"Lower anchor," the young sailor Tam said, "and wait for the harbourmaster to come. It'll be too soon for me."

They dropped anchor some distance from the shore and all were given a double ration of rum to celebrate their safe arrival. All were tense and jumpy, feeling the weight of uncertainty now the journey was at an end. Finn was jumpiest of them all, the sheer height of the island's cliffs reminding her what a time it had been since she had had to climb a wall.

It did not take long for the harbour officials to row

out to the resting caravel. It was suggested, without much subtlety, that Enit and the others should take the opportunity to rest below decks. They agreed with alacrity, hiding in one of the storerooms until the officials had gone.

"They have ordered us to appear afore the General Assembly tomorrow, to explain how we come to be here and to assure them we are free o' any form o' heresy or witch-taint," Captain Tobias told a tense and silent little group. "Ye have one night and one night only, to do what ye came here to do. Tomorrow we flee, regardless o' your success. Trust me when I say none o' us wish to appear afore the General Assembly."

"But why do they mistrust ye?" Enit asked, her dark-skinned face as pale as it was possible to be. "Should they no' be welcoming ye wi' open arms, a captain with the courage to flee the Rìgh's fleet?"

"They do no' think it is possible for us to have sailed the Skeleton Coast without witchcraft," the captain replied tersely. "And though I tried, I fear my eyes fell and my cheek whitened. I am no' used to lying."

They waited until night had fallen. Dide sat and strummed his guitar as if nothing could go wrong, but the others found it hard to endure the hours. Ashlin gnawed his knuckle raw, Bran fiddled with her short blonde pigtail, and Dillon bent his head over the shaggy white dog and said not a word, while Finn paced back and forth like a caged wolf.

At last all was dark and still. The prison loomed over the ship, more impregnable than any building Finn had ever seen. Now that she was here, the cat-thief was prey to gnawing doubts. Despite the dark, heavy presence of the magic cloak in her pocket and the warmth of the elven cat around her neck, Finn was cold and light-headed with fear. Dide had worked out every step of the operation, every variable, every trick Lady Luck could play, but still Finn could not sit still. *We have come so far,* she thought. *I could no' bear it if I was the one to fail . . .*

As soon as it was fully dark under the cover of night they took the long boat and rowed with muffled oars to a place where the cliff hung over the sea with a dark and frowning aspect. Dillon sat in the prow with his hand on his sword, while Jay and Dide worked the oars and tiller. All were dressed in black, with their faces and hands blackened with soot.

"Finn, are ye sure ye think it wise for ye to free the prophet yourself?" Dide whispered. "I'd be much happier if ye'd let us come into the Black Tower wi' ye."

"Ye with your great clumping boots and propensity to burst into song at the drop o' a hat?" As Dide protested, she went on, "Nay, believe me, it'll be much better if there's only one o' us to attract attention. I've been trained to this; ye three have no'. If I have need o' ye, I'll call ye through the golden ball ye gave me, as ye taught me."

Dide nodded reluctantly.

"Have a care for yourself, Finn," Jay said urgently, as the boat bumped against the rock.

"Och, dinna ye worry about me," Finn answered, heaving her bulging satchel on to her back and checking the rope was secured to her waist. "Though if I am no' back by dawn, make sure ye are gone from here, do ye hear me?"

Jay made an inarticulate protest and she smiled reassuringly and said, "Do no' fret, you great goose-cap. I'll be fine!"

Pulling on her climbing gloves, she looked up at the shelf of rock over their heads. Even in the darkness, she could see how it bulged out over the water, slick with spray.

"The easier slopes are all heavily guarded, but they think this side is inaccessible," Dide said. "Wha' do ye think, Finn? Can ye climb it?"

"Can a cat scratch its fleas?" Finn replied with false insouciance. "Watch and learn, my hearties!"

She reached up and thrust a long steel spike into the stone overhanging their heads, hammering it in with one quick, almost silent blow. In an instant she had belayed her rope around the spike and had hauled herself out of the boat and onto the rock, clinging as close as any spider to a leaf. She took pride in clambering out of sight in the time it would have taken one of her comrades to blink, pausing once she was over the bulge of rock to calm her galloping nerves.

Five hundred feet of steep, treacherous rock, all damp with seaspray and shrouded in the dark of a moonless night. Finn climbed slowly, carefully, taking the time to be sure her spikes were hammered in firmly and quietly. Many times her foot slipped or her hand fumbled, but each time she was able to recover her balance and cling close to the rock-face, her face pressed against the cold granite. Sometimes the elven cat climbed ahead of her, showing Finn a safer route. Sometimes she clung to Finn's shoulder, the sting of her claws keeping the girl alert and focused. Occasionally Goblin hung from her claws, mewing in distress, terrified by the steepness and inaccessibility of the cliff. Each time Finn found some crack in which to wedge a steel spike, some clump of weed to cling to, some high shelf to scramble to, dragging the elven cat behind her.

At last Finn crawled over the lip of the cliff. She lay in the darkness, panting harshly. Goblin lay beside her, trembling, her silky coat damp and filthy. Both would have happily curled together and slept, but at last Finn forced herself to her knees, and then to her feet. Above her the prison walls loomed, two hundred feet high and broken only by rows of narrow arrow slits. "Easy as pissing in bed," Finn said.

She scaled the closely fitting stones of the wall as swiftly as a carpenter climbing a ladder. The very top of the wall had been built out, however, making it impossible for Finn to climb up and over. She hung for a while, thinking, then slid down her rope until she came to the last row of arrow slits. There she belayed her rope firmly, before looping it loosely around the pin once more to allow easy release. She then crept within the embrasure, struggling to squeeze her long body through. She could not help wishing she was as skinny as she had been in the old days, when she had first been trained as a sneak-thief.

At last she fell through, her shoulders scraped raw, landing on her knees in a long, badly lit corridor. There she took the precaution of drawing out the little square of silk she carried in her pocket and shaking it out around her. At once all the hairs on her arm stood up, her skin shuddered, her nerves jolted with cold.

With an effort she shook off the lassitude and chill the cloak of invisibility always gave her, cuddling the warm little cat close to her chin. She took off the specially designed shoes and gloves she wore and stowed them away safely in her pack.

Feeling no fear, she then set off down the corridor, looking for the doorway out onto the battlements. She knew exactly where to find it, Elfrida NicHilde having drawn up a rough map of the prison that Finn had studied till she could see its shape behind the darkness of her closed lids.

A patrol of guards marched down the corridor, dressed in heavy armour and long white surcoats emblazoned with the design of a black tower. Finn simply stood against the wall until they had passed, confident they would not see her. She then went on until she reached the end of the corridor, leaning her ear against the huge, iron-bound door to listen.

She could hear the murmur of voices within and hesitated, gnawing her lip. After a while, she slowly turned the handle and eased the door open a crack. Keeping the cloak wrapped closely about her, she insinuated one arm through, then her head, then her leg. She was just sliding the rest of her body through when one of the guards said irritably, "shut the door, will ye, Justin? It be colder than a witch's tit out there!"

Finn just managed to whip her leg through before the door was slammed upon her. She stood very still against the wall, the guard that had shut the door only a few inches away from her. As he turned, his armour brushed against her but he did not notice, only shivering and beating his hands against his arms. "Brrrr!" he said. "So much for summer!"

The door to the battlements was on the other side of the guardroom. Finn waited for the soldiers to resume their game of trictrac before tiptoeing across the little room. She could not resist stealing one of the guards' pouch of tobacco on the way, for it had been some weeks since her own store had run out and Finn had been dying for a smoke. The door creaked as she opened it and the guards jumped, startled.

"Happen one o' the ghosts be walking," one said nervously. "Och, this be a bad place to work!"

As Finn slipped through she heard the other guards laugh at the nervous youngster and fought down the impulse to make an eeerie wailing sound. Closing the door very gently behind her, she made her silent way across the top of the battlements. She found the point where she had climbed up, then tied her sash around the elven cat and carefully lowered her over the battlements, Goblin mewing a little in distress. Swinging rather wildly at the end of Finn's sash, she at last came to the steel spike where Finn had left the rope loosely looped. The elven cat caught the rope in her mouth and as Finn tugged her upwards, the rope jerked free and was dragged up with the elven cat.

At last Goblin was dragged safely over the battlements, spitting and hissing in rage. Finn hugged her fiercely, but the elven cat struggled free and then sat with her back to Finn, smoothing down her ruffled fur with one well-dampened paw. "Ye did well, sweetie," Finn whispered, stroking the top of her head. "Thank ye!"

Goblin only hissed in reply, her tail lashing.

Taking care to make as little noise as possible, Finn hammered in another belay hook, ran the rope through it and then let the great length of it fall. After a long wait, when she began to feel rather sick with nerves, the rope jerked under her hand and she knew one of her companions was climbing up to join her. She did not wait, knowing it would take Dide and Dillon a long time to make the climb. She jerked the rope twice to let them know she was on her way to free the prophet, then crossed silently to the inner wall of the battlements.

The prison was built in the shape of a great square,

with a tower at each corner and battlements on top
that ran the length of each wall. Within the square
was another, smaller tower, built of black, shiny stone.
So carefully had the tower been built that the cracks
between the huge blocks of stone were no thicker than
a hairsbreadth. Soldiers stood sentinel outside the one
entrance, a massively thick iron door at the base of
the tower, while more soldiers patrolled the courtyard.

Finn leant over the crenellations for a long time,
scrutinising the central tower carefully. It was here
that Elfrida had lived most of her life, and here that
all the most important prisoners were incarcerated.
No-one had ever escaped the Black Tower before, it
was said, let alone tried to break in. Finn knew it
would be death for her if she was caught.

She waited for the wind to die down, then raised
her crossbow, winding it on with the hook at her belt.
She took careful aim and fired.

The crossbolt flew across the distance between the
towers and embedded itself deep in the stone, carrying
with it a length of stout rope. Finn instinctively
crouched low, despite the concealment of the magical
cloak. When it was clear none had heard the whine
of the bolt, she screwed another hook into the wall
and secured the rope tightly. She then took a deep
breath and stepped out onto the rope.

The wind caught at her, causing her to sway. She
regained her balance with some difficulty, her arms
stretched wide. Far below her the soldiers marched in
tight formation round the foot of the tower but none
thought to look up. Finn resisted the temptation to
look down, fixing her eyes firmly on the opposite wall.
She slid one foot forward, then the other, trying not
to think what would happen if she should slip. Step by
slow sliding step she crossed the tightrope, her cheek

curving in a grim little smile as she remembered how Dide and Morrell had alternately coaxed and goaded her into practising her rope walking until she was accomplished indeed. Finn had thought it a mere game to while away the weeks of travelling and to give her something to do when the jongleurs performed. She should have known Dide never did anything without good reason.

At last she made it to the opposite side, crawling over the battlements with her heart slamming and her palms sticky. Goblin unwound herself from Finn's neck, washing herself thoroughly while Finn rubbed her claw-scored throat ruefully. She would have given much to have lit up her pipe but dared not risk anyone noticing the flare of the flint or the smell of tobacco smoke.

She found the door to the tower but it was locked and barred on the inside. Finn sighed and pulled out her lock-picking tools. Kneeling on the ground she inserted first one, then another, then another, until at last the lock sprang free. Lifting the bar was another difficult struggle and Finn had to subdue her impatience, knowing it would only make her difficult task harder. Although the dark hours of the night were trickling away, kicking a door and swearing were not going to make the minutes pass more slowly.

At last she had the door open, and crept down the winding stairs until she had reached the corridor below. She pressed her back against the cold black stone and pulled the prophet's wooden cross from her backpack.

Finn felt him straight away, as loud as if he was blowing a trumpet. To her dismay he was deep in the bowels of the building. She had hoped he would be in the heights, close to her rope and her route to safety. She thrust the cross into her pocket and set off down the corridor at a jog. Time was running out.

Black as a living shadow, the tiny cat slunk along the dim corridor, her long tufted ears twitching back and forth, sniffing at the doors and in the corners. Suddenly she froze, one paw raised, her tail stiff. Finn bent over her. "What can ye smell, Goblin? What can ye hear?"

*Mouse,* she hissed and looked up at Finn with gleaming aquamarine eyes, her fangs showing white and sharp.

"No' now, sweetie! We're looking for a smelly auld man, a very smelly man if the reports be true. They say the Tìrsoilleircan mystics think it a sin to wash so ye should be able to smell him a good way off!"

Goblin wrinkled her nose fastidiously.

The corridor led out into another wider hall, lined with heavily barred doors. At the end of the hall was a landing leading to a wide sweep of stairs. Finn's eyes brightened and she hurried towards it.

Suddenly she heard the sound of singing. Finn stopped mid-step, entranced. It was a woman's voice, singing a lament. Finn recognized the tune. It was a song she had heard Enit sing many times.

> "I wish, I wish my babe was born
> An' smiling on yon nurse's knee;
> An' I myself were dead and gone,
> Wi' green, green grass growing over me,
> Aye, wi' green, green grass growing over me."

The song faltered and broke off. Then, very low and piteous, Finn heard the words again, spoken not sung: "Aye, wi' green, green grass growing over me."

Finn paused for a moment, irresolute, then shook

her head irritably, drew the cloak more tightly about her and hurried towards the stairs.

Safe within the camouflage of the cloak of invisibility, Finn took no more than ordinary care, concentrating on haste rather than stealth. She passed many guards, some standing sentinel outside doors, others patrolling the halls with white cloaks swinging.

On the ground floor she paused in a quiet corner and held the wooden cross again, reorienting herself. It took some time, watching and listening, before she discovered the way down into the dungeons. They were locked and closely guarded so she bided her time, fidgeting with impatience, until the hourly patrol came round once more. She slipped in through the door behind them, almost treading on one soldier's heels as she hurried to make it through the door before it clanged shut again.

Down here the halls had been hacked out of living rock and the walls and floor were rough and uneven. Set all along the sides of the corridor were doors made of iron, with little barred windows set at eye height, and a flap down at floor level for food to be shoved through. Every now and again the corridor branched, but Finn showed no hesitation in choosing which way to turn. She had no need to touch the wooden cross again. She could feel where the prophet was as surely as if she were a compass and he true north.

She followed another flight of steps down, these ones narrow, with the steps set at different heights so she had to descend with care. The stone was slimy to the touch and when she passed a torch, she saw the floor shone with puddles.

At the end of the corridor was a large iron door, with two guards sitting in front of it. One was having difficulty keeping his head from nodding forward on to his chest, jerking it back every few minutes. He yawned widely, took off his helmet to scratch his head vigorously, then jammed the helmet back on again.

"Och, I hate the graveyard shift," he grumbled. The other one made no response other than to snore, loudly and comfortably. His companion looked at him, sighed, and nudged him in the leg with his toe. "Wake up, Dominic!"

There was no response. The guard sighed again, very noisily, then took a swig from a ceramic tankard by his feet. "Why, oh why did I join the army?" he said.

Finn knelt on the ground as quietly as she could and slowly, cautiously, slid the straps of her satchel off her back, being careful to keep all parts of her body beneath the cover of the cloak. She unbuckled one of the straps, slid her hand within and groped about. There was a clink as Dide's golden ball rolled against her hammer. Immediately Finn froze.

The guard looked up rather blearily. Unable to see anything, he rubbed the back of his neck with his hand and said to his sleeping companion, "The least ye could do, Dom, is stay awake and keep me company!"

Finn's fingers closed upon a little packet of folded paper. Carefully she drew it out and unfolded it. The paper crackled and again the guard looked up, this time more sharply. Finn kept very still, as still as the elven cat crouched at her feet. He stood up and peered down the corridor, paced a little, then at last sat down again. His hand reached down, groped for his tankard of ale, brought it up to his mouth for a long swig. He sighed, wiped his mouth, and went to set the tankard back down on the ground. As his eyes rolled back in his head, the tankard fell from his nerveless fingers and broke on the ground, ale splashing out.

"Well, that sleeping powder certainly works well," Finn whispered to Goblin as she bent, unhooked the keys from the guard's belt and unlocked the door.

Finn recoiled as soon as she stepped inside. A thick miasma closed about her, so thick as to be almost palpable. Composed of mould and sweat and urine and human excrement and something darker, like terror, it caused her to choke and retch with revulsion. She muffled her nose and mouth with the cloak, and peered about.

It was black inside, black as a chimney sweep's arse. Finn wished she had thought to bring in one of the lanterns hanging outside the door. She groped her way out again, took great breaths of air that tasted sweet in comparison, then seized the lantern and stepped back inside.

Within was a small cell. Lying on a filthy pallet of straw and rags was an old man. He woke as soon as the light penetrated the cell, cowering back with a cry. Upon his papery skin were the ugly marks of torture: angry red burns, deep cuts and lacerations all weeping with pus, old bruises in yellow and green and new ones, black as ink.

Finn tried to reassure him but it was clear he could not understand her. She knelt by his side and pressed the wooden cross into his hands. His wildly dilated eyes stared at the cross, then back at her. Suddenly his face came alive with hope and joy and he kissed the cross passionately.

Finn helped him to her feet. He was dressed in only a few damp and filthy rags, and was shivering with cold. She had come prepared for this. Finn dragged a long black robe out of her pack and indicated that he

should dress in it. For some reason she did not understand he recoiled at the sight but she pressed her
hands together pleadingly and reluctantly he nodded.
She turned away as he stripped away the rags and
dressed himself in the robe. She passed him a pair of
soft shoes and he crammed his long, bony feet into
them. She saw that the soles of his feet were suppurat-
ing with sores where he had been whipped again
and again.

When he was ready, she slowly eased open the door
and checked outside. All was quiet, the two sentries
snoring away. Finn chewed her thumbnail thoughtfully. The plan had been for her to steal one of the
soldier's uniforms and to pretend to be a guard escort-
ing a pastor through the prison. Such a sight was not
uncommon in the prison, apparently, since the pastors
spoke rites over those close to death, and many in the
prison died every day. The prophet's filthy, emaciated
state would not occasion much surprise, since many of
the Tirsoilleirean pastors starved themselves willfully
and refused to wash the filth and lice from their bodies, considering such peculiar behaviour holy. Finn was
hesitant to strip the guard, however, in case the one
whose sleep was natural should wake.

After a moment she decided to take the risk, however. Indicating the prophet should wait inside the
cell, she stripped the drugged guard of his armour as
quietly as she could. It was impossible to avoid some
clinks and clanks, however, and once or twice the
other guard stirred and once half-opened his eyes,
only to mutter something incomprehensible and close
them again. Finn dragged the half-naked guard within
the cell, dressed herself rapidly in his unpleasantly
smelling chain-mail armour, then put his helmet on
her head and his gauntlets on her hands. It was all

very heavy and very smelly, and Finn wrinkled her nose in distaste. At last she was ready and able to lock the cell again, hanging the keys on her belt.

The prophet was very unsteady on his feet and Finn was beside herself with impatience as he shuffled along the corridor. She took his arm and tried to urge him along faster. There was no hurrying him, though, and so she stamped down her anxiety and helped him as best she could.

It was in the wee small hours of the night and all was quiet. Finn managed to avoid most of the guards and those they did pass did not pay them much attention, even though the prophet was so clearly barely able to totter. Once they reached the stairs it was easier for he was able to lean heavily on the balustrade, and she was able to push him from behind.

They were on the top floor when Finn heard again the sound of singing. She stopped in her tracks, once again entranced by the power and beauty of the voice. It sang of running along the sea-strand, the wind in her hair, the birds calling in her ears, finding shells that sang of the ocean. Some sound must have penetrated the old man's maimed ears as well, for he lifted his grime-caked face to hers and said softly, "Be that the sea witch I hear?"

It was the first time he had spoken and Finn gaped at him in surprise. He frowned a little and said, "They may have cut off my ears but I can still hear, lad. I hear sounds, though indistinctly, and I hear with the ears o' the spirit. That is something they could never take away from me, no' till they took my life. And then I'd be with God and should hear the singing o' angels, which indeed I long to do."

He sighed. "I remember the sea witch, though. I used to be in the cell next to hers. I'd press my ruined

ear against the wall and hear her as she sang. How
sweetly and how sadly she would sing! Indeed, I do
no' think the singing o' the angels could be as sweet,
for she sang o' things I love, spring and apple trees
and children playing . . ."

Finn nodded and smiled. She listened to the pure,
angelic voice a little longer, her mind racing. She had
been present at many of the early war conferences,
when the Bright Soldiers of Tìrsoilleir had first attacked the free lands of Eileanan. There had been
much puzzlement as to how the Bright Soldiers had
managed to sail the Skeleton Coast, with the seas thick
with Fairgean and the coast unknown to any living
sailor, since it had been three hundred years since any
merchant ships had sailed from Bride. Once Meghan
had said, "If it was anyone else, I would think they
must have had a Yedda to sing them to safety, but I
ken the Bright Soldiers abhor all witchcraft and would
never have a trained sea witch to help them."

Lachlan had replied, "Unless they captured that
ship I sent to Bride five years ago. It had on board
the last remaining Yedda that I had been able to find.
They may have forced her to sail with them and sing
the Fairgean to death. If that was so, it would also
explain how the Bright Soldiers kent the way through
the Bay o' Deception, for there were many canny sailors on board that ship that kent that coast like the
backs o' their hands."

No Yedda had ever been found on board any of
the Tìrsoilleirean ships captured during the war and
Finn had never heard her mentioned again. Now she
remembered, however. She stood and listened, and
wondered, and somewhere inside her a germ of an
idea took root.

Hearing the sound of marching feet behind her she

hustled the old man along the corridor and into the safety of the side hall. The patrol marched past. Once they were safely gone, Finn hurried the old prophet up the narrow flight of stairs to the battlements. They stepped out into the fresh air, both taking deep gasping breaths, relief buoying their blood.

Finn was a little dismayed to find the darkness was already fading. A few seabirds wheeled overhead, screaming plaintively. It was light enough for her to see the shape of the battlements dark against the sky. She led the old prophet across to her tightrope, still stretched between the two buildings. On the other side she could see the dark shape of Dide and Dillon as they rose from their hiding place behind the crenellations. Although she could not see their faces, their hunched stance and urgent movements told her how tense and anxious they were.

"Shut your eyes," Finn told the old man, riffling through her bulging satchel for the leather harness and then fastening it securely round his skinny body. She led him to the wall and made him climb on top of it, clipping the strap of the harness to the tightrope. The old man opened his eyes and gave a shriek of dismay as he realised he was standing on the very edge of the battlement.

"Sssssh!" Finn hissed urgently and Goblin hissed as well, lashing her tail. "Shut your eyes and keep your mouth shut too, unless ye wish to betray us all!"

Trembling, the old man obeyed. Finn gestured to the two men on the other side and then gave the old man a vigorous push. He fell, wailing. The rope jerked and held. Hanging from the tightrope by his harness, he sailed across the distance, his bare legs kicking wildly. Dide caught him at the far end and hauled him up and over the wall.

"Go! Go!" Finn made wild gesturing motions with her hands and Dide nodded and half-dragged, half-carried the old man across the battlements to where the rope hung all the way down to the sea, past seven hundred feet of sheer rock.

Finn waited till they were busy strapping the old man to Dillon in preparation for the long descent back to the boat, then ran back to the door and down the stairs, her mind scurrying with excitement and fear. As she ran she dragged out the magical cloak and flung it around her once more. It was almost dawn and soon the prison would be stirring. If Finn was to rescue the Yedda, she would have to be quick.

The sea witch was singing no longer but Finn knew where she was incarcerated and wasted no time getting there, clanking in her borrowed armour as she ran. Goblin bounded before her, ears pricked forward. Finn reached the door, which was unguarded, knelt outside it and picked the lock with her tools. Within seconds the lock had flown open and she was able to swing open the door.

A very thin, pale, haggard woman sat on a low trestle bed, her blonde-grey hair hanging free all around her, a comb in her hand. She looked up in surprise and stared, puzzled and frightened, her hand to her sunken cheek. Finn realised she still had the hood of the cloak over her head and pushed it back. The Yedda gasped.

"Witchcraft!" she cried. "It must be. One minute there was no-one there and now, here ye are! Who are ye?"

"My name is Finn. There's no time for chitchat. I have come to rescue ye. Quickly! Ye must come with me now."

"But I . . ."

Finn seized her hand and dragged her to her feet. "Quickly! The guards will patrol past soon. We must be gone. Come on!"

"But I be in my nightgown . . . just let me . . ."

"For Eà's sake, will ye no' come?"

The Yedda was dragging on her stockings but at Finn's words she looked up, her eyes glowing. "Eá! It has been long since I heard her blessed name. Aye, for Eà's sake I shall come and gladly."

She thrust her feet into shoes and caught up a plaid from where it hung over her chair. As she flung it round her, she seized a few belongings from the low table and tried to shove them into a reticule. Finn dragged her away. "Come away!" she cried in a frenzy. "Do ye no' realise it is dawn?"

"What about the others?" the Yedda cried, suddenly dragging back against Finn's hand. "Do ye no' save them too?"

"What others?" Finn asked as she pulled the door closed behind them.

"John and Peter and Captain Banning, and auld Ballard, and Ferris . . ."

"I do no' ken who they are," Finn said indifferently. "Come, let us no' tarry."

The Yedda stood firm. "They are the crew o' the *Sea-Eagle*. We have suffered much together and I canna be leaving them. Come, they are in the next rooms, it will no' take but a minute!"

"We do no' have a minute!" Finn cried in a frenzy of impatience. The Yedda pleaded with her though and so Finn flung herself to her knees before the next door down and manipulated the lock with hands shaking with fear and haste. "Goblin, keep watch!" she hissed through her teeth and the elven cat slunk away down the corridor, her aquamarine eyes narrowed.

At last the door swung open. Within was a long room, all crowded with trestle beds upon which men lay sleeping, or sat up, yawning and questioning. At one end was a barred window and through the grime Finn could see the wall opposite, just fingered with light. "The sun is up!" she cried. "Come on, come on, all o' ye!"

As the men woke, exclaiming in surprise, Finn motioned them all forward. The men quickly began to scramble into their breeches and shoes, and she waved her arms furiously. "Hurry!"

Without waiting to see if they obeyed her, Finn bent over to pick the lock of the next door along. She roused the men within with a hiss and a shake, then hurried along to the next door, her heart hammering. At last the final door was unlocked and the man within, a tall man with a weather-beaten face and an air of command, was woken by Finn's urgent hand.

The Yedda leant past her. "Captain Banning, come on; we must flee. They have come to rescue us at long last!"

The captain did not ask for an explanation, nodding and pulling on his breeches. "We do no' have time!" Finn cried, hurrying back out into the corridor. "Please, please, hurry!"

"They bring us some food in the early hours," the Yedda whispered, her hand shaking. "They will find that we have gone then. How are we to escape?"

"Follow me," Finn said as they all hurried along the corridor, boots clattering against the stone. "Canna ye walk more lightly?" Finn hissed and they tried to tiptoe, making even more noise in the process. Finn rolled her eyes.

From behind her came a squalling mew, as loud and

high as the little elven cat could manage. Finn dragged one slow man out of his room with a determined heave.

"The guards come!" she cried. "Be quick! Be quiet!"

She heard the sound of marching feet and looked about her in despair. There were close on twenty men milling about in various states of undress, some wearing nothing but their shirts. The marching grew closer. Everyone froze, panic on their faces.

*Stall them!* She projected her urgent mind-message to the little cat, while beckoning the men forward, her other finger held against her lips. They hurried round the corner into the little side corridor. They heard a cat yowling, then laughter and a scuffle. Finn was white to her lips. "Please, Eà, keep Goblin safe," she whispered.

The yowling faded away, and after a confused moment, the marching resumed, accompanied by low voices and laughter. There was no time for them all to get out on to the battlements and in the growing light, it was too much to hope that none would notice them huddling in the antechamber.

So Finn motioned them all close to her. "Huddle in under my cloak," she whispered frantically. "Creep in as close ye can get and make sure no hands or feet stick out. Oh, blessed Eà, let the cloak stretch far enough!"

Miraculously it did. The stretch of black silk that could fold up small enough to fit inside Finn's pocket billowed out to cover twenty-four men and two women with ease. Finn did not stop to wonder how. She merely gave fervent thanks to Eà as the patrol marched straight past them, then urged the free captives up the stairs and out on to the battlements.

"Dide is going to kill me!" she mouthed, then

shrugged, calling out anxiously to Goblin with her mind.

"Who is this goblin that ye call to?" the Yedda asked, causing Finn's eyes to widen in amazement. "Do ye have faery assistance?"

"Goblin is my cat," Finn explained, urging them to hurry.

"Ah, your familiar," the Yedda replied. Finn nodded, calling to Goblin again. As the Yedda went through the door Finn turned back anxiously to look behind them and saw the elven cat turn the corner and come limping up the corridor. *Hoarweasels follow* . . . the cat said, her mind-voice wincing with pain.

*Are ye hurt, sweetie?*

*Those feral hoarweasels kicked me!* the cat answered, her mind-tail lashing. *They are close behind me.*

Finn pushed the last man through the door, and scrambled through herself. As Goblin leapt up the stairs to join her, she saw a guard turn the corner. Goblin whisked through the door and Finn slammed it behind her.

"Hold this shut for me!" Finn cried. "Quick! Ye must swing across that rope to the far side! Make haste!"

As some of the men put their shoulders to the door, Finn hastily locked it with her lock-picking tools. Blows began to fall upon it from the other side. "We are discovered!" Finn cried. "Oh, Eà, make haste!"

One by one the men swung across the rope to the battlements of the opposite tower. Dide stood there, livid with anger, but he helped them over the wall and then instructed them to start climbing down the rope. The Yedda could not swing hand over hand across the rope and so Finn ran lightly over the rope, and seized the leather harness that had been strapped to Killian the Listener. Dide tried to grab her arm, hissing angry questions at her, but she shook him off. "We are discovered!" she panted, before running back across the rope as swiftly and easily as if it were a plank over a burn. She strapped the Yedda into it and pushed her off vigorously. As she hung over the battlements she saw soldiers down below pointing up at them and shouting. Some were running into the outer fortress and Finn had no doubt they would soon be attacked from within.

Then the door splintered and broke. Soldiers in white surcoats poured out, but those men still remaining on the battlements grappled with them fiercely. Finn leapt out of the fray and hastily drew her crossbow, firing bolt after bolt at the attacking guards. They fell, screaming. Those she did not shoot down were battered into insensibility by the freed sailors, who seized the guards' swords before swinging across to the opposite battlements. Finn picked up Goblin and ran across the tightrope after them, just as more soldiers burst out on to the rampart. With a single slash of his dagger, Dide cut the rope free.

"Ye porridge-head," he snarled, seizing Finn's arm so tightly she thought he would break the bone. "Wha' are ye about?"

"They are Lachlan's men," she panted, wincing and trying to drag her arm free. "She be a Yedda. I could no' leave them."

"How are we to save them all?" he cried. "Once the soldiers get out on to the heights, all they need do is cut the rope and we shall all die!"

"We had best get down quickly then," Finn said

and pushed him towards the rope still hanging over
the wall. "No time for squawking, Dide, climb!"

He tried to make her go first but she shook her
head. "Do not be a porridge-head, Dide! I have secured the rope just below. Once ye are past that point,
I can cut the rope here free. Then they canna stop us!
I can climb down without it. Do no' argue! Climb!"

Dide swore at her, swung his leg over the rampart
and began to climb down the rope. Finn heard the
crack of breaking wood and turned. Soldiers had broken through the door and were running towards her,
brandishing swords. She looked back. Dide was swinging down the rope but he had not yet reached the
point where Finn had secured the rope. She took a
deep breath, turned and raised her crossbow.

One, two, three bolts slammed into the running soldiers. They fell, screaming. Finn loaded again, and
wound on the crossbow as fast as she could. The bolt
took the soldier in front between the eyes and he fell,
right at Finn's feet. Then the others were upon her.
She thrust them off with the crossbow, and Goblin
leapt for them, claws raking, hissing like a snake. For
a second they faltered. It was time enough for Finn
to leap on to the wall, seize the rope in her hand and
swing out and down. The cat leapt with her, landing
on her head and digging all her claws deep into Finn's
skull. Although she shrieked with pain, Finn slid down
the rope as fast as she could. There was no time to
hammer in any spikes so as soon as she was past the
overhang, Finn simply let go of the rope, clinging with
all her strength to a tiny ledge of rock where moss
had crumbled away the cement. The rope slithered
down past her, cut by the soldiers above who now
hung over the battlement, trying to see if she was

falling. Finn hung there, all her muscles screaming, and looked down herself.

Relief flashed through her. Dide hung on the rope, just below the belay hook where Finn had fastened the rope. He looked up at her, his face white. Finn jerked her head at him urgently, mouthing, "Go! Go!"

He nodded and began to slide down once more. Below him Finn could see other men, all hanging on to the rope for dear life. She began to feel about with her feet for another ledge, her fingers white with the strain. Just as she thought she could not support her own weight any longer, she found a little crack in which to rest her foot. Letting go of all her breath in a gusty sigh of relief, Finn eased one hand down and then her other foot. Slow inch by slow, painful inch, she climbed down the wall.

The tower guards shot at them from the arrow slits but the angle was so steep and the men hanging so close to the wall, few were injured. Alarm bells rang out, causing sea birds to rise in a cacophony of white wings that did more to endanger those descending than the arrows. Since most were sailors, they were swift and nimble in their descent, however, and it did not take long before all were down in the water, clinging to the sides of the longboat. Finn fell the last ten feet, so faint with exhaustion that she could no longer manage to hold on to the rope. She hit the water with a great splash, and was dragged into the boat by Jay. She opened her eyes and looked up into his white, anxious face. "Told ye I'd be fine," she said.

"Fine as a proud laird's bastard," he answered.

She smiled, closing her eyes again.

# HELL'S GATE

**C**annons boomed. "By the Centaur's beard, that one was close!" Dide coughed as black smoke enveloped the *Speedwell*. They leant over the rail, staring at the ships that pursued them, their yards straining under full sail. The lead ship was so close they could see the yawning black mouths of the cannons and see the men scurrying about on her deck.

"They be big, those ships," Bran said anxiously. "Will they catch us, Dide?"

"Nay, o' course no'," he reassured her. "Ye can conjure a wind to sweep them away if they come close enough."

Bran looked even more unhappy than before. The roar of the cannons sounded again and all were drenched by the lash of spray as the cannonballs missed the little caravel by a whisker.

"Why do we no' shoot back?" Finn demanded.

"Our range is no' as long as those cannons," the young sailor Tam replied. "Why waste cannonballs shooting at the waves?"

"Once we are past the Devil's Vortex we should be safe," Dide said. "They will no' dare follow us through the whirlpool."

Finn's stomach muscles clenched at the thought of facing that whirling maelstrom of water again. Somehow she had never given any thought to what would happen after they had rescued Killian the Listener. She had assumed their adventure would be over and Tìrsoilleir conquered. Yet she realised now how naïve that assumption had been. They still had to take Killian the Listener and the other rescued prisoners to meet Lachlan and his army at the border with Tìrsoilleir. It could be months before the words of the earless prophet had ignited a fire strong enough to sweep away the Fealde and the General Assembly, and restore the monarchy. It could be years.

And in the meantime, they still had to escape the angry retribution of Tìrsoilleir's ruling council, who had sent a fleet of great ships in pursuit. If the journey along the Skeleton Coast had been dangerous before, it was doubly so now, with the great galleons of Tìrsoilleir chasing them with all the power and speed of their massive, billowing sails and their decks of long-range cannons. Already the *Speedwell* had suffered some damage to her hull and rigging, but with all the extra willing hands, they had been able to repair the damage quickly, without slackening their headlong speed.

The Devil's Vortex could only be crossed at high tide, when the rocks and reefs that caused the great tumult of water were almost fully submerged. The *Speedwell* had been tacking about waiting for the tide, and that was how the galleons had managed to come close enough to fire once more. The tide was running high, now, though, and the *Speedwell* changed course once more, heading straight for the treacherous stretch of water. Finn sank down, gathered Goblin in her arms, and shut her eyes determinedly. She had no desire to watch.

"Six times! Alphonsus the Sure will go down in legend!" Jay shouted after an eternity of roaring, spinning darkness. "Open your eyes, Finn; we're safe."

Finn obeyed with alacrity, scrambling up to join the others at the rail. To their dismay, the galleons had not changed course but were racing along the outskirts of the maelstrom in pursuit. As they watched, one was caught in the rip and capsized, masts and rigging smashing down into the churning water. Men leapt into the water, only to be dragged under by the rip, their despairing hands disappearing under the water.

"There must a hundred ships on the sea-bed just there," Tam said somberly, his face white under his sunburn. "It is well named, the Devil's Vortex."

Although the other galleons found it difficult to maintain control, they were not so unlucky and soon were once again bearing down upon the *Speedwell* as she tacked to and fro amidst the Teeth of God.

"We should be able to shake them now," Dide said with his usual optimism. "They may be bigger, but the *Speedwell* is quick and agile. She can turn much faster than those ponderous beasts and will be able to sail where they canna."

At first it seemed he would be proven right, for the *Speedwell* was able to sail close to the cliffs, once racing right through a tall arch of stone where part of the cliff had crumbled away. Being much deeper and wider, the galleons had to head out to the open sea to avoid the rocks. For several days they were nowhere in sight, and the sailors of the *Speedwell* were able to relax a little.

But with the rising of the sun a few days later, the sailors were horrified to find the fleet of galleons bearing down upon them from the east. The Tìrsoilleirean ships had been able to gain much time by not having constantly to tack to avoid the many rocky islands. In addition, they were better able to use the light and fitful wind because of their greater sail power. Soon they would be within firing range again. Once again all hands were called on deck, and they laboured to regain their lead.

It was no use. The billowing white sails grew larger and larger, the great hulk of the galleons looming over them. Then they saw puffs of black smoke and heard the dull roar of the cannons. Confusion reigned as part of their rigging was again torn down, smashing down upon the deck and trapping many of the sailors beneath it.

"Canna ye whistle up a wind to take us out o' here, Bran?" Finn begged.

The cannons boomed once more. They coughed as foul-smelling smoke poured over the deck, then saw with horror one of the galleons looming up close beside them. They saw the cannons being reloaded and the smile on the face of the ship's captain as he raised his hand for the order.

Bran hesitated. She wished that the Yedda they had rescued was strong enough to advise her, at the very least, but the strain of the escape had proven too much for Nellwyn. Weakened by years of deprivation and harsh treatment, the sea-witch had collapsed as soon as she had reached the deck of the *Speedwell,* and was still weak and disorientated. Besides, Bran knew that Nellwyn was no weather witch, having been trained in the use of the songs of sorcery, not in the ways of wind and water. She probably knew no more about controlling the forces of weather than Bran herself.

"Happen I could try . . ." She said at last, closing her eyes and clenching her hands into fists. Her lips moved soundlessly.

The black smoke swirled apart. They felt a freshen-

ing breeze on their cheeks. The *Speedwell*'s flapping
sails billowed out and they felt the boat surge forward.
The galleon's cannonballs fell harmlessly into their
wake.

"Ye did it!" Finn cried and hugged her cousin ec-
statically. "I always kent ye could!"

"I'm glad ye did," Bran replied wryly.

"What do ye mean?"

"I was never sure myself," Bran said, dropping
her eyes.

"But the MacSian clan have always been powerful
weather witches. Why . . ."

"But they were all trained at the Tower o' Storms,"
Bran cried. "They were all taught from birth how to
raise the wind and calm it. I was only two when witchcraft was outlawed on pain o' death. I was punished
severely if I even talked about magic! I remember
once getting into terrible trouble because I chanted a
little rhyme my auld nurse had told me, and almost
drowned myself calling up the wind to fill the sails o'
my wee dinghy. I could no' control the wind once it
came and it caused terrible damage to the crops and
all the crofters' cottages, and I had to be rescued when
my dinghy capsized. I never tried again, in fear o'
getting into trouble again and in fear o' what I might
do. I do no' even remember the rhyme . . . so ye see,
I really did no' ken if I could do it. I've been so afraid
ye'd all be realising I dinna have any Talent . . ."

"No Talent!" Finn cried, amazed. "But ye are the
NicSian!"

"Exactly," Bran answered. "Ye can see my problem."

"And ye were always going on about it, stopping
me from riding out because ye said a storm was coming or . . ."

"I ken, I ken," Bran said. "No need to rub it in."

"So ye really do no' ken how . . . but ye must, ye just called up wind then!"

Bran nodded, smiling rather sheepishly. "Aye, lucky, wasna it?"

"Ye mean . . ."

"I had always thought ye needed to be taught all the right words and rituals," Bran said, "and so when we met up with the MacAhern's caravan, I begged the Loremaster to teach me. He told me witches' talents were innate powers, born into ye. He said that learning to draw upon and use such power could be taught, but that ye either had or did no' have the ability. He said if I had managed to do so as a bairn, I must have been born with the Talent and I could train myself to try and use it. He suggested that I try and learn as much about the weather as I could, listening and watching and figuring out how it works. Well, oddly enough, a boat is an ideal place to learn about such things. We are so dependent upon the wind and the tide. I have been practising calling the wind and keeping it steady . . ."

"That is why the winds were so fair most o' the time!" Finn cried. "I've heard the sailors marvel it should blow so steady and always from the right quarter. Tam said having an auld witch bless the fleet with flowers and goldensloe wine works much better than one o' their parsons with his holy water . . ."

"Aye, but I was no' sure if it were truly me or if it was just coincidence. And then the storm came . . ."

"But ye bound the storm."

Bran nodded. "I canna tell ye how happy I was when that auld spell o' my nurse's actually worked. I had no' been sure afore then . . . and that could have been coincidence too, ye ken. But now I truly ken it was me! That wind came from nowhere and see how strong and steadily it blows."

She turned and gestured up at the sails. Only then did the two girls realise that the galleons were close upon either side of the ship, so close that sailors were leaning down with grappling hooks to try and catch them in their ropes. The wind that filled the *Speedwell*'s sails had also filled the galleons' and brought the great ships close upon the caravel's stern.

For a second Bran stared, her mouth agape. Then she dropped her hands and swiftly untied her sash, still knotted in three places from where she had bound the storm. She ran up on to the aftercastle and leant over the railing, undoing the knots as fast as she could. Then she waved her sash at the two galleons bearing down so close upon them, shouting:

"Wind and rain and lightning, I release thee! I release thee! I release thee! Hailstones, hurricane, thunderclap, I release thee, I release thee, I release thee! By the powers o' air and fire and earth and water, I command thee, storm, to rage!"

There was a great roar as sheet lightning suddenly leapt from the end of Bran's flapping sash, irradiating the sky with white fire that set the galleons' sails ablaze. The air stank of sulphur. Everyone cowered down, screaming in shock, all their hair standing up from the static electricity in the air. Thunderclap after thunderclap boomed out, and the wind roared. When Finn opened her eyes, her hands still clamped over her ears, she saw Bran's slim figure outlined against a great sheet of lightning, the ships' masts black and smoking behind her, her sash billowing wildly in the gale. Then it began to rain, so heavily that it seemed dusk had fallen over the Tìrsoilleirean fleet while the *Speedwell* raced on through sunshine.

"God's teeth!" Arvin the Just roared. "What witch-craft is this?"

"Who cares?" Captain Tobias cried. "Look!"

They all looked back and saw the galleons tossed wildly about in the storm, their masts broken, their sails tearing free. Hailstones large as pebbles battered the decks, and they could hear cries of pain and terror that soon dwindled away as the *Speedwell* raced along, her sails full of wind, the water creaming along under her bows.

Bran swayed and crashed to the deck, the sash still clutched in her fist. Finn ran to her, kneeling beside her. Bran was unconscious, her cheek as white as the hailstones. At first Finn's trembling fingers could find no pulse but then she felt a faint, erratic flutter, and sobbed aloud in relief.

"They that sow the wind shall reap the whirlwind," Arvin the Just said with gloomy satisfaction.

Finn leapt to her feet. "Canna ye ever shut up, ye frog-faced lout!" she cried.

His granite-hard countenance did not even quiver. "Fools think their own way is right, but the wise listen to advice. Fools show their anger at once but the prudent ignore an insult."

"Flaming dragon balls, if I hear one more o' your bloody awful sayings I swear I'll cram them down your throat with your own balls!"

She advanced on him with her fist raised high and he folded his massive arms and looked down at her impassively. Dide caught her arm and said soothingly, "Settle down, wild cat! Ye'd only bruise your knuckles. Come, help me carry Bran downstairs for the Yedda to look at. All Tower-trained witches are taught some healing skills. I ken Nellwyn's weak still but she will ken better than anyone what to do for sorcery sickness. Never mind Arvin, he ate too many sour crabapples as a bairn!"

"All the words o' my mouth are righteous," the first mate said sternly. "There is nothing twisted or crooked in them."

"I'll give ye something twisted," Finn muttered, but allowed Dide to drag her away.

Nellwyn took one look at Bran's clammy skin, as blue as skimmed milk, and crawled out of her bunk, her plaid clutched close about her nightgown. Though she was almost overwhelmed with dizziness, the Yedda at once took command, sending Finn to fetch boiling water and blankets and listing any number of herbs that Finn had never heard of, and was certain could not be found on board the ship. She did her best, meagre as that was, but was not allowed to linger by Bran's bedside, the Yedda sending her back above deck. All that could be seen of the storm was a single black thundercloud shaped like a fist, reaching from the sea to the heavens, the deluge of rain below it shrouding the galleons from view. Everywhere else the sun danced on the waves and sea birds circled, crying aloud mockingly.

All that afternoon and evening the wind blew steadily, even though Bran was sunk in a restless sleep like the one that had fallen upon Enit and Ashlin after the singing of the song of love. The young NicSian was gripped with fever and nightmares, tossing and turning on the bunk-bed, her skin slick with perspiration. Killian the Listener was in no better state, his blood poisoned by the infection that had sunk its claws deep into his many wounds, his temperature dangerously high.

Nellwyn the Yedda shook her head over them, wishing there was a properly trained healer with a bag of herbal tinctures to attend them. The tossing of the ship and the close, dank air below deck did not help, but she had a group of eager lads to assist her and the old sea-cook Donald had many a country remedy up his sleeve which helped greatly, rather to her surprise. Just after dawn Bran's fever dropped a little and she slept more naturally, and Finn and Ashlin and Jay were at last able to curl up and sleep on the deck.

"We come close to the border with Arran," Arvin the Just told them the following afternoon. "Only a few more days' and we shall have reached Kirkinkell Firth, no' far from the village where your winged Rìgh has made base camp."

"No' just our Rìgh," Dide said sternly. "Lachlan MacCuinn is your Rìgh now too, remember."

Arvin the Just sighed heavily. "Aye, happen that be true," he answered. "Times are changing and we with them."

Finn was just settling down to her breakfast the next day when she heard the lookout's cry. "Sails ahoy!"

Immediately the crew were all on their feet, leaning over the bulwark and examining the horizon anxiously. Finn once again climbed to the very top of the topgallant mast to borrow the farseeing glass from the lookout boy. When she saw the ship on the horizon, her breath caught. She could clearly see marked on its white sails and flags the device of a scarlet fitch cross. It was another Tìrsoilleirean galleon.

The great ship gained on them rapidly, straining under full sail. The *Speedwell*'s crew leapt to haul up the mizzensail but by mid-afternoon, the galleon was close behind. There was no sign of any damage so it was clear this was a ship that had not been caught in Bran's witch-storm.

The captain ordered the helmsmen to bring the *Speedwell* about.

"If we canna outrun them, we shall need to engage," he said grimly. "We shall see if we canna slip in close and hit them low with our own cannons."

"If only Bran was awake, he could conjure another storm to sweep it away," Finn lamented, staring down at the restless figure of her cousin, entangled in sweat-dampened sheets.

"He'd kill himself if he did," Nellwyn said tersely. "Or send himself mad. He's untrained in the art o' sorcery and has exhausted himself dangerously with this storm-raising. It will be some months afore he will have strength to even light a candle."

"I do no' think he can light a candle," Finn replied with a grin.

"He conjured lightning, he can light a candle. Ye are no' a bairn anymore, lad, do no' act like one."

The Yedda looked more haggard than ever, the bones of her faces and hands pressing up against her grey-hued skin as if seeking to break through. The nursing of Bran and Killian had obviously exhausted her badly, and her hands trembled as she set a fresh poultice upon the bruised face of the sleeping prophet. There was fire in her voice, however, and Finn was given a glimpse of the strength of character that had kept the Yedda alive through her years of cruel imprisonment.

"I'm sorry," Finn said, chastened. "I do no' mean to. It is just my way. I joke when I am most worried."

Nellwyn stared at her grimly, then suddenly the thin line of her mouth softened into a smile. "Very well then. Be off with ye and get your work done. This cabin be small enough without a great, tall lad like ye taking up all the room. Your cousin will be just fine and the auld prophet too."

Finn opened her mouth to reply, thought better of it, and went back up on deck, catching up her crossbow as she went.

The galleon was closer than ever, the round black mouths of her cannons staring at them across the stretch of water. Finn ran to join Enit, Jay, Dillon and Dide in the bow. The old jongleur was sitting in her chair as usual, her twisted fingers gripping the wood. "What can we do?" Finn asked anxiously.

"If we were close enough, I could try and sing them all to sleep," Enit replied, "but then I'd sing all our own crew to sleep as well."

"Unless they blocked up their ears," Jay suggested.

"Then they could no' hear the captain's orders," Dide objected.

Enit made an impatient gesture. "It is o' no use anyway. They will sink us long afore we get close enough to sing the song o' sleep."

"They are more likely to try and board us," Dillon said. "We shall just have to fight them off." His fingers caressed his sword-hilt lovingly.

"Why?" Dide asked. "Why no' just bombard us with their cannon until we sink?"

"They could have done that afore," Dillon answered. "All the cannon shots were aimed at disabling us, no' sinking us. I would say they want to capture us alive."

"But why?" Finn asked.

Dillon shrugged. "To make an exhibition o' us. If the folk o' Bride watched us all burn, it would be a much sharper lesson than if they were simply told we had been caught and sunk. Nay, the Fealde would wish everyone to ken we died an agonising death.

They would think less lightly o' rebelling against her rule that way."

It made horrid sense. Finn swallowed, feeling sick to her stomach, and saw both Dide and Jay were pale under their tans. They all looked up at the galleon, bearing down upon them on the starboard side. Suddenly the great ship's cannons boomed. Once again the cannonballs sliced through the sails and rigging, bringing the mizzen-yard smashing down upon the deck. The *Speedwell*'s crew scrambled to clear the deck of the wreckage as the helmsman swung the great wheel so that the caravel turned broad on the port quarter. She slipped up close beside the galleon, so that its high poop deck cut out their sun. Then the captain gave his terse order, and the *Speedwell*'s cannons were fired for the first time.

The noise was deafening, and it was hard to breathe with thick, black clouds of smoke choking the air. Again and again the *Speedwell* fired, her cannonballs hitting the galleon just above the water line. The galleon was unable to retaliate, since her cannons had a much longer range and were set so high above the *Speedwell*'s deck. Her sailors were able to leap into the caravel's rigging though, firing down upon the crew with their heavy pistols or leaping down to engage in hand-to-hand combat. For a time all was confusion, with the smoke obscuring the combatants' vision so everyone was fighting blind. The caravel's cannons kept firing away, however, and the galleon began to take in water, causing her to begin to keel over.

Dillon had drawn his sword with a wild joyous yell and as the smoke drifted away, Finn could see him fighting off four Tìrsoilleirean sailors, his teeth bared in a grin. Jed fought with him, the great dog leaping up to close his heavy jaws on one swordsman's arm so that Dillon could run him through or using his substantial weight to bear another to the ground before he could attack Dillon from behind.

So ferociously did Dillon fight that Finn was frozen for a moment in a sort of awe. He had no hesitation in using his fists and feet as well as his sword and Finn recognised some of Iseult's techniques in the way he somersaulted high into the air to land behind his attackers, or jabbed one in the throat with his elbow at the same time as he kicked another in the stomach. Iseult was trained in the art of the Scarred Warrior and most adept at hand-to-hand fighting, and had evidently passed on many of her secrets to the young squire. Dillon's sword was not still for a moment, and he often tossed it from one hand to the other, taking his attackers by surprise. All his movements were as swift and graceful as if he engaged in a dance, not a fight to the death, and he laughed as he fought.

Finn had no opportunity to watch for long, for more of the enemy were swarming down the ropes to land on the forecastle where she crouched by Enit's feet. Finn shot down two in quick succession, but they came faster than she could reload. Dide was fighting by her side, however, throwing his silver daggers with quick and deadly accuracy.

"Come about!" the captain roared. The *Speedwell* turned swiftly and slid away from the galleon, causing many of the enemy clinging to her rigging to fall screaming into the water or crash down upon the deck.

With Dillon fighting like a madman at their head, the *Speedwell*'s crew slowly overcame those of the enemy still on board. The Tìrsoilleirean dead and wounded alike were thrown overboard as the caravel sought to put as much distance as possible between them and the crippled galleon. "Look, she's going down!" Tam shouted, pointing over the port bulwark. "We hit her where it really hurts!"

Finn turned and stared, amazed at how quickly the galleon was keeling over with all the weight of its sails and the huge carved poop and forecastle dragging it down. Suddenly the cannons on its near side fired again.

Finn screamed as the cannonballs tore their way into the *Speedwell*'s hull, causing the ship to lurch and shudder. She was thrown down, a tangle of rope falling across her back and pinning her to the deck. She fought to free herself, sick with anxiety as she heard the moans of injured men. At last she could scramble free and looked about her. Once more the *Speedwell* was listing at an unnatural angle, the deck sloping sideways. Men everywhere were trying to get to their feet, cradling their heads or shoulders. Many lay unmoving.

Finn crawled up on to the forecastle, feeling her pulse hammer in her skull as she saw Enit's chair overturned. The old jongleur lay unconscious on the deck, the carved chair broken and half-covering her limp body. Finn turned her over and saw blood seeping from a bruised cut on Enit's temple.

"Abandon ship!" came the captain's stentorian roar. "She's going down!"

The crew hurried to unlash the boats. Ashlin came staggering up the ladder, Bran's drooping body in his arms, and tenderly laid her down in the little dinghy with Donald beside her to watch over her. Enit was laid out in the long boat, with Nellwyn tending her bleeding head, then Jay came running up from below with his precious viola, which he tucked in tenderly beside Enit's unconscious body. Donald was hard at work passing up sacks of grain and vegetables which were hastily stacked into the boats, then he clambered up the ladder with his arms full of a side of mutton, his wrinkled old face unusually grim.

"Can ye swim, lassie?" he asked Finn and she shook her head.

"Och, neither can I," he answered. "Happen ye'd best try and hang on to a plank o' wood then. Take off your boots and leave your bow and arrows. They'll only weigh ye down."

"Tuck them here in the boat," Nellwyn said. "By the looks o' those rocks, ye'll be wanting your boots."

Finn nodded and did as she said, then scooped up Goblin and dropped her into the long boat too. "She doesna like water," she said to Nellwyn rather pleadingly. "She be only a wee thing; she willna take up much room."

Nellwyn nodded and went to pat the frightened little cat, who hissed and struck out with her claws. Nellwyn snatched back her hand, then cast Finn an angry, embarrassed glance. Finn said, "I'm sorry. She is still an elven cat, ye see. Ye canna tame an elven cat."

"Happen I should've reminded your mother o' that," Donald said affectionately. "Come, Finn, jump in. Hang on to the back o' the long boat and ye should have no trouble staying afloat."

Finn smiled at him, though her face was so stiff with fear it took a real effort to move her cheek muscles. She stood on the ship's deck and stared down at the wild waves tossing about below, throwing up spray and spume. Quite a few heads were already bobbing away down there, clutching broken planks and struggling to keep their heads above water.

There was a wrenching, groaning sound and the caravel suddenly lurched sideways. Everyone shouted.

Jay seized her hand. "Come on, Finn, jump!" he urged. "Else the ship'll take ye down with her."

Finn hung on to his hand and jumped when he did. They fell down and hit the water below with a great splash that knocked the breath out of her body. Deep into the water she plunged, then she felt the drag of Jay's hand as he kicked for the surface. Finn kicked too and at last her head broke through and she was able to gasp a breath of air.

Then another wave broke over her head and she sank again, choking on water. Jay dragged her up, putting his arm under her armpit. "Kick!" he ordered.

Desperately Finn obeyed. Occasionally she saw one of the boats rising up beyond the waves, or a glimpse of the sinking *Speedwell*, but otherwise the whole universe was heaving grey water, bitter as grief and cold as death. Then Jay found a plank and heaved her on to it, and she was able to rest for a moment as he clung to its edge. She put down her head and closed her eyes, and found she was choking now on tears instead of seawater. *I wish I had said goodbye to her,* she thought. *My poor mam!*

They drifted for a while, too exhausted to kick any longer. "Are we coming close to the shore?" Finn whispered, her throat raw from the salt.

Jay raised his head, wiping his salt-stung eyes with his hand. "I canna see," he answered. "I canna see anything."

Finn peered through the dusk but the waves all about were too high and wild for her to see anything but their white-veined grey backs, their curling white-maned crests. She sobbed aloud and Jay shifted his hand so it rested on her back. "Do no' weep, Finn," he whispered. "There be salt enough in this water.

Try and rest. The current will take us to shore, never ye fear."

Finn sniffled and wiped her nose with her hand. Every now and again she hiccuped with tears again but otherwise they were quiet, clinging to the plank, as darkness fell about them.

Suddenly they heard a high-pitched whistling and then the smack of water as some great sea-creature leapt out of the water close to hand. Finn stifled a shriek. "Are . . . are there . . . sharks in this water?"

"Are they no' sharks everywhere?" Jay replied grimly. "I do no' ken, Finn. Crawl a wee bit higher on the plank, there's a dear." His face was a smudge of white in the dark. Finn obeyed, lying on the plank with nothing but her feet in the water. Jay had all of his body in the icy-cold water, only one arm hooked over the plank as he paddled with the other. They heard the smack of water again.

"What about ye?" she whispered anxiously. "Jay, canna ye climb up too?"

"There be no' enough room," he answered. She could hear the strain in his voice. "Come, Finn, let's kick again."

She kicked as hard as she could, straining to see through the darkness. Again and again a wave surprised her with a shock of cold, filling her eyes and her mouth with water, and sending her pulse hammering. Then suddenly she felt something brush against her bare foot. She recoiled with a shriek, falling off the plank into the water. Jay called her name anxiously.

"Something touched me!" she gasped, grabbing hold of the plank again. "Something scaly! Oh, Jay, what if it be the harlequin-hydra?"

Right in their ears, they heard the whistling sound.

Jay raised himself up on his arms so he could hear more clearly. Then suddenly a long body thrust up through the waves, shining oddly in the darkness.

Finn leapt back, flailing her arms as the water closed over her head. Then strong arms seized her and lifted her up so she could breathe. Coughing and retching, Finn kicked out and the arms tightened, twisting her away. Finn felt silky scales against her skin and saw, frighteningly, a strange flat face with tusks curving up on either side. "It's a Fairge!" she cried hoarsely.

She stopped fighting, even though she was so frightened she thought her heart would pound right through her ribcage. She fully expected the Fairge to drag her down under the water and drown her, and there was not a thing she could do about it. This was the Fairge's natural element, and Finn was the alien here. In a way it was a relief, to know the fight was over and she could relax and let the sea swallow her. Fatalistically she lay back in the Fairge's arms and waited to drown.

The sea-faery held her securely, however. She could feel the powerful motion of his tail as he swam through the waves, his arms holding her high so that she could breathe easily. The two moons were rising, casting a silvery radiance over the sea. She could see the black mass of the cliffs ahead of them, and the white break in the waves at their feet. Again her body tensed with fear but the Fairge quickened his speed and she felt the power of the wave as it caught them and sped them towards the shore. Then she was being flung up on the shore. She landed with a thump that knocked all the breath out of her body. The sea tried to drag her back, but Finn grasped at the wet, slippery rocks, ignoring the pain of her bruised and cut limbs. Frantically she dragged herself higher, feeling the tug of the water as it swirled back into the sea. At last her legs were free of the water and sobbing, she glanced back. All she could see was the flash of a silver tail as the Fairge dived back into the moonlit waves.

The Skeleton Coast was a wild, inhospitable place. The cliffs reared several hundred feet from the sea, with nothing but sharp black rocks at their base. All along the coast crags of fantastic shape rose from the waves, some near as high as the cliffs themselves. The only sign of life was the sea birds, who screeched and fought and soared all about.

As the sun rose slowly out of the sea, giving the water a strange red shimmer, the survivors of the ship-wreck slowly gathered together on the shore. With their clothes torn and stained, their eyes red-rimmed and their faces bruised, they were a pitiful sight but, as they all agreed, miraculously alive. Thanks to the Fairgean, not one of the crew or passengers of the *Speedwell* had drowned. The sea-faeries had even saved Jed, Dillon's big shaggy hound.

Dide was able to light a fire for them, despite the dampness of the driftwood, and Donald cooked up a salty stew. Nellwyn the Yedda tended the worst of the injuries, as best as she could without any medicinal supplies and still so weak herself. She was astounded by the action of the Fairgean, having thought of them as implacable enemies all her life and having always used her magic to destroy them. She had heard about the jongleurs' singing the song of love and had thought it foolish, but was now quick to admit that perhaps she and the Coven had always been wrong.

"Who would've thought they would rescue drown-ing men," she said as she bandaged up cuts and splinted broken limbs. "I've never heard o' such a thing!"

Once all were warmed and fed, there was much discussion about what to do next. Although they were still alive, they had little food and even less fresh water. Many among them were incapable of walking, let alone climbing the great height of the cliffs. The Bright Soldiers would be searching for them and it surely would not take them long to find the floating wreckage of the *Speedwell*. It was clear that an expedition had to set off in search of help as soon as possible.

"Could ye climb these cliffs, Finn?" Dide asked.

She nodded and shrugged. "All my climbing equipment went down with the *Speedwell*, so it would no' be easy," she answered.

"There is naught but a few farms up top," Captain Tobias said. "And they be strict, dour people. I do no' think they would offer assistance willingly, no' even to help Killian the Listener."

The old prophet was sitting hunched by the fire, his spindly arms and legs clutched close to his body. His wrinkled face turned from one person to another as they spoke but he showed no sign of comprehension on his bruised face.

"I wish I kent exactly where we were on the coast," Alphonsus the Sure said. "The last time I marked our position on the map we were only two or three days sail east o' our meeting place with the MacCuinn. We had a fair wind and so had been managing a hundred and fifty or so miles a day. No' matter how swiftly any party travelled, they would still be on foot. We are talking about three weeks at least afore they reached the rendezvous point. Then the Rìgh would need to travel back to reach us and that would be another week or two, even if they whipped the horses. No' even the strongest man among us could survive that long without food and water, let alone the auld man and woman."

There was a long silence. Everyone looked at the frail old prophet and then at Enit, who had regained consciousness but looked very sick and weak, with a great dark bruise discolouring one side of her face. All knew that she was crippled with arthritis and could not walk a step unaided. They then glanced around at the injured men lying uncomfortably on the sharp rocks and at the sea which surged and swirled a scant few paces away.

"It's low tide now," Arvin the Just said dourly. "Soon the waves will be rising again. Tide nor time tarries for none."

"Och, he's such a joy to have along; he be like the honey bee and brings us naught but sweetness and light," Finn whispered to Ashlin, who choked trying to stifle his involuntary burst of laughter. Arvin turned his granite-hard countenance upon them in disapproval and both giggled again.

"Well, happen our first task should be to find a less exposed spot in which to make camp," Dide said, casting Finn an exasperated glance. "Happen there may be a cave or grotto somewhere along here where we may get some shelter both from the elements and from anyone searching for us."

"Excuse me, sir," Tam said rather hesitantly, "but there be some caves along here somewhere, I do ken that. I do no' think we'd want to be sheltering in them though."

"Och, that's right," Captain Tobias said. "Ye were born hereabouts somewhere, were ye no', young Tam?"

"Aye, sir."

"Do ye ken where we are?"

"Well, sir, if I be no' mistaken, those two tall rocks along there, sort o' leaning against each other, they be what folks round here used to call the Two Lovers."

"So do ye ken where these caves might be?"

"Aye, sir, but truly, if the tales be true, we do no' want to go into those caves. They say they be haunted, sir."

"Ye sound like a witch-lover, lad," Arvin the Just said sternly, "talking o' haunted caves. Do ye no' ken there are no ghosts?"

"So the pastor used to say, sir," Tam replied equably, "but he also used to say all witches were evil and ugly, and indeed sir, ye canna say that about young Bran, for she be a bonny lass indeed and sweet as a nut."

His words caused Dide, Jay and Finn to start upright and Finn said indignantly, "What do ye mean by calling him a lass, Tam?"

The young sailor grinned at her. "Do ye think I be blind and foolish as a newborn pup? I been working and eating and sleeping alongsides the lot o' ye for weeks on end now. I ken a lass when I see one, lass."

Finn flushed scarlet and Dide laughed and slapped Tam across the back. "Indeed, I always kent Bran would never pass off as a lad, no' with that skin and hair."

"Och, it were the figure I was noticing," Tam said with a grin, though he coloured up nearly as red as Finn.

"What about me?" Finn demanded. "How did ye guess I was no lad?"

"Och, lassie, your figure be no' so bad either," Tam replied. "Besides, I couldna help but notice how yon other lads were always looking out for ye two, and holding your hand when ye were afeared."

"I always said letting a passel o' women on board would do us no good," Arvin the Just said gloomily. "We were doomed afore we even set sail from safe harbour. 'All wickedness be but a wee to the wickedness o' woman.'"

"Och, what is done is done," Captain Tobias said. "Is it no' said that 'a cheerful heart is good medicine but a downcast spirit dries up the bones?' Please stop with your lamenting, Arvin, and let us think how to save our lives."

"We mun find these caves, and quickly," Dide said impatiently. "Already the waves are rising and we sit here and flap our jaws. We'll worry about the ghosts when we encounter one. Tam, ye mun lead the way. Come, let's get moving."

They struggled over the rocks with litters made of broken planks, carrying those who could not walk, as the wildly tossing waves splashed their faces with spray and made the rocks beneath their feet even more slippery. Finn walked at the head of the expedition with Jay and Tam, the elven cat riding on her shoulder. As she walked she often glanced up at the towering cliffs, searching for a place where a climb to the top could be accomplished more easily. Several times they had to wade through deep rock-pools or scramble over great boulders near as large as a cottage, and once a wave caught one of the sailors and swept him off the shore. They managed to pull him to safety but all were shaken by the close call, and hurried their step.

At last they came to a narrow crack in the rock where a shallow stream of water tumbled out over slime-green rocks and down into the sea. Donald tasted the water and then, with great excitement, pronounced it fresh. They all drank eagerly, and no water had ever tasted as sweet as that brackish liquid from the heart of the rock.

"How much further to these bluidy caves?" Nellwyn asked, easing her swollen feet in the cool water.

"We be here," Tam said. "That be the entrance. They call it Auld Clootie's Cleft."

The Yedda looked at the crack with disfavour. "The cave canna be very large. Shall we all fit in?"

"The cave be huge," Tam said. "If the tales are true, it runs for miles and miles all along the coast and under the land. Some foolhardy lads tried to explore it with ropes and lanterns. They came out at Lucifer's Leap, sixty miles north-west o' here, those o' them that survived."

The Yedda withdrew her feet, dried them on her skirt and put her stockings and shoes on again. "Well, I be no' afraid o' ghosts," she said calmly. "Ghosts are naught but a psychic memory o' some powerful emotional energy. They canna hurt ye unless ye let them and most can be banished by filling a place with laughter and goodwill. I swear if I can find a place to rest my weary bones I'll be generating enough goodwill to banish a thousand ghosts, no matter how malevolent."

Tam looked at the crack with disfavour. "Well, so long as we do no' go too far in," he said and helped one of his fellow sailors to heft up a litter.

Dide went first so he could conjure some fire to light their way. When he squeezed through the high, narrow crack, he gave a low whistle of amazement as he held up the ball of witch-light. Finn pushed her way to the front of the queue, her hazel green eyes alight with curiosity. As she clambered through, she too let out a little gasp.

The cave beyond was enormous. Dide's ball of silvery-blue light was barely able to illuminate the further-most reaches. It was far larger than the great banquet room at Rhyssmadill, larger than any hall Finn had ever seen. Down its centre wound the little shallow stream, forming little pools here and there that glimmered blackly.

By the time all had clambered in, Dide had lit another fire, using dried seaweed and driftwood they had gathered along the way as kindling. They ate a sparse meal, and Donald tied hooks onto fishing lines in the hope they would be able to catch some fish off the rocks.

"And I warrant those screeching sea birds wouldna taste so bad roasted over a slow fire," he said with a grin. "Lucky I made sure my bow and arrow were tucked into the long boat."

After lunch they made further plans for an expedition to go in search of Lachlan and the Greycloaks. Now they had shelter and fresh water, everyone's hopes had risen that they might still be able to get out of the shipwreck alive. It was decided that Dide should be the leader of the expedition, with Tam as their guide. Otherwise the exploratory party would include Dillon and his dog Jed, Finn, Jay, Ashlin, and a squad of sailors. They were to take with them most of the rope, the compass, and as much food and water as they could carry. Those left behind in the big cave would be able to hunt and fish to supplement their diet but it was unlikely that those exploring the caves would be able to do so.

The afternoon was spent resting, making torches from driftwood, torn material and lamp oil, and making up packs of supplies. At last all was ready, and the party set off with much false cheer and optimism.

They followed the stream, that being as good a

place to start as any. Deep into the cliffs they clambered, sometimes having to scale high rocks where the water tumbled down in a little cascade. The roof continued lofty and elevated so they had no need to bend or crawl, which made their passage easier.

They rested often but never for long, very conscious of the need to make haste. The compass was rarely out of Tam's hand and many times he paused to try and judge where they were in relation to the geography above ground. They had no way of telling the passage of time so far underground, and this only increased their anxiety. Soon it felt as if they had been clambering through the cave system for days on end and all grew impatient to breathe fresh air again and feel the sun on their skin.

The walls began to narrow dramatically, and the ceiling closed down upon them so they were climbing a steep, stony passageway, the rocks all slippery with moss. Soon they had to crawl and all were unable to resist feeling rising panic. When they were having actually to slide forward on their elbows through the icy cold stream, many began to suggest it was time to turn back.

"Are ye sure this is the way the men ye kent came?" Dide asked Tam and the young sailor nodded, his face white under all the mud. Dide instructed the majority of the party to wait where there was room for them all to sit and he crawled on alone.

It was not long before he was calling to them all to follow and rather reluctantly they shouldered their packs and again began to creep up the low passageway. It was difficult to keep the torches dry and so they were doused, leaving only Dide's flickering blue light to see by.

They clambered out through a small damp hole into

another cavern, all wet through and shivering with cold. They huddled together under their few damp blankets and at last fell into an uncomfortable sleep.

Dillon was the first to wake and he roused the others roughly. Dide summoned fire to light the torches, which had been laid out to dry on the stone. To their horror, one of the sailors, a sturdy man named Jack, could not be woken. He was dead, his flesh white and slack and cold as ice. Examining him under the fitful light of the torches, they found three dark puncture holes up near his ear.

"This happened to some o' the men I kent," Tam said rather shakily. "There be a big black bug that lives in these caves and feeds on warm blood. They say its drool stops ye from feeling pain so ye do no' even ken ye've been bitten, and if it spits at ye and it gets in your eyes, ye'll lose your sight. They call it the assassin bug."

There was much angry muttering among the men, and Dide said rather sharply, "I wish ye'd mentioned this bug afore, Tam."

"I was only a laddiekin when they tried to explore the caves," Tam said defensively. "I did no' remember till now."

"Is there anything else ye do no' remember?"

"How am I meant to ken until I do remember?" the young sailor retorted.

They divided Jack's pack up amongst the rest of the party and hurried on, unwilling to break their fast with the dead man lying there beside them. They ate later, all keeping a close eye out for bugs.

They were now in a system of small caves all connected by short passageways. Many times they could have left the stream to explore up a side passage but all were unwilling to leave their only link to the out-

side world, even though it meant they were not ever
able to fully dry off. After several days of constantly
wet feet, some of the men were finding big blisters
forming on their skin where their boots chafed but
they bound them up as best they could and stumbled
on. Jed the dog whined miserably, his black-patched
white fur stiff with mud, his tail slunk down between
his legs.

They came to a tall natural archway and paused to
thrust their torches in, wrinkling their noses at the
odd smell. There was a sudden high shrill shrieking, a
strange leathery rustling noise, then they were all
plunged into darkness. A few of the men cried aloud
in alarm and all leapt back. The rustling noise slowly
died away and then there was silence, a heavy, humid,
ominous silence. Dide lit his torch again and slowly,
cautiously, peered within the chamber.

"Bats!" he cried. "Look, thousands o' them."

As he stepped forward into the chamber, the bats
once again took flight, shrieking in dismay. Dide's
torch was again snuffed out but he brought witch-light
to life in his palm and raised his hand high. All the
others could see was the blaze of roiling blue-white
energy, the shadow of his arm and body, and thousands of tiny black shapes with sharply serrated, out-
spread wings darting all about him.

"Come in," Dide whispered, "but tread carefully.
The floor is all mucky." They obeyed, tiptoeing
through the pools of bat guano that covered the floor.
"The stream leads upward again," Dide whispered.
"Do no' fear, bats willna hurt ye. I will light the
torches again once we are free o' their home."

Gingerly they clambered up the rocky stairs at the
far end of the cavern. Occasionally one of them ut-

tered a low but heartfelt curse as they put their hand in something soft and squishy.

Beyond was another sequence of small caves, also occupied by bats. They filed through them slowly and cautiously, following the stream as it tumbled down over slippery grey rocks. At last they came out into another great cavern, almost as big as the cave by the sea. All cried aloud in joy, for far above their heads they could see a circle of dark blue light that twinkled with stars. The stream poured down over the lip of the hole in thin ribbons of water that gleamed with starlight.

"I ken where we are!" Tam cried in amazement. "This be Hell's Gate. We have come an awful long way, near sixty miles by my reckoning. Hell's Gate be up near Lucifer's Leap. They say that on certain nights o' the year the demons o' the Archfiend escape from hell through this hole and fly about the sky all night, seeking the weak and sinful to tempt them from the way o' the Lord. They say their wings blacken the moons, there be so many o' them. I remember as a lad my brother once dared me to throw stones down the hole to see if we could awaken a demon, and a whole flock o' bats came shrieking out. We dinna stop running until we reached home."

"Well, we canna do much about getting out until dawn," Dide said when he stopped laughing. "Let's grab some sleep and we'll see if our wee cat can climb out when there's some light to see."

They slept more comfortably than they had since the *Speedwell* had been sunk, despite the dampness and hardness of the stones, sure they were close to getting out of the caves at last. They would then beg, borrow or steal some horses and ride as fast as they could for Kirkinkell and the Rìgh's army, and all would be saved.

The dawn brought a brutal end to their hopeful imaginings. They all stood and stared up at the circle of blue so far above them and raged in despair. It was clear to all of them that no-one without wings could get up to that small hole into the open air. The walls were more than a hundred feet high, sheer as glass and slick with spray. They curved in sharply to the roof, so that any climber would have to crawl twenty feet or more whilst hanging upside down from the ceiling.

"I might have been able to do it if I had my climbing equipment," Finn raged. "Why, oh, why, did I no' think to make sure it was thrown in to the boat with my other stuff?"

"How were ye meant to ken?" Dide said wearily.

"I saw the cliffs from the boat," Finn cried. "I should've kent I would have to climb at some point. Now it's all at the bottom o' the sea, all my rope and tackle and my spikes and hammer. Och, how could I be such a porridge-head?"

"No use fraitching," Jay said, though his voice was heavy with disappointment. "Those other explorers could no' have got out this way either, yet Tam said they got out somewhere near here. There mun be some other way."

Unhappily they shouldered their packs once more and retraced their steps, groaning aloud as the soft natural light once more gave way to darkness and the close, fetid air of the caves.

They reached the cavern of the bats and made their way through another high stone archway they had not explored before, carefully piling a small pyramid of stones by its entrance so they would know where they had been.

They heard a soft rustling sound, a gentle murmur like the wind through a forest in autumn. In the flickering light of the torches they looked at each other in mingled hope and fear.

"It could just be more bats," Ashlin said.

Dide nodded. "Aye, I'd say it's just bats."

They walked on, pressing close together in their eagerness. The roof began to slope upwards and then they stepped out into yet another wide cavern, raising their torches high to try and pierce the darkness.

There was a rush of sound and motion, a blck whirlwind of shadows that blew their hair into their eyes and snuffed out the torches. They huddled together as Dide tried without success to re-light the brands, each spark he conjured just sinking away into nothingness. He gave up with an impatient oath, cupping his hands and bringing witch-light springing up in his palms.

Finn screamed. Hovering all about were tall dark figures, thin as twigs, with huge batlike wings, staring down at them with great, slanted eyes that shone with a peculiar blue light. The sailors fell down on their knees with strangled cries, muttering garbled prayers, holding their crossed fingers before them in the age-old sign against evil. There was an angry murmur from the shadowy figures and they closed in, lifting their long, bent fingers as if to seize them.

Startled, Dide let the witch-light die. As darkness plunged down upon them once more, many among the little party cried aloud to their god and wept for mercy. There was the sound of swords and daggers being drawn and Dide once more conjured light, crying, "Back to back, lads!"

Alone among all the men, Dillon had not drawn his sword. He was staring at the tall, shadowy figures with joy and amazement on his face. As Dide raised his dagger to throw, Dillon cried, "Nay, nay, drop your arms! They be nyx. Do no' harm them! They be nyx!"

For a moment Dide was frozen in astonishment, then he seized the arms of the men closest to him, forcing them to lower their daggers. Dillon did the same and after a moment Finn joined them, though the men were filled with superstitious fear and horror.

"They be demons," one cried.

"The Archfiend's minions," shouted another. "Look at their black wings and evil eyes."

"Nay, nay, they be nyx," Dillon repeated. "Faeries o' the night. They are our allies; one o' their kind signed the Pact o' Peace. Ye must no' harm them."

As the men lowered their weapons, the nyx stirred and rustled, drifting away from the little group of humans. They muttered among themselves in their own strange language, then one drifted down and stood before them.

He was tall, almost twice as tall as Finn, and his leathery wings covered his body like a cloak. His black hair hung all down his back in wild elf locks, matted with leaves and twigs. His dark face was long and narrow, and dominated by his enormous slanted eyes. Although they were black as ink, his eyes shone with an unearthly blue light like those of the elven cat perched on Finn's shoulder.

"Who are you, that you know the nyx?" the faery asked. Although he spoke their language, they had trouble understanding him for he spoke in such a low, hoarse voice and with such a strong accent.

"They call me Dillon o' the Joyous Sword. I ken

one o' your kind, an auld nyx they call Ceit Anna. She lives in the caves under Lucescere."

The nyx muttered together. "We had thought that there were no other nyx left living," the faery said. "It is glad news that you bring us, even though you come with flame in your hands."

"Please forgive us," Dillon said. "We mean ye no harm. We would never have brought light into your caves if we had kent ye were here. We do no' wish to destroy ye."

Again there was a murmuring like dry leaves blown in the wind. The nyx were slowly circling around them, like the smoke of candle flames, wavering and flowing all about them. The men shifted uneasily and some closed their grip tighter upon the hilts of their weapons.

"Are ye no' of human blood?" the nyx asked bitterly. "Those of your kind hate and fear those of our kind. For centuries we the nyx have been hunted, tormented, subjected to the light so that we dissolve. You come with flame in your hands and fear and hate in your hearts, we can feel it. And one among you carries an evil thing, a thing woven of the hair of dead nyx, woven in terror and loathing."

The muttering rose, the drifting, circling motion quickened, the queer slanted eyes of the nyx all shining malevolently. Finn suddenly swallowed, sliding her hand within her pocket to feel the cold silk of the magical cloak within her pocket. The eyes of the nyx followed her movement.

"Aye, you stroke that dead thing, that evil thing, you stroke it with longing," he hissed. "Do you think to slide it about you and disappear? You shall not disappear from our eyes, I warn you, black-hearted human."

Dide and Dillon were frowning in puzzlement, looking about them at the others and shrugging in confusion. Finn stepped back and felt Jay's eyes fly to her face.

"I did no' ken it was made o' nyx hair." Her voice came out in a childish squeak. "I promise ye, I did no' ken."

The nyx laughed, a strange dry sound. They drifted closer, their great black wings extended, their long, spindly arms stretching out as if to strangle them all. The men huddled even closer together, daggers falling from nerveless fingers.

"Finn?" Dide asked.

"I swear I did no' ken," Finn repeated. She took the cloak out of her pocket, clutching it to her breast. Folded up, it was no larger than a handkerchief.

"The cloak o' invisibility!" Jay cried.

"So that is how ye hid the prisoners!" Dide cried. Finn lifted her chin defiantly. "But how? It went missing after the Samhain rebellion. Did ye take it?" Dide searched her face. "Did ye no' ken the Keybearer was anxious indeed about it? They searched for it everywhere . . ." He paused momentarily then said with a slight hardening of his voice. "Ye must've kent. They asked your *dai-dein* to locate it. He said he could feel it nearby."

"And nearby it was," Finn replied cheekily. The colour rose in her cheeks.

Dide was white with anger. "Why did ye no' tell us? So what was why ye insisted on going into the Black Tower alone. And we were sick with worry over ye! Ye could have told us."

Her eyes fell again. "I be sorry," she said contritely. "I do no' ken why I did no'. Somehow I could no' talk about it with anyone."

"It is an evil thing," the nyx said hoarsely. "It is made of dead hair, murdered hair. It was woven with dread and hatred. It wraps the wearer in darkness, coldness. It makes them care for naught."

"Aye," Finn said thoughtfully. "That is true. It makes ye cold." She gave a little shudder and suddenly held the little bundle of silk away from her.

"You must unravel it," the nyx said.

Involuntarily she clutched it to her again. "I canna."

"You must."

"I willna!"

"You must, else we shall unravel it for you. But I warn you, with its unravelling so too shall you unravel."

The nyx were now so close their dry papery skin and leathery wings were brushing against them all, causing everyone to shrink closer together. The dark-winged faeries were never still for a moment, lifting, drifting, hovering, encircling, rustling, muttering. Finn stared at them defiantly, the cloak clutched to her heart.

"If you do not unravel it yourself," the nyx whispered hoarsely, "you shall die. For it is now your shadow."

"Your shadow, your shadow," the others whispered, their wings rustling.

"Destroy it, Finn!" Jay cried.

"Ye must destroy it," Dide echoed.

"Finn, ye must do as the nyx says!" Dillon ordered sharply.

She stared round at them with greatly dilated eyes, her breast rising and falling rapidly. Mutely she shook her head.

Then the tiny black elven cat reached down from Finn's shoulder and caught a corner of the bundle in her sharp claws. She leapt away, the material shredding with a loud tearing noise. Finn cried aloud as if she had been hurt herself. She fell to her knees, cradling the cloak against her. It had billowed out like a living shadow, and where it brushed against her, all her skin twitched and stung. The nyx bent over her, cutting her off from the others, their great wings surrounding her with darkness.

"Your shadow, your shadow," they whispered.

Finn closed her eyes, took a deep breath, and felt delicately all over the cloak with the tips of her fingers. She found the gash where Goblin's claws had caught. With a sharp cry, she inserted her fingers into the break and tore the material apart. It felt like something inside her was tearing apart, but she did not stop, tearing and tearing until the cloak was mere scraps of black silk. The nyx stepped back. As the blue witch-light fell upon the scraps, the threads began to dissolve until nothing was left but a fine black dust that swirled up in the wind of the nyx's wings and was gone.

Finn covered her face with her hands and wept.

Although she could hear the others talking above her head and the low, hoarse voices of the nyx replying, Finn could make no sense of what anyone said. She was cold, cold and lost, wandering in a strange cold land of shadows and phantoms. Suddenly she felt something warm and silky touch her hand. She recoiled. The warm, soft silk brushed her hand again, as the little elven cat crept into her lap, rubbing her head and back against Finn's wet face, licking her with a tongue as rough as sandpaper, purring lovingly. Finn gathered her warm, soft body close, drying her tears on Goblin's soft fur.

After a moment she stood up, finding it hard to meet anyone's gaze. The others bent close, however, peering into her face, asking after her anxiously.

"I be grand," she said abruptly.

"Grand as a goat's turd stuck with buttercups?" Jay asked with a grin and she tried to smile back, though she felt as thin and empty as a bellfruit seed.

"It takes much strength to unravel one's own shadow," the nyx said, bending over her and staring into her eyes with his own great, dark, slanted eyes. Finn stared back and felt something of the coldness within her ease. "The souls of those murdered nyx are now free, part of the night once more. We of the nyx thank you."

Finn nodded, cuddling Goblin close under her chin.

"We wish to thank you and return the act of kindness," the nyx said, while his companions murmured and rustled all about. "What is it that we can do for you?"

Finn raised her head. "We need to get out o' here," she said pleadingly. "I canna stand the dark anymore. We need to get out."

"We can carry you out," the nyx answered. "That is a task of no hardship. We often fly out the sky-crack to walk the night and fly the wind."

"We are in desperate need o' reaching our friends. They are somewhere to the south-west o' here, several weeks walking," Finn said. "Can ye possibly carry us so far?"

The nyx murmured together, bending close together and swaying away.

"We will carry you, unraveller of the cloak of darkness," he replied after a long time. "We are filled with joy to know that another of our kind lives and filled with joy that the souls of the murdered nyx are at last

part of the night once more. We will fly the night to
rejoice and you shall fly with us, unraveller."

That evening, when the sun had set and Hell's Gate
was once again twinkling with stars, the nyx carried
Finn up and out of the caves in an explosion of
midnight-black wings, shining eyes and wild, streaming
hair. The others were left staring in awe and envy,
before turning to crawl back through the caves on
their own mundane elbows and knees.

Below Finn the rolling hills and forests were all
dark, only the occasional burn or loch reflecting back
the silvery radiance of the moons. The sky however
shone darkly, burning with a thousand far-distant suns.
The wind was in her eyes, in her mouth, in her hair.
All about was the susurration of the nyx's wings, dark
and angular against the round moons, and the sound
of their joyous singing. Finn flung wide her arms, un-
afraid, letting the night and the song pour through
her, erasing the last of her grief and regret and rage.
All night they flew and when the first silvery gleam of
the dawn began to show above the curving line of the
horizon, they circled down and down until Finn could
see below them a thousand red gleams, like the scattered coals of a fire. Down, down, they flew until Finn
could see it was not one scattered fire, but a thousand
fires, burning amidst orderly circles and rows of tents
and wagons and pickets of sleeping horses. Further
down they flew, until the great burning arch of sky
was no longer all their world, but a mere curve above
them. Finn could hear the sounds of the sleeping
camp, muffled snores and snorts and the occasional
clink of metal.

"We can fly no lower," the nyx whispered in her
ear. "Else we shall dissolve in the light o' those red

flames. I shall weave ye a rope o' my hair and lower
you down. Do you trust me?"

"With my life," Finn answered, her voice thrilling
with emotion. The nyx hovered there in the darkness,
his hands playing with his hair. Slowly, slowly, it spun
itself into an impossibly long rope that dangled down,
its end too far away to see.

"I thank ye," Finn whispered.

"We, the nyx, thank you," he answered and gave
the rope into her hand. Swiftly Finn slid down it, her
eyes straining up through the darkness for a last
glimpse of the faeries of the night. All she saw was
darting, swirling shadows, too swift for the eye to follow. Then her foot touched the ground. The rope suddenly went limp and tumbled down about her. Finn
stared up into the starry sky and suddenly saw the
shape of many serrated wings against the moon, darkening its light. Then Gladrielle shone brightly once
more.

# TO THE RESCUE

The soldier standing guard outside the royal pavilion suddenly tensed, bringing his spear forward defensively. Out of the shadows stepped a thin, exceedingly dirty boy, dressed in rough, tattered clothes. He stepped into the smoky light of the torches with great confidence, saying, "I need to see the Rìgh!"

"Where the hell did ye spring from, haggerty-taggerty? What do ye do here?"

"I'm here to see the Rìgh," the boy repeated impatiently. "It's important. Take me to see him right now!"

"Ye mun be joking! As if I'm going to take a beggar-lad to see His Highness! How did ye get here? What do ye want?"

"I do no' see that is any concern o' yours, frog-face! Take me to the Rìgh now, else ye'll be exceedingly sorry."

"Is that so? It's the sergeant on duty I'll be taking ye to see and I'll wager a week's grog he'll flay the skin from your backside afore he boots ye out o' camp."

"Porridge-head," the boy replied scornfully.

The guard made a lunge for the beggar-lad who avoided his grasp nimbly, leaping over the tent-rope and disappearing again into the darkness. The guard broke into a run but tripped over the rope, falling hard on his face. When he at last untangled himself and got to his feet, there was no sign of the dirty little beggar-lad. Angrily the sentry shouted the alarm.

In the royal pavilion, Lachlan and Iseult were looking over the maps with Duncan Ironfist and Leonard the Canny, a Tìrsoilleirean soldier who had surrendered to Lachlan during the Bright Wars. He had since been appointed seanalair to Elfrida NicHilde's small army, due to his undeniable fighting prowess and tactical brilliance. Lachlan and Iseult both hoped that his knowledge of the terrain and the Bright Soldiers' fighting methods would help swing the war their way.

He was a tall, broad-shouldered, slim-hipped man with grizzled brown hair cut very close to the scalp, an aquiline nose and a clean-shaven chin. His silver armour was polished to a high gleam, and he wore a long red cloak with a black gauntleted hand holding aloft a golden sword. Above the sword unrolled a ribbon with the MacHilde's motto upon it, *Bo Neart Gu Neart,* which meant "From Strength to Strength."

There could have been no greater contrast to Leonard the Canny than Lachlan's seanalair, Duncan Ironfist. Dressed in a faded blue kilt under a battered leather breastplate, Duncan's bushy black beard flowed down over his enormous barrel chest. His square face was much weathered, with a shapeless nose, a thick knotted scar that showed white against his tan, and rather battered-looking ears. On his back he carried an enormous black claymore.

After an initial distrust and coolness, the two seana-lairs had grown to respect each other, though Duncan would always think the Tìrsoilleirean a cold fish and

Leonard would always think of Duncan as a very rough sort of fellow.

At the growing commotion outside, Duncan raised one thick black eyebrow and put his head outside the tent flap. "What be all the ruckus?" he demanded.

"Saw a beggar-lad sneaking around, sir; tried to catch him but he 'twas slippery as an eel and got away," the soldier reported breathlessly. "The sergeant wants to make sure he's caught and put under lock and key, sir."

"Och, well, try and keep it down, lad," Duncan replied and drew his head back through the tent-flap to report to Lachlan.

Lachlan was not interested in beggar-boys. He was tired and stiff after a hard day's riding and wanted to have the next day's progress plotted out before he went to bed. At Duncan's explanation he merely nodded and then repeated his last question to Leonard, who did his best to answer.

At last all the logistics were fully worked out and the seanalairs could pass on their orders to their officers and seek their own beds. They wished the Rìgh and Banrìgh good night and went out into the night, securing the tent flaps behind them. Iseult sat down on the pallet bed, undoing her boots thankfully.

"We've made quick progress so far," she said. "Only a few minor skirmishes, naught at all to bother us. Happen we've managed to take the Fealde by surprise at last."

"Och, I doubt it," Lachlan answered. "I'd wager the Fealde is preparing an ambush o' sorts. We must ride up through a narrow pass a week hence. That would be a good place for it. Or happen she's moving her army round behind us by ship, planning to attack us from the rear. My scouts say there's been a grand fleet o' galleons sailing offshore the past week or so."

He sat beside Iseult on the bed, so she could unlace the back of his breastplate. All of Lachlan's clothes and armour had to be made to accommodate his magnificent black wings, making it rather difficult for him to dress or undress without assistance. He had long ago got used to it and no longer found it humiliating to ask for help. Normally his squire would have assisted, but Lachlan had sent the boy to bed long ago and so the task fell to Iseult.

Suddenly she glanced up, her hands stilling.

"What is it? Lachlan asked.

"I heard . . . nay, it must have been naught. A leaf scratching against the side o' the tent." She helped him take off his armour and hung it on a stand against the wall, then Lachlan unbuckled the belt from his kilt so the great length of plaid could be folded and laid ready for the morning. He yawned and stretched and lay down on the pallet, saying sleepily, "Come to bed, *leannan.*"

Iseult was turning down the flame in the lantern when she suddenly heard a slight scuffle to one side. She turned swiftly, the eight-sided *reil* flying to her hand from her weapons belt which hung over a chair. Then she strode forward, reaching down one hand and dragging out a small figure from the shadows. Fiercely she held a glittering blade to the intruder's throat.

"What do ye do here?" she cried. "How dare ye sneak into the royal tent." She shook the figure roughly.

"There's no need to be so rough," the beggar-lad said plaintively. At the sound of the voice, Iseult let the *reil* drop and dragged the figure closer to the lantern. "Finn!" she cried. "By the gods! What do ye here?"

"I've come to make my report," Finn replied, still in that plaintive tone of voice. "I would've been here sooner but your block-headed guard wouldna let me in."

"How did you get in here?" Iseult demanded.

Finn grinned. "Slit the side o' the tent."

"With none seeing ye or hearing ye?" Lachlan was incredulous.

"Och, I am the Cat," Finn replied with a touch of hauteur. "They couldna hear me if I dinna wish them to."

"And ye made your way here to the very centre o' the camp with none o' the sentries sighting ye?" Incredulity was giving way to anger.

"Well, I am the best," Finn replied complacently.

"Someone will hang for this," Lachlan said ominously. "What if ye had been an assassin in the pay o' the Fealde?"

Finn was anxious. "Och, do no' be angry, Lachlan, I mean, your Highness. Indeed, they couldna have seen me. I was dropped right in the very centre o' camp and unless they'd been looking up, they couldna have seen me. Do no' be hanging anyone for it!"

"My sentries should be looking up, down and all around," Lachlan snapped.

"What do ye mean, ye were *dropped*?" Iseult asked.

"The nyx carried me here." Finn was enjoying herself. "I flew through the night with them. I wager no-one's done that afore!"

"The nyx!" Lachlan exclaimed. "What do ye mean? The nyx are all gone, all except that auld one that lives in the caves under Lucescere."

"Nay, they are no'," Finn replied. "There are more,

hundreds o' them. We found them when we were trying to escape the caves."

"If this is your idea o' making a report, Fionnghal NicRuraich, ye'll never make a soldier. In the name o' the Centaur and his Beard, tell us what ye do here! Where is Dide and Enit? Are they safe? Was your mission successful? Did ye free the earless prophet?"

Finn stood straight and saluted smartly. "Finn the Cat, sir, here to make her report. Mission successful, prophet removed from Black Tower along with a Yedda and the lost crew of the *Sea-Eagle*. However, the *Speedwell* was lost at sea due to enemy fire, crew all safe thanks to rescue operation by Fairgean, hiding in caves but very short on supplies, need to be rescued as soon as possible, sir!"

For a moment there was a flabbergasted silence and then Lachlan said rather faintly, "Thank ye, Finn, everything is perfectly clear now."

The full telling of her tale took a very long time, for Iseult and Lachlan wanted to hear every detail of her amazing journey. They were particularly astounded by the rescue of the *Speedwell*'s crew by the Fairgean.

"It scarce seems possible," Lachlan said wonderingly. "Who has ever heard o' a Fairge saving a drowning sailor? Usually they're the ones drowning them!"

"It was the song o' love," Finn replied with conviction. "They had to be the same ones that heard Enit sing! I tell ye, 'twas amazing, that song. It made me wish . . ."

"What?"

Finn shrugged. "I canna describe it. All I ken is I felt that my heart was big enough to love the whole world and that by loving it, I could save it. We all felt the same, all o' us."

"Imagine the possibilities," Lachlan cried, his golden eyes glowing with fervour. "If we could sing the Fairgean to love and peace . . ."

"Aye, all hundred thousand o' them," Iseult said drily. "Ensorcelled by a singer, a guitarist and a fiddler. That'd be a miracle indeed."

"Ashlin played too," Finn said in defense of her piper.

"And others could be taught. Ye ken *I* can sing the song o' love, *leannan*," Lachlan said with a seductive rasp in his voice.

Iseult returned his gaze steadily. "Aye, but I was receptive indeed to the hearing o' it. Ye ken even better than I that the songs o' enchantment can only cast their spell when the listener hears with their heart as well as their ears. These Fairgean, they must have wanted to hear, they must have wanted peace and friendship, for the spell to have worked so powerfully."

"It worked on me and Bran, and I certainly never wanted to be friends with her nor her with me," Finn said.

"Ye never hated your cousin, Finn, do no' tell me ye did," Lachlan cried. "The soft-hearted wee thing that ye are? Nay, ye were just like cats, hissing and showing your claws and defending your territory. Ye would've become friends without the song o' love."

"Maybe," Finn replied, her colour rising. "Though it was more than that. I dinna like anyone back then. It was the cloak o' invisibility. It made me cold and sort o' . . . detached, like I dinna care for aught at all."

So at last Finn had to confess her theft of the cloak of invisibility and how it had been unravelled in the cave of the nyx, who had then flown with her through the night to find the Rìgh's army. Again Lachlan and Iseult exclaimed and asked questions and demanded explanations until Finn was swaying on her feet with exhaustion. It was then that Lachlan cried, "Enough, my wee cat! Tell us the rest in the morn. Ye look as white as whey. Get ye to bed!"

He called for his squire, a tall, sturdy boy with a mop of corn-yellow curls. His face was vaguely familiar but it was not until he spoke that Finn recognised him as Connor, who had been the youngest of the League of the Healing Hand. Last time Finn had seen him he had been a little boy of only six, whom Dillon had carried on his shoulders. Now he was twelve and dressed in the blue kilt and cloak of the Rìgh's personal bodyguard, the charging stag badge worn proudly on his breast.

Finn exclaimed with surprised pleasure and embraced him, but Connor wriggled out of her grasp and stood to attention, asking formally what orders his Highness had for him.

"As ye can see, the League of the Healing Hand still serves me loyally," Lachlan said with a smile. "When Dillon set sail with ye and Dide, I temporarily promoted Connor from pageboy to squire, and indeed he serves me well."

"I canna believe how tall he has grown," Finn answered. Then she cried in excitement, "Are Johanna and Tòmas here too? Oh, glory be! We'll have a grand reunion o' the League."

"Aye, Johanna is one o' our most promising healers," Iseult said. "And o' course Tòmas is here; we couldna ride to war without him."

"Has he grown as tall and strong as ye?" Finn asked Connor with a grin.

Connor looked sombre. "Nay," he answered. "Tòmas is still a poor wee thing, weak as a wisp. Jo says he gives all his strength to the healing and none to growing, poor laddiekin."

Finn looked troubled. "It'll be good to see him again though, and Jo too," she answered. "It has been such a long time."

Connor nodded. "Och, aye, that it has. Can I be doing aught else for ye, my laird?"

"Nay, Connor, get ye back to bed and take the Cat to hers. Every time she yawns I yawn too, and my jaw will crack with the strain soon. Finn, we'll see ye in the morning. Johanna will take good care o' ye!"

Finn nodded, yawning again and rubbing her scratchy eyes. Then she asked, rather hesitantly, "Lachlan, I mean your Highness . . . have ye any news o' Rurach?"

Lachlan and Iseult exchanged glances, then the Rìgh said cheerfully, "I must admit we wondered why ye'd never asked. Finn, all is well. Your father was able to drive off the Fairgean at last, and they retreated back into the sea as we hoped. Unfortunately, most o' the ships we sent west were attacked by pirates and their cargo lost, but we sent wagonloads o' supplies and medicines to help and the last we heard the riots had stopped and they had managed to get the plague o' disease under control."

"And my mam?" Finn asked in a small voice. "Has she . . . did she . . . ask for news o' me?"

"Indeed she did," Iseult said warmly. "We were able to tell her that we'd seen ye at Midsummer and that ye were looking hale indeed. And now that we have seen ye again and ken that ye are safe, we shall send a homing pigeon to Lucescere with messages for her. They'll make sure she hears ye are safe."

Finn thanked her with a lighter feeling around her heart than she had had in months. She bowed and said goodnight, and followed Connor through the dark quiet camp to a large tent some distance away. There the young squire gave her some lukewarm stew to eat, surprisingly delicious despite its tepidity, and unrolled a thin pallet for her to sleep on, finding room for her among the many sleeping bodies who sighed and snored all round her. Finn pulled the rough woollen blanket over her head with a sigh of relief and fell at once into sleep, more comfortable than she had been in months.

When she woke it was morning. Sunlight struck through the open flaps of the tent, warming her toes. Goblin slept on her neck as usual, almost choking Finn with thick black fur. She lifted the elven cat away and repositioned her in the crook of her arm. For a while she lay still, listening to the bustle of the camp about her. She could hear heavy wagons trundling over rough ground, the neigh of horses and clink of bridles, the bleat of chickens and the occasional soft *maaa* of a goat. Men shouted and swore, and there was the occasional higher pitch of a woman's voice.

The tent was now empty. The pallets were all rolled and stacked against one wall, beside six small brown chests. Arranged neatly on top of the chests were a number of small haversacks, each with a blanket rolled up and strapped on top. Already the grass was springing up from where it had been flattened by the weight of sleeping bodies. Only Finn's pallet remained where it had been unrolled. She could not help marvelling that she had slept through everyone else's waking and packing up, and thought they must have all been very quiet and deft.

Just then a woman bent and looked through the

tent flap. "Och, ye're awake at last! I was beginning to think I'd have to roll ye up in your pallet and load ye on the wagon still fast asleep," she said with a warm inflection of humour in her voice.

"Jo!" Finn cried, and leapt to her feet. "Hell's bells, look at ye! I would never have recognised ye."

"Have I changed so much?" Johanna said whimsically. "I suppose I have. It's been six years. Though ye haven't changed at all! I thought ye were meant to be a banprionnsa now, Finn? Look at ye! Ye're as filthy and ragged as ye used to be in the auld days."

"Aye, but I've been having adventures," Finn cried joyously. "Ye canna fight battles and almost drown and crawl through caves and no' get a wee bit dirty."

"Nay, I suppose ye canna," Johanna said. "But ye're going to come and wash up now, and put some decent clothes on, that I can promise ye."

"Indeed?" Finn replied, marvelling at the ring of authority in Johanna's voice. The beggar lass she had known had been a thin, anxious-faced girl afraid of everything. She was now a tall, strong-looking woman with rough, capable hands and a determined face. She looked as if she was afraid of very little.

"If ye want breakfast, ye will," Johanna answered. "No-one sits down at my campfire with hands as black as a chimney-sweep's!"

"Very well then," Finn answered meekly. She was very hungry indeed.

Rather to her dismay, Johanna's idea of a wash up included a scrubbing brush, buckets of very hot water, a great deal of soap and the removal and burning of all of Finn's clothes. Finn protested once or twice but soon found that resistance did her little good. The impression of strength Johanna had given her was not mistaken. It was not till every inch of Finn's body was pink and glowing, including her toenails, that Johanna desisted with her scrubbing and rubbing. Finn was then given clean linen drawers and a chemise, a shirt of undyed linen, a long grey coat, a pair of grey woollen breeches that tied under the knee, long knitted stockings and some sturdy brogues to wear. She dressed thankfully in the warm, clean clothes, combed out her damp curls and came out from behind the screen to present herself for Johanna's inspection.

Johanna looked her over critically then smiled and nodded in approval. "Ye'll do," she said. "Now come and eat, 'cause I havena any more time to be wasting on ye."

Finn grinned back and followed her over to the fire eagerly. Goblin was curled up on her pack, waiting for her, having had no desire to stay in Finn's company while so much water was being sloshed around. Finn sat down beside her and eagerly ate two big bowls of porridge loaded with nuts and dried fruit and sweetened with honey. While she ate, Johanna cooked her some bannocks on the griddle, which proved to be as light and airy as Finn had hoped.

"This is all awfully good," she said. "I do no' remember ye being a good cook, Jo."

"Isabeau the Red taught me to cook," Johanna answered. "She's one o' the best, ye ken. She taught me most o' what I ken, about herbs and healing and distilling and everything. If it was no' for her, I'd still be an orphan lass with no home and no way to support myself. I am aye grateful to her."

Finn lay back on her elbows, wishing fervently for a smoke. Her pouch of tobacco had been ruined in the shipwreck, however, and she had not had time to steal another.

Johanna stood and stretched, saying, "Are ye fin-

ished? We're behind schedule, thanks to ye, sleepy-
head, so I really need to get these washed up and
packed away. I need to speak to the other healers
afore we ride out, and make sure they think to look
out for any willow trees. We can never have enough
willow-bark and the porridge-heads never see a thing
if it's no' pointed out to them."

"How about I wash up and ye do what ye need to
do?" Finn offered.

"That would be grand," Johanna answered with relief and bustled away.

Within ten minutes she was back. Finn tucked Goblin in her pocket, picked up her satchel and followed
the healer through the camp to where a squadron of
soldiers were preparing to ride out. Lachlan and Iseult
were both there, the Rìgh mounted on a magnificent
black stallion, the Banrìgh upon a tall, grey mare with
a flowing white mane and tail of great silkiness. Both
were wearing cuirasses of hard leather, with light
leather helmets on their heads and their plaids slung
about their shoulders. Upon his gauntleted wrist,
Lachlan carried a snowy white gyrfalcon that regarded
the world through the slits of its leather hood. Finn
recognized the beautiful hawk immediately, for
Stormwing had been a gift to the Rìgh from Finn's
father Anghus MacRuraich.

Strapped to Lachlan's saddle was a quiver of arrows
and the great longbow that had once belonged to his
ancestor Owein MacCuinn. He wore his heavy claymore strapped to his back so it hung down between
his wings, a short sword at his waist and a dagger in
his boot. Iseult was also heavily armed, with her crossbow and quiver of arrows near to hand, and a belt
heavy with weapons about her slim waist.

At the sight of Finn, Lachlan raised his hand and

beckoned to her. She crossed the meadow eagerly, nodding her head to Iain and Elfrida who stood by the horses' heads, waiting to say their farewells.

"As ye can see, we are all ready to ride," the Rìgh said with an affectionate smile. "I hope ye are well fed and rested, my cat, because we have a long, hard gallop ahead o' us!"

"Finn, how was Killian himself?" Elfrida asked anxiously.

"Och, he was no' grand," Finn answered. "He seems very dazed and confused. I think he sometimes did no' understand what was going on but he were so very weak he could no' protest or fight, just let us heave him about like a sack o' potatoes." She described the marks of ill-use that covered the old man's emaciated body and saw Elfrida's eyes fill with tears of pity.

"Och, that be bad news indeed," she said. "Did he understand ye had come on my behalf?"

"I be no' sure," Finn answered. "There was so little time for explaining. He recognized the cross."

"Well, that be something at least," Elfrida said with a sigh. "I wish I could be coming wi' ye."

"No, ye do no'," Iseult said coolly. "We ride hard, Elfrida. Ye ken ye will be much more comfortable travelling in your carriage at the rear o' the army, with your maids to serve ye and your bodyguard to protect ye. Ye would only slow us down if ye came."

"Aye, I suppose so," Elfrida replied unhappily. "Well, I hope ye find him in better shape and all those who helped him too." She raised her hand in farewell. "Godspeed!"

"Godspeed," Lachlan answered with a smile and a little salute.

"May Eà be with ye all," Iain said, sliding his hand

within Elfrida's arm. They then both turned and walked away. It was clear from the droop of Elfrida's shoulders that Iseult's words had hurt her but the Banrìgh showed no sign of remorse. As usual, her beautiful pale face was calm and rather stern.

"Aye, it is hard to believe Elfrida is the descendant o' the bright warrior-maid," Lachlan said, as if Iseult had offered some explanation for her harshness. "She was no' brought up to be warlike, though, Iseult; ye should no' expect it."

Iseult returned his gaze squarely. "I do no' expect it."

"Then why be so cold to her all the time?" he asked. "She be a sweet lass and tries hard to be friends with ye."

Iseult gave a small shrug of her shoulders. "Am I cold? I do no' mean to be. It is just she is always wringing her hands and weeping, instead o' doing what needs to be done." She paused, then said with a faint heightening of colour in her cheeks. "All ye men think her so sweet and gentle, yet she always gets what she wants without the least effort on her part. I find it exasperating."

"Aye, she is bonny," Lachlan said infuriatingly. He looked down at the avidly listening Finn with a grin. "Come, enough o' this idle chitchat. Let us make ready to ride!"

Finn grinned and followed Johanna through the rows of mounted soldiers. Apart from the Rìgh and the Banrìgh, there were the fifty Yeomen of the Guard, led by Duncan Ironfist upon an enormous brown gelding with shaggy white fetlocks and mane. Connor sat beside the Rìgh on a pretty bay pony, carrying the Rìgh's standard. Finn stared at him enviously as Johanna instructed her to climb up into a small wagon with the court sorcerer, Gwilym the Ugly, and the other healers.

"Why canna I ride too?" she asked rebelliously. "I hate bouncing around in wagons!"

"I dinna ken ye could ride," Johanna answered. "Besides, we havena any horses to spare."

"O' course I can ride," Finn replied crossly. "I can ride anything!" She thought rather longingly of her black mare Cinders, left in Nina's care in Rhyssmadill along with the other horses. "Surely someone must have a horse I could borrow? Flaming dragon balls! How can I direct Lachlan which way to go if I'm stuck in the rear eating everyone's dust?"

"Ye should call the Rìgh 'His Highness'," Johanna replied austerely. "Wait here, Finn. I shall speak to the cavalry-master and see if ye can borrow one o' the cavaliers' spare destriers. They shall no' be happy, I warn ye. Destriers cost a great deal o' money and are much loved by their riders. Ye had best be as good a rider as ye say!"

She went away across the field and Finn leant against the wagon, swinging her foot impatiently.

"Hello, Finn," a soft, rather plaintive voice said. "Do ye no' remember me?"

She glanced up, startled. Sitting right beside her in the wagon was a small, thin boy with pale gold wisps of hair and enormous blue eyes. His skin was so pale it was translucent, the trail of blue veins at temple and eyelid clearly visible. Deep violet shadows curved under his eyes, and the knobs of his collarbone stuck up rigidly at the base of his throat. He wore a small black gauntlet on the hand hanging limply over the side of the wagon.

"Tòmas!" Finn cried. "Oh, Tòmas."

To her surprise tears started to her eyes. She leant

up and embraced him fiercely, blotting her tears on the soft wool of his coat. "O' course I remember ye! I just dinna see ya."

"I heard ye were here," Tòmas said. "They say ye were dropped out o' the night sky by a flight o' nyx."

"I was indeed."

"I would've liked to have seen that," he answered with a sad little sigh.

"It was very late. Ye would've been asleep."

He stirred a little, lifting his hand and then letting it drop again. "I do no' sleep very well," he answered listlessly. "There are always so many sick people. I can feel their pain, even though they will no' let me touch them all. They say I must save my strength for those who need me most."

"That be good advice," Finn said briskly. "Ye canna be touching everyone, ye ken."

"I feel their pain," he answered sadly.

Again there was that unexpected rush of hot tears to Finn's eyes. She wondered what was wrong with her, that she should be so troubled so easily. It had been many months since she had felt like crying and here she was, weeping all the time like some soppy sentimental girl. She sniffed back the tears and said, even more briskly, "Well, ye should learn to block it out. Ye'll be making yourself sick if ye try and heal every silly gowk that has a sniffle or a sneeze."

"That's what Jo says."

"Well, listen to her. Jo is right."

"Och, o' course I am," Johanna said, coming up behind her. "Though I have no idea what ye're talking about. Come on, Finn, I have found a horse for ye. Ye had best take care o' him and no' hurt his mouth or score his side with spurs, else ye'll be making an enemy o' his owner. Come, his Highness is growing restless and wants to be on the road. It's long past dawn!"

Gladly Finn hurried to mount her horse, a big chestnut with a proudly curved neck named Harken. He was much taller than Cinders and, as Finn found as soon as she mounted, much stronger as well. He pranced and jibbed at the unfamiliar lightness of her weight and she had some trouble bringing him into line with the other horses. She hid her dismay however, and kicked him forward so that she was near Lachlan and Iseult, both watching her critically.

"Are ye sure ye can manage him, Finn?" Iseult said.

"O' course!"

"Very well then," the Rìgh said. "Let us ride!"

By the end of the first day, Finn was ready to weep with exhaustion. She had never ridden so hard and for so long. The horses were given their heads at every opportunity, galloping over the long stretches of meadow and through the green dales of trees. Only when the forest grew too thick were the horses reined in, and then to an uncomfortable jog that rattled the teeth in Finn's head and chafed her inner thighs raw.

It had taken Harken less than ten minutes to unseat Finn and she had hit the ground very hard, falling from a great height and at full speed. Goblin had been clinging to her shoulder and she leapt clear, landing nimbly on her feet and then tidying up her whiskers as a shaken and furious Finn tried to catch the gelding.

Harken was too well trained to bolt but she had to remount him without the assistance of a mounting block or a helping hand, all while clutching a protesting elven cat who was not averse to punishing Finn for the insult with her sharp little claws. Aware that the healers were all watching from the wagon, Finn

scrambled up with flaming cheeks, dragged the chestnut's head around and kicked him forward, galloping
in the muddy tracks of the other cavaliers who had
cantered on without pause.

Soon after, the gelding swerved under a low branch
and Finn had only been able to keep her seat by slipping sideways out of the saddle, gripping the stirrup
leather with both hands. He threw her again half an
hour later with an unexpected sidestep at full gallop,
and again at midday, stopping abruptly to drink at a
slow-moving brown stream. Finn was thrown over his
head and into the water, much to the amusement of
the cavaliers. Duncan Ironfist himself leapt down to
pull her up out of the stream, saying over his shoulder,
"Well, Harken has decided this is as good a place as
any to stop for lunch! Let us stand down and let the
horses rest a wee while."

Wet and deeply mortified, Finn waded out on to
the bank, surreptitiously rubbing her bruises and refusing to meet anyone's eyes. Goblin stalked out in
her wake, her black fur plastered flat to her bones,
her tail dripping. She sat with her back to Finn and
licked herself dry, hissing at Finn when she tried to
pick her up.

No-one paid the embarrassed girl and her cat any
attention, busy loosening their girths and unpacking
their saddlebags. Finn could only be glad the gloomy
first mate of the *Speedwell* had not been there to see
her ignominious descent. Arvin the Just had told her
many times that "pride goest afore destruction and a
haughty spirit afore a fall," and she could not help
thinking it would have given him great satisfaction to
have been proved right.

Finn could have curled up under the trees and slept
all afternoon, but to her consternation they stopped

only long enough to eat a rough meal of cheese, bread and ale before once again riding on. Goblin made her feelings clear by jumping up into the wagon and curling up on a pile of blankets, not deigning to look at Finn when she tried to coax her back on to her shoulder. Finn was by now so stiff and sore she would gladly have joined the elven cat in the wagon but her stubborn pride would not allow her to admit defeat and so she mounted the chestnut with a wince and a curse, and clung on with gritted teeth as he once again trotted forward.

At last the sun began to sink down behind the high round hills, but to her dismay they rode on long after twilight had darkened to night, their way lighted by flaming torches. At last they made camp, but Finn was so very stiff and sore she could hardly walk. Without comment Johanna gave her a pot of salve which burnt like fire when rubbed into her bruises and aching muscles but relieved the pain enough for Finn to finally get some sleep.

The second and third days were unadulterated torture. Finn found herself heartily sorry that she had boasted of her riding prowess, since the destrier was far too strong for her and fought her hand on the rein constantly. She was determined to show no weakness before the soldiers, however, and so used every ounce of strength in her body and will to force the horse to obey her. She was thrown several times but each time sprang back into the saddle and rode on without complaint.

By the fourth day her muscles were growing used to the hard pace and the soothing balm Johanna had given her had eased the pain of her chafing. By the fifth day, Finn felt in full command of the destrier, who had finally stopped trying to knock her off with low branches or unbalance her with a cunning sidestep at full gallop. By the sixth day, she was able to enjoy the excitement of their headlong pace and even to begin to notice the beauty of the scenery around them.

The cavaliers were riding through the downs that swept down towards the sea, ending abruptly at the edge of the high cliffs that Finn had last seen from the deck of the *Speedwell*. Streams wound down through the wide valleys, often meandering through small stretches of forest where they were able to hunt for birds or coneys to supplement their diet. Here and there were lonely farmhouses, usually strongly barricaded behind high stone walls. Often they saw a farmer out working in the fields. At the sight of the squadron of soldiers, he would turn and run back to the house, shutting the gates tight against them. The cavaliers never stopped, even though all would have liked to buy some fresh food or ask for a comfortable place to sleep.

On the seventh day they fought a skirmish with a company of Bright Soldiers on patrol. Lachlan was not interested in fighting a pitched battle. The aim of their expedition was to rescue the shipwrecked crew of the *Speedwell*, not to further the war against the General Assembly. So they simply rode through the company at top speed, laying about them with their swords. The gyrfalcon Stormwing plunged down from the sky at frightening speed, killing one soldier with a single blow of its clenched talons. Gwilym the Ugly conjured an illusion of snakes that had the enemy's horses rearing in panic and then, once the Yeomen were out of sight beyond the curve of a hill, concealed their trail with magic. A few soldiers were sent off to create a false trail leading their pursuers off on a wild goose chase, and their journey continued with the same discipline as before. Finn had to admit she was impressed with the speed and calm with which everything had been accomplished. The Blue Guards were seasoned veterans indeed.

On the eighth day they drew closer to the coast so that Finn could begin looking out for any landmarks that she recognised. Everyone was conscious of anxiety, for there were so many spectacular formations of rock rising from the wild sea that all wondered how Finn would be able to tell one from another. She just laughed scornfully, however, saying, "Flaming dragon balls, have ye forgotten I be a NicRuraich? I could find them in the dark with my eyes blindfolded, my ears stuffed with wax, and my hands tied behind my back!"

That day they saw a fleet of galleons sailing up the horizon and took cover behind the rocks for an hour or so, not wishing anyone on board to see them through their far-seeing glass. At last the white sails had disappeared from view and they were able to ride on, picking their way carefully over the uneven ground.

Suddenly Finn gave a shout. "Look! The Two Lovers! That's what Tam called them. See those rocks leaning together as if embracing? That's near where we came on shore. Auld Clootie's Cleft is hereabouts somewhere."

The shadows were growing long and the light had that effulgence that comes just before the sun sinks out of sight. Lachlan wanted to make camp in the cover of a small forest some distance away, returning in the morning so Finn could climb down the cliff and find her shipwrecked companions. Finn was determined to search them out straightaway, however.

"The cliff be no' much more than two hundred feet

high, I can slide down that in minutes!" she cried. "Please, Lachlan? They'll be so anxious. Then I can get all ready to haul them up first thing in the morning and we shallna be wasting any more time."

"But the tide be coming in," Lachlan said. "What if ye canna find them in time?"

"Och, I ken exactly where they are," Finn replied. "I'll go down the cliff right above Auld Clootie's Cleft and just swing in. I shallna need to set foot on the shore at all."

"Finn, can ye tell if all are still alive and well?" Iseult asked.

Finn hesitated. "No' really," she admitted. "I can feel a tumult o' minds but there is so much rock between us."

"I can feel pain," Tòmas said miserably.

"What about the prophet?" Lachlan leant forward, frowning. "Can ye tell if he still lives?"

Finn shrugged. "I think so. I do no' have the cross anymore, I gave it back to him, so I do no' have anything o' his to touch to make sure. I think he is still alive, though his minds feels very faint."

She had dismounted as she spoke, readying her rope and pulleys in preparation for the descent. While she had slept that first night in the army camp, Lachlan's quartermaster had been preparing new climbing equipment for her. One of the army blacksmiths had forged her some stakes and a square-headed hammer like the ones that had gone down with the *Speedwell,* and she had the great length of the nyx-hair rope, which coiled up into a surprisingly small knot that she wore hanging from her belt.

Finn buttoned the elven cat up securely in her coat pocket, belayed the nyx-hair rope firmly about a rock and swiftly, nimbly, descended the cliff-face.

It was shadowy in the lee of the cliff but Finn had climbed many a cliff in full darkness and had no difficulty in finding her way down. The rope was so slippery she was able to slide down at great speed, but so silky she did not burn her hands with the friction. Every now and again she bounced off the cliff with her feet, gaining extra momentum. By the time she reached the bottom the white-crested waves were growling and snapping about the rocks. Finn swung her body round so she hung upside down over Auld Clootie's Cleft. "Hey, Scruffy," she whispered.

There was a faint sound of movement within. "Finn?" The voice was incredulous.

"Aye. Can I come in or will ye stick me with that bloody happy sword o' yours?"

"Nay, o' course ye can come in." Dillon had stepped forward and was peering out into the darkness. "Where the blazes are ye, Finn, in the water?"

She rapped him on the top of his skull. "Up here, porridge-head."

He looked up, startled, rubbing the crown of his head. "Flaming dragon's balls!"

"Step back, ye lout, do ye want me to land on top o' ye?" As Dillon stepped back, muttering under his breath, Finn lithely swung herself down and through the cleft, landing gracefully before him.

"Good to see ye, Scruffy; how are ye yourself?" she asked.

He laughed, still rubbing the top of his head. "I'll give ye this, Finn, ye do ken how to make an entrance!"

"Thank ye kindly, I try."

"How in Eà's name did ye ken I was on guard tonight?"

"It's my business to ken such things," she replied haughtily. "I am the Cat, after all."

He grinned. "Thank Eà ye've come, Finn, we were sick with anxiety. No' to mention hunger. Have ye brought food? We've eaten naught but seaweed and barnacles for days!"

Finn nodded, shrugging her shoulders so her heavy pack bounced up and down. She looked past Dillon into the gloom of the cave, seeing dark figures huddled about a fire lit at the far end of the enormous cavern. No-one had yet noticed her arrival and she was struck by the despondent slump of their shoulders.

"Lachlan and Iseult and their men are up top," she said. "They've brought healers too, for they ken some o' the sailors were injured. How are everyone else themselves?"

Dillon looked grim. "We've lost a few, I'm afraid."

"Och, no' the prophet!" Finn was dismayed. To have Killian the Listener die when they had travelled so far and endured so much to rescue him!

"Nay, he lives still. He's a tough auld boot, for all he looks like a bundle o' sticks and rags. He's in better shape than some o' them!"

"No' Enit?" Finn cried.

"Nay, though she is very weak. She can barely lift her head from her blankets and if ye had no' come when ye did . . ."

"Well, then," Finn said, relieved. Though she was naturally sorry that some of the injured sailors had died, she could only be glad it was not Killian the Listener or the old jongleur with the silvery voice. She started to move forward once more but Dillon stopped her with a hand on his arm.

"I be real sorry, Finn, but I'm afraid your auld gillie Donald . . ."

"No' Donald?"

"Aye, Donald. He was fishing off the rocks and got swept away by a wave. Dide and I tried to save him but it all happened too quickly . . ."

Finn was numb with shock. It had never occurred to her to fear for the gillie's life, although he was near as old as Enit or Killian. She stared at Dillon, then suddenly her face crumpled and she broke into tears. Dillon put his arms about her clumsily, patting her shoulder.

"Do no' greet, Finn, do no' greet," he whispered.

Finn wiped her eyes. "I canna believe it. He was so . . . so doughty." She could think of no better word than the one Donald had used so often himself.

"We have missed him badly indeed. None o' us are much o' a hand with a bow and arrow, and the fishing line went down with him. We've done our best but it's been hard."

He led her over to the fire, where she was greeted with a great commotion. The contents of Finn's haversack were received with almost as much excitement and she set about handing around food and the big flask of whiskey, her heart swelling with grief and pity. All of the castaways were very thin and pale, their clothes more ragged than ever. Most were still heavily bandaged, some with limbs tightly splinted. Enit lay in a restless doze that not all the noise could awaken her from. Bran was still weak and listless from her bout of sorcery-sickness, though her green eyes had lit with joy and relief at the sight of Finn. Ashlin could only get to his feet with an effort, a hacking cough causing him to double over with pain. His eyes, like Bran's, were fever-bright. He bowed to Finn, though, saying in a hoarse voice, "Thank Eà ye be safe, my lady! I have been in such a fret over ye."

"Do no' call me that," Finn said impatiently. "I be just Finn."

She looked round for Jay and Dide and found them waiting to embrace her. "Och, Finn, it be grand to see ye!" Jay cried, hugging her so hard she gave a little yelp. "We havena been able to help fretting about ye. When we saw ye disappearing into the sky like that, surrounded by all those strange, wild faeries . . ."

"The nyx be wonderful," Finn protested indignantly.

"I'm just glad to see ye alive and well," Jay said and embraced her again.

"Well, I'm glad to see ye too," Finn said awkwardly. "No' that ye look well. Ye look bloody awful!"

Indeed, both Dide and Jay were thin and grey, their skin moist with perspiration, their voices roughened from too much coughing.

"Some kid o' cave fever," Nellwyn the Yedda said. "We've all got it. Comes from the dampness and chill, I'd say. We havena dared show our faces outside, for the galleons have been scouring the coast for us."

Finn nodded. "Aye, we saw them. Never mind. We'll have ye out of here and into the fresh air first thing in the morning. Tòmas is there and Johanna too. They'll make ye all better."

It was a difficult task, hauling all the castaways up the cliff the next dawn. Few were strong enough to even attempt to climb and so the Yeomen had to drag them up on stretchers suspended from ropes. Dillon's dog Jed howled the whole way up, struggling feebly against the ropes that bound him. He was gaunt beneath his shaggy white fur, having lived on nothing but cave rats for weeks.

Killian the Listener was one of the first to be dragged over the lip of the cliff. The first thing he saw when he weakly lifted his head was Lachlan, bending over him with a frown of concern. The young Rìgh was all gilded by the brightness of the rising sun, his golden-topaz eyes blazing in his dark face, his magnificent black wings framing all the strength and power of his tall figure. Killian gazed up at him with reverent awe, then struggled to his knees, seizing Lachlan's strong, brown hand and kissing it.

"Indeed, ye are the angel o' the Lord!" he cried.

"Nay, I am no angel," Lachlan said gently. "I am naught but a mortal man, struggling like all men to do what is right."

"Nay," Killian said. "I have seen ye in my dreams. Ye are the messenger o' God our Father, sent to do His will."

"Happen that is true," Lachlan said, "if it is his will to try and bring peace to all the land. For indeed, that is what I intend to do, even if I must fight to the very death."

"It is always His will to bring peace," Killian said, a smile trembling on his ancient mouth. "Love, joy and peace, this is what He tells us to seek, no' this greed for power and material things, this selfish ambition, which drives the Fealde, she who they call the Whore o' Bride."

"Love, joy and peace," Lachlan said slowly. "Indeed, that is all I want. And with your help, may Eà grant we find it."

Johanna and her healers had swung into action as the first white face had appeared above the lip of the cliff. Those that had suffered serious injuries were carried across to where Tòmas sat, pale and grave-faced. The little boy peeled away his black gauntlets and laid his hands upon their foreheads. From his fingers the pink glow of health flowed down over the grey counte-

nances. Broken limbs knitted together, pus-filled
wounds dried and healed over, congested lungs
cleared, and bruises faded.

After the little boy had touched Enit, the old jongleur opened her eyes and smiled up at the boy, saying
"Bless ye, laddie! I feel like a young lass again. I feel
like I could dance a jig!"

She flexed her gnarled fingers wonderingly, then
rose to her feet with the aid of an eager-faced Dide
and took a few tottering steps, the first she had taken
in some years. The extensive damage to her joints
caused by her rheumatoid arthritis could not be repaired—Tòmas could not restore what had been lost—
but much of the swelling and pain had subsided, so
that Enit was more comfortable than she had been for
a very long time.

"Indeed, his is a marvellous talent," Dide cried.
"We had thought Grandam would never walk again!"

"A miracle indeed," Killian the Listener said,
watching with great interest. "Indeed, the ways o' the
Lord our Father are many and wonderful."

Tòmas looked up at him. "Would ye like me to
touch ye too?" he asked timidly. "I cannot give ye
back your ears, but happen I can heal your other
wounds. I can feel your pain."

The old prophet nodded his head, his emaciated
face very solemn. He bent and Tòmas laid his hands
upon his bony forehead. When at last he lifted his
head away, the prophet stood tall and sure, his dark
eyes flashing. There was no sign of the wounds of
his torture.

"I heard the voices o' the angels as ye touched me,"
he cried. "I had feared they spoke to me no longer,
so many months I have heard naught but the scrab-
bling o' my own dark thoughts. But now, now! I heard

the trumpet call o' their commands, I hear the heavenly choir o' their rejoicing. I had feared myself forsaken but now I ken I had closed the ears o' my soul as the Fealde had closed the ears o' my body. Hallelujah! The wrath o' God shall smite these false leaders who have led the people o' my land into this dark age o' sin and deceit, where the word o' God is twisted and made foul. Let us put on the armour o' God, let us gird ourselves with truth, let us buckle on the breastplate o' righteousness! Raise high the sword o' the spirit, which is the word o' God our Father, and let us throw down these false preachers, these proud, vain, deceitful leaders!"

# THE TAPESTRY
# IS WOVEN

# THE CLOVEN HOOF

⚜️

A fire was lit in the shelter of a small grove of trees and a meal hurriedly prepared for the famished castaways. Duncan Ironfist passed around a great flask of whiskey, "to warm all their bones," as he said.

There was much talk and laughter as they ate and drank, the League of the Healing Hand together again after so many years. Many old adventures were recalled and new ones recounted, old jokes revived and fresh ones made up. The thought of those members of the old gang who had not survived the Bright Wars brought a moment of sadness, but all were too happy and relieved to be melancholy for long and soon all were laughing again. After hearing of Bran, Tam and Ashlin's role in the adventure of the Black Tower, they were declared honorary members of the League of the Healing Hand by Dillon, who was still and would always be, their general. A toast was drunk and Finn made an impromptu speech that had them all in fits of giggles.

Just then, Lachlan came and smiled down at them and they all leapt to their feet and bowed. "I just wanted to say thank ye to ye all," he said. "For the first time I feel confident that we can prevail in the

Forbidden Land. I dinna ken how I can show ye my gratitude but show ye I will."

"Another pouch o' tobacco wouldna go astray," Finn said hopefully. Lachlan laughed and promised to find her some, then said seriously, "I mean it though, all o' ye. Ye have achieved the impossible once again. I do no' ken what I have done to deserve such true and loyal friends."

They had not known how to answer, all choked with pleasure. Then Finn had grinned at Lachlan and bowed with an extravagant flourish of her hand. "Always a pleasure to serve ye, your Highness."

Lachlan laughed. "Why do I feel suspicious when ye are polite, my cat?"

"Because it happens so rarely," Brangaine said.

Lachlan smiled. "Aye, that must be it."

"I do no' ken what ye mean," Finn said, pretending to be hurt. "I am always the very soul o' courtesy."

Just then there was a cry from the lookout boy, who had been deputised to keep a close watch out while everyone else ate and relaxed. Lachlan turned and left the fire abruptly, creeping up the ridge to lie next to the sentry and look where he pointed. Finn and the rest of the league swarmed up behind him, peering over the rocks.

White as wings, the sails of a galleon billowed out in the wind.

"They sail close," Captain Tobias said in a low voice, who had taken the farseeing glass from the lookout and was holding it to one eye.

"Have they spied us?" Lachlan asked grimly.

"Impossible to tell." The captain retracted the telescope and tucked it again in the pocket of his ragged greatcoat. "I dare no' watch any longer for the sun is against us and could flash in the glass, giving us away."

"Come, we had best be moving on then," Lachlan said.

Iseult was watching the ship with keen eyes. "They are waving flags about," she said. "I can see the flash o' colour."

"Bad news," Arvin the Just said gloomily. "They are signalling to shore."

"Let us away from here," Lachlan said. "If there is a squadron o' Bright Soldiers about, I do no' wish to be meeting them!"

"Where shall we go?" Finn asked eagerly.

"If only we had a safe house in this area," Lachlan mused. "But I ken o' none within a day's ride. Leonard the Canny has already warned us that the people o' the downs be the dour, pious sort and no' likely to offer any help to heretics like us."

The young sailor Tam looked up with a flush. "I beg your pardon, your Highness, but although it be true that the down folk are pious indeed, they have no liking for the General Assembly and think them most corrupt and ungodly. We are far from the city here. We live close to the land and the ways o' our fathers and our fathers' fathers are thought good enough for us. There are many in my village who mourn the overthrow o' the MacHildes as if it happened yesterday and who cling to the auld ways, when a farmer who worked all day in the fields was no' expected to throw down his tools and attend the kirk three times a day when the harvest must be got in." He finished with some heat, his words tumbling over each other.

"Is that so?" Lachlan said thoughtfully. "I take it from all this that ye come from hereabouts, my lad?"

Tam nodded. "Indeed I do, your Highness. Born and raised a downsman."

"Then I can see ye being most useful to us, lad. If ye are willing to be so."

Under Lachlan's intense scrutiny, the colour rose in Tam's cheeks again but he made a rather clumsy bow and said, "Tam o' Kirkclanbright at your service, my laird."

"I thank ye, Tam o' Kirkclanbright, and very pleased I am to be making your acquaintance. Now, do ye think ye can find us a safe house where we can hide from those misbegotten Bright Soldiers?"

"I'll take ye to my Da's farm, Rowanglen," Tam said simply. "He be a stern man and loyal indeed to the Kirk, so do no' be expecting him to be falling at your feet, your Highness. He has a very nice sense o' right and wrong, however, and has a great respect for the prophet, so I am sure he shall take ye in when ye hears how ye rescued him and healed him."

"As long as he gives me a hot bath and some decent food, I do no' care if he spits in my face," Lachlan said with a grin. "Lead the way, Tam, my lad!"

Rowanglen was a prosperous little farm tucked in the side of the downs. It had a wide stream running through its golden fields, a pond where ducks swam, and a sturdy house with high pointed gables. A long avenue of rowan trees led up to the farm, which was protected all along the road with a high wall set with an iron gate.

They all waited at the edge of a wide swathe of forest, watching the farm. All was quiet. Grey smoke curled lazily from one of the chimneys and horses grazed in the home meadow. Enormous haystacks filled the fields, and birds hopped amongst the golden stubble. The leaves of the trees were all turning russet, yellow and brown, and here and there were rowan trees heavy with red berries. The shadows were growing longer and already it was cool under the trees.

It had been a hurried, furtive journey through the countryside. Tam had led them through torturous byways and fields, the overloaded wagon often becoming bogged down in the mud and having to be levered free by the soldiers. As far as possible they had tried to avoid being seen, but there were many people working in the fields and they were a sizable company now, with the crew of the *Sea-Eagle* and the *Speedwell* as well as the soldiers, healers, jongleurs and witches. The wagon was overcrowded with those who could not walk with ease, and many of the weary horses carried more than one passenger. All were greatly travel-stained, with most of the shipwreck survivors dressed in little more than rags. It was impossible for them not to attract a great deal of attention, or for them not to leave marks of their passage in the mud of the fields and the broken twigs of the hedgerows.

"I fear we do your family no favours," Lachlan said grimly. "If there are Bright Soldiers about, they will soon have wind o' us."

Tam looked anxious.

"Do no' fear," Iseult said. "Our army has had instructions to march this way. We shall soon have plenty o' reinforcements."

Tam's look of anxiety only deepened and he looked out at the peaceful valley with foreboding. Across the stream was an apple orchard, golden fruit peeping out between the leaves, which half-concealed a house with a green gabled roof. The road led down through bare fields and copses of trees to a small village, smudged with smoke from its chimneys, and dominated by the grey hulk of its kirk. The square tower of the kirk was topped with a tall cone-shaped spire that soared high above the trees and roofs and was crowned with a gilded cross.

Everywhere people were working with the slow grace of those who work with the land all year long. A big wagon was being loaded with hay in one of the fields. Elsewhere, a boy was tending a herd of fat black pigs. A strong-looking woman was splitting kindling with an axe by the side of one of the crofts. By the river the sails of a mill turned slowly in the fitful breeze, and a cart laden with sacks of grain was being unloaded by three men in rough brown clothes. In the village square children were playing hopscotch or squatting in the dust, tossing sheep's knuckles. They could hear the occasional bleat of sheep, the ringing of a blacksmith's hammer, and the piping of the goat-keeper who sat amidst the herd grazing on the river-bank.

"It has been many years since we had war here in Kirkclanbright," Tam said unhappily.

Just then they heard bells ringing out the hour. Six times the bells rang, and the hidden watchers saw the workers in the field lay down their hoes and scythes, and trudge through the stubble towards the kirk.

"It be vespers," Tam explained in a whisper. "Once they are all in kirk, there shall be none to watch us pass by."

"How often must ye all go to kirk?" Finn asked, as he began to cautiously lead the party out of the shelter of the wood.

"It used to be once a day and twice on Sundays, but these days the General Assembly demands we all must attend at least three times a day and six times on Sunday. It is fine for us who live only a wee while away from the kirk but for those who live away from the villages it is difficult indeed, and has caused much bad feeling."

"Why do they make ye go so often?"

Tam shrugged. "Happen if we spend all day on our knees praying we shallna have time for anything else," he said with deep irony.

The valley now lay deserted and they were able to move out into the dusty road, moving as quietly as they were able. The evening was so still they could hear the sound of chanting from the kirk, and the murmur of the river over stones. Rowanglen's iron gate stood open and they passed through it and up the cool dusk of the avenue.

"Happen ye'd best all hide in the barn and wait for my family to come home," Tam said. Obediently they crowded within the great building, filled with shadows and smelling of dust and straw. There the exhausted horses could at last be unsaddled and rubbed down, with Tam spreading hay for them and showing the soldiers how to work the pump. The men and women made themselves nests in the straw and lay down where they could to rest, all tired after the long day's walking. Everyone was conscious of tension. They were deep in the heart of the enemy's territory, badly equipped for any battle, and vulnerable to betrayal. Even if the Greycloaks had made excellent time, they must still be some leagues away, without any way of knowing where Lachlan and his men had taken shelter. They could only trust in Tam and his family.

Nearly an hour later they heard the sound of voices. Tam rose. His colour was high, his eyes eager. "That be my mother's voice I hear. And that's my wee sister laughing! Wait here. I shall go and explain everything. All will be well, I promise."

He hurried out of the barn into the deepening dusk,

calling to his mother. They heard a babble of excitement, the bang of a door, and then silence.

It was a long, long wait. At last, though, they heard the barn door being opened and Tam came in carrying a lantern. Behind him strode a tall man with a stern, clean-shaven face and grey hair cropped very short. He was dressed in grey breeches, long boots, a rough shirt and a black coat that had seen better days. He carried himself with authority, however, looking around at the crowd of men and women with angry disdain.

"Who is this man who says he be the prophet?" he demanded.

Killian had dropped into a doze but Johanna gently woke him and helped him to his feet. He looked around with dazed eyes, settling his gaze at last on the farmer and his son. Tam lifted the lantern higher so that the light fell full upon Killian's maimed head, with the ugly scars that showed where his ears had once been.

The farmer stared for a long while and then said, in a slightly gentler tone, "Many men have lost their ears at the behest o' the Fealde, aye, and their hands and noses too. How am I to ken that ye are indeed Killian the Listener, the prophet?"

Killian peered at him uncertainly. "I am Killian, he they call the Listener."

The farmer frowned and stuck his big, red hands in his belt. He looked around at the crowd.

"And the one calling herself the NicHilde?" There was an odd note in the farmer's gruff voice, a wistful yearning imperfectly concealed behind belligerence.

Elfrida rose gracefully and came forward, her dark red plaid wrapped close around her slim body. Although her hair was tumbling out of its severe bun, stuck here and there with straw, and there was mud on her skirt, she somehow managed to project an air of quiet dignity. "I am the NicHilde."

He looked her over for a long moment. "Ye be as fair as a MacHilde," he said at last, the belligerence gone from his voice.

"That is because I am a MacHilde," she answered, no trace of anger or offence in her gentle voice. "It is a sad day when a man o' Kirkclanbright doesna recognise a MacHilde when he sees one. Have ye forgotten how this valley came to be so named? Is this no' the place where the bright warrior-maid bore her first son, thus laying the foundations o' my clan? Is your kirk no' the first kirk ever built in the Bright Land?"

"Aye, that it is," the farmer answered, rubbing at his bristly chin. "But few care to remember that these days."

"I care to remember," she answered softly.

The farmer shifted uncomfortably, glancing about him at the men and women crowded close together in the shadowy barn. "They say ye have taken up with witches and demons, though, my lady."

"Berhtilde was a witch herself and proud o' it," Elfrida answered, her colour rising. It was the first time any of them had heard her admit such a thing and Iain smiled and stepped closer to her, his arm brushing hers. "But it is an evil lie to say I have dealings with demons! Those that support and help me are all good, brave men, and as human as ye or me."

"But what o' this winged *uile-bheist* who has set himself up as Rìgh?"

Lachlan stepped forward, his feathers rustling. His brows were drawn over his golden eyes in a forbidding frown. "I am the MacCuinn."

The farmer looked him up and down, noting the MacCuinn plaid pinned with the device of the crowned stag, the long black wings springing from his back, the Lodestar thrust through his belt. He then looked round at the crowd, absorbing every detail of their muddy, ragged clothing, the horses with their heads sunk low, the old woman with her crippled hands, the youthfulness of some of the faces. Then his eyes went back to Gwilym the Ugly, leaning on his tall staff, his fingers all laden with rings. Although the sorcerer was dressed as plainly as any of them, with a long cloak of rough grey wool over breeches, the staff and rings proclaimed him as one of the Coven to those who knew the signs. The farmer clearly did.

With disgust in his voice, he said abruptly, "Ye be a witch."

"Aye, that I am," Gwilym replied in his deep, harsh voice.

"Do ye no' ken that they burn witches in these parts and those that harbour them?"

"So I believe," Gwilym answered.

"So what do ye do here, risking your life and ours?"

"I am here to serve my Rìgh," Gwilym answered.

The farmer pondered him for a moment longer, his mouth compressed with anger. "Do ye no' ken witchcraft is the working o' the Archfiend!" he suddenly hissed at Tam. "Ye defile our land by bringing these abominations here!"

"But *dai-dein*! The prophet himself has declared the Rìgh the messenger o' God! And this wee lad here, he is the one that heals wi' the laying on o' hands. I have seen it wi' my own eyes and I swear there is no evil-doing there. He is as innocent as a newborn babe."

"Auld Clootie has many faces, no' all o' them foul," his father responded.

"As does God our Father, and no' all o' them fair," a woman suddenly said. They all looked at the door where a short, middle-aged woman stood, regarding them all with twinkling hazel eyes just like Tam's. She was dressed very plainly in dark grey, with rough sabots on her feet and a white apron tied around her plump waist. Her hands were red and coarse, but the skin of her round face was very soft and pale, wrinkled like hands left too long in water.

"What sort o' welcome is this to give to our guests, father?" she scolded, coming forward to seize her husband by the elbow, and shaking his arm none too gently. Her head only came up to his chest but to all of their surprise, the big, grim-faced man hung his head, abashed. "Has Tam no' told ye again and again that the auld prophet has sworn that these be no workings o' the Archfiend but the servants o' our God the Father, come to put the NicHilde back on her throne? What are ye about, to call the angel o' death himself an *uile-bheist*? One would think ye had never heard the reading o' the Guid Book!"

"But mother . . ."

"No buts about it! I be ashamed o' ye, father. Have we no' heard tales o' the miraculous doings o' this dark angel? Did no' the beasts o' the field and the birds o' the air fight at his command? Did he no' show great mercy to those that had fallen, bidding the lad wi' the healing hands to help them? Have we no' all muttered against the cruel and corrupt Whore o' Bride and wish that she and her loose-lipped bootlickers would all be swallowed up by a crack in the earth?"

"Och, aye, but . . ."

"Such a great gowk ye are!" the little plump woman

said affectionately. "It is only in stories that the earth opens up and swallows the evil-hearted. In real life, we must do what we can to hasten things. Is it no' said that God helps those that help themselves?"

"Aye, but . . ."

"Well then! Look at the puir things, so dirty and ragged. We must bustle about and get them some hot water to wash in and something to eat, and ye, Great Tam, must go across to Jock o' the Apples and Miller Dan and to the pastor, o' course, and tell them what be towards. And rouse up Peter Goatkeeper too; he be a wily lad, and Joe the Smith, and Jack Woolly too. Oh, and happen ye should send Wee Tam across valley way and tell Dick Dickson, for if he's the last to ken he'll be stirring up trouble and better he be here under my eye."

"Very well, mother," Great Tam said obediently.

"Happen ye'd best go to Dick Dickson, Da, he might take offense if it be only me," Tam said. "I'll go and rouse up Jock o' the Apples."

His father gave a slow grin which greatly mellowed his face. "Aye, lad, and give my best to young Bessie too. She'll be aye glad to see ye!"

Colour flamed in Tam's cheeks. He ducked his head and hurried out of the barn, leaving the lantern hanging from a hook. His father was quick to follow him, casting one last doubtful look about the barn and muttering, "Whatever be the world coming to, when we have witches and *uile-bheistean* breaking bread and tasting salt wi' us!"

"All things are possible with God," Killian suddenly said, taking them all by surprise.

"Aye, that be the truth indeed," Tam's mother answered, nodding her round grey head. "Indeed that be the truth." She suddenly came forward in a rush to kneel at Elfrida's feet and kiss her hand. "Och, welcome home, my lady, welcome home!"

"Thank ye," Elfride said with tears in her voice.

"We've been a long time waiting for ye," the old woman said. "But I always kent ye'd come home to us."

That night the men of the district all gathered in Great Tam's parlour to look Lachlan and Elfrida over and to listen to Killian the Listener speak. Killian had been bathed and dressed in a long white robe of homespun cloth, his wispy hair and beard combed out. Around his neck he wore his wooden cross on its knotted thong of leather. His dark eyes were tragic as he told them how the Fealde had ordered him tortured in order to force him to sign a confession saying that all he preached was dictated to him by the Archfiend and not God himself.

"But I would no', for I kent I had heard the true singing o' the angels," the prophet said and all the farmers shifted and muttered among themselves.

Then he told of his daring rescue, and how the Rìgh's people had risked everything to save him. Now his dark eyes glowed with fervour and his voice trembled with gratitude. He described how Tòmas had healed him and how he had heard a chorus of heavenly singing at the first touch of his miraculous hands.

"Indeed, we are blessed, for God our father has heard our prayers and sent this winged angel to save us from the dreadful tyranny o' the corrupt General Assembly, and this young boy with the miraculous touch to heal the wounds o' our people, and He has kept our sweet young NicHilde safe from harm so that she may rule us as was always God's will, for is she no' the appointed one, the heir to the golden sword?"

Finn had been unable to bear the suspense and so she eavesdropped on the whole proceedings from outside the window, telling herself she was standing guard in case of betrayal. To her surprise it was the local pastor who proved to be Lachlan's most fervent supporter. A roly-poly man with a shiny bald head fringed all round with cherubic grey curls, he was dressed in a long black cassock with a plain wooden cross at his waist. He looked as if he thought of little more than his dinner but he proved to be of a romantic temperament. The story of Elfrida, the disinherited young banprionnsa fighting to free her people, stirred his imagination. He had no difficulty in believing Lachlan to be the angel of death so many prophets had foreseen, clasping his hands together at his very first sight of the Rìgh and murmuring "Night-winged and flame-eyed, the angel o' death shall smite them, for they have forgotten the word o' God!"

Dick Dickson proved to be a thin, oily man who continually rubbed his hands together as if washing them, and whose narrow dark eyes darted from one face to another. When he first came in, he had said with deep foreboding, "He who sups with the Devil should have a long spoon, Great Tam."

"Aye, but better a dinner o' green herbs where love is than a stalled ox and hatred within," the pastor had immediately returned.

Dick Dickson shook his head lugubriously. "The Devil can aye quote scripture for his own ends, Pastor."

Indignant colour surged up in the pastor's round cheeks. "A fool may give wise men counsel, but they rarely thank him for it," he snapped.

Patchy colour rose in Dick Dickson's narrow cheeks. He sought for a riposte but finding none, merely shook his head sadly and said no more, though his ferret eyes watched everyone's faces avidly.

Long into the night the discussion wound. The men of Kirkclanbright were by nature conservative and prudent, and reluctant to throw in their lot with pagans and heretics. Even Tam's mother was troubled by the presence of witches in Lachlan's retinue, even though Lachlan pointed out most persuasively that witchcunning was born into all people and therefore must be seen as a gift from God.

"By Him all things were created that are in heaven and earth, visible and invisible, human and unworldly, whether thrones or dominions or principalities or powers. All things were created through Him and for Him, He is afore all things and in Him all things consist," Killian the Listener said, clasping his wooden cross tightly, and the pastor nodded, though his kindly face was troubled.

"And what shall happen to us if this winged pagan does win through to Bride and puts the NicHilde back on the throne and throws down the Great Kirk?" Dick Dickson said then. "We shall be made to dance naked around the kirkyard and say our prayers backwards and boil the bones o' murdered children for evil spells . . ."

Lachlan interrupted him with a great shout of laughter. "Is that what ye think the Coven does?" he cried when at last he caught his breath. "By Eà's green blood! Och, well, happen it be like the stories we always heard about how ye sacrificed babes on your altars."

There was an indignant outcry. Lachlan laughed again. "I can promise ye this, there's no boiling up children, though it is true witches often dance about naked. Never fear! The Coven would never make ye do so if ye did no' want to. We o' the Coven believe all must be free to think and worship as they please. None would be forced to pray in a kirk six times a day if they would rather be ploughing their fields, that I assure ye! We believe that living a good and compassionate life and having a care for others is a better way to worship the sacred forces o' life than kneeling in a cold, draughty building, but each to their own!"

"But is it no' true that yon witches worship the Archfiend and do his bidding?" the pastor asked anxiously.

"Witches do no' believe in the Archfiend," Lachlan said, a tinge of exasperation in his voice. "I had never heard o' your Auld Clootie afore your soldiers came and invaded my land!"

"Ye do no' believe in the Archfiend?" The pastor was perplexed. "But do ye no' swear allegiance to him and all his evil minions, and chant the Lord's prayer backwards and hang the cross upside down on your altars and . . ."

"No, we do no'," Lachlan said shortly.

"Gracious me," the pastor said. "I always thought ye did."

The humour suddenly returned to Lachlan's face. "Nay, I'm afraid ye have as untrue a picture o' the Coven as we used to have o' ye, afore the NicHilde set us straight. Happen we shall all have to try and find the kernel o' truth amidst the chaff o' lies."

"If ye do no' believe in the Archfiend, surely that means ye canna believe in God our Father?" Dick Dickson suddenly asked. Immediately the whole room stilled, the men turning shocked eyes from him to the Rìgh.

Lachlan thought carefully before replying. "No' at all," he said at last. "We believe there is a life-force

that animates the universe, though we do no' divide
it into black or white, good or evil, male or female,
night or day. We call this life-force Eà and believe
she contains all these opposites within her, or him if
ye so prefer. We believe Eà is all gods and goddesses,
all devils and angels."

There was a little indrawn breath of displeasure and
he went on with a sudden rush of words. "Eà has
had many names and faces, no' all o' them good and
beautiful. We choose what aspects o' that godforce we
worship. To the Coven it is the Eà o' green forests
that we look to for our blessing. Most o' the folk o'
Blèssem see Eà as a farmer, a strong, kindly man who
sows the seed and reaps the harvest. If I understand
your religion correctly, ye look to the power o' the
sun and the heavens as your inspiration. Some choose
to see Eà's dark hideous face, the face of Gearradh,
she who cuts the thread. That is their right, though it
would no' be my choice. One o' the things we will do
once we have overthrown the Fealde is make sure that
ye all have the chance to believe as ye wish. If you
choose to pray in the kirk six times a day, so be it. If
ye choose to dance naked in the forest, so be it."

Many of the men were shocked by this and Finn,
crouched cold and stiff outside, though Lachlan had
blundered. However, when at last the group broke up
and went home through the dew-silvered fields, many
looked thoughtful indeed. And the next day Killian
the Listener spoke in the kirk, the light shining down
through the tall plain windows upon his wispy white
head. Every pew in the kirk was crowded with people,
and many more stood at the back, twisting their hats
in their hands and listening with rapt faces. Finn listened from the front pew, and though she did not
understand much of what he said, the rhythm of his

words broke over her in waves, filled with the sound of trumpets.

"The time o' God's vengeance is at hand, for ye have been led astray by false words and false promises! Ye have lost your way and wander frightened in the wilderness because o' the blindness and folly o' your vain hearts. Ye have been seduced into sin, ye have been led into war and wickedness, ye have set yourselves on pedestals, thinking yourselves the judge o' God's intentions when the great workings o' our Lord the Father are invisible to our eyes and inconceivable to our hearts. Ye have allowed proud, greedy, deceitful masters to rule our land and our thoughts, you have cowered down afore their faithless commands in fear and cowardice, ye have forgotten the words o' the Lord who spoke always o' forgiveness and understanding, love and humility. Have ye forgotten that all things that creep and walk, fly and swim and slither, were made by our Lord the Father, and were good in his eyes? Och, aye, ye who call evil good and good evil, who mistake darkness for light and light for darkness, who put bitter for sweet and sweet for bitter, the time o' God's vengeance is at hand!"

Many in the crowd sobbed and cowered in fear; many were white-faced with trembling hands. It seemed Killian the Listener's words struck deep into their hearts. His tone softened then. He spoke for a long time about forgiveness and compassion, about sacrifice and redemption. Finn was unable to help being moved by all he said, even though her sceptical mind found many things to question in his beliefs. Elfrida wept in the front pew and her husband Iain and Ashlin were absolutely engrossed. Even Lachlan was clearly touched by all the prophet said, once applauding spontaneously. At one point Jay leant across Finn to whisper to Dide, "The prophet has magic in his voice, same as ye or Enit. He could convert a cursehag, he could." The jongleur nodded in agreement.

A new mood swept over the crowd. They wept now in repentance and shame, they lifted faces shining with new resolve. When at last the prophet ended with a resounding call to arms many shouted and threw up their hats. As Lachlan and his retinue walked out of the kirk, the last to leave, they found the people of Kirkclanbright waiting for them outside in tense silence. Elfrida stopped on the steps of the kirk, the sun shining on her fair head, facing the crowd with flushed cheeks. The people of the valley went down on their knees before her, the men holding their hats to their hearts, the women with their heads bowed low. All swore as one to give their allegiance to Elfrida Nic-Hilde the true banprionnsa of Tìrsoilleir, and through her to the MacCuinn, Rìgh of all Eileanan.

So it was that when Lachlan rode out of Kirkclanbright the next day, his company was augmented by a platoon of men and women armed with axes, scythes, cleavers, pitchforks and spades. Lachlan was greatly heartened by this first sign of the power of the prophet's influence and began to hope they might have a repeat of their miraculous victory at Dùn Eidean, when they had broken the siege without needing to strike a single blow.

The company was in good spirits as it marched along the road towards the downs rising ahead of them. They did not sing, as most soldiers were wont to do when on the march, and Finn heard to her amazement that the Tìrsoilleirean frowned down upon music, singing and dancing, thinking them vain and frivolous. She wondered how Dide would be able to contain himself, for since she had been in his company a day had not gone by without the jongleur entertaining them all with his guitar-playing and singing.

He showed no sign of strain, however. His battered old guitar was tucked away out of sight and he was every inch the sober soldier. Again his appearance and behavior had undergone a subtle transformation. Instead of the rolling gait of a sailor, he walked with the brisk steps and upright posture of a military man. Instead of the rough oaths of a sailor, he spoke like a soldier, saying no more than was necessary and with absolutely no trace of humour. The golden earring had vanished and his dark hair was neatly tied back under the cockaded blue tam-o'-shanter of a Yeoman of the Guard. He carried a sword strapped to his back and had a slim black dagger thrust into his highly polished boots, and wore a blue kilt and cloak like all of Lachlan's general staff. He stood to attention when addressing the Rìgh and saluted smartly after being given his orders. It was as if he had never lived any other life than one of the Rìgh's most trusted officers. Finn was sure that if she had told any of their Tìrsoilleirean companions that Dide was indeed a roving minstrel, juggler and acrobat, they would have scorned to believe her.

Tam had reluctantly bid farewell to his sweetheart Bessie once more, having being appointed the company's guide through the downs. Although they were no longer so concerned about running into enemy squadrons, given their increased size and strength, Lachlan had decided that they should still try and keep a low profile until they had rejoined the Greycloaks. Consequently Tam had led them away from the highway, taking them along a little known route that wound across the downs and into the valley beyond, where Lachlan's scouts had located the rest of the army.

The downs were open, rolling hills, bare of any trees but covered in long grasses that waved in the breeze. Here and there great grey boulders thrust up out of the grass in uncanny formations. Tam knew the name of every cluster of stones and the stories behind them. Most had names like the Devil's Anvil, Satan's Steps, Temptation Rock or Auld Clootie's Footstep, so that Finn marvelled how much this Devil of the Tìrsoilleirean religion dominated their imagination.

Their path led them to a black cleft in the rock face called the Cloven Hoof. It reminded Finn of Ogre Pass at Cairncross, for the walls of the cliffs rose up high on either side, casting the pathway into deep shadow. It was an eerie, uncanny place. The downs fell away on either side, empty of any life. Tall grey rocks rose out of the rippling grass like crooked fingers, casting sinister shadows across the path. No birds sang. No coneys hopped about. No lizards baked in the sun. There was only the melancholy sigh of the wind amongst the time-weathered rocks.

Lachlan surveyed the Cloven Hoof grimly, saying, "I dislike the look o' this, my lad. Is there no other way through?"

Tam shook his head.

"Och then, happen we should hurry through afore we begin to lose the light," Iseult said. "Tell everyone to make haste and keep a close eye out, for I've never seen a likelier spot for an ambush."

"But who would ken we came this way?" Tam objected. "And if they kent, who would tell?"

Lachlan and Iseult exchanged a glance. "There are spies and traitors everywhere, Tam," the Rìgh said grimly.

The young sailor swallowed, losing some of his sun-burnt colour.

"Let us hope none have betrayed us, though," Lachlan said with a smile. "Our luck may still hold. Come, lead the way, lad!"

As the soldiers began to march through in single file, all keeping a cautious eye out, Lachlan beckoned to Gwilym who limped forward, leaning on his staff. "Ugly, can ye sense any hostile minds about? I have an uneasy feeling about this."

"So do I," Gwilym answered, his beetling brows drawn down upon his hooked nose. "This be an evil place, though. There has been murder done here before, and much blood shed. And ye ken as well as I do that it be difficult to sense an ambush when there already be such a crowd o' people here, all jostling with thoughts and emotions. If ye would all draw away for a while, happen I could get a clearer idea."

"Too late," Iseult said. "Already we have begun to march through and, besides, we do no' have time for loitering. Already the sun is beginning to go down and we want to reach the Greycloaks while there is still light, if we can."

Duncan Ironfist trotted up beside them, saying with a smart salute, "Are ye ready to ride through, your Highness?"

Lachlan nodded and the captain of the Blue Guards wheeled his horse about so he rode before the Rìgh, his sword drawn. Dillon rode next with his hand clasped on *Joyeuse*'s ornate hilt, his big shaggy dog loping along at his horse's heels. Iseult fell into place behind her husband, and Dide spurred forward his mount, the big chestnut Harlen, so that he too guarded her back. The other officers trotted close behind, surrounding Iain and a pale-faced Elfrida, all with swords drawn or bows at the ready.

Finn was at the rear of the company with Ashlin, Brangaine, Jay, Enit, Killian, Nellwyn, Tòmas, Johanna and the other healers, all of them crowded into three wagons drawn by big carthorses donated by the village of Kirkclanbright. They had their own guard of twenty-five soldiers, led by one of Lachlan's officers, a young man called Sweeney. Although Finn had protested when Lachlan had insisted her horse be given to Dide, she was secretly rather glad to be travelling in the wagon with her friends instead of battling the big chestnut. It was like old times, having the League of the Healing Hand back together again, after so many years apart.

At last it came time for them to move forward into the Cloven Hoof. Jay slapped the reins on the carthorse's brown rump and clicked his tongue, and the horse strode forward, the little wagon bouncing over the ruts of the path, already greatly churned by the boots and hooves of those that had gone before.

The sunlight was blocked out and a chill fell upon them. Brangaine pulled her plaid more tightly about her, saying, "Ooh, I dinna like this place. I'll be glad when we are on the other side and safe within the army camp."

Finn nodded her agreement, cuddling Goblin up to her neck. She stared back at the narrow gash of sunlight behind them. Her heart suddenly lurched. "Look!" she cried. "Flaming dragon balls, I just saw . . ."

Jay quickly turned around. "What?"

"I do no' ken . . . movement . . . a flash."

Jay stared back, then suddenly he dropped the reins to lift both hands to his mouth, giving a long resounding cry like that of a hunting horn. The sound bounced around the narrow canyon, causing horses to sidestep uneasily and men to cry aloud in alarm. Anyone who still had their weapons sheathed drew them and Lachlan launched Stormwing up into the sky, the hawk giving a long whistling cry as it flew up into the bright slit of sky.

Suddenly it shrieked a warning. In response, archers stood up all along the ridge and shot a deluge of arrows down into the ravine. Luckily Lachlan's men had had time to lift their shields or take cover behind the wagons, but the air was still rent with the sound of men and horses screaming as arrow after arrow found a target.

Then soldiers began to pour along the canyon, attacking the calvacade from the rear. They all wore heavy metal armour with long white surcoats emblazoned with a scarlet fitché cross.

"Bright Soldiers!" Johanna screamed. She had been present at many a battle between the Greyclocks and the Bright Soldiers and knew they were in acute danger indeed. She thrust Tòmas behind her and drew her dagger.

The gyrfalcon was harassing the archers with its swift, sudden descent, knocking down one after another with its clenched talons, slashing at their faces with its beak and blinding them with a flurry of white wings. One of the archers lifted his bow and aimed straight for the great white bird's breast. Just as he pulled back the string, an arrow from Lachlan's longbow struck him through the heart and he fell with a cry.

Man of the Blue Guards were attempting to swarm up the steep sides of the ravine so they could grapple with those attacking from above. Both Lachlan and

Iseult flew straight up out of the ravine, as swift as any bird, and began shooting the enemy with their bows and arrows. There were so many of the Bright Soldiers, however, that even with their deadly accuracy both Lachlan and Iseult were soon out of arrows and had to land on the ridge and fight hand-to-hand.

Meanwhile, the Bright Soldiers attacking from the rear were getting ever closer to the wagons. Sweeney and his men were fighting desperately to protect the wagons' precious load but they were being overwhelmed by the sheer force of numbers. Finn had her crossbow to her shoulder and was firing bolt after bolt at the attacking soldiers, but she was hampered by the heads of her friends which kept getting in her way.

"Get down, get down, ye gowks!" she screamed.

To her horror she saw Sweeney fall, then the Bright Soldiers were reaching up their gauntleted hands for the sides of the last wagon in the calvacade. In that wagon were Johanna, Tòmas, Killian and the team of healers. All it would take were a few quick strokes and all would be dead.

Finn leapt across the narrow gap between the two wagons, landing nimbly on the swingletree slung between the two carthorses harnessed to Johanna's wagon. The carthorses were all rearing and plunging in wild distress, for none were trained to battle, being only gentle farm animals more used to pulling a plough than hearing the screams of wounded men. Clinging to their harness, Finn swarmed across their backs and over the driver's seat, her dagger in her hand. Behind her, Jay was attempting to dodge the enormous flailing hooves, at last managing to dart past, attacking one of the soldiers with his narrow sword.

Johanna was slashing at the soldiers' hands with her

knife but they all wore steel gauntlets and she could
do no damage. One already was throwing his mail-
clad leg over the side of the wagon, though the healers
sought to throw him down again with all their
strength. The wagon lurched forward as the carthorse
tried to bolt, and the soldier fell back to the ground,
screaming as the wheel of the wagon rolled over him.

Finn looked about her wildly, then glanced up. The
deluge of arrows had faltered as the archers converged
on Lachlan and Iseult fighting desperately further
along the ravine. Quick as a thought Finn seized the
coil of nyx-hair rope that she wore at her waist, knotted it to one of her crossbow bolts and fired straight
up. The bolt flew up and embedded itself in a rock at
the height of the cliff. She tested it swiftly, then bent
and dragged up Tòmas, crouched white-faced against
the floor.

"Cling to me, laddie," she cried. "Do no' let go."

With the slight weight of Tòmas hanging about her
neck, she swarmed up the rope. A soldier grabbed her
leg. She kicked him in the face and he let go, clutching
at his broken nose. Another thrust at her with his
sword but she swung out of reach. It seemed to take
her mere seconds to reach the top of the cliff. She
crawled over, heaved Tòmas off her back, and peered
over the edge. Down below all was chaos. Finn lifted
her crossbow and fired at the soldier about to run Jay
through. The solider crumpled back, his sword falling
from his lifeless hand.

"Jay! The prophet!" she cried.

Jay cast her a wild glance but bent and picked up
the old man, who was shrinking back against the headboard in bewildered fear. Jay staggered under his
weight but managed to heave him over his shoulder.
He then seized the rope and tried to swarm up it as

Finn had done. He was no trained cat-thief, though, and frail as the old prophet was, he was still far heavier than Tòmas.

As Jay struggled with the rope, a soldier cut his way through the healers and raised his sword high, about to bring it down upon the young jongleur and his burden. Suddenly a small black fury leapt for his face with sharp claws raking. The soldier screamed and clutched at his bleeding eyes, and Goblin dashed away into the shadows again.

The elven cat had bought Jay a few seconds and in that time Finn desperately began to haul on the rope, even though she knew she did not have the strength to drag both Jay and Killian up the cliff. To her surprise, the rope was as light and easy to haul as if two men did not dangle on the end of it. She looked down with her heart springing into her mouth, afraid that they had fallen down, but Jay still clung to the rope, Killian draped over his shoulder.

*Nyx magic!* Finn thought with a glad spring of her heart. In seconds Jay was heaving himself over the lip of the cliff, dropping Killian to the ground. The young jongleur was panting with the effort but his hazel eyes were alight with triumph. "Well done, Finn!"

"We have to save the others too, if we can," Finn cried and leant over to call, "Johanna! All o' ye! Grab the rope!"

She tossed the rope back down and Johanna seized it with one hand, ordering her healers to grab hold of it.

"Pull them up," Finn ordered. "It's a nyx rope. It's magic! It'll help ye. I'll guard them."

She raised her crossbow and shot down a soldier thrusting his sword at one of the healers, then another seeking to drag down those clinging to the rope.

Slowly at first, then more swiftly, the rope slithered up the side of the cliff, three young women clinging to it. Jay helped them over as Finn continued to harass the soldiers below with her crossbow, then tossed the rope down again for Johanna and the other two remaining healers.

The ferocity of the battle in the ravine was beginning to die down. Many of the Rìgh's soldiers had managed to scale the cliffs and were fighting with those that had been concealed along the ridge. Others had run back to help protect the defenseless passengers in the wagons. Lachlan and Iseult were still fighting back to back, surrounded on all sides by a great pile of dead and wounded Bright Soldiers. The gyrfalcon fought with them, a bolt of white lightning that struck without warning from the twilight sky.

In the other wagon, Nellwyn and Enit had joined hands and raised up their enchanting voices. Sleeping soldiers were draped all round her wagon, their armoured chests rising and falling peacefully. Among the sleepers were Brangaine and Ashlin, both looking altogether too comfortable. "Think o' how we'll be able to tease them when they wake," she panted to Jay. "We're fighting to the death and they're snoring!"

"The fight's no' over yet," Jay said grimly, picking up his sword from where he had dropped it. "Finn, look out!"

Finn spun round and saw six Bright Soldiers racing to attack them, deadly intent on their faces. They had seen the white robes of the old prophet and knew they would achieve great distinction if they were the ones who managed to kill him.

The healers were not armed and Finn had used up all of her crossbow bolts. She drew her dagger with a curse, and stood shoulder to shoulder with Jay and

Johanna, all of them without shields or armour and untrained in the art of war. Suddenly a slim figure somersaulted over their heads and stood before them, a glittering eight-sided star in her hand. One arm was bleeding and her red braid was unravelling wildly, but Iseult was otherwise as cool and unflustered as if she was out for an evening walk.

"So, ye attack bairns and auld men, do ye?" she asked. "Cowards!"

The six soldiers yelled in response and charged. The *reil* spun out of her hand, circling round to slice through two of the men's throats, cutting through the heavy chainmail like a knife through butter. They fell, gurgling horribly, and Iseult drew her long skewer, the only weapon she had left in her belt.

The four remaining soldiers had not even faltered, merely leaping over the fallen bodies of their comrades and thrusting their swords straight towards Iseult's heart. She spun round on one foot, knocking one down with a powerful kick to the head and disarming another with a skilful flick of her wrist. His sword spun up into the air and she caught it and engaged the other two soldiers in a flurry of thrusts and feints too fast to follow with the eye. The disarmed soldier tried to grasp her from the back, and she kicked back with her boot, striking him in the groin. He wore heavy armour though, so he hardly flinched, smashing her in the face with his gauntleted fist. She fell, and Jay lunged forward with his narrow sword, shouting in horror. He stabbed the soldier right through the visor of his helmet, and the Bright Soldier fell back, the sword embedded in his eye. The other two soldiers were upon them, though, and they had only Johanna and Finn's daggers left.

Finn tossed hers to Jay and then quickly knelt and

tugged at her rope. To her amazement the knot slithered free instantly. *I canna have tied that very well,* she thought. *Lucky it did no' come undone afore!*

She spun round, her nimble fingers tying a running bowline so that the rope was tied into a loop that could be loosened and tightened at will. Then she spun the rope as she had seen the horsemen of Tìreich do and threw it at one of the soldiers. To her delight, it fell down about his shoulders and tightened with a jerk that knocked him off his feet. As he went down his flailing legs caught his comrade behind the knees and he fell too with a great huff as his breath was knocked out of him. Iseult had staggered to her feet, blood masking her face from her nose and mouth. She brought her sword to rest on the soldier's throat. "I would no' try to rise," she said conversationally and he lay still, staring up at her through the slits in his visor. "Good decision," she said, and wiped her bloody mouth with the back of her hand. Then she glanced across at Finn. "Nice rope trick," she said. "Where did ye ken to do that?"

Finn was still rather astounded at the success of her stratagem. "Saw a Tìreichan spinning a rope like that and thought I'd give it a go," she answered rather breathlessly. Iseult raised one thin red brow and Finn confessed, "Nyx rope. I think it's magic."

Iseult nodded. "The gifts o' the nyx are like that, it seems. Well, quick thinking anyway, Finn! Ye're a worthy addition to the company indeed."

Finn flushed with pleasure as Dide came running up behind them, to help disarm the remaining soldiers and march them away with the other prisoners. Despite having every advantage of surprise, numbers and terrain, the Bright Soldiers had proved no match for the Blue Guards. They had suffered heavy losses indeed and, although many of Lachlan's supporters had been killed or wounded, the key players were all still alive. Tòmas was able to lay his hands upon the injured and heal them, and within half an hour all were almost ready to march on again, the dead laid out on one of the wagons and the prisoners all bound and herded together in the centre.

After close questioning, one of the Bright Soldiers had let slip the name of the man who had betrayed them. To no-one's surprise it was Dick Dickson and Lachlan had sent back a messenger to the pastor of Kirkclanbright with the news, knowing the people of the valley would exact their own rough justice.

Finn and the others were all sitting on the edge of the ridge, recovering their strength after the strenuous battle and teasing Brangaine and Ashlin about having slept through it all. The sun was now very low in the sky, and the downs were all lit with a dim red light while to the east stars were already beginning to prick through the twilight.

Tòmas was lying with his head on Johanna's lap, his hand over his eyes. As usual, the effort of healing so many had exhausted him and he was looking very white. Suddenly he lifted his head and said in a small voice, "Something bad is happening."

"What, dearling?"

"Something bad is happening."

Finn and Johanna exchanged worried glances. They had heard the little boy say that before.

"Where, dearling?"

Tòmas raised himself on the elbow and pointed back the way they had come. "Over there."

Finn stared off into the twilight. With a sinking heart she saw a faint smudge of smoke, almost invisible against the twilight sky. They all stared at it for a few minutes, then Finn got slowly to her feet. "Toasted toads, I'd best go tell Lachlan and Iseult."

She found the Rìgh and Banrìgh on the far side of the Cloven Hoof, making the final preparations before giving the order to ride out. They looked at each other in dismay at the news.

"Kirkclanbright?"

"I hope no'," Lachlan replied. In all of their mind's eye was a picture of the serene little valley with its slow river and the tall spire of its kirk soaring above the golden-brown trees. "I fear it is but a vain hope, though, *leannan*." Suddenly he smashed one hand into the palm of the other. "I should've kent, I should've suspected! Damn that Dickson and his nasty sly face."

"What should we do?" Duncan Ironfist asked, distress on his battered face. "If we can see the smoke from here it is too late to do aught but try and succour those left alive."

Lachlan nodded angrily. "We must go back. It is on our account that they incurred the displeasure o' the Bright Soldiers. We must take Tòmas and the healers and see what we can do." He gave a deep sigh then straightened his shoulders once more. "The purpose o' battle is slaughter and the price o' victory is blood," he quoted. "I do no' ken why I always find it so hard to remember this."

Iseult took his face between her hands and kissed him. "Because ye are at heart a good and gentle man," she said. "And that is why I love ye."

Weary of heart and body, the company turned round and headed back the way they had come. It seemed like a very long time ago. As they came down the road into the valley of Kirkclanbright, they could see flames still leaping high all through the valley. The kirk blazed like a torch, casting rippling orange reflections across the river. Where Rowanglen had stood was a smoldering ruin.

Tam was hurrying at the head of the calvacade, and he cried aloud in pain. "No, no! Da! Mam!"

Beside him were the other folk of Kirkclanbright, who had set out so blithely that morning. Many of them cried aloud in distress. Some wept, leaning on their pitchforks.

"The Bright Soldiers may still be about," Lachlan said grimly. "Och, no, Tam! Take care!"

Tam had gone running up the avenue of rowan trees, not heeding the Rìgh's shout. Dide dashed after him, his sword drawn, and the others followed in close formation.

Tam's father and mother and sister were all working to douse the flames, their faces black with soot. Tam threw himself on his mother with a great sob of relief. "Ye're alive!"

"We took refuge in the woods," Great Tam said shortly. "Bessie o' the Apples came running to warn us. They saw the kirk being torched and guessed what had happened."

"I'm so sorry, I'm so sorry," Tam wept.

"Och, lad, it is no' your fault," his mother said, setting down her buckets with a sigh. "It is the Fealde's black-hearted soldiers that set the fires, no' ye."

"The Bright Soldiers always have to burn," Lachlan said sombrely. "Ye should have seen what they did to Blèssem. It was a black char-pit when they finished with it, no' a tree or head o' corn left standing."

As he spoke the Rìgh was signaling to his soldiers to help put out the fire and although all had marched a long way and fought a hard battle, they set to with willing hands.

"I am so very sorry that your help to me should be so cruelly rewarded," Lachlan said.

Great Tam shrugged. "Well, we truly be at war now." He spoke stiffly, gazing at his ruined house with sombre eyes, but there was no rancour in his voice.

"Aye," Lachlan said unhappily. "I am sorry but we must ride on. There are others that must be helped too. I will leave a squad o' soldiers to guard ye and assist ye."

"Well, thank ye for that," Great Tam replied.

All night they worked to douse the flames and help the injured. The Bright Soldiers had been swift and brutal in their reprisals, but luckily many had been forewarned and had taken refuge in the forest. Only a few had lost their lives, among them the rotund little pastor, struck down while trying to save his kirk.

A patrol of Lachlan's soldiers found the Bright Soldiers camped only a few miles away, all enjoying a good night's rest after their long day's labour. The captain had not expected any trouble and so had set only one sentry who was easily overcome, allowing the patrol to capture the entire encampment without the shedding of a single drop of blood. They were taken back to Kirkclanbright and lashed in with the other prisoners, stripped of their armour and weapons, with chains about their wrists and necks.

"I hate prisoners," Lachlan said gloomily. "What am I meant to do with them?"

"Set them to work rebuilding Kirkclanbright," Iseult said.

"Whatsoever a man soweth, that shall he also reap," Killian said in agreement.

Lachlan sighed and nodded. "Very well. I shall leave a company o' soldiers here to assist and guard them, and to scour the countryside for any more o' the blaygird things. Eà's green blood, I hate Bright Soldiers!"

Just then Duncan Ironfist came riding up with a squad of Yeoman. Across his lap was slumped the figure of a man. Duncan let him fall to the ground. It was Dick Dickson. He lay in the dust, his head twisted unnaturally, his eyes closed. Blood seeped from three deep wounds in his breast.

"We found him impaled to his front door with a pitchfork," Duncan said shortly. "No way o' kenning who the pitchfork belongs to. Every house in this valley has a few."

Lachlan nodded. "Very well. Bury him with the others." He sighed and rubbed his eyes with his fingers. "Well. What now?"

"Now we bide a wee and rest up," Iseult said. "Tomorrow we'll ride out once more."

He nodded, his face shadowed. She laid her hand on the back of his neck, under his curls.

"I am sick o' the stench o' death and ashes," Lachlan said. "I seem to carry it round with me, like Gearradh's cloak."

"We are at war," Iseult answered.

"Fancy that," Lachlan replied. "Who would have guessed?"

She smiled at him wearily. "Come and wash your face and hands. Ye're as black as chimney sweep's arse, as Finn would say. Happen when ye are clean ye shall no' think ye spread the stench o' death like Gearradh!"

# SAMHAIN WISHES

$\mathcal{A}$utumn laid its bright mantle over the land of
Tìrsoilleir. Stags bellowed in the forest, and the
swineherds knocked down nuts from the trees
to fatten the pigs before they were slaughtered for the
winter. The villages were pungent with the smell of
freshly brewed ale. In the mornings mist lay heavy
over the valleys, the bare crests of the downs rising
like islands out of a white sea. Although the days remained warm, the nights were cool and crisp and the
Greycloaks were all glad to huddle close around their
campfires.

Bride, the capital city of Tìrsoilleir, lay just on the
other side of the bay but the Greycloaks were in no
hurry to besiege the home of the Great Kirk just yet.
They had won all of southern Tìrsoilleir to their cause
with only a few battles and minor skirmishes, and were
now intent on moving at a leisurely pace across the
Alainn River and through northern Tìrsoilleir to approach Bride from the rear. All hoped the northern
lairds would be as quick to pledge their support to
Elfrida NicHilde as the southern lairds had been.

At first Lachlan had been restless and edgy, wanting
to thrust towards Bride in a great rush of raw energy,
hoping they would carry all before them. He was sick
of the war and anxious to be at home with his wife

and children, enjoying the fruits of peace. His firstborn son and heir, Donncan, was now five and half years old while the younger children, the twins Owein and Olwynne, were only eighteen months in age. Their mother and father had been absent for a quarter of their entire life. It hurt Lachlan greatly to be missing out on this stage of their growth, when they were all wonder and delight. Although they received regular news of home, Lachlan wanted to be there with them, not hearing it all second-hand.

Iseult missed her children terribly too but it was she who had counselled patience. "Now is the time to be like snow," she told him. "Snow is gentle, snow is silent, snow is inexorable. Fight hard against snow and it will always smother you with its softness and silence. Submit to snow and it will melt away afore you."

Lachlan had been impatient with her Scarred Warrior maxims, but to his surprise Leonard the Canny and Duncan Ironfist had agreed with her.

"Aye, ye should let the rumour mill work on your behalf," Leonard said. "Already the tales o' your rescue o' the auld prophet are racing around the country like wildfire. Allow time for speculation and wondering. Let the people talk amongst themselves and, as much as possible, give them the chance to hear Killian speak so that he can sway them with his words. Allow time for the lairds to approach us and discuss terms, and weigh the matter carefully. None will throw in their lot with us quickly. They need time to consider the consequences."

"This is the one time when biding our time will be to our advantage," Duncan agreed. "The Bright Soldiers are in the superior position here. They are all trained from birth, while our soldiers were being apprenticed as farmers and blacksmiths and cobblers.

They are fighting on their own terrain and have all the advantages of supplies and numbers. Let us no' waste our strength on futile charges. Let us remember the lessons we learnt during the Bright Wars. Remember the tactics that worked so well at Dùn Eidean and Rhyssmadill? Let us allow the prophet to do his work, as Jorge the Seer did so well; let us use trickery and deception where we can; let us build up a fearsome reputation so that they truly believe we have the hand o' their god upon us, and see if we can win this war without striking a single blow."

"By biding our time, we shall be making the Fealde very nervous," Leonard said in satisfaction. "And that can only bode well for us."

So Lachlan repressed his homesickness and his impatience and did as they counselled. Killian the Listener preached in every village square and kirk, and the crowds that came to listen to him grew greater every week. Elfrida rode out on her white palfrey, visiting the sick and the poor with the healers, meeting with the local lairds and guildmasters, and stopping to talk to plump matrons in the marketplaces. With her sweet face and demure manner, she soon became a favourite with the countryfolk, many of whom retained a romantic longing for the old days when the MacHilde clan had ruled.

Strict discipline was maintained amongst the army. It moved slowly and inexorably, accompanied by its own supply wagons laden with sacks of grains, bales of hay and poultry in coops, and its own herds of pigs, sheep and goats. Any extra supplies that were needed were paid for by the quartermaster, a shrewd and canny man known for his excellent bargaining ability. Consequently, the dismay which the sight of the Greycloaks had once engendered was replaced by eagerness amongst the local farmers and merchants, confident that their women and possessions would be in no danger and that a fair price would be paid for their merchandise.

There were many clashes with bands of Bright Soldiers, but the Greycloaks were never persuaded into pursuing their enemies, concentrating on choosing their ground well and keeping a tight formation, making it difficult for the Tìrsoilleirean army to do more than harass their edges. The closer the Greycloaks drew to the Alainn River, the more frequently the skirmishes occurred but the sheer size and weight of the Rìgh's army and the hilly terrain discouraged any major confrontations.

Lachlan and Iseult passed the days studying with Gwilym the Ugly, learning as much as they could about the Tìrsoilleirean religion and culture, and practising their fighting skills. Dide was often to be found studying with them, although he was still reluctant to pledge himself fully to the Coven. He was fascinated by magic, however, and eager to learn more. Jay, Finn and Brangaine also joined the lessons daily, all finding to their pleasure a natural adeptness at the use of the One Power. Gwilym the Ugly was a stern taskmaster, but an excellent teacher. He imbued them all with a love of knowledge for its own sake, so that Finn found herself borrowing books to read later and pestering him with questions about all sorts of things. Gwilym had spent the years of the Burning at the Tower of Mists, the only witches' tower where the ancient library remained intact, so he had an extraordinary breadth and depth of knowledge.

Dide and Jay also spent much of their time with Enit and Nellwyn, learning more about the use of magic through music. Ashlin often joined them there, leaving Finn and Brangaine to their own devices. They helped Johanna and the other healers gather leaves, flowers, roots, nuts, seeds and bark, and learnt how to grind them or distill their precious essences to make medicines, healing salves and pain-numbing potions. They accompanied Elfrida on her expeditions, sat in on many of the war conferences, and played many a game of trictrac or cards, Finn puffing away on her pipe. Brangaine even joined Finn in her daily fighting lessons with the other soldiers, learning how to draw a bow, wield a short sword, and repel an attacker with one quick, fluid movement.

They crossed the Alainn River a week after the autumn equinox, and fought their first bloody battle. Though the cost was high, the Greycloaks were eventually victorious, driving the Bright Soldiers back and securing the land all the way up to the Great Divide. Once again Lachlan wanted to press their advantage, but was counselled again to bide his time. Reluctantly he submitted to his advisors and set up camp at a strongly walled town called Kirkenny, built within the deep curve of the river so it was surrounded on three sides by water. From there they rode out in small, well-guarded expeditions, Killian preaching in the kirks, Lachlan and Elfrida meeting with the local powers, the soldiers clashing with those who still stood against them. On each occasion the Greycloaks were able to overwhelm the Tìrsoilleirean army with their speed and ferocity, or unnerve them with clever tricks. The Greycloaks began to be regarded with superstitious awe, the countryfolk whispering that they were protected by God and could not be beaten.

One night, in late October, a pigeon arrived from Lucescere with letters for the Rìgh and Banrìgh. Lachlan had been absent from his lands for four months and had been anxious indeed for news. Eager to hear what had been happening in the rest of the country, Finn and the others clustered close around the Rìgh's pavilion. As usual, they had joined Lachlan and Iseult for their evening meal, which was served on a long trestle table set with candelabra and fine tableware. Gwilym the Ugly, Elfrida, Iain, the two seanalairs Duncan and Leonard, and Lachlan's staff of officers also joined the meal every night. Dinner was usually followed by much talk and laughter, some soft-voiced performances from Nellwyn and the jongleurs, and games of chance. Tonight, however, all gathered round to hear the news.

The package had to be small by necessity, since it was carried by a pigeon, but it had been written in very small writing and contained much news of interest. The Fairgean were on the rise again, returning to their winter home after spending the summer in the southern seas. A new coast watch set up by the MacRuraich had proved most helpful in tracking their movements, however, and some defensive measures had been taken that had proved to be of use. Also from Rurach came the news that Gwyneth NicSian was once again with child. Finn was both happy and astounded by this news, whispering to Jay, "Och, well, Da must have managed to spend *some* time at home this summer!"

"Isabeau also writes that the NicThanach has finally given birth to a very healthy little boy, which be glad news indeed," Iseult said. She was reading the letter out, being the only one able to decipher her twin sister's cramped handwriting. "They have called him Fymbar, because he be so tow-headed, then Lachlan for ye, *leannan*."

"Och, that be nice o' them," Lachlan said smiling. "Fymbar Lachlan MacThanach is a grand name!"

"She says Meghan is very happy with the progress o' the students in the Theurgia, though she willna admit it, o' course, calling them all woolly-headed slowpokes."

Lachlan grinned and made a wry comment, and Iseult went on, "Apparently she has taken on a new apprentice now Isabeau is a fully fledged witch. He's a young boy with a shadow-hound for a familiar. Fancy that! Isabeau says all the dogs in the city come to his whistle."

"That must be a sight to see!" Lachlan grinned. "What about the laddiekins, *leannan*. Does she no' write o' them?"

"Isabeau says the lads are as artful as a bagful o' elven cats. Look, Elfrida, she's enclosed a letter for ye from Neil. She says his lessons are coming along well."

Neil was Iain and Elfrida's son, only three months younger than Donncan. He had been sent to stay in the safety of Lucescere while his parents rode to war, for Donncan and he were the very best of friends. Elfrida received the roughly scrawled missive with an upwelling of tears, turning it over proudly and exclaiming at how well he was forming his letters now.

"*Leannan*, Isabeau says Olwynne is talking quite well now but that Owein hardly says a word, letting his sister do all the asking for him. We shall have to do something about that when we get home! Oh, but she says Owein has taken his first flight! Oh, Lachlan, he be only nineteen months auld. Did Donncan fly so young?"

"I canna remember, *leannan*. I do no' think so," Lachlan replied proudly. He and Iseult smiled at each other, both feeling a tightness in their throat at the thought they had missed their baby boy's first flight.

"What else does Isabeau say?" Dide asked eagerly. "Has she truly decided to stay at the Tower o' Two Moons now?"

Iseult nodded. "Aye. I told ye she sat for her Third Test o' Powers on Midsummer's Eve, the night we were all meeting clandestinely at Rhyssmadill? Well, she says here that she has already sat her First Test o' Elements and won her ring o' fire. She is wearing the ruby ring that she found at the Cursed Towers, the one that belonged to our ancestor Faodhagan the Red."

"Och, she mun be aye powerful, this sister o' yours," Nellwyn said. "To be only twenty-two and already admitted into the Coven as a fully fledged witch, and then to win her first elemental ring within only a few months!"

"Aye, the Keybearer believes she may be the strongest young witch the Coven has found since the Burning," Gwilym said. "Definitely a chance for a new sorceress there, I'd say."

Dide had been staring into the depths of his goblet, but now he raised it to his lips and tossed back the dark wine within. "Well, that would make the Keybearer happy," he said wryly and poured himself another cup, slopping some of the wine on the white tablecloth. "Let us drink to Isabeau the Red and her ruby ring!" he cried, leaping to his feet and holding his goblet high.

"To Isabeau!" the table echoed, sipping their wine.

"And to Fymbar Lachlan MacThanach, heir to Blèssem," Lachlan said, and everyone toasted the new baby enthusiastically.

"To those we've left behind," Elfrida said tearfully, clutching her little boy's letter. This toast was drunk with eagerness, many sighing and looking pensive.

"To my mam's belly!" Finn cried.

"Aye, to the expectant mother," Lachlan said and drank deeply.

"To peace," Dide said sombrely and the laughter died away, everyone at the long table nodding and repeating, "To peace," as they drank.

"Well, that be all the news," Iseult said, folding the pages away.

"How about some music, Dide?" Lachlan said.

The young jongleur looked up from his goblet. "Aye, why no'?"

Connor was sent running to fetch his guitar, and everyone refilled their glasses and sat back to enjoy his song. For once, Dide did not play some ribald song of seduction or a humorous ballad designed to set everyone laughing. He strummed his guitar softly, the candlelight flickering over his olive-skinned face, with its straight, fine nose, sensuously curved mouth, and dark eyes now brooding with shadows. Then he began to sing a very old, very plaintive tune. So very unhappy was his voice, so full of heartfelt emotion, that many of those present cleared their throats, thinking of their own loves they had left far behind. Lachlan reached out and took Iseult's hand, and Elfrida nestled her head on Iain's shoulder, the ready tears once again springing to her eyes.

"Long have we been parted, lassie my darlin',
Now we are met again, lassie, lie near me.
Near me, near me, lassie, lie near me,
Long have ye been away, lassie lie near me.
All that I have endured, lassie my darlin'
Here in your arms is cured, lassie, lie near me.
Near me, near me, lassie, lie near me,
Long have ye been away, lassie lie near me.

Say that ye'll aye be true, say ye'll n'er deceive
    me
And I'll love none but ye, my darlin', lassie lie
    near me.
Near me, near me, lassie, lie near me,
Long have ye been away, lassie lie near me.
If we were n'er to part, lassie my darlin'
My joy would be complete, lassie, lie near me.
Near me, near me, lassie, lie near me,
Long have ye been away, lassie lie near me."

His voice sighed away into silence, the last chords of
the music dying away. Then the long hush was broken
by uproarious applause. Dide bowed, unsmiling, and
then came back to his seat.

"Och, ye are such a performer, Dide," Finn cried.
"So wistful ye sounded, anyone would think ye really
felt the bitter pangs o' unrequited love." She rolled
her eyes, her hand to her heart.

Dide stared down at her, colour running up into his
cheeks. Then abruptly he turned and walked out of
the pavilion and into the dusk, his shoulders very stiff.

"Flaming dragon balls, what's up with him?" Finn
asked in bewilderment.

Jay hesitated then leant forward, saying very softly,
"Ye should no' tease him so, Finn."

"But what's his problem?"

Brangaine leant forward, her face soft. "He's in
love, is he?"

Jay nodded. "Aye, he has loved her a very long
time. He says since he first saw her, when they were
but bairns."

"But why . . . Does she no' love him too?"

Jay shook his head. "I do no' think she even kens."

"But, roasted rats, that's ridiculous," Finn answered. "What's wrong with the lass? Dide's as bonny a man as I've ever seen, quick and clever and funny. And he fights like a lion and sings like a nightingale, and is the Rìgh's best friend. What more could she want?"

Jay cast her a quick glance, full of trouble and anger. "Love is an unaccountable thing. Like lightning, it strikes at random. Who is to say why one person loves another?" His voice was stifled with emotion and Brangaine looked at him with a little frown.

Finn did not notice, however, saying, "What a gowk that girl must be! Who is it? Anyone we ken?"

Jay would not answer but Brangaine said, "This evening, when Isabeau the Red was mentioned, I saw such a look in his eye, a look of such longing, I could no' help but wonder . . ."

Jay shifted uncomfortably, colour rising in his lean cheeks.

"Isabeau?" Finn cried. "But o' course. When we were at Lucescere he was always dancing with her and singing her love songs, and hanging on her shoulder. Why did I no' see it?" She gave a sigh. "Isabeau the Red. How romantic."

Brangaine was shocked, however. "But is she no' the Banrìgh's own sister? No wonder he looks so unhappy. Such a union would be impossible."

"Why?" Finn demanded.

"I am sure the Rìgh has planned a grand wedding for her, one o' great advantage to the throne. The Rìgh would never allow his sister-in-law, a NicFaghan, to marry a mere jongleur."

Jay was silent, staring broodingly into his wine. Finn leapt immediately to Dide's defense.

"Why not? Dide is Lachlan's greatest friend, I have often heard him say so. And Isabeau is no simpering corn-dolly to be married off to some rich laird just because it would be to Lachlan's advantage! She's a powerful witch, ye heard them say so tonight. She has always gone her own way!"

"Even so, there are few enough o' the blood left to make it unwise for her to choose her own destiny," Brangaine said. "Isabeau NicFaghan has a duty to her family, just like ye and I do, Finn. We canna be marrying just anyone, or directing our lives to suit ourselves."

Colour rose in Finn's cheeks. "Flaming dragon balls, why no'?" she demanded, scrambling to her feet. "Why should we be sacrificed just because our ancestors were witches o' the First Coven? I never asked to be a banprionnsa. There's no way I'm going to let myself be married off to some fat auld hog o' a laird just because he be rich!"

With Goblin stalking after her, tail raised high, Finn strode off into the darkness, leaving Jay and Brangaine staring after her.

"Poor Finn," Brangaine said. "She does no' realise that being a banprionnsa has its duties and responsibilities as well as privileges. She will learn in time."

"Are Finn's parents like that?" Jay's voice was troubled. "Will they really try and marry her off for some kind o' political advantage?"

"O' course they will," Brangaine answered. "Och, they are kind and loving indeed, and very indulgent o' Finn's wildness. But she is heir to the throne o' Rurach. It has been a troubled decade in our part o' the world. There has been much hardship and both Siantan and Rurach have lost much o' their wealth. A good marriage will do much to mend matters, as well as setting up new trade opportunities and political treaties. The MacRuraich will be considering all possible suitors very carefully indeed."

There was a long pause, then Jay said, "And be that true o' ye too, Bran?"

"Och, o' course," she answered. "I am the NicSian. My people depend upon me. As soon as I come o' age, the management o' the country will be in my hands. I must make a good marriage. My husband must have strength and wealth enough to help me rule my country as it should be ruled. I have always kent that."

"Someone auld and powerful then," Jay said bitterly.

Brangaine smiled. "He must be young enough to breed up heirs."

"That's sickening!"

"Nay, why? It's the reality o' life as a banprionnsa. I have been brought up to it and ken the importance o' it. Finn, unfortunately, has no'. She will have to learn."

Jay said nothing but there was such a condemnatory quality to his silence that Brangaine said defensively, "She will be the NicRuraich."

The next morning Finn sought Dide out and apologised to him, and he laughed at her and said that it was him that should be saying sorry. "I was just in a bad mood, Finn. I want this war to be over and all o' us back in our rightful places."

"I do no' ken where my rightful place is," she said rather unhappily.

He stared at her. "But ye have a family and a home. Ye will return there, o' course."

"I suppose so."

"Do ye no' wish to?"

"It's no' that," she said. "It's just I really do no' want to be a banprionnsa. I wish I could do this forever."

"This?" Dide said mockingly. "Hang around waiting for the war?"

"Well, nay. But travel about and have adventures and see new places. Like ye do."

"Och, ye mean, ye wish ye could be a spy and an adventurer like me," Dide said. Although he spoke laughingly there was a bitter shade to his voice that made Finn look at him questioningly. "Be careful what ye wish for, Finn; ye just might get it."

"But, toasted toads, I'd love to get it," Finn said.

"Ye do no' ken what ye are saying, lass. Be happy with what ye have. Many girls dream o' being heir to a throne and a castle."

"Porridge-heads," she said.

Dide could not help but smile. "I mean it, Finn. Mine is a hard and dangerous life, and lonely too. I slip in and out o' people's lives, always playing a part, always ready to betray them for my master. I am his ears and his eyes in the countryside, scenting out rebellion, searching for traitors, telling the tales the Rìgh wants told. I can trust no-one but my own family and even them I doubt sometimes, so cynical that I get. Ye do no' want that, Finn. When this is all over ye will go home and hunt in your hills and dance with the young men o' the court. And when ye are a wee bit aulder, ye will fall in love and marry and have bairns, and be happy and at peace. These are all good things, Finn; do no' be throwing them away for the lure o' adventure. It's naught but a will-o'-the-wisp that will lead ye into danger and misery, and ultimately to your death."

Dide spoke with real feeling in his voice. Finn stared

at him, feeling doubt for the first time. He had given her the opportunity she had been waiting for, however, and so she said boldly, "Why do ye no' give it up then, Dide? Marry and have bairns and be happy, if that is what ye want?"

"Marriage is no' for me, Finn."

"Why no'?"

Goaded, he cried, "Because I canna have the lass I want and if I canna have her, I dinna want anyone."

"But I'm sure if ye told her . . . Ye could make her fall in love with ye; all the lassies are always falling in love with ye, Dide. Why do ye no' just seduce her?"

He quirked up one side of his mouth. "Och, I've tried that."

"And she dinna want ye? I never thought Isabeau was a fool!"

Immediately he stiffened, colour surging up his lean, brown cheeks. Finn quailed a little before his angry look but said, "I'm sure if ye let her ken how ye feel, Isabeau would . . ."

"Isabeau is a NicFaghan and I am a nobody," Dide snapped. "What do I have to offer her: a life on the road, sleeping under a caravan and juggling oranges for a living? She has already told me such a life is no' to her taste."

"What a dray-load o' dragon dung! Ye're no' a nobody, ye're a Yeoman o' the Guard and the Rìgh's best friend," Finn snapped back. "I canna see why ye canna retire from being a jongleur if ye wanted to. There's plenty o' other things ye could do. And I'm sure Isabeau does no' care if ye do no' have a last name. I wouldna!"

"Well, thank ye, Finn," Dide answered sarcastically. "But there's more to it than that. Isabeau wants to be a sorceress and ye ken they do no' marry."

"But . . ."

"Thank ye for your concern, Finn, but if ye dinna mind, I'd really rather no' talk about it." He resettled his sword at his waist and walked away, his shoulders under the blue cloak set very rigidly indeed. Finn sighed and pulled at Goblin's tufted ears.

To Finn's dismay, a constraint grew up between her and Dide after this conversation and, to her bewilderment, between her and Jay. Up until the night of Isabeau's letter, all had been comfortable between them, Finn having forgotten or forgiven Jay's kiss on Midsummer Eve and falling into her old habit of easy discourse with him. She thought it might have been because Jay had told her about Dide's feelings for Isabeau, which the jongleur clearly did not like being common knowledge.

Finn took to spending much of her time with Ashlin the Piper, for he seemed to find everything she did right and appropriate and never regarded her with Brangaine's air of faint disapproval or Jay's miserable silence. He flushed with pleasure every time she stopped to speak with him and was the only one who did not lecture her for gambling at cards or puffing away on her pipe all the time.

She also spent a lot of time with Dillon, having persuaded him to give her extra lessons in fighting. The young squire was already one of the most skilled and powerful fighters in the Rìgh's retinue and Finn hoped he would teach her some of the Scarred Warrior tricks he had learnt from Iseult. Although Finn in many ways missed the Scruffy she had known, she found a new respect growing in her for the sombre, reserved man Dillon had become. The shadow of the cursed sword he carried had transformed him from a cocky beggarboy, quick with his fists and his tongue, to someone who was thoughtful and deliberate in his every word and action. Dillon knew that once he drew *Joyeuse* he must fight until all his opponents were dead and so he never drew her unless under great duress. When he and Finn sparred, they always use wooden practice swords, though *Joyeuse* was never far from Dillon's hand or eye.

Samhain Eve came as dark and silent-footed as Goblin the elven cat, a heavy mist lying in all the valleys and shrouding Kirkenny in a thin, cold veil. In Lucescere, the night of death was defied by the lighting of many lanterns and bonfires, the ringing of bells and the wearing of lively colours. Here in Tìrsoilleir, the people locked themselves in their houses and drew their curtains. Samhain Eve was the night when ghosts walked and evil spirits were about. No Tìrsoilleirean dared brave such a night.

Lachlan and his retinue had debated what to do about Samhain Eve for some time. Lachlan had no desire to alienate his new allies by flaunting his paganism but believed he must celebrate the differences between their cultures while still staying true to his heritage. Consequently, Samhain Eve was to be celebrated as it had always been in his youth. A great fire was to be lit in the great hall of Keep Kirkenny, chains of lanterns had been strung along the walls, hollowed-out turnips carved into the semblance of fearsome faces grinning with fiery eyes and mouth, and a magnificent feast was spread out on the tables. Everyone in Kirkenny, from the laird of the castle to the humblest chimneysweep, was welcome to attend the festivities but none would be condemned for staying away.

Rather to Lachlan's surprise, quite a few of the townsfolk of Kirkenny braved the mizzling weather and the ghosts to attend, some even making some effort to brighten their sombre dress with the last leaves of the year or a knot of grey ribbon. None of the Greycloaks had brought any party clothes with them, but all had managed to find some vivid article of clothing so that the great hall was filled with colour and movement. All the musicians had dug out their instruments and played in public for the first time since arriving on Tìrsoilleirean soil, and squares and lines of dancers swung back and forth across the hallway. Although none of the Tìrsoilleirean guests dared join in, a few seemed to enjoy the spectacle and any condemnation was politely concealed, much to Elfrida's amazement.

"I never thought I'd see music and dancing in *Tìrsoilleir,*" she said to Iseult, "let alone the laird o' the castle tapping his foot to it!"

"Times change," Iseult replied.

"I hope for the better," Elfrida said rather anxiously and Iseult smiled at her.

"Definitely for the better. Why do ye no' go and dance?"

"I do no' ken how," Elfrida admitted.

"Och, it be easy enough. I'm sure Iain kens how. Why do ye no' ask him to show ye?"

Elfrida hesitated. "The elders may no' like it," she said. "Word would be sure to get back to them."

The elders were the most powerful group in the community, chosen from all walks of life by the congregation to oversee the running of the kirk by the pastor. The General Assembly which ruled Tìrsoilleir was composed of the most powerful elders and churchmen, and were very strict in their ideas. They frowned down upon any form of entertainment, called a pack of playing cards "the devil's prayer book," a pair of dice "the devil's bones" and a violin "the Archfiend's box." Any form of personal adornment was abhorrent to them, so that a woman could be lambasted in the kirk for tucking a daisy in her belt. Dancing was particularly loathsome to the elders, who regarded it as inherently licentious. None of the elders of the Kirkenny parish had come to the Samhain feast, all no doubt considering it a lewd and heretical event, but Iseult knew as well as Elfrida did that they would have their spies among the gathering there tonight.

"So?" Iseult said. "When ye are banprionnsa it will be your job to change things around here. Ye may as well let them ken now."

Elfrida hesitated then shook her head. "Nay, I'd better no'."

"Then I shall," Iseult said and put down her cup of spiced ale and rose to her feet. Lachlan met her glance with a smile and crossed the floor to meet her, the two of them joining in the dancing with enthusiasm.

Finn was dancing too, her green-flecked hazel eyes alight with excitement. As always, the infectious melody of Jay's fiddle was working its magic so that even some of the most disapproving locals were nodding their heads and tapping their toes in time. When the air was finished, Finn found herself right next to Jay and impulsively she cried, "Och, I love your fiddle, Jay! Ye have magic in your fingers indeed."

"Thank ye," he answered gruffly, not looking at her, and lifted his bow and swung at once into another tune. Finn's excitement ebbed away. She found herself feeling rather low and stepped out of the line to refill her cup of Samhain ale, sweet with apples, honey, whiskey and spices. She saw her elven cat Goblin curled on a cushioned chair near the fire and went to seek the comfort of her soft fur and affectionate purr.

Many of the locals looked at her askance as she lifted the elven cat to her shoulder, and Finn stuck out her tongue at one rude boy who made a less than surreptitious sign against evil.

She watched Jay from her vantage point by the fire, but not once did he glance her way or show any sign that he was aware of her regard. She was used to a current of silent communion always running between them, a wordless connection fed by their shared sense of the ridiculous, their reverent love of music, and their knowledge of each other's minds.

Her misery at his coldness soon gave way to anger. When Dide and Nellwyn began to sing a very sweet and proper love song together, allowing Jay to lay down his viola and take a rest, she marched over to confront him, Goblin riding on her shoulder.

"Why are ye angry with me?" Finn demanded. "What have I done?"

"I'm no' angry with ye," Jay replied coolly, filling his cup with spiced ale.

"Then why are ye being so peculiar? Am I no' your friend anymore?" Anxiety replaced anger in Finn's voice.

He looked down at her then, and twisted his mouth wryly. "I'm sorry. O' course ye're still my friend. It's just . . ."

"What?"

He made a vague gesture with his hand. "I canna . . . I ken it's no' your fault . . . it's just . . ."

Just then, the song came to an end and Gwilym the Ugly limped forward, his hand raised high for silence. He was dressed now in his flowing white witch's robes, with his long dark hair unbound and rings heavy on his fingers. As usual his witch's staff was as much a crutch as a symbol of his communion with the Coven, for Gwilym had lost one leg in the torture chambers of the Awl and now wore a wooden peg strapped to his thigh.

"Samhain Eve marks the turning o' the season, the beginning o' winter and the dead months," he said. "It is the night when the souls o' the dead may return if they choose, to haunt those that have done them harm or speak with those that they have loved. On Samhain Eve the doors between all worlds are open, the door between the dead and the quick, the door between the past and the future, the door between the known and the unknown. It is a fearful time, for no' all spirits o' the dead are welcome and no' all visions o' other places and times desired.

"It is a time to think o' the past and what we may have done better and o' the future, and what shape we wish for it to take. So on this night we o' the Coven encourage all to cast away the faults and failings o' the past and seek to make ourselves stronger and wiser, more courageous, more compassionate, truer to our secret self. In pursuit o' this intent, we ask that all o' ye present write down upon a piece o' paper your greatest weakness or failing and cast it into the Samhain fire, making a wish as ye do so. This is a time to be truthful with yourself, to see yourself with clear eyes as others may see ye, and to think about what is your heart's true desire."

He then relaid the fire with logs of the seven sacred woods—ash, hazel, oak, blackthorn, fir, hawthorn, and yew—and tossed upon it salt and powdered herbs so the flames leapt up in brilliant colours of violet, green and blue, sending sweet-smelling smoke out into the room.

Slowly, one by one, people took the quill and parchment offered to them, wrote upon it after long deliber-

ation, crossed the room to the fire and cast their
Samhain wish upon it. Some did so with embarrassed
laughter and coy looks at each other. Others were
very serious, watching their paper devoured by flames
and disintegrate into ash with intent eyes and a prayer
murmured under their breath.

"Do ye remember the last time we all did this together?" Johanna said as the League of the Healing
Hand gathered together to ponder their wishes. "Ye
were no' there, Finn, but the rest o' us were. We had
no ink so Dillon made us write it down in our own
blood." She gave a little shiver at the memory, half-
serious, half-mocking. "We were in the ruined witches'
tower and all o' us were terrified o' the ghosts."

"Ye may have been," Dillon said. "I wasna."

"I wished I was no' such a scaredy-cat." Johanna
smiled in reminiscence. "And just after I had to go
out into the storm with all those ghosts and wolves
howling and ring the tower bell. I thought I would die
o' terror!"

"But ye did it," Connor cried proudly, and his sister
smiled at him.

"Aye, I did it. Since then I havena really been
scared o' anything much. I suppose that was the most
terrifying thing for me, having to do that alone, yet I
managed to survive it."

"Ye made me write 'tyrant' on my bit o' paper,"
Dillon said. "I suppose I was rather autocratic."

"Just a wee," Finn laughed. She turned to Jay, colour running up into her cheeks. "What did ye write?"

He glanced at her then away, scuffing his boot
against the carpet. "I dinna remember."

"I ken ye wished for someone to teach ye to play
the auld viola the way it should be played," Johanna
said. "So your wish has come true too."

"I suppose so," Jay said, without any pleasure in his voice.

"What did ye wish for, Tòmas?" Brangaine asked with a gentle smile.

He looked up at her with huge cerulean-blue eyes. "For peace, so that I could go home to my mam." They all fell silent, troubled. Tòmas said, "So ye see, I am the only one whose wish did no' come true."

"Except Anntoin, Artair and Parlan," Jay said harshly.

The celebratory mood now truly broken, everyone looked unhappy, glancing down at the bits of paper in their hands with anxious eyes.

"Well, I ken what I'm going to write," Brangaine said cheerfully. "I want to be the best laird to my people that I possibly can be, and I think that means I have to unbend a wee, and try and have more understanding for people's faults and weaknesses. I dinna want anyone calling me a muffin-faced prig again." She grinned at Finn and wrote, in her beautiful courtly hand, "muffin-faced prig" on her scrap of paper.

"Flaming dragon balls!" Finn cried. "Who would've guessed it?"

"Well, I want to be the greatest healer in the world," Johanna said. "And a great healer should always be patient and compassionate and sensitive to the feelings o' others. I found one o' the other healers crying last week because I'd called her a numbskull and a twit, and I ken they hate the way I order them around all the time. So I guess it's my turn to burn the word 'tyrant'!"

"If ye're going to write what I wished for last time, I'll take what ye wished for," Dillon said with no trace of laughter. He bent over the table, laboriously writing "scaredy-cat" in his clumsy scrawl.

"To no' be afraid anymore?" Johanna asked softly. "But why, Dillon? I do no' ken anyone more courageous than ye."

He met her eyes, his hand caressing the ornate silver hilt of his sword. "She will have blood," he answered simply. "One day it will be mine."

Johanna nodded, her eyes soft with sympathy. Together they crossed the floor and cast their wishes into the fire, watching them disappear into smoke with an intent gaze.

Without saying a word, Tòmas wrote "peace" in his round, childish script and Connor quickly followed suit, with a shy smile for his friend. Together the two boys crossed the floor, both with fair hair and wide blue eyes, but one a thin, frail figure, the other much taller and sturdier, even though there was only a few months of age between them.

"What are ye going to write, Ashlin?" Brangaine asked.

He flushed, looking quickly at Finn and then away again. "Och, to no' be such a gowk all the time," he said awkwardly. "To be brave and strong so I can serve my lady well."

"Och, do no' call me 'my lady,' I'm no lady," Finn said automatically and he flushed even redder than before. He turned round so none could see what he wrote on his scrap of paper and then, with one final glance at Finn, went to the fire with Brangaine.

"What will ye wish for, Dide?" Finn said rather diffidently, hoping he would not snub her again. He glanced at her, then said softly, "I ken I should wish to lose this futile longing for what I canna have, but I shall no'. I can no'. So I shall go on wishing for what I've always wished for, and go on longing." And with great deliberation he wrote Isabeau's name upon his piece of paper and went to the fire to throw it on to the coals.

Finn felt a sting of tears in her eyes. She knuckled the edge of one eye and turned back to find Jay's eyes upon her. "What?" she said, flushing.

"Naught," he said. "Just wondering what it was ye were going to write."

"I have so many faults it'd be hard to find just one," Finn answered with a sigh. "I'd need a whole scroll o' paper."

Jay laughed. "What's your worst fault then? Write that down."

"They're all so bad, it's hard to choose. I'm impatient and loud-mouthed and always have to stick my nose into other's people's business. I punch people who irritate me and smoke too much and drink too much and my fingers are made o' lime-twigs. I find it hard to resist filching someone's pocket when they leave their swag in such easy reach." She sighed. "Ye see my problem."

"But ye wouldna be Finn the Cat if ye were no' so curious and interested in everything, and did no' have such amazing turns o' speech. Ye ken everyone is always quoting ye."

"Aye, much to my mother's horror. Happen I should try no' to be such a filching-mort. Picking people's pockets is no' the way for a banprionnsa to behave."

"Nay, I think ye're probably right," Jay said with a laugh in his voice.

"Well, I do try but the temptation is just too much sometimes. I usually put it back again later, unless it's tobacco which really they should guard more carefully, it being so rare these days."

Again Jay could not help laughing, though he said

with a great deal of sympathy in his voice, "So that's what you're going to write? No more stealing so ye can be a better banprionnsa and laird to your people?"

"I suppose so," Finn said unhappily. Jay said nothing, just looked at her inquiringly. "I ken what I'd really like to wish for," she burst out.

"What's that?"

"To go on like this," Finn said, flushing. "The League o' the Healing Hand together again, having adventures, saving auld prophets from prisons, outwitting the enemy, breaking into castles, fighting back to back. I've been so happy these last six months, happier than I've been since we helped Lachlan win his throne."

"Is that really what ye'd wish for?" There was more warmth in Jay's voice than there had been in some weeks.

Finn nodded. "I ken I should no'. I ken I have to go back to dreary auld Rurach and be a dreary auld banprionnsa, but when I think it might be years afore I see ye again, or any o' the others . . ." Her voice broke.

Colour rose in his cheeks. "Happen ye can," he cried eagerly. "There must be some way. Canna ye do what your aunt did and join the Coven? Ye canna rule if ye be a sorceress; they never let ye do both."

Finn's eyes kindled. "Happen I could do that," she said thoughtfully. "I'd like to be a sorceress. We could go to the Theurgia together; it'd be grand! We could be witches together and travel about . . . Oh, I wish I could!"

With sudden resolve she uncrumpled the paper clutched in her hand and wrote on it, "To stop being what other people want me to be. To be myself. Finn

the Cat, adventuress, sorceress, thief." She showed it
to Jay, who said, "Are ye sure?"

She nodded. "What about ye?"

"I canna write," he said in a stifled voice. "I canna
do anything but play the fiddle."

"What a dray-load o' dragon dung," Finn said
rudely. "Here, let me write it for ye. And then tomorrow I'll start teaching ye to write so that next year ye
can write it for yourself." She seized his scrap of
paper, smoothed it out, and wrote upon it, reading the
words aloud: "Jay's wish. To stop being such a silly
gowk and start being proud o' who he is, Jay the Fiddler, adventurer, sorcerer, the best fiddler in the land
and the best friend anyone ever had."

They grinned at each other, then seized each other's
hands and ran across to the fire, throwing in the scraps
of paper with excited laughs.

"Wish with all your heart?" Jay said, colour surging
into his cheeks. She nodded, crossing her fingers and
closing her eyes, scrunching up her face as she wished
with all her will and desire. Then they retreated back
to the corner, still clutching each other's hands. "Oh,
I'm so happy," Finn cried. "Though my *dai-dein* is
going to be angry!"

"I think your mother will be rather relieved," Jay
said. "She always kent ye were no' cut out to be the
ruler o' Rurach!"

"I'll rebuild the Tower o' Searchers," Finn said,
going off into a daydream. "People will come and ask
me to search things out for them, magical swords,
dragon's treasure, kidnapped heirs . . ."

"Lost puppies," Jay said.

She punched his arm. "I'll be able to go off on
quests all the time and they'll pay me a fortune to do
so! I'll restore Rurach's fortune for my *dai-dein*."

"Just try no' to steal too much o' it," Jay replied dryly. "Ye dinna want to be the first banprionnsa to lose her hand."

"I shall only steal things back for the rightful owners," Finn promised. "Ye shall have to come and help me. Ye'll play the dragon to sleep while I steal his treasure."

"I'll rescue ye when they throw ye into prison for picking someone's pocket," he replied, laughing.

"It's a deal!" she cried. "Let's shake on it."

And solemnly they shook hands, as behind them the Samhain fire sunk into ashes.

# TRIAL BY COMBAT

∙∙∙∙∙∙∙∙∙∙∙∙∙∙∙∙∙∙∙∙∙∙∙∙∙∙∙∙∙∙∙∙∙∙∙∙∙∙∙∙∙∙∙∙∙∙∙∙∙∙∙∙∙∙∙∙∙∙∙∙∙∙∙∙∙∙∙

T he city of Bride sprawled along the shore of the bay, hundreds of tall spires competing to see which could soar highest into the sky. Many gleamed with gilt in the pale spring sunshine, which sparkled upon the blue waters. The bay was filled with ships, most of them fighting galleons with ornately carved figureheads and a great mesh of rigging which showed black against the pale sky. The ships guarded the city from attack from the sea, allowing the Fealde to concentrate her troops on protecting the city walls.

Enormously thick and high, the city walls were all topped by cruel steel spikes that curved out and down, making them almost impossible to breach. There were only four gates, each stoutly defended with immense barbicans. Each gate had to be approached via a long, enclosed tunnel, with heavy iron gates at one end and a massive iron-bound oak door at the other. Narrow machicolations in the tunnel walls were protected by archers, so that any enemy attempting to storm the gates would be slaughtered long before they reached the inner door.

As if those defenses were not impregnable enough, Bride had been built in three concentric rings, so that it was indeed three cities, one within another. The outer city was crammed between the external walls and the first of the inner walls, a labyrinth of small, dark, cramped buildings where the poor scratched out a meagre living. The middle city was protected from their impecunious neighbours by another high wall, broken once more by four heavy gates. Within this area lived the merchants and the artisans. The further away from the inner wall one lived, the wider the streets and the bigger the houses. There were parks here and wide avenues of flowering trees and many grand mansions.

Then there was the inner city, built within the last circle of high stone walls and protected by many stout watchtowers. There soared the spires of the Great Kirk, a most magnificent building with many tall lancet windows of crystal that glittered in the sunshine and a square belfry where enormous bells tolled out the hours. Clustered about it were the mansions of the aristocracy and the highly ranked churchmen, surrounded by formal gardens and esplanades.

Beyond stretched a great park of velvety green, broken here and there by copses of ancient trees. A long avenue of flowering starwood led the eye to the royal palace, Gerwalt, set like a jewel within its gardens and reflected within the waters of a long rectangular pool, lined with intricate knots of hedges and tall cypress trees. Built of soft grey stone, Gerwalt was both an impregnable fortress and a palace of immense elegance, with many small turrets rising up to the central tower, which was topped with a cone-shaped spire. From the flagpoles fluttered the all-too-familiar white flag with its design of a red fitché cross.

All this the Greycloaks could see from their position on top of the hills which surrounded the bay. They had set up camp outside Bride a week ago, but not all their long observation could see any way of breaking the city's defenses.

"We could besiege them for a year and no' break the stalemate," Lachlan said gloomily.

"And unless we can seize control o' the harbour, we canna prevent them from bringing in supplies anyway," Duncan Ironfist said just as gloomily. "We could sit here and twiddle our thumbs for the rest o' our lives and no' manage to break the city."

"We shall just have to make the Bright Soldiers come out and fight us here," Iseult said.

"But why would they?" Leonard the Canny said. "The Fealde kens she is safe within the city walls. She will never come out."

Lachlan strode back and forth along the ridge, scowling darkly, his wings rustling. "Canna we challenge the Fealde to single combat?" he said suddenly. "Is that no' an important ritual here, far more important that in Rionnagan or Blèssem?"

"It is an important aspect o' our law," Elfrida answered in her high, sweet voice. She was sitting on the grass, her skirts spread round her, picking daisies and weaving them into a chain. "Anyone who has been accused o' a crime can undergo trial by battle, in which their guilt or innocence is decided by a test o' arms. Clergymen, women, bairns, or those who are blind or crippled in some way can nominate a champion to fight on their behalf."

"Ye mean ye do no' have a trial in which evidence is heard and weighed, and eyewitnesses called?" Duncan Ironfist exclaimed.

"Aye, but eyewitnesses often lie and evidence can be falsified," Elfrida answered. "Trial by ordeal puts the judgement in the hands o' God."

"But surely whomever is the strongest and most skilled at arms is the one who wins?" Duncan objected.

Elfrida nodded. "Aye, that is true and since the Fealde's champion is specifically trained in single combat, it is rare indeed that a criminal escapes justice."

"But what if they are falsely accused?"

"Then God would ensure their safety," Elfrida replied with childlike naiveté.

Duncan and Iseult exchanged an incredulous glance, and the Banrìgh said with spurious sweetness, "Tell Duncan about the other ways a criminal can be tried and judged."

"Well, there be ordeal by fire, where the accused must pass through flames in order to prove their innocence. Any sign o' burning is seen as proof o' guilt. Then there be the ordeal by water, where criminals are held below the water. Water is the blessed medium o' baptism, so if it receives the accused, it is a sign they be innocent but if it buoys them up, then they be guilty."

"So if they can swim, they are dragged out and executed, and if they canna swim, they drown. Neat, isn't it?" Iseult said.

This time, Elfrida heard the sarcasm in Iseult's voice and flushed vividly. "Ye may mock our judicial system but we have very little crime," she cried angrily. "No' like Lucescere where ye have to carry your purse hung inside your clothes because o' all the pickpockets."

"I did no' think to hear ye defend the Fealde," Iain said with a faint stress of reproof in his voice. "Surely ye can see such a trial is terribly flawed. Ye yourself were wrongfully imprisoned most o' your life, dearling, and Killian the Listener too. He was never given a fair trial, ye ken that. Did he no' suffer the ordeal by water? Would he no' have died if the crowd had no' broken through the ranks o' the soldiers and dragged him free o' the dunking-pool?"

"Being the instrument o' God's will in doing so," Elfrida replied obstinately. She stood up, the daisy chain falling unheeded from her lap.

"Happen that is so," Leonard the Canny said placatingly. "God moves in mysterious ways."

Elfrida nodded in agreement, though her face was still set in stubborn lines.

"So if we challenged the Fealde to prove her innocence by ordeal by combat, would she be required to submit?" Lachlan said impatiently. "It is in my mind that we could win Bride without having to waste our strength by trying to breach all those walls. Canna we contrive it so that the whole outcome o' the war rests upon one single battle, between the champions o' Elfrida and the Fealde?"

All stared at Lachlan, fascinated and afraid. "But what if we lost?" Iseult objected.

"We shallna lose," Elfrida said. "Right is on our side."

"We canna lose," Lachlan said. "The whole country must see the Fealde defeated. For if Elfrida is right about the significance o' trial by combat, her defeat will be seen as a clear sign from their god that her reign is over and that she has been found guilty by both the judicial system and by the kirk. Do ye understand? This must be a spectacle that all will watch, and there canna be any confusion about the outcome. The Fealde's champion must die."

"She will no' be easily defeated," Leonard said, troubled. "The Fealde's champion has never lost a trial by battle. She is a woman o' incredible strength and skill, trained in the use o' all hand weapons. I am a cavalier, used to fighting from horseback. Although

I have been taught to fight hand-to-hand, as all Bright Soldiers are, I must admit to some trepidation."

"I do no' mean for ye to fight," Lachlan said. "I ken ye are a brave man and loyal indeed to your banprionnsa, but if this ordeal by single combat is to achieve all I want it to achieve, I must be the one to face the Fealde's champion."

Immediately there was an outcry.

"Nay, master! Ye canna risk yourself so," Dide cried.

"But *leannan,* ye ken ye were no' trained to fight from the cradle as this berhtilde would have been," Iseult objected. "I myself taught ye to fight and ye were already a grown man. I ken ye are a strong and bonny fighter now, but she would have the greater experience . . ."

"Your Highness, I am your captain; I will fight," Duncan Ironfist said, going down heavily on one knee before his Rìgh.

Lachlan smiled at him affectionately. "Thank ye, my friend. I do no' doubt that ye would be a better choice, the stoutest-hearted man I have ever kent. But nay. It must be I who fights."

Dillon flung himself on his knees, gripping the intricately coiled hilt of his sword with both hands. "Please, your Highness, let me fight for ye. Ye ken *Joyeuse* has never been defeated!"

Lachlan raised him with one strong hand, then bent and pulled Duncan to his feet also. "Such loyal, true men I have to serve me," he said, his voice rather thick. "But would I send a lad to die for me, or a man who will never see forty years again? Nay, I would no'! More importantly, I do no' fight on my own behalf but on Elfrida's. Have we no' told the people o' Tìrsoilleir that I am this angel o' death, come to lead her army and win back her throne for her? Do I no' proclaim myself the sword o' their god? Canna ye see this is a true test? It is no' just the Fealde I need to convince here but every Tìrsoilleirean man, woman and bairn!"

They were all silent. Iseult was white to the lips but she showed no other sign of her fear. After a long moment of stillness, she came forward and laid her hand on Lachlan's arm. "Are ye sure ye are willing to risk your life so?"

"Every time I fight in battle I risk my life! At least here there will be only one foe and I shall ken she's attacking!"

"We must plan this carefully," Leonard said. "There is no use fighting such a battle beyond the city walls. Even if ye should win, your Highness, they will just shut the gates against us and we shall have gained naught."

"Aye, it must be within the inner sanctum," Donald said. "And we must have a force with us, for they shall plan treachery, no doubt o' that."

"It must be within a public arena," Iseult said. "If the whole point is to prove Elfrida's right to rule to the people o' Bride, the people must be able to see her."

"We shall have to goad her into agreeing," Leonard said. "We must make any refusal seem like an admission o' guilt. We must give her no other course o' action but to send her champion against ye."

Lachlan nodded. "Let us sit down and write the charges against the Fealde, and let us make the wording as contemptuous and mocking as possible!"

The next day a long procession rode out of the army camp, led by Lachlan upon his high-stepping black stallion. The Rìgh was dressed all in white and gold, with a gold circlet upon his black curls. He held aloft a gilded sword, blade upwards, which shone in the long rays of sunlight pouring down upon the Rìgh's head. Heavy clouds, rumbling with thunder, hung over the city but where the Rìgh's procession rode, all was bright.

On either side of the Rìgh trotted the standard-bearers. Dillon carried a square banner of forest green, upon which the white stag of the MacCuinns leapt, a golden crown in its antlers. Connor, acting as Elfrida's squire, carried the red flag of the MacHilde clan, with its black gauntlet holding a golden sword. Behind fluttered the flags of all those that supported Elfrida, in every device and colour possible, including those of the ten prionnsachan.

Before Lachlan marched the pipers and the drummers, skirling and pounding away. They came to a halt before the main gate of Bride, and there was a loud flourish of trumpets. Then Leonard the Canny dismounted and strode forward. He was dressed in full armour, the visor of his helmet lowered, his red cloak blowing back in the wind. With great deliberation, he removed his heavy gauntlet and flung it to the ground.

"I, Leonard Adalheit, Duke of Adalric, Earl of Friduric, Baron of Burnaby, due hereby charge thee, Ulrica of Bride, self-proclaimed Fealde o' the General Assembly o' the Great Kirk, o' the following crimes, in the name o' our blessed banprionnsa and lady, Elfrida Elise NicHilde, the only daughter and heir o' Dieter Dearborn MacHilde, and direct descendant o' Berhtilde the Bright-maid, bearer o' the golden sword and founder o' the great land o' Tìrsoilleir, the Bright Land."

Then, with a great many flourishes, he read out the

proclamation which he and Lachlan had laboured over until the wee small hours. It accused the Fealde and the elders of the General Assembly of murder, manslaughter, false arrest and imprisonment, treason, sedition, embezzlement and fraud. Leonard would have included many more, such as heresy, unorthodoxy, lewdness and licentiousness, but Lachlan wished to make this a political matter, not a religious one.

Leonard the Canny had a strong, carrying voice and Gwilym the Ugly was able to use his magic to amplify the sound so it boomed out over the city, causing birds to rise screaming in their thousands and horses to neigh and rear. The only answer was the booming of the city cannons, which failed to cause any damage to the ranks of Lachlan's supporters, who had been careful to stop well out of range.

He repeated his challenge at sunset, a pronounced sneer in his voice, and again at dawn the next day. This time there was a response, an angry refutation of the charges and counter-accusations against Elfrida and Lachlan, who was described variously as a foul demon, a heretic, blasphemer and apostate, a *uilebheist* and monster, and a false idol. Leonard the Canny did not retire to ponder the charges but immediately and angrily threw down his gauntlet.

"In the name o' Elfrida NicHilde, banprionnsa o' Tìrsoilleir, I challenge ye to prove these false and vile charges in a trial o' arms, where the judgement o' God our Father shall prove her faith and innocence beyond the faintest shadow o' a doubt. Name your champion!"

The challenge caused a flurry of surprise on the battlements. There was a long pause, during which Leonard stood straight and tall, then finally there came a response. The Fealde herself stood upon the battlements, dressed in golden armour, carrying a great golden sword that caused Elfrida to cry out in anger and dismay, "That be my father's sword! How dare she!"

The Fealde had a brusque, uncultivated voice, showing her origins as a cobbler's daughter. With many coarse swear words and calls to the heavens, she accepted the challenge, crying contemptuously, "If this devilish *uile-bheist* be indeed the angel o' death and wields the sword o' God let *him* prove it so on the field o' combat, in a fight to the very death!"

"And so the trap is sprung," Lachlan said with satisfaction.

"Let us just hope that ye are no' the mouse," Iseult replied curtly.

It took a week of negotiations before the location of the ordeal by combat was agreed upon, and marshals appointed to ensure a fair fight, and weapons determined upon. The Fealde was understandably reluctant to open her gates to the Greycloaks, and it took much jeering and taunting before she agreed. Leonard the Canny tried to force her to have the battle in the public square before the Great Kirk, but the Fealde was too canny to agree to allowing a force of enemies within all three rings of Bride's walls. So at last it was agreed to hold the ordeal in the massive public arena in the center of the merchants' quarter. Here there were tiers of stone seats where hundreds of the city folk could sit and watch, as well as grandstands where the principal parties could sit and still be well-protected from any enemy attack.

"I do no' trust that cursehag as far as I could throw an elven cat," Duncan Ironfist said. "Are ye sure this is a wise manoeuver, your Highness?"

"The Bright Soldiers are bound by a rigid code o' chivalry and honour, Ironfist, ye ken that," Lachlan replied. "Any obvious act o' treachery will be hissed upon by both the army and the common folk, I am sure o' that. It is the hidden act o' treachery I must guard against, the hidden blade in the tip o' the boot, the poison-dipped dagger, the dust thrown in the eyes."

"Ye will have a care for yourself?" Duncan said anxiously and Lachlan nodded, smacking him on his burly shoulder.

"Aye, o' course, auld friend. It is your job to guard Iseult and Elfrida, and to watch my back."

At last the day arrived, a cool spring day with the sun veiled behind grey clouds and very little breeze. It was perfect fighting weather, and Lachlan smiled at Gwilym and thanked him, for he knew the sorcerer had a talent for weather and would have arranged it so Lachlan did not have to contend with heat, flies and the sun in his eyes.

"I wish I could do more, my liege," Gwilym answered.

"Ye could give me Eà's blessing," Lachlan said grimly and Gwilym made the mark o' Eà upon his brow, murmuring, "May Eà shine her bright face upon ye this day."

Leonard the Canny had tried to persuade Lachlan to don the heavy metal armour of the Tìrsoilleirean but Lachlan had refused. He was not used to the extra weight or lack of mobility, and so wore only his battered leather cuirass over a light, closely woven chain-mail shirt that had been a gift to him by the silver-smiths of Dùn Gorm. On his head he wore a light helmet with a broad brim and pierced visor, giving exceptional protection to his head, face, and neck. He wore his kilt, as always, his legs protected by long leather boots. On his back was strapped his heavy claymore, with a short court sword and dagger at his belt, and his little *sgian dubh,* a narrow but deadly dagger, thrust in the boot. Over it all he wore a dark green surcoat with a white stag leaping across his breast.

Lachlan was not allowed to carry the Lodestar, since that was a magical weapon, forbidden under the rules of the trial by combat. Since it was death to anyone but a MacCuinn to touch it, it had been rolled in silk and locked securely in a chest which was left back in the army camp in the care of one of the Blue Guards. If Lachlan should fall this day, it was the guard's sole responsibility to escape Tìrsoilleir and take the chest back to Lachlan's five-year-old son, Donncan Mac-Cuinn, who would then be Rìgh.

As the procession approached the gates into Bride, all felt the hairs on the back of their necks lift. Once they had passed through that long, ill-lit tunnel, there was no retreat. If the Fealde broke her surety of safety, all could be cut to pieces in minutes.

Lachlan had tried to limit his retinue to the three hundred soldiers agreed upon by the Fealde and Leonard the Canny, but Iseult had refused to stay behind and so had Elfrida, rather to Iseult's surprise.

"Ye risk your life on my behalf," Elfrida had said. "I must go."

The League of the Healing Hand had also insisted on accompanying Lachlan's retinue, though Lachlan had at first been incredulous and then angry. But as Finn said, "As if we want to miss the battle o' the century! I'd rather eat roasted rats than no' be there. Besides, if there is treachery, happen we'll be able to help."

Given how helpful the League of the Healing Hand had been in the past, Lachlan had protested no longer, though their presence only added to the heavy weight he carried. Now that it was time to face the Fealde's champion, Lachlan was conscious of a sick, cold feeling in the pit of his stomach. No sign of it showed on his face, though, which was set as pale and cold as carved marble.

As he strode through the gateway into the public arena, there was a great uproar from the stands, much hissing and cries of "demon" and "heretic". In the grandstand, Elfrida clenched her hands together, closing her eyes and muttering a prayer under her breath. Iseult sat still and proud, dressed as a Banrìgh in heavy white damask all edged and scalloped with gold. Her red hair was plaited into a thick, heavy braid that hung down her shoulder, reaching past her waist. Although none there knew it, her dress had been designed to be loosened with a single tie so that, if need be, Iseult could discard her ornate gown and be ready to fight at a moment's notice.

The Fealde's champion strode out to meet Lachlan and they bowed to each other and then to the two grandstands at opposite ends of the stadium. The champion was a tall, heavy figure, clad all in silver armour, with a long white surcoat emblazoned with a scarlet fitchè cross. All that could be seen of her was a pair of glacial-grey eyes, glaring from the slit of her helmet. Her armour had been forged in order to proclaim her status as a berhtilde, having been shaped to fit only one large breast, the left side being fashioned into a hollow. She too carried a heavy, two-handled sword, with her dagger and court sword hanging at her waist.

There was a long flourish of trumpets and then both Lachlan and the berhtilde each in turn swore that their case was just and their testimony true, and that they carried no weapons other than those decided upon by the marshals and no magical aids.

"Then let the ordeal by combat begin!" the Fealde declared in her coarse, angry voice. Again she wore the suit of golden armour, her face concealed behind the visor of her ornate helmet, her gauntlets resting on the hilt of the sacred golden sword.

At first the two combatants tested each other's strength and looked for their weaknesses. Claymores were heavy, double-bladed weapons, designed for hacking rather than thrusting. Since both hands were engaged, there was no opportunity to use the dagger to feint or parry. Occasionally one or the other was able to kick or elbow their opponent, but otherwise there was only the clash of sword against sword, the constant circling and rushing forward, sword swinging, the dance back out of reach, the sudden duck or roll when the enemy drew too close.

Although Lachlan was a shade taller and heavier, his upper body strongly developed as a result of his wings, it was clear the berhtilde was his master at the art of swordplay. She had many a tricky swing or parry stroke that came close to disarming Lachlan on a number of occasions, and she fought relentlessly, without anger or fear. Once the blade of her sword sliced along Lachlan's arm, tearing the chainmail so that blood came welling up, making the ground beneath his feet slippery. Many in the Rìgh's box sucked their breath in sharply but Iseult sat as still and poised as ever, her hands clasped loosely in her lap.

The sting of the wound seemed to excite Lachlan to action. He attacked the berhtilde in a wild flurry of blows, causing her to retreat back across the stadium. Her movements here were ponderous. It was clear to all watching that her armour weighed her

down, made her slow to respond to Lachlan's lithe
and graceful movements. Suddenly she spun on one
foot, her sword held low and close to her body. It
seemed Lachlan would be sliced in half, so swift and
powerful was her movement, but he spread his wings
and leapt high into the air, the sword passing below
his boots. Then one foot suddenly lashed out, kicking
the berhtilde hard in the face. She fell with a crash of
armour. Lachlan landed lightly, bringing his sword
down in one quick, hard blow. It smashed into her
chest, denting the concave of her left breast but not
piercing it. She cried aloud in pain, but knocked Lachlan's sword away with her gauntlet, bringing her own
sword up in a rather wild swipe. Lachlan leapt back,
and she scrambled to her feet, one hand to her chest,
her breath coming harshly.

For a long time they fought with neither regaining
the upper hand. Lachlan's face could be seen to gleam
with sweat behind his visor, and occasionally the berhtilde paused for breath, leaning on her sword instead
of pressing the attack. There were many cries and
moans from the crowd, all caught up in the drama of
this fight to the death between two combatants so
evenly matched in strength and skill.

Then the berhtilde seemed to decide the battle must
be finished. Whether she was growing tired in her
heavy armour, or whether she felt she now knew all
Lachlan's weaknesses was impossible to tell, but she
attacked with blow after heavy blow, forcing Lachlan
ever further back. Soon the wall was pressing up behind him and he had nowhere else to go.

He glanced behind him, then suddenly set his sword
in the dust and used the wall behind him as a spring-
board, somersaulting high into the air. This was a
Scarred Warrior trick and had never been seen before

by the Tìrsoilleirean audience, who all cried aloud in amazement. Lachlan lifted his sword as he somersaulted high over the berhtilde's head, smashing her on the crown of her helmet with the massive hilt of his claymore. As he landed behind her, she rotated drunkenly to face him, overbalanced and fell with a clash of steel. Lachlan leapt forward and drove his sword down between the join of her breastplate and guardbrace, deep into her shoulder. She screamed and struggled to rise, but she was pinned there, the sword having passed through her body and into the ground below. With her other hand she seized the hilt of Lachlan's sword and slowly, painfully, dragged it out. Using the sword as a crutch she staggered to her feet, and stood there, facing Lachlan, leaning on his sword, her own sword held out in defense. Slowly she straightened, then turned and flung Lachlan's sword out of the arena.

"She be as strong as a horse," Duncan Ironfist hissed in amazement. "That should've ended it, that blow."

"But now Lachlan be without his sword," Finn said, gripping her hands together.

The Rìgh had drawn his court sword and his dagger, both much shorter and lighter than the great broadswords. She swiped at him with her sword, and he ducked under it, came up close to her body and stabbed at her visor with his dagger. It glanced off the edge of the metal, scoring it deeply but failing to penetrate. So he bashed at her injured shoulder with the hilt of his sword and she staggered back, dropping her sword. Lachlan kicked it aside, lunging at her with the court sword and tearing the chainmail at the join of her thigh and groin. She seized his arm and threw him over her shoulder and to the ground. Before

Lachlan had a chance to regain his feet, she was stabbing down with her short sword. The Rìgh rolled first one way, then the other, then came to his feet with a nimble backflip, spinning on one foot and kicking out with the other. His boot took her full in the chest, and she stumbled backwards, lost her balance and fell heavily. For a moment her arms and legs moved weakly, like an overturned beetle trying to regain its feet. In that instant, Lachlan bent and dragged her helmet free, seeing his opponent's face for the first time.

She was only young, with a square, brutish face that stared up at Lachlan without expression as he knelt upon her chest, his blade against her throat. "Do ye ask for quarter?"

The berhtilde did not reply. Her glacial-grey gaze did not waver. Lachlan leant a little on the sword. Blood ran up its edges. Still she did not speak. With a sigh Lachlan stepped back, lifting his sword. She did not hesitate, scrambling to her feet as quickly as her heavy armour would allow her and attacking him ferociously with sword and dagger.

"The chivalrous fool," Duncan Ironfist said affectionately.

The clash of steel against steel filled the arena. The short sword was a different weapon entirely than the great claymore. It was much lighter, with a sharp point made for thrusting and edges designed for parrying, rather than slashing. Because wielding it involved only one hand, the other could be used to feint and stab with the dagger, to jab or throttle or throw dust or poke at undefended eyes. In the next few, frantic minutes, both combatants took full advantage of this freedom. It was soon clear, however, that here Lachlan had the advantage. Aided by his wings, he was able to leap and sidestep nimbly. He had been trained to fight by a Scarred Warrior. Swords were not weapons used on the Spine of the World; fists and feet and elbows and the side of the hand were employed as deadly weapons, and so Lachlan had many tricks and manoeuvers the berhtilde was not familiar with. In addition, she was weary and sorely wounded. Soon it was clear she was failing. Then Lachlan suddenly lunged forward, his sword at shoulder length. Cleanly it pierced the berhtilde's unprotected throat, emerging on the far side smeared and bloody. She gave a horrible little gurgle and fell back, her weapons falling from nerveless fingers. Lachlan was dragged down by her weight, falling on one knee beside her body.

For a moment there was a stunned silence, and then the three hundred Greycloaks were on their feet, cheering. Elfrida leapt up and flew into Iain's arms, laughing and weeping. Iseult dropped her face into her hands, surprised by a rush of tears, while the League of the Healing Hand leapt about in their joy, banging each other on the back.

Suddenly Iseult started to her feet, her face all scrunched and crimson, wet with tears. "Lachlan!" she screamed.

At that moment an archer concealed in the Fealde's grandstand rose to his feet, lifting a longbow to his shoulder. Swiftly he fired, the arrow hissing down towards Lachlan's kneeling figure.

At Iseult's scream, Lachlan leapt to his feet, his closed eyes springing open. The arrow was curving down towards his breast. Everyone stood, frozen in shock and horror. Automatically Lachlan threw up his hand and caught the arrow only a few inches from his heart. Again the archer fired. Again Lachlan caught the arrow in mid-flight, just before it plunged into his throat. There was an amazed sigh from the crowd.

"How did he do that?" Brangaine whispered.

"I do no' ken how," Iseult said, weeping again. "I have seen Meghan do it, but she be the most powerful sorceress in the land. I did no' ken Lachlan could do such a thing."

"God's hand protects him," Elfrida said.

Lachlan stood alone in the centre of the stadium, his fist holding the arrows, black anger in his face. Then deliberately he broke them over his knee and flung them away. He bent and hauled his sword free of the dead berhtilde's body then advanced, limping, upon the Fealde's grandstand.

Again the archer fired, though the crowd in the stands were hissing and booing. Lachlan spread his wings and soared high into the air, the arrow curving down and clattering uselessly on the ground. He landed gracefully before the cowering Fealde, his sword held to her throat. "Is this how ye receive God's judgement, ye treacherous bitch? Well, now shall ye suffer his retribution!"

And thus the Bright Wars were finally ended, the Forbidden Land finally conquered, in that final act of thwarted perfidy. So sensational had been the battle, so dramatic its outcome, that there was remarkably little resistance to the Greycloaks taking control of the city. Indeed, so complete had Lachlan's victory been that most truly believed him to be the angel of death he had declared himself to be. When he limped from the stadium, the people of Bride pressed close all about, touching his dusty, disarrayed feathers, his bloodstained surcoat, some weeping with joy. Elfrida was greeted as uproariously. Few disavowed her right to rule when her champion had proved her claim so triumphantly in the trial of combat. The gates of the inner city were flung open for her and she was swept towards her family's ancient stronghold on a wave of shouting, cheering Tìrsoilleirean.

The euphoria did not die for several days. The hated elders of the General Assembly were all arrested and imprisoned in the Black Tower, awaiting trial. To everyone's dismay, the Fealde was not included among them. The woman in the golden armour who had watched the ordeal by combat so impassively was not the true Fealde, but only her servant. While her champion had been fighting to the death for her cause, the Fealde had been escaping from the city with as much of the royal treasury as she could carry.

Lachlan had been healed by Tòmas so that he was returned to his usual strength and vigor less than an hour after the ordeal by combat. He was exhilarated by his success, his golden eyes blazing, his dark face alive with excitement. Again and again he relived the battle, describing this thrust and that feint, until at last Iseult laughingly begged him to desist. "That was one o' the longest hours o' my life and I never want to suffer such an hour again," she said.

On the afternoon of the spring equinox, when the hours of daylight finally lasted as long as the hours of the night, Elfrida Elise NicHilde was crowned banprionnsa of Tìrsoilleir by the new Fealde of Bride, Killian the Listener. She was dressed very simply in white, with the red MacHilde plaid flung over her shoulder and fastened at her breast with her clan badge. Over the other shoulder she wore the heavily ornamented baldric from which hung her father's golden sword, that had been carried by every MacHilde since Berhtilde the Bright Warrior-Maid herself.

She looked very young and frail with the heavy crimson and gold crown on her head, but very regal. When she drove back to the palace in an open carriage drawn by four white horses, the crowd went wild, throwing flowers and sweet cakes to her and tossing their hats high in the air.

The League of the Healing Hand were all guests of honour at the feast last night. They were given new clothes to wear and, although these were rather drab by Lucescere's standards, were much grander than the rough clothes they had been wearing for months. Brangaine was particularly happy to be dressed as a girl again, though her hair was still too short to be put up, hanging below her ears in a silken bob.

When Finn came down the stairs, dressed in a dark brown velvet gown, with the elven cat riding on her forearm, Jay bowed to her and said, "Look at ye, fine as a proud laird's bastard."

"Hey, ye're stealing my patter!" Finn protested. "Next ye'll be saying I'm grand as a goat's turd stuck with buttercups."

"Indeed ye are," he answered, offering her his arm. "Grander."

"Well, are not we the courtier tonight," she said. "I must say ye look grand too in that suit, though rather sombre. And look at the NicHilde! She's really flying the flag tonight, with a wee bit o' white lace at her neck. Are they no' a peculiar race o' people? Remember Captain Tobias and his disapproval o' our buttons?"

The feast was as subdued as their clothes, with no fire-eating or sword-swallowing, acrobatics or music to amuse them while they ate. The feast had been organised by the ladies of the court, who were clearly a long way away from daring to put away their habit of austerity. The Rìgh's quartermaster had rolled out some barrels of wine, however, which Lachlan's retinue all drank rather surreptitiously. Much to Finn's disgust, she and the others not yet of age were given only fruit juice to drink.

After all had eaten their fill, Elfrida began to formally receive the lairds and ladies of the court. Lachlan beckoned Dide, Finn and the others and they bowed, made their farewells and retreated to one of the magnificent antechambers, where decanters of whiskey and jugs of wine and ale had been set out for them.

"By the beard o' the Centaur, what a dreary party!" Lachlan exclaimed. "We must just hope that Elfrida has learnt something about the art o' hospitality while living in our lands, else she'll never be able to persuade any o' us to visit her again!"

Dillon poured them all wine or warm ale, and they settled themselves comfortably on couches around the fire. Although it had been a warm day, Gerwalt was a cold and draughty palace and all were glad of the fire's warmth.

"Ye'll all be glad to ken that I shall return to Lucescere a much richer man than I was when I left," Lachlan said with satisfaction. "Although the former Fealde, Eà curse her black heart, did her best to empty Elfrida's coffers, the NicHilde has still been able to pay restitution to me for the cost o' the Bright Wars as well as a very handsome tithe. This is good news indeed, for I promise ye, if I had levied any more taxes the people o' Eileanan would have risen up in rebellion once more, I be sure o' it."

They all congratulated him and he described with a great deal of enthusiasm the beautiful war galleon Elfrida had given him as part of her tithe. Lachlan had

decided to call it the *Royal Stag* and he was looking
forward to sailing home in it very much. "I was most
envious o' all your adventures on the *Speedwell*," he
told Brangaine and Finn. "Brangaine, ye shall have to
sail with me so we are sure to have fair winds all the
way home. No more slogging along on foot for me!"

Remembering the Devil's Vortex, the attack by the
sea serpent and the terror of their shipwreck, Finn
could only stare at him in amazement. "Ye're stark
raving mad, your Highness!" she cried. "I'd be happy
if I never had to set foot on a ship again."

"Aye, but like all cats, ye dislike getting wet," Lachlan teased. He lifted his goblet for Dillon to pour him
some more wine, then said, "The war is over at last!
Let us drink to victory!"

They all joined in the toast enthusiastically, then
Iseult said, "To celebrate our triumph, Lachlan and I
have prepared a few gifts for ye all, to thank ye for
all that ye have done."

"Firstly, I think," Lachlan said, "we should reward
Dillon, who has been the best squire any Rìgh could
hope for. Indeed, I am very sorry to lose him."

"Lose me?" Dillon said anxiously. "What do ye
mean, your Highness?"

"Dillon o' the Joyous Sword, will ye kneel down
afore me?"

Looking rather dazed, Dillon obeyed. With a few
light touches of his court sword, Lachlan knighted him
and appointed him a Yeoman of the Guard, one of
the Rìgh's personal bodyguards. "Arise, Sir Dillon,"
he said.

Smiling, Iseult held out a small pile of clothing for
him. There was the blue kilt and jacket that all Yeomen wore, a long blue cloak, a plaid, and a silver
brooch depicting a charging stag, the badge of the

Yeomen. Dillon took them, unable to speak with joy and surprise, though Jed the scruffy white dog barked enthusiastically and knocked over a goblet with his wagging tail.

"Connor, I ken ye are young to be a squire but ye did such a good job while Dillon was away in my service, the job is yours again if ye wish it," Lachlan said to the boy, who flushed crimson and cried, "Would I!"

Iseult then gave him back the livery of the Rìgh's squire, which he had surrendered so reluctantly to Dillon upon his return. Connor gave a squeak of excitement and scampered away to change.

Tam was given a heavy purse of gold, to help him buy his own farm or business. He accepted it with stammered thanks and shining eyes and Iseult said teasingly, "I hope we shall soon be hearing some happy news o' ye, Tam."

"It be only three months until Midsummer's Eve— plenty o' time for ye to return to Kirkclanbright and ask that bonny lassie from the apple orchard to be jumping the fire with ye," Lachlan said encouragingly, not having the same subtlety as his wife.

Tam blushed bright red and stammered inaudibly.

Ashlin was given a beautiful silver flute, which he clutched to his breast with trembling fingers, unable to even mutter a thank you. Brangaine was promised help and money in rebuilding Siantan, with a purse of gold in payment of the first installment. She accepted it graciously, saying, "I thank ye, your Highness. There is naught ye could have given me that would have pleased me more. I shall use it to feed my people, who have been hungry indeed these past few years."

"Ye are a good NicSian," Lachlan said. "I hope to

see Siantan returned to prosperity under your benevolent rule."

"If ye are true to your promises to help drive out the Fairgean, I believe that hope will be fulfilled," she returned.

He sighed. "No' a week has gone past since we finally conquered the Forbidden Land and already she wants me to start attacking the Fairgean."

"It canna be soon enough for me," she answered.

He nodded. "Nor for any o' us, Brangaine. Let us no' talk about it now though, please? This is meant to be a joyful occasion."

"I am sorry, your Highness," she said with a graceful curtsey and retired back to her seat, her point made.

"Johanna, o' all o' the League o' the Healing Hand, ye have seen the uglier aspects o' this war," Lachlan said. "Ye have worked hard and willingly for years now, and we have watched ye grow into a good woman, with a gentle heart and hands. On this journey, ye have no' had the skill o' Meghan or Isabeau to assist ye, yet ye have shown good judgement every step o' the way. We therefore have great pleasure in telling ye that ye have been appointed head healer."

Everyone cheered and Johanna thanked him with tears in her eyes. Iseult had had a long green robe prepared for her, embroidered on the breast with a bunch of healing herbs and a mortar and pestle. Johanna slipped it over her head, then stood holding out its silken folds with wonderment in her eyes. "Are ye sure?" she said. "There are so many talented healers in our team . . . and I still have so much to learn."

"We're sure," Iseult assured her and Johanna sat back down in silence, stroking the pale green robe with reverent fingers.

Lachlan then knelt before Tòmas, who sat quietly on the edge of the couch, regarding him with wide blue eyes. "Tòmas, I have no words to express the thanks I feel in my heart for all that ye have done for us. So many men and women can still walk and laugh and play with their children because o' ye, myself included. I shudder to think o' the feast Gearradh would have devoured these past few years if it was no' for ye. Indeed, it was a wonderful thing for us, that ye should have such power in these two small hands o' yours. I ken ye have paid a terrible price for your magic and for that I am very sorry. I have tried and tried to think how I can repay ye, but it is impossible. All I can say is that I hope this is the end o' it, that we can all go home to our families and be at peace now."

"I should like that," Tòmas said gravely. "I miss my mam."

Lachlan nodded and rose to his feet. "I swear that ye and your family shall never want for anything as long as I and my heirs live," he said. "I shall have a special decree prepared, so that ye shall be fed and housed and clothed and shod all o' your life, and all your needs met and all your desires fulfilled. In pursuit o' that aim, I have ratified a coat o' arms and a badge for ye, so that all your heirs ever after shall be known to be descended from Tòmas the Healer."

With her blue eyes bright with love and sympathy, Iseult lifted another pile of material from the table. It was a beautifully made flag, featuring a golden-rayed hand on a bright blue background, all edged with gold braid and tassels. There was also a very small surcoat and a golden badge in the same design. Finn remembered the clumsy little flag that Johanna had sewn them so many years before and marvelled that Lachlan should have remembered it.

There was also a small pile of golden medals hung from blue ribbons. Embossed upon the medals was the design of the rayed hand and the words, "League of the Healing Hand." These were passed out to all the members of the league, who pinned them to their coats with great excitement.

"Well, now we come to the last three o' ye," Lachlan said. "I must admit, I have had the most trouble thinking o' appropriate gifts for ye three. Dide, ye were the first to swear fealty to me, in those dark and terrible days when I was first transformed back into a boy after so many years trapped as a bird. I was only fifteen and ye were only nine, but in all those years ye have never once faltered in your allegiance, never once hesitated in risking everything to help me, never once failed me. How can I reward such love and loyalty?"

"Ye canna, master," Dide said steadily. "I do no' seek reward."

Lachlan nodded, bending and pulling Dide to his feet so he could embrace him warmly. "I ken. But for once I am going to ignore your wishes. Nay, do no' say anything. This reward is as much for dearest Enit as for ye." He smiled at the old jongleur, who sat huddled in her shawls by the fire. She smiled back at him affectionately.

"Now, I canna deny that Dide the Juggler has been my most useful spy. He can travel anywhere in Eileanan and be welcomed by all. He can listen to gossip as much as he likes and no-one lifts an eyebrow. He sings songs in my praise for the common folk to hear and tells tales o' my bravery and wisdom with so much conviction none thinks to disbelieve him. I must admit I would hate to lose all this and so, as long as Dide feels the itch in his feet, well, I shallna be discouraging him.

"One day, however, he may begin to be bored with the road and long for a nice cosy house with a warm fire. So I hereby bequeath to ye the lands and castle o' Caerlaverock in Rionnagan. It is a most bonny estate, Dide, overlooking Kilvarock Loch and rich too. The castle itself is only small but very pretty and the lands are fertile. There is a manager in there now, who can look after things as long as ye want him to."

Dide sat down heavily. "Ye've given me a castle?"

"Aye. Caerlaverock. Is it no' appropriate, since I am giving it to a family that sings as beautifully as any skylark? And if ye are to have a castle, ye must have a surname, Dide, and a plaid and badge and a motto too. I thought we could figure all that out later, though the shield must feature larks in it, since that is to be your name."

"My name?"

"Aye. Dide, will ye kneel afore me?"

Dide looked across at his grandmother, who nodded, smiling. So Dide obeyed, though he looked pale and troubled.

"I name thee Laird Didier Laverock, the first earl of Caelaverock, in gratitude for the many services ye have done me."

"But I be naught but a jongleur," he protested. "Can ye just turn me into an earl like that?"

"I be the Rìgh, I can do anything I like," Lachlan replied, very pleased with himself.

Dide sat down, looking rather dazed, as Lachlan turned then to Jay. "I did no' ken what to do for ye, Jay," the Rìgh admitted. "I would have given ye a bonny new fiddle but ye have the viola d'amore and there is no finer instrument in all o' Eileanan."

"And I'd want no other," Jay said earnestly. "Indeed it was a kingly gift when ye gave it to me and one that was no'. deserved."

"Deserved then and deserved now," Lachlan said with a grin. "I would like to do something for ye, though, Jay, if ye would tell me what ye'd like."

"I want for naught," Jay said. "I already have all I want, my viola and being taught to play it properly. That is all I have ever wanted."

Lachlan nodded. "I thought that was the case. But come, there must be something else? Gold, fine clothes?"

"I'd like to be taught to read and write," Jay said, surprising them all.

"Och, that is definitely something I can do for ye," Lachlan said when he had recovered from his astonishment. "Nellwyn says ye have a real talent, the brightest talent she has ever kent. Ye could be a Yedda if ye chose, she said, and ye will definitely need to be able to read and write if ye seek to join the Coven."

Hot colour rose in Jay's lean cheeks. "I would like that, if she truly believes I have talent," he said. "Though I willna be a Yedda. I do no' wish to use my music to murder."

Lachlan nodded slowly. "I respect that, Jay, though one's choices are no' always as easy as all that. If ye truly wish to study to be a witch, though, I can arrange for a scholarship to the Theurgia for ye. Caerlaverock is only a day's ride away from Lucescere so ye will be able to visit Enit and study music with her whenever ye want."

"Thank ye, your Highness," Jay cried, his hazel eyes very bright. "I would love that!"

Finn stared at him enviously, then looked at Lachlan with desperate hope in her eyes. So far the Rìgh had understood all of their heart's desires as well as if he had read the Samhain wishes they had all burnt on the sacred fire. Would he know hers as well?

Lachlan smiled at her. "So I hear ye want to be an adventuress, Finn?"

Her heart leapt. "Aye, your Highness."

"And happen a sorceress too, if ye have the talent?"

"Aye, your Highness."

"I do no' think your father would be happy to ken that."

"He has Aindrew," Finn pointed out, "And this new wee babe that's on its way. He doesna need me."

"But he loves ye and wants the best for ye," Iseult said gently.

"Surely the best thing for me is to be happy?" Finn said desperately, feeling tears welling up. "Indeed, your Highness, I'd rather eat roasted rats than be buried alive in that dreary auld castle! Canna I go to the Theurgia with Jay and study to be a witch? And then, whenever ye need me, I'd be right there. I could saddle up and ride out that very night, and do whatever it is ye need doing. Why, I could hunt down that curse-hag the Fealde for ye and get back Elfrida's money. Or I could find the Lost Horn of Elayna or the Ring of Serpetra. Will ye no' speak to my father on my behalf, your Highness? Please?"

Lachlan nodded. "Aye, Finn, I shall. Indeed, it would be a waste o' your talents for ye to be naught but a banprionnsa! I can see ye being very useful to me and the Coven."

"Thank ye," Finn cried.

"But if ye are to become a sorceress, ye must learn to mind your manners," Iseult said, her eyes dancing.

"Ye shall have to stop smoking that filthy pipe, and learn to speak without scorching people's ears, and most importantly, ye'll have to learn humility. No more boasting, Finn!"

"Och, what a dray-load o' dragon dung!" Finn cried. "I shall no'!"

# GLOSSARY

*Aedan MacCuinn:* the first Rìgh, High King of Eileanan. Called Aedan Whitelock, he was directly descended from Cuinn Lionheart (see *First Coven*). In 710 he united the warring lands of Eileanan into one country, except for Tìrsoilleir and Arran, which remained independent.

*Aedan's Pact:* Aedan MacCuinn, first Rìgh of Eileanan, drew up a Pact of Peace between all inhabitants of the island, agreeing to live in peace and not to interfere in each other's culture, but to work together for amity and prosperity. The Fairgean refused to sign and so were cast out, causing the Second Fairgean Wars.

*Ahearn Horse-Laird:* One of the First Coven of Witches.

*Aislinna the Dreamer:* One of the First Coven of Witches.

*Anghus MacRuraich:* the Prionnsa of Rurach and Siantan. He uses clairvoyant talents to search and find.

*Arran:* southeast land of Eileanan, consisting mainly of salt lakes and marshes. Ruled by the MacFóghnans, descendants of Fóghnan, one of the First Coven of Witches. Independent from the rest of Eileanan.

*Aslinn:* deeply forested land ruled by the MacAislins,

descendants of Aislinna, one of the First Coven of Witches.

*autumn equinox:* when the night reaches the same length as the day.

*Awl:* Anti-Witchcraft League, set up by Maya the Ensorcellor following the Day of Reckoning.

*Ban-Bharrach River:* the southernmost river of Lucescere which, together with the Muileach River, makes up the Shining Waters.

*banprionnsa:* princess or duchess.

*banrìgh:* queen.

*Beltane:* May Day; the first day of summer.

*Berhtfane:* sea loch in Clachan.

*Berhtilde the Bright Warrior-Maid:* one of the First Coven of Witches.

*berhtildes:* the female warriors of Tìrsoilleir, named after the country's founder (see *First Coven*). Cut off left breast to make wielding a bow easier. Say they are "married to the spear."

*blaygird:* evil, awful.

*Blèssem:* The Blessed Fields. Rich farmland lying south of Rionnagan, ruled by the MacThanach clan, descendants of Tuathanach the Farmer (see *First Coven*).

*Blue Guards:* The Yeomen of the Guard, the Rìgh's own elite company of soldiers. They act as his personal bodyguard, both on the battlefield and in peacetime.

*Book of Shadows, The:* an ancient magical book which contains all the history and lore of the Coven.

*Brangaine NicSian:* the daughter of Gwyneth NicSian's sister. She is named Banprionnsa of Siantan in the Second Pact of Peace.

*Bright Soldiers:* name for members of the Tìrsoilleirean army.

*but and ben:* a small crofter's cottage, usually of only two rooms.

*Candlemas:* the end of winter and beginning of spring.

*caravel:* a small fighting ship, fast and maneuvrable, with a broad bow and a high, narrow poop deck. It was rigged with three or four masts, of which only the foremast carried a square sail. The other masts carry triangular lateen sails, making the caravel easier to sail in fickle winds.

*carrack:* strongly built, three-masted vessel, carrying two courses of square sails on the foremast and mainmast, and a lateen sail on the mizzenmast. Such ships are equipped with only a limited amount of armament and are designed primarily for carrying cargo.

*Carraig:* Land of the Sea-Witches, the most northen county of Eileanan. Ruled by the MacSeinn clan, descendants of Seinneadair, one of the First Coven of Witches. The MacSeinn clan has been driven out by Fairgean, and taken refuge in Rionnagan.

*Celestines:* race of faery creatures, renowned for empathic abilities and knowledge of stars and prophecy.

*Clachan:* southernmost land of Eileanan, ruled by the MacCuinn clan.

*clàrsach:* stringed instrument like a small harp.

*claymore:* a heavy, two-edged sword, often as tall as a man.

*cluricaun:* small woodland faery.

*corrigan:* mountain faery with the power of assuming the look of a boulder. The most powerful can cast other illusions.

*craft:* applications of the One Power through spells, incantations and magical objects.

*Cuinn Lionheart:* leader of the First Coven of Witches. His descendants are called MacCuinn.

*cunning:* applications of the One Power through will and desire.

*cunning man:* village wise man or warlock.

*cursehags:* wicked faery race, prone to curses and evil spells. Known for their filthy personal habits.

*dai-dein:* father.

*Day of Betrayal:* the day Jaspar turned on the witches, exiling or executing them, and burning the Witch Towers.

*Deus Vult:* war cry of the Bright Soldiers, meaning "God wills."

*Dide:* a jongleur.

*dragon:* large, fire-breathing flying creature with a smooth, scaly skin and claws. Named by the First Coven for a mythical creature from the Other World. Since they are unable to adjust their own body temperature, they live in the volcanic mountains, near hot springs or other sources of heat. They have a highly developed language and culture, and can see both ways along the thread of time.

*dram:* measure of drink.

*Donncan MacCuinn:* eldest son of Iseult and Lachlan. Has wings like a bird and can fly.

*Dùn Eidean:* the capital city of Blèssem.

*Dùn Gorm:* the city surrounding Rhyssmadill.

*Eà:* the Great Life Spirit, mother and father of all.

*Eileanan:* largest island in the archipelago called the Far Islands.

*Elemental Powers:* the forces of air, earth, fire, water and spirit which together make up the One Power.

*elven cat:* small, fierce wild cat that lives in caves and hollow logs.

*Enit Silverthroat:* a jongleur; grandmother of Dide and Nina.

*equinox:* when the sun crosses the celestial equator; a time when day and night are of equal length, occurring twice a year.

*fain:* gladly, willingly.

*Fairge; Fairgean (pl):* faery creatures who need both sea and land to live, and whose magic is strange and brutal. The Fairgean were finally cast out of Eileanan in 710 by Aedan Whitelock when they refused to accept his authority. For the next four hundred and twenty years they lived on rafts, rocks jutting up out of the icy seas, and what small islands were still uninhabited. The Fairgean king swore revenge and the winning back of Eileanan's coast.

*Fang, the:* the highest mountain in Eileanan, an extinct volcano called the Skull of the World by the Khan'cohbans.

*Faodhagan the Red:* One of the twin sorcerers from the First Coven of Witches. Particularly noted for working in stone; designed and built many of the Witch Towers, as well as the dragons' palace and the Great Stairway.

*Feich the Raven-Winged:* witch who wove a cloak of invisibility; descendant of Brann, one of the First Coven of Witches.

*Firemaker, the:* honorary term given to the descendants of Faodhagan (see *First Coven*) and a woman of the Khan'cohbans.

*First Coven of Witches:* thirteen witches who fled persecution in their own land, invoking an ancient spell that folded the fabric of the universe and brought them and all their followers to Eileanan. The eleven great families of Eileanan are all descended from the

First Coven, with the MacCuinn clan being the greatest of the eleven. The thirteen witches were Cuinn Lionheart, his son Owein of the Longbow, Ahearn Horse-Laird, Aislinna the Dreamer, Berhtilde the Bright Warrior-Maid, Fóghnan the Thistle, Rùraich the Searcher, Seinneadair the Singer, Sian the Storm-Rider, Tuathanach the Farmer, Brann the Raven, Faodhagan the Red and his twin sister Sorcha the Bright (now called the Murderess).

*fraitching:* arguing.

*General Staff:* the group of officers of the Yeomen of the Guard that assists the Rìgh in the formulation and dissemination of his tactics and policies, transmits his orders, and oversees their execution.

*Ghleanna NicSian:* mother of Anghus MacRuraich, and the last Banprionnsa of Siantan. After Ghleanna married Duncan MacRuraich (Anghus's father), the thrones of Rurach and Siantan were merged into one, and Anghus inherited both. He later dissolved the Double Throne so that his niece Brangaine NicSian could inherit.

*gillie:* steward to a laird.

*Gladrielle the Blue:* the smaller of the two moons, lavender-blue in colour.

*glen:* valley.

*gravenings:* ravenous creatures that nest and swarm together, steal lambs and chickens from farmers, and have been known to steal babies and young children. Will eat anything they can carry away in their claws. Collective noun is "screech."

*Great Crossing, the:* when Cuinn led the First Coven to Eileanan.

*Gwyneth NicSian:* daughter of Ghleanna NicSian's sister, Patrice, and married to Anghus.

*harlequin-hydra:* a rainbow-coloured sea serpent with many heads that lives in the shallow waters near the coast of Eileanan. If one head is cut off, another two grow in its place and its spit is deadly poisonous.
*harquebus:* a matchlock gun with a long butt, usually fired from a tall stock.
*harquebusier:* soldier bearing and firing a harquebus.
*horse-eel:* faery creature of the sea and lochan; tricks people into mounting it and carries them away.

*Isabeau the Red:* apprentice to Meghan of the Beasts.
*Iseult of the Snows:* twin sister of Isabeau.
*Ishbel the Winged:* wind witch who could fly. Mother of Iseult and Isabeau.

*Jaspar MacCuinn:* eldest son of Parteta the Brave, former Rìgh of Eileanan, often called Jaspar the Ensorcelled. Was married to Maya the Ensorcellor.
*jongleur:* a travelling minstrel, juggler, conjurer.
*Jorge the Seer:* witch who can see the future. Was burnt to death by the Bright Soldiers.

*Khan'cohbans:* Children of the Gods of White. A faery race of snow-skimming nomads who live on the Spine of the World. Closely related to the Celestines, but very warlike. Khan'cohbans live in family groups called prides, which range from fifteen to fifty in number.
*The Key:* the sacred symbol of the Coven of Witches, a powerful talisman carried by the Keybearer, leader of the Coven.

*Lachlan the Winged:* Rìgh of Eileanan.
*Lummas:* first day of autumn; harvest festival.
*League of the Healing Hand, The:* formed by the band

of beggar children that fled Lucescere with Jorge the Seer and Tòmas the Healer.

*leannan:* sweetheart.

*lickspittle:* a sycophant or toady.

*Linley MacSeinn:* the Prionnsa of Carraig.

*loch; lochan (pl):* lake.

*loch serpent:* faery creature that lives in lochan.

*Lodestar:* the heritage of all the MacCuinns, the Inheritance of Aedan. When they are born their hands are placed upon it and a connection made. Whoever the stone recognises is the Rìgh or Banrìgh of Eileanan.

*Lucescere:* ancient city built on an island above the Shining Waters. The traditional home of the Mac-Cuinns and the Tower of Two Moons.


*Mac:* son of.

*MacAhern:* one of the eleven great families; descendants of Ahearn the Horse-Laird.

*MacAislin:* one of the eleven great families; descendants of Aislinna the Dreamer.

*MacBrann:* one of the eleven great families; descendants of Brann the Raven.

*MacCuinn:* one of the eleven great families, descendants of Cuinn Braveheart.

*MacFaghan:* descendants of Faodhagan, one of the eleven great families, newly discovered.

*MacFóghnan:* one of the eleven great families; descendants of Fóghnan the Thistle.

*MacHilde:* one of the eleven great families; descended from Berhtilde the Bright-Warrior Maid.

*MacRuraich:* one of the eleven great families; descendants of Rùraich the Searcher.

*MacSeinn:* one of the eleven great families; descendants of Seinneadair the Singer.

*MacSian:* one of the eleven great families; descendants of Sian the Storm-Rider.

*MacThanach:* one of the eleven great families, descendants of Tuathanach the Farmer.

*Magnysson the Red:* the larger of the two moons, a crimson-red in colour, commonly thought of as a symbol of war and conflict. Old tales describe him as a thwarted lover, chasing his lost love, Gladrielle, across the sky.

*Maya the Ensorcellor:* former Banrìgh of Eileanan, wife of Jaspar.

*Meghan of the Beasts:* wood witch and sorceress of seven rings. She can speak to animals. Keybearer of the Coven of Witches before and after Tabithas.

*Melisse NicThanach:* newly crowned banprionnsa of Blèssem.

*Mesmerd; Mesmerdean (pl):* a winged ghost or Grey One; faery creature from Arran that hypnotises its prey with its glance and then kisses away its life.

*Midsummer's Eve:* summer solstice; time of high magic.

*mithuan:* a healing liquid designed to quicken the pulse and numb pain.

*moonbane:* a hallucinogenic drug distilled from the moonflower plant. Grows only in the Montrose Islands, to the south-west of the Fair Isles.

*Morrell the Fire-Eater:* a jongleur; son of Enit Silverthroat and father of Dide and Nina.

*Muileach River:* the northernmost river of Lucescere, which together with the Ban-Bharrach River, make up the Shining Waters.

*Murkfane:* lake in the centre of Arran.

*Murkmyre:* largest lake in Arran, surrounds the Tower of Mists.

*murkwood:* a rare herb only found in Arran. Grows on trunks of trees and heals anything.

*Nic:* daughter of.

*nyx:* night spirit. Dark and mysterious, with powers of illusion and concealment.

*One Power:* the life-energy that is contained in all things. Witches draw upon the One Power to perform their acts of magic. The One Power contains all the elemental forces of Air, Earth, Water, Fire and Spirit, and witches are usually more powerful in one force than others.

*prionnsa; prionnsachan (pl):* prince, duke.

*Ravenscraig:* estate of the MacBrann clan. Once their hunting castle, but they moved their home there after the Berhtfane castle fell into ruin.

*Ravenshaw:* deeply forested land west of Rionnagan, owned by the MacBrann clan, descendants of Brann, one of the First Coven of Witches.

*Red Wanderer:* comet that comes by every eight years. Also called Dragon Star.

*reil:* eight-pointed, star-shaped weapon carried by Scarred Warriors.

*Rhyllster:* the main river in Rionnagan.

*Rhyssmadill:* the Rìgh's castle by the sea.

*rìgh; rìghrean (pl):* king.

*Rionnagan:* together with Clachan and Blèssem, the richest lands in Eileanan. Ruled by MacCuinns, descendants of Cuinn Lionheart, leader of the First Coven of Witches.

*Rurach:* wild mountainous land, lying between Tìreich and Siantan. Ruled by MacRuraich clan, descendants of Rùraich, one of the First Coven of Witches.

*Rùraich the Searcher:* one of the First Coven of Witches. Known for searching and finding Talent. Located the world of Eileanan on the star-map, allowing Cuinn to set a course for the Great Crossing.

*sabre leopard:* savage feline with curved fangs that lives in the remote mountain areas.

*sacred woods:* ash, hazel, oak, blackthorn, fir, hawthorn, and yew.

*Samhain:* first day of winter; festival for the souls of the dead. Best time of year to see the future.

*satyricorn:* a race of horned faeries called the Horned Ones by most of the woodland faeries. The women often take male captives to breed with, since male satyricorn are rare.

*Scarred Warrior:* Khan'cohban warriors who are scarred as a mark of achievement. A warrior who receives all seven scars has achieved the highest degree of skill.

*Scruffy:* formerly a beggar boy in Lucescere. Also known as Dillon the Bold.

*scrying:* to perceive through crystal gazing or other focus. Most witches can scry if the object to be perceived is well known to them.

*seanalair:* general of the army.

*Seinneadair the Singer:* one of the First Coven of Witches, known for her ability to enchant with song.

*seelie:* tall, shy race of faeries known for their physical beauty and magical skills.

*sennachie:* genealogist of the clan chief's house. It was his duty to keep the clan register, its records, genealogies and family history; to pronounce the addresses of ceremony at clan assemblies; to deliver the chief's inauguration, birthday and funeral orations and to invest the new chief on succession.

*Sgàilean Mountains:* Northwestern range of mountains

dividing Siantan and Rurach. Rich in precious metals and fine marbles. Name means "Shadowy Mountains."

*sgian dubh:* small knife worn in boot.

*shadow-hounds:* very large black dogs that move and hunt as a single entity. Are highly intelligent and have very sharp senses.

*Shining Waters:* the great waterfall that pours over the cliff into Lucescere Loch.

*Sian the Storm-Rider:* one of the First Coven of Witches. A famous weather witch, renowned for whistling up hurricanes.

*Siantan:* north-west land of Eileanan, between Rurach and Carraig. Famous for its weather witches. Once ruled by MacSian clan, descendants of Sian, the Stormrider.

*Sithiche Mountains:* northernmost mountains of Rionnagan, peaking at Dragonclaw. Name means "Fairy Mountains."

*skeelie:* a village witch or wise woman.

*Skill:* a common application of magic, such as lighting a candle or dowsing for water.

*solstice:* either of the times when the sun is the furthest distance from the earth.

*Sorcha the Red:* one of the twin sorcerers from the First Coven of Witches. Also called Sorcha the Murderess, following her bloodthirsty attack on the people of the Towers of Roses and Thorns after the discovery of her brother's love affair with a Khan'cohban woman.

*Spine of the World, The:* a Khan'cohban term for the range of mountains that runs down the centre of Eileanan; also called Tìrlethan.

*Spinners:* goddesses of fate. Include the spinner Sniomhar, the goddess of birth; the weaver Breabadair, goddess of life; and she who cuts the thread, Gear-radh, goddess of death.

*spring equinox:* when the day reaches the same length as the night.

*summer solstice:* the time when the sun is furthest north from the equator; Midsummer's Eve.

*syne:* since.

*Tabithas the Wolf-Runner:* Keybearer of the Coven of Witches before she disappeared from Eileanan after the Day of Betrayal. Turned into a wolf.

*Talent:* witches often combine their strengths in the different forces to one powerful Talent; eg, the ability to charm animals, like Meghan; the ability to fly, like Ishbel; the ability to see into the future, like Jorge.

*Test of Elements:* once a witch is fully accepted into the Coven at the age of twenty-four, they learn Skills in the element in which they are strongest; i.e., air, earth, fire, water or spirit. The First Test of any element wins them a ring which is worn on the right hand. If they pass the Third Test in any one element, the witch is called a sorcerer or sorceress, and wears a ring on their left hand. It is very rare for any witch to win a sorceress ring in more than one element.

*Test of Powers:* a witch is first tested on his or her eighth birthday, and if any magical powers are detected, he or she becomes an acolyte. On their sixteenth birthday, witches are tested again and, if they pass, permitted to become an apprentice. The Third Tests take place on their twenty-fourth birthday and, if successfully completed, the apprentice is admitted into the Coven of Witches.

*Theurgia:* a school for acolytes and apprentices.

*thigearn:* a horse-laird a rider of a flying horses.

*Tìreich:* land of the horse-lairds—most westerly country of Eileanan, populated by nomadic tribes famous for their horses and ruled by the MacAhern clan.

*Tìrlethan:* Land of the Twins; once ruled by Faodhagan and Sorcha, twin sorcerers. Called the Spine of the World by Khan'cohbans.

*Tìrsoilleir:* The Bright Land, also called the Forbidden Land. North-east land of Eileanan, populated by a race of fierce warriors. Was once ruled by the MacHilde clan, descended from Berhtilde, one of the First Coven of Witches. However, the Tìrsoilleirean have rejected witchcraft and the ruling family in favour of militant religion. Have dreams of controlling Eileanan.

*Tòmas the Healer:* one-time acolyte of Jorge the Seer.

*Towers, the:* the Towers of the Witches. Thirteen towers built as centers of learning and witchcraft in the twelve lands of Eileanan. The Towers are:

*Tùr de Aisling* in Aslinn (Tower of Dreams)

*Tùr na cheud Ruigsinn* in Clachan (Tower of First Landing; Cuinn's Tower)

*Tùr de Ceò* in Arran (Tower of Mists)

*Tùr na Fitheach* in Ravenshaw (Tower of Ravens)

*Tùr na Gealaich dhà* in Rionnagan (Tower of Two Moons)

*Tùr na Rabin Beannachadh* in Blèssem (Tower of the Blessed Fields)

*Tùr na Rùraich* in Rurach (Tower of Searchers)

*Tùr de Ròsan in Snathad* in Tìrlethan (Towers of Roses and Thorns)

*Tùr na Sabaidean* in Tìrsoilleir (Tower of the Warriors)

*Tùr na Seinnadairean Mhuir* in Carraig (Tower of the Sea-Singers)

*Tùr de Stoirmean* in Siantan (Tower of Storm)

*Tùr na Thigeanrnean* in Tìreich (Tower of the Horse-Lairds)

*tree-changer:* woodland faery. Can shift shape from tree to humanlike creature. A half breed is called a *tree-shifter* and can sometimes look almost human.
*trictrac:* a form of backgammon.
*Tuathanach the Farmer:* One of the First Coven of Witches. (See *Bléssem*).
*Tuathan Loch:* the loch near Caeryla, the first in the Jewels of Rionnagan.
*two moons:* Magnysson and Gladrielle.

*uile-bheist; uile-bheistean (pl):* monster.

*weaverworm:* a caterpillar that spins a cocoon of silk, used by the Celestines to make their gowns.
*Whitelock Mountains:* named for the white lock of hair all MacCuinns have.
*will-o'-the-wisp:* faery creature of the marshes.
*winter solstice:* the time when the sun is at the most southern point from the equator; Midwinter's Eve.
*Wulfrum River:* river that runs through Rurach.

*Yedda:* Sea-witches.
*Yeomen of the Guard:* Also known as the Blue Guards. The Rìgh's own personal bodyguard, responsible for his safety on journeys at home or abroad, and on the battlefield. Within the precincts of the palace, they guard the entrances and taste the Rìgh's food.

*zimbara:* large, doglike creatures that pull the caravans of the Tìreichans. Known for their faithfulness and great strength.

# AUTHOR'S NOTE

...................................................

For those faithful travellers in the world of Eilea-nan who have missed Isabeau in this adventure, do not fear! Isabeau has been pursuing her own destiny while Finn, Jay, Dide and the others have been fighting sea serpents, surviving shipwrecks and helping Elfrida win back her crown. You can read all about Isabeau's adventures in the next book in the series, *The Skull of the World*.

Much of the action of *The Skull of the World* takes place at the same time as Finn's adventures, though in a very different part of the world. Isabeau has immersed herself in the life of the Khan'cohbans but she still hopes to return to Lucescere from her self-imposed exile upon the Spine of the World. First, though, she must undertake her journey of initiation to the Skull of the World, where the cruel and enigmatic Gods of White will reveal her destiny to her. On this journey she will face many dangers but, by overcoming them, will finally discover her true Talent. And when she finally does return to her own people, she will find that she is the only one who can finally face Margrit of Arran and overcome her . . .

I hope that you have enjoyed the tale of Finn the

Cat, and that you look forward to once again travelling in the strange and marvellous world of Eileanan.
May Eà shine her bright face upon you!

—*Kate Forsyth*

## Carly's eyes were heavy, mirroring his own need.

He lowered his head. Her eyes fluttered closed; her soft, plump mouth parted. With a groan his mouth found hers.

But then with a shaky breath, Max pulled away, knowing it was all about to get out of control. He ran a hand along his jaw. "Forgive me." She began to protest but he shut her down. It would be easier if they both pretended that this was something he had gotten wrong, that he was the only one who wanted this kiss, this fire. He pressed on. "That was inappropriate. I would like to apologize."

He stepped back, gestured to the villa. "I'll walk you to your room."

Carly removed his jacket and passed it to him. Tilting her chin she said, "There's no need."

She swooped down and picked up her heels.

Max watched her walk away. And closed his eyes when she went inside, a wave of frustration washing over him.

A kiss that was so wrong it shouldn't have felt so perfect.

Dear Reader,

I began this novel wanting to tell the story of single dad Max Lovato trying to negotiate the tricky toddler years with his single-minded daughter, Isabella. As a parent who has had her share of sleepless nights, I thought there could be no better love interest for this struggling father than a sleep consultant in the form of wise and empathetic Carly Knight.

I think all new parents constantly question if they are doing right by their child, and Max embodies the fears and hopes we all experience.

This is a love story about two wounded people learning to trust others but also themselves. I love the mischievousness that plays out between Max and Carly as they fall in love. I hope you find this book to be an uplifting and heartwarming read, and one that allows you to escape to the glamour and warmth of stunning Lake Como in Italy.

Happy reading!

*Katrina*

# Resisting the Italian Single Dad

*Katrina Cudmore*

⬦ **HARLEQUIN**®ROMANCE

Recycling programs
for this product may
not exist in your area.

ISBN-13: 978-1-335-49920-2

Resisting the Italian Single Dad

First North American publication 2018

Copyright © 2018 by Katrina Cudmore

**Printed in U.S.A.**

**HARLEQUIN®**
www.Harlequin.com

A city-loving book addict, peony obsessive
**Katrina Cudmore** lives in Cork, Ireland, with her
husband, four active children and a very daft dog.
A psychology graduate with an MSc in human
resources, Katrina spent many years working in
multinational companies and can't believe she
is lucky enough now to have a job that involves
daydreaming about love and handsome men!
You can visit Katrina at katrinacudmore.com.

### Books by Katrina Cudmore

### Harlequin Romance

#### *Romantic Getaways*

*Her First-Date Honeymoon*

*Swept into the Rich Man's World*
*The Best Man's Guarded Heart*
*Their Baby Surprise*
*Tempted by Her Greek Tycoon*
*Christmas with the Duke*

Visit the Author Profile page at Harlequin.com.

To Harry, my night owl.

## Praise for
## Katrina Cudmore

# CHAPTER ONE

THE EXACT SECOND her office clock hit midday, Carly Knight grabbed her laptop bag and the yellow cardboard box jammed with the natural sleeping aids she brought to all her parent talks. She was about to leave her office when the angry blare of a car horn from the road outside had her pause by her office window to watch a taxi driver angrily weave past a silver car that had pulled in on the double yellow line.

The driver's door slowly opened. A tall, powerfully built man climbed out. He moved to the other side of the car. Wasn't he worried about getting a parking fine? But then, given the car he was driving, a parking fine would probably be nothing more than pocket change to him.

He came to a stop at the rear door of the car and bowed his head for the briefest of seconds before sending his gaze heavenwards. There was an aloneness, a heaviness of spirit in how he stood stock-still, his feet firmly anchored to the ground, staring upwards. The man's lips moved briefly in speech as though he was talking to someone.

She needed to leave or she'd be late for her talk,

but she couldn't drag herself away from watching him. She moved closer to the window, placed her palm against the cool glass.

Opening the rear door, he leant into the car for a moment before reappearing with a little girl in his arms.

He kissed her forehead, tenderly smoothed her soft brown curls and attempted to place her down on the footpath. But the little girl, dressed in a yellow jacket and blue pants, and who Carly guessed was about two years of age, refused to let go.

The man shook his head and then began to pace the footpath, the little girl in his arms, glancing all the while down the street. Who was he waiting for?

Carly soon had her answer when a petite, dark-haired woman, holding hands with a similarly dark-haired boy of four or five, rushed towards him. She hugged the man warmly, stroked the little girl's cheek. They were a beautiful family. Carly's heart tightened at their intimacy. But then the man attempted to pass the little girl to her mother, but she clung to him, refusing to let go. In the end, he was forced to remove her baby stroller from the boot of his car one-handed, refusing the mother's offer of help. When he lowered the little girl into the stroller, Carly could hear her cries of protest. Kneeling before the stroller, the man stroked the little girl's curls, but her leg smacked against his forearm and pushed him away.

The woman said something to him and hugged him again before rushing off with both children.

Fists tightly bunched at his side, the man stared after his family for a long while before turning in the direction of Carly's building. Carly's head jerked back at the desolation etched on his face. She stepped back from the window, out of his view, feeling like an intruder on his suffering.

Should she go down and ask him if everything was okay?

The man's chest rose heavily and when he exhaled, the torment in his eyes disappeared. An aloof, guarded expression took its place. He removed his phone from his pocket, answered a call and strode in the direction of her office block.

Carly frowned. Could this be Mr Lovato? Her client who was supposed to have been here half an hour ago? But why didn't his wife come in with him?

Locking the office door behind her, she went out onto the stairwell and was on the turn of the stairs when the door to the reception area burst open.

A blur of dark wavy hair, a phone pressed to hard jawbone, an expensive grey suit, the jacket spilling backwards as he climbed the stairs two at a time, raced towards her.

Carly's heart lurched; it was rather disconcerting to be faced with such male perfection on a Tuesday lunchtime on the concrete stairs of an office block desperately in need of refurbishing.

Light, misty green eyes flicked in her direction as he passed her by.

Turning, she saw that he had already reached the turn in the stairs. 'Mr Lovato?'

He came to a stop and looked down towards her. Standing still, he was even more devastatingly handsome than when he had been in motion. He considered her through a serious gaze, his mouth shaped like a soft wave, turning ever so slightly downwards at the corners.

He rolled his impressively wide shoulders and gave a nod.

'I'm Carly Knight, the sleep consultant you made the appointment with. Is everything okay?'

His eyes narrowed. 'What do you mean?'

There was a defensiveness to his tone that had Carly wavering. She wanted to ask if she could somehow help in whatever had been troubling him outside, but the proud tilt of his head told her he would not welcome her intrusion.

Instead she climbed the stairs to stand a few steps below him. 'I'm sorry but I have another appointment that I have to leave for. If you speak to Nina on reception she will schedule another appointment for you.'

He considered her for a moment, the ever so slight tightening of his jaw the only indicator of his unhappiness. 'I apologise for my lateness. I promise I won't delay you for more than ten minutes.'

His voice was deep and—okay, so she'd admit it—*really* sexy. Where was his accent from? His surname, Lovato, was that Italian or Spanish? His smooth tanned skin and dark hair suggested long, sun-kissed Mediterranean days in whitewashed villages with views of a glistening sea.

For a moment, a deep longing for some sunshine and freedom washed through Carly. After a long icy winter, spring in London had proved to be cold and miserable. And it felt as though she hadn't seen daylight for years thanks to the ongoing task of establishing her fledgling sleep consultancy business, which entailed working late into the night on far too many evenings.

'I'm sorry, Mr Lovato, I really have to leave for another appointment.'

'It's important that I meet with you *now*.'

Carly attempted to give him a sympathetic smile, but in truth her earlier irritation with Mr Lovato, which had temporarily disappeared in the face of his upset, was quickly reappearing at his insistent tone. Only this morning, he had somehow managed to sweet-talk an appointment with Nina, the office-block receptionist who provided a diary booking service for all the tenants, despite the fact that Carly's diary was already full for the

day. Nina usually guarded the diaries like a Rott-
weiler on steroids.

When Carly had questioned Nina on why she
had given him an appointment, Nina had given her
a soppy smile that was alarming in itself and said
he had been referred by Dr Segal, a paediatrician
who was increasingly referring patients to Carly,
and that she hadn't had the heart to turn him away;
that he had sounded so lovely and sincere and such
a concerned dad for his daughter who wouldn't
sleep at night. Tough-as-nails Nina had obviously
fallen for that deeply accented voice that no doubt
had the potential to melt granite.

'It's now close to ten minutes past twelve, you're
over half an hour late for your appointment,' Carly
pointed out. From his expensive suit, glistening
black leather shoes and a car even her stepfather
couldn't afford, Carly guessed that Mr Lovato was
rich. Seriously rich. And no doubt used to getting
his own way. But not now. Not with her. She had
spent her teenage years being manipulated by a
stepfather who had used his wealth to get his own
way regardless of the consequences to others. If Mr
Lovato was anything like her stepfather he would
have no problem in making Carly late for her appointment with a group of other parents, as long as
his own needs were met. Money talked for some
people and it gave them an inflated sense of enti-
tlement. 'My receptionist shouldn't have given you

an appointment today. My diary was full. She tried calling you back to make alternative arrangements but you didn't answer her calls.'

'I was working from home today—between taking care of my daughter and client calls I never managed to call Nina back.' He shrugged, gave her a hint of an apologetic smile. 'When it was time to leave I couldn't find my daughter's shoes. And when we were finally on our way I realised that I had left her changing bag in the hallway so I had to turn around. You know how it is when you have children—time seems to disappear into a void of chasing your own shadow.'

Carly cleared her throat, ignoring the nudge of pain in her chest at his not unexpected but incorrect assumption she had children of her own. It was a common assumption many clients made. 'I don't have any children of my own but from working with them for the last decade I agree that you have to be very organised around them.'

His gaze narrowed. Carly pressed on, knowing she had to leave for her meeting despite a nagging feeling that she should give Mr Lovato some time. 'Nina should be able to schedule you in for some time next week, after the bank holiday.'

Moving down the steps towards her, he came to a stop directly in front of her. Carly tilted her head to meet his gaze. He was tall. Very tall. At least six feet four, and over eight inches taller than herself.

He carried himself with a smooth ease, which, combined with his prominent angular features and soul-searching eyes, had the effect of making you forget all that you were thinking, and everything you were about to say.

'I want us to speak now.'

Carly blinked at the smoothness of his tone, at the bluntness of his words. 'That's not possible. I'm giving a talk to a parent group in Kilburn at one. I have to leave now or I'm going to be late.'

His eyes narrowed but did not move from hers for a moment. Carly had to force herself not to look away, hating the heat that was growing on her skin at his nearness, the strange feeling of undoing that was unravelling in her insides.

'How are you getting there?'

Carly frowned. 'The underground.'

'I'll drive you.'

Carly stared after him as he moved to the reception doors. He held one of the scruffy blue doors in need of a repaint open for her. Carly followed him down. 'That's not necessary, Mr Lovato.'

His beguiling mouth curved upwards into a hint of a smile. 'My name is Maximiliano but you can call me Max. We can talk on the journey there. It's the least I can do considering my lateness for our meeting. Can I carry your box out to the car for you?'

Irritated, Carly shook her head. 'No…and I don't

think it's appropriate you driving me. After all, we have just met.'

To this he let out an amused exhalation before saying, 'I'm a seriously sleep-deprived father. I can assure you that you have nothing to fear from me.' He looked towards reception where Nina was staring in their direction and added in a teasing tone, 'Nina, I'm driving Ms Knight to her appointment in Kilburn. Should anything happen to her you have my address and telephone number, which you can pass onto the police.'

Unbelievably, Nina giggled at this. Carly eyed her with exasperation but Nina was too busy ogling their visitor to catch her annoyance.

'I really don't think—'

Before she could add anything else, Max interrupted her, his voice low, the intensity of his proud gaze flipping her stomach. 'I urgently need your help, Ms Knight…as does my daughter.'

Carly Knight's cornflower-blue eyes disappeared in a slow blink behind her long and lush eyelashes as she considered his words.

Max wanted to walk away. He hated asking for help. It wasn't in his nature. He found it degrading—a sign of weakness. He valued his privacy, disliked having to expose himself and his family to the scrutiny of an outsider. From a young age he had understood the importance of self-reliance.

His mother, a strict disciplinarian, had constantly told him that to be dependent on others made you weak. And growing up in a tough suburban neighbourhood of Rome, he had quickly learned that to survive he had to be strong, resilient and, most important of all, never show weakness.

Carly Knight was not what he had expected. When he had reluctantly called the number his paediatrician had given him, he had imagined meeting an older woman, a grandmother perhaps, with sensible hair and sensible shoes to match her sensible personality. A woman with years of experience dealing with strong-willed toddlers hell-bent on testing their parents.

He hadn't expected a woman who hadn't experienced first-hand the exhausting reality of parenting. He hadn't expected sparkling white trainers under ankle-length faded blue jeans, a white blouse covered in red stars. He hadn't expected tumbling blonde hair or creamy skin so smooth he wanted to touch his thumb against her high cheekbones. He hadn't expected the attitude that said he was an inconvenience in her life.

He wanted to walk away; to tell her he didn't want her help after all. But that would be a lie. He did need her help. And so did Isabella, his beautiful, inspiring, contrary-as-a-hungry-goat daughter. They could not go on as they were. As much as he hated to admit it, they were both miserable.

He clenched his jaw as the constant slow burn of guilt for failing his family intensified under Carly Knight's critical gaze.

Her brow wrinkled but then something softened in her eyes. She let out a deep breath. 'Okay, I'll take the lift.'

Torn between the relief that she had said yes and the deep wish that he had never needed to ask for her help in the first place, he took hold of her box, which she released reluctantly, and guided her out to his car.

She had resisted even taking a lift from him. How on earth was she going to respond when she learnt of everything he wanted from her?

Outside she folded her arms and stared pointedly at the double yellow line his car was parked on. He opened the passenger door for her, and nodded down towards the box. 'Do I smell lavender?'

'As part of bedtime routines, I recommend to parents that they use aromatherapy creams and oils in baths and in massaging their children—lavender and camomile being just some they can use. I take samples along to my talks to give to parents.'

He placed the box in the rear seat of his car, beside Isabella's car seat, sure that Isabella would never tolerate him massaging her. Thankfully.

When she got into the car, Carly's gaze flicked over the leather and walnut interior, her head twisting to take in the rear seat. 'This must be the cleanest family car I've ever seen. Most of my clients' cars are covered in toys and crumbs and empty wrappers.'

'I'm away with work a lot. My daughter isn't in my car that often.'

She frowned at that. Max punched the buttons of his satnav, wondering not for the first time if he had done the right thing. Was Carly Knight about to judge him, to confirm that, yes, he was an inadequate father? Knowing your inadequacy was one thing, allowing someone else to see it, exposing yourself to their criticism, was another matter.

Carly gave him the address of her appointment and he pulled away from the kerb, following the instructions of the satnav voice.

Beside him Carly asked with a hint of surprised amusement in her voice, 'Is your satnav speaking in Italian?'

'Yes… I like some reminders of home.'

Her bee-stung mouth carved upwards into a light smile. 'I wondered if you were Spanish or Italian.'

Despite himself he smiled and faked indignation. 'How could you confuse the two? I'm Italian and very proud to be.'

'So why are you in cold and damp London? Why not the Amalfi coast or somewhere as gorgeous as that?'

'I like London, the opportunities here. I've a home in Italy too—on Lake Como—but my work commitments mean I rarely get to visit there.'

'I've never been but I would love to one day.' She gave her head a small shake and, sitting more upright in her seat, she clasped her hands together. 'Okay, tell me how I can help you and why it was so urgent that we talk today?'

Her voice had returned to its formal professionalism. Max waited for a break in the traffic to turn right out of Rowan Road, fighting the reluctance to confess the problems in his family. Eventually he forced himself to admit, 'My daughter Isabella is twenty-two months old. She's a terrible sleeper. The worst in the world. I thought as she got older it would improve but in recent months it has only worsened.'

Carly twisted in her seat and he glanced over to find her studying him carefully. 'What do you mean by a terrible sleeper?'

Her tone held a hint of censure, as though she didn't quite believe him. Frustration tightened in his chest. 'She won't go to sleep—it can take hours and has tried the patience of even the most chilled-out nannies that I've managed to employ. She wakes frequently at night and refuses to go back to sleep. It's causing havoc. She's tired and irritable during the day and my job is very demanding—her sleeplessness is killing my concentration. I can't retain nannies. They all walk out eventually. My neighbours have a boy of a similar age who's been sleeping through the night since he was five months old.'

'No two children are the same. Don't compare Isabella to other children—on this or anything else. Trust me, it's the quickest route to insanity for any parent. Studies vary in their results but some say that fewer than half of all children settle quickly at night and sleep through. Isabella is in the majority by waking.'

Max shook his head, picturing Isabella's brown eyes sparking with anger last night as she stood beside her bed and shook her head each time he told her it was time to go to sleep. *È ora di andare a letto, Isabella.'*

His daughter's word count was slowly increasing but her favourite word continued to be a defiant, 'No.' And last night she had used it time and time again, her chestnut curls bouncing about her face as she dramatically shook her head.

He had been so tempted to crawl into bed beside her, to hold her in his arms, sniff her sweet baby scent, listen to her soft breaths when she eventually fell asleep. But to do so would be to do Isabella a disservice. She needed to learn to go to sleep on her own, learn to be independent of him.

He rolled his eyes. 'I bet she's an outlier though; I bet she's in the top one per cent for waking at night. My daughter doesn't do anything by halves.'

She smiled at that. He felt a surprising pleasure that she got his attempt at humour. 'Waking at night is normal. Children wake for a variety of reasons: shorter sleep cycles, hunger, being too hot or cold, their room being too bright, or the need for comfort and assurance. I find that unrealistic expectations cause parents the most stress. How does Isabella's mother feel about her sleeping?'

Max cursed under his breath at a car that swerved into his lane on the Hammersmith flyover without indicating. The tight fist of guilt that was his constant companion these days squeezed even fiercer. Would talking about Marta ever get easier? Would the guilt of her death—how they had fought in the hours before—ever grow less horrific? 'Isabella's mother, Marta, died in a car crash when Isabella was three months old.'

'I thought…' She glanced in his direction, confusion clouding her eyes. 'I saw you from my office window earlier…'

Now he understood her confusion. 'My wife's friend Vittoria agreed to take Isabella this afternoon so that I could meet with you.'

He waited in the silence that followed for her response to hearing of Marta's death. Most people responded with panic, a keen urge to change the subject or preferably, if circumstances allowed it, to find an excuse to get away.

'I'm very sorry to hear about your wife. It must have been a very difficult time for you.'

Her softly spoken words sounded heartfelt. He glanced in her direction and swiftly away again, not able to handle the compassion in her eyes.

'Do you have other children?'

'No, just Isabella.'

'Have you family or friends nearby, who support you?'

'I have some friends, like Vittoria...but they have their own families to look after.' Max paused, pride and guilt causing him to add more fiercely, 'Anyway, we don't need support.'

'It can't be easy coping on your own since Marta died.'

He didn't answer for a while, focusing his attention on merging with the traffic on the Westway, but also thrown by all her questions, what she was saying...how easily she said Marta's name. Most people skirted around ever having to mention Marta's name, as though it was taboo to say it out loud. He swallowed against a tightening in his throat, suddenly feeling bone tired. At work he deliberately kept a professional distance from those who worked for him. The few friends he had in London, friends that in truth had been Marta's friends and had probably stayed in his life out of duty and respect to Marta, had stopped asking him about how he was managing a long time ago. In the early months after Marta had died, he had made it clear it wasn't up for discussion.

He saw a gap in the traffic open up in front of him and he pressed on the accelerator. He needed to get back to the office and he was keen to get this conversation over and done with. He wanted Carly Knight to show him how to get Isabella to sleep, not ask all these questions. 'I grew up in a one-parent household, my mother raised me single-handedly. It's a fact of life for a lot of people.'

'Yes, but it's not the future you had envisioned, and losing that must be very hard.'

He wanted to thump the steering wheel hard with the palm of his hand. Carly's words were resonating deep inside him. He didn't just miss Marta, he missed the future they had mapped out together, he missed the support of co-parenting, he missed having someone to talk to. All selfish things that only added to his guilt that Marta had died so young, that she would never see Isabella grow up. Marta would despair over just how out of sync he and Isabella were—their relationship was more often than not a battle of wills, and at the moment Isabella was winning. Of course he adored his daughter but he worried deeply about how dependent she was on him, which only seemed to be worsening in recent months, given her tendency to cling to him and her refusal to be cared for by others. How would she cope if anything ever happened to him?

'Isabella's nanny walked out yesterday. Dr Segal referred me to you this morning when I took Isabella to see her. She said you have helped some of her other patients.'

'Your nanny walked out on you because of Isabella's sleeping?'

'Yes.' He glanced over and saw that she had an eyebrow raised, not buying it. He shifted in his seat, gripped the steering wheel tighter. 'The fact that I'm away a lot of the time is probably a factor too.'

'How often are you away?'

'Two…sometimes three nights a week. When she was younger I took Isabella with me but the travel was too much for her.'

'She's probably missing you a lot—and the fact that you are coming and going means she has no consistency, which will have an impact on her ability to sleep.'

Her voice was calm, matter-of-fact, which annoyed him as much as what she had to say. 'It's the nature of my work… I don't have a choice.'

'I've never come across a situation that doesn't have alternative choices, or solutions. What is it that you do?'

Maybe she should try living his life some time. In architecture, you were only as good as your last design and winning bids was a never-ending cycle of late nights and client meetings. 'I'm an architect and property developer—my main office is here in London with other offices in Milan and Shanghai. My clients are worldwide, as are my properties.'

'My guess is Isabella needs more stability and routine to sleep better at night.'

Reluctantly he nodded. She was right. And he needed Carly's help in establishing that routine. It was time he started broaching his plans with her. 'I have to leave for my second home on Lake Como later this week. My in-laws live there, and my father-in-law is celebrating his sixtieth birthday on Friday evening, and on Sunday my brother-in-law, Tomaso, is marrying. I have no choice but to go—Isabella is a flower girl at the wedding. I've no idea how she will behave. I need her to sleep in the nights before—that way hopefully she might not throw a tantrum, which she's prone to do at the moment.'

Along Harrow Road they came to a stop while the driver of a concrete mixer ahead in the road tried to manoeuvre into a narrow construction site entrance. He turned to her and asked, 'Will you work for me for the rest of this week, come to Lake Como this weekend, to help me in getting Isabella to sleep? I'll pay you generously.'

Carly looked at him and then turned to stare at a nearby billboard advertising happiness via a deodorant, trying to contain her irritation. He was a client, clearly in need. But seriously! She turned back to him, cursing once again that he was so distractingly handsome, and tried to keep her voice calm. 'I'm a sleep consultant, Mr Lovato, not a nanny.'

'I know that.'

She forced herself to hold his gaze, even though his misty green eyes did something peculiar to her heartbeat. 'Do you?' She waited a pause before adding dryly, 'I'm busy with other clients all of this week and have my own plans for the weekend.'

'Nina told me earlier that you were on annual leave Friday—can't you at least come to Lake Como with us?'

Nina! What had got into her this morning? 'No—I've rented a cottage in Devon; I like to surf. I've been planning this trip since the New Year.' Why was she telling him this? Why did she feel she had to justify saying no to him?

'I'll pay for you to rebook.'

'I don't provide the type of service you are looking for. Yes, I visit clients' homes but I don't stay overnight or get involved in childcare. I provide a bespoke plan that parents follow over a period of months. Isabella is not going to be sleeping through the night any time soon—it doesn't work that way. My approach to your child sleeping contentedly takes time, patience and consistency.'

The traffic ahead of them began to flow again. Max eased his car forward, the expensive engine barely making a noise. 'I'm not asking you to get involved in the childcare.' His tone was one hundred per cent exasperation. 'Isabella barely slept last night. I flew in from Chicago yesterday. She's exhausted. I'm jet-lagged.' He rubbed his brow and continued to stare forwards. 'We need help.' His voice was so low, Carly had to lean towards him to hear him. 'This weekend…with Marta's family, the wedding…it's going to be trying. I want them to see that Isabella is happy and well cared for.'

Carly dropped her head and studied her hands, thrown by the honesty of his words. 'I've bookings all of this week. I can't—'

'Come to Lake Como with us this weekend.'

She closed her eyes to the soft appeal in his voice. The image of him standing alone on the street staring after Isabella's stroller, looking so alone, and then the anguish she had witnessed when he had turned towards the building had her tempted to say yes. But she needed to think this through. How many times had she believed others only to find out a very different truth? Not only did she have a stepfather who used his wealth to keep her at a distance, who thought throwing cash at her made up for a lack of love and affection and his poorly disguised belief that she would never be as good as his own three daughters, but Carly had trusted her own father when he promised he would visit her when her mother had ended their marriage. That promise had lasted all of twelve months until he decided to emigrate to New Zealand. Men had a habit of smashing her trust in them—her ex, Robert, had told her he loved her only to break off their engagement weeks before their wedding, telling her that he couldn't marry her because he was still in love with his ex. Carly had learned never truly to believe or trust in others, always to dig deeper to find out the truth.

She needed more facts and details before she made any decision…and Isabella's father needed to understand that she provided no magical cure for disturbed sleep. She buzzed down her window, needing some air. 'I don't sleep train. I don't give you any magical formulas. I just assist in building a routine and developing the correct expectations in parents as to how children sleep. There's no instant cure. There's just slow improvement over weeks, if not months.'

'I will take on board everything you have to say.'

'Yes, but will you actually implement what I suggest? It takes a lot of time and patience.'

His jaw worked for a moment. 'It depends on how persuasive you are.'

The hint of humour in his voice was matched

by a glint of defiance in his eyes when he glanced in her direction.

Despite herself, Carly found herself having to fight the temptation to smile. 'That sounds like a challenge.'

'Lake Como is beautiful. You said earlier that you'd like to visit it some time. Why not now? The forecast is great for the weekend. Unlike here in England where rain is predicted. Surfing in the rain or boating in the Italian sunshine on Lake Como… there's not much competition, is there? I promise you lots of free time. Isabella and I will show you around the area, even take you for the best ice cream, not only in Italy, but in the entire world.'

She folded her arms, telling herself not to fall for his promises that were so, so tempting. 'That's some claim.'

He shook his head, clearly amused. 'What's your favourite flavour of ice cream?'

'Dark chocolate.'

He nodded. 'Good choice. I meant it when I said I'd pay you well. I'll quadruple your fees.'

Carly closed her eyes, disappointment slamming into her. Why did he have to ruin it all by mentioning money again? 'I don't want your money,' she said sharply.

He gave her a quizzical look. 'It was not my intention to insult you.'

'I don't like people who use their wealth to get

what they want in life regardless of the consequences and how they affect others.'

'And what are the consequences of you coming to Lake Como with me?'

Carly held his gaze for a moment too long, felt heat travel up along her neck at his softly spoken words. She grabbed her phone from the central console where she had placed it earlier, checking the time, trying to ignore a deep instinct that in going to Lake Como with Max Lovato her life would never be the same again. It wasn't a rational feeling, yet it sat there in her stomach like a long trail of worry beads. 'I'll be cancelling my holiday. And I don't know you—for all I know you could be an axe murderer.'

Before Carly knew what was happening, Max had his paediatrician, Dr Segal, on the loudspeaker confirming that he wasn't a danger and, worse still, enthusiastically agreeing that Carly's intervention was badly needed. Then he put a call through to Vittoria, who laughed when Max asked her to give him a character reference and proceeded to say that, though he was much too stubborn when it came to letting others help, she admired him greatly for how he was coping on his own. Max quickly ended the call with Vittoria, looking uncomfortable and taken aback by what she said.

By the time those calls had ended they had

reached the offices of the family support group that was hosting her parent talk.

Outside the car, Max lifted her cardboard box from the rear seat. She went to take it but he wouldn't let it go. Instead he held her gaze and said softly, '*Vieni con noi.* Come with us.'

Carly swallowed hard, hating the effect his voice, his gaze had on her. Max and Isabella clearly needed some help but something deep inside her was telling her not to go. 'I need some time to think about it.'

'When will you give me an answer?'

'I'll call you tomorrow.'

'Isabella is bright and intelligent—you'll really get along.'

Carly could not help but laugh at the mischief sparkling in his eyes. 'Are you trying to bribe me with a little girl?' Not waiting for his answer, she walked away, saying, 'I'll call you with my decision tomorrow.'

# CHAPTER TWO

IT WAS LATE Wednesday afternoon and instead of chairing his weekly major projects review meeting, Max was sitting on a much-too-small chair in a Montessori school, surrounded by other similarly exhausted-looking parents.

Early on in his career, Max had been shortlisted in a prestigious competition for the design of an art gallery in Seville. He had been certain he'd win. His design had been stronger than all his competitors'. Winning the competition would not only have brought much-needed finances into the fledging practice but, more importantly, would have brought his name to international attention. But another practice had won. He had sought out the chair of the selection committee after the announcement, desperate to understand why his design hadn't been selected. The chair had revealed that his competitor had brought the committee out to see their other completed projects and had organised for them to meet the building contractors who had vouched for their ability to flex to the ever-changing nature of big projects but still bring those projects in on budget. In short, his competitor had chased the business and had anticipated every issue the client would have concerns over. Max had learnt that, no matter how great the design, it was no match for the trust and reassurance that came from the strong connections face-to-face meetings brought.

Which was why he was here, listening to Carly Knight give a talk to parents on helping their children to sleep.

When he had entered the room, ten minutes late, she had done a double take. He had smiled, apologised for being late and explained that he had spotted on her website that she was giving the talk here this afternoon.

He had waited all day for her call and when none came he knew he needed to take matters in hand.

Carly spoke with a professional enthusiasm to the group, explaining her approach to sleep with the aid of an overhead presentation and a detailed account of some of the previous families she had successfully worked with. Max listened to her talk, realising it would be so easy to believe in everything she said. But Max knew that life wasn't so simple. He raised his hand when she spoke about the importance of initially staying with your child as they fell asleep.

Her brow furrowed. 'Yes, Max?'

'Shouldn't we be encouraging our children to be independent? Everything you are saying will make them even more dependent on us.' Max was gratified to see some of the other parents nod in agreement.

'The most independent and contented people are those who are secure in their love—isn't that the gift we want to give our children?' Without waiting for him to answer, Carly continued her talk.

Max shook his head. Didn't she understand the importance of making a child independent? All of her *tenderness* and *comforting* talk was nonsense. Children needed to learn to cope on their own. Just as he had done growing up. His mother had rarely been around when he was a child as she had often worked a double shift in her job as a hotel chambermaid. Being independent hadn't done him any harm…how many other people were running a billion-euro business at thirty-three? And he had coped when his mother had died when he was nineteen. He'd got on with his life. Isabella was without a mother too. She was at a greater disadvantage than other children so it was important that she learned to be strong. Not to rely on others. What if anything happened to him and Isabella was completely reliant on and attached to him? How would she manage? One thing was for sure, Carly Knight's tenderness and comfort would be of little help then.

At the end of the talk Carly patiently answered the other parents' questions. Begrudgingly he admitted that some of what she said made sense, especially the need for routine and consistency. He knew he needed to revise his work commitments, but his clients expected him on location to personally present at design bids, and with a workforce of over five hundred staff, it was his responsibility to make sure that work continued to flow into the practice. And as loath as he was to admit it, sometimes a hotel room was preferable to facing the emptiness of his house late at night when Isabella had eventually fallen asleep. The loneliness that engulfed him in those late hours often felt as though it were eating him up from the inside out.

As the other parents drifted out of the room, after giving Carly enthusiastic applause, he stood and approached her as she packed away all the sleeping aids she had shown around the group.

She raised one of her perfectly arched eyebrows. 'It was an unexpected surprise to see you here.'

Hidden in her teasing tone was a hint of scepticism. He shrugged, leant against the wall next to a table filled with pots of tender, newly sprouting plants, name stickers haphazardly applied to the terracotta-coloured plastic. 'I thought it would be a good opportunity to get a head start in understanding the techniques you'll use with Isabella.'

Carly placed the lid on the yellow cardboard box. 'In other words, you're here to try and persuade me to come to Lake Como with you.'

'Yes.'

She shook her head. 'At least you're honest, unlike a lot of other people.'

Surprised by her jaded tone, he said, 'I thought in your line of work you'd see the positive in everyone.'

Today she was wearing a knee-length, primrose-yellow summer dress. She rested her hand against her upper chest, where the top buttons were undone to reveal smooth creamy skin. 'I try to be...' She eyed him carefully as though trying to weigh up just how much she could trust him.

He hesitated for a moment, but decided to go for broke...no matter how humiliating it was to be practically begging this woman. He cleared his throat. 'I'm a proud man who doesn't like to admit when he's getting things wrong...' he paused, taken aback by the sudden need to unburden himself in the face of Carly's attentive blue gaze '...but I've been getting things wrong with my family for far too long. I need help. I need *your* help. Will you come?'

'I don't usually——'

He stepped forward, handed her the paper sheet he had folded into his jacket pocket earlier this morning. 'Isabella created this drawing yesterday with Vittoria, I thought you might like it. I think she has an artistic flair.'

She took the sheet and smiled at the tiny pink

handprint that had then been covered in a rainbow of assorted Pollock-like paint drips. 'Considering your profession it's no wonder that Isabella would have an artistic flair too. What type of projects is your firm involved in?'

'We mainly specialise in large commercial contracts.'

She nodded and lifted her laptop bag. 'Any that I would be familiar with?'

He went and picked up the cardboard box. 'The Ayer building in New York, Yumba International Airport.'

She held the classroom door open for him to pass through, her eyes widening. 'The Ayer building—wow, I've seen photos in the press. It's a stunning building.'

After she said her goodbyes to the owner, who was in her office, they walked out into the school garden and then to the road beyond the security gate. 'What did you think of my talk?'

'You have a flair for public speaking—really engaging.'

His answer seemed to amuse her, but then with a more serious expression she said, 'I meant the content, the substance of my approach.'

She had said earlier that she liked his honesty. He didn't make it a habit to talk about his past, or anything to do with his family. But he knew he had to open up to Carly if he wanted her support. He lowered the box to the ground, shrugged on his jacket against the chill in the evening. 'It's very different from how I was brought up—I had to be independent from a young age. I can see the benefit to a lot of what you say…but I need help implementing it.'

She gestured for him to pass the cardboard box to her. Nodded down the road. 'My underground station is in that direction. I have to go—I'm meeting a friend later.'

'Can I give you a lift?'

She shook her head. 'The underground will be faster.'

'So, have you made a decision about this weekend?'

She frowned and indecision shone in her eyes. Why was she so reluctant to go to Lake Como with him? His instinct told him that there was more to it than just her planned weekend away. She didn't trust him. He smiled. 'Honestly, the ice cream in Lake Como is really good.' He gestured to the dull day surrounding them. 'And you can't say that you'd prefer to stay here with this weather.'

Her eyes narrowed. 'What time is your flight tomorrow?'

'My plane has a slot for five p.m. at London City jet centre.'

'I've a full schedule tomorrow until three.'

'A driver from my office can collect you if you

give me your address. We can board immediately, so provided you are there by four-forty we can go. Will that work for you?'

Carly inhaled a deep breath. Looked down at Isabella's painting she was still carrying in her hand. 'I'll go because of Isabella. You can pay me my standard fee but also make a charitable donation to the family support group I gave the talk to on Tuesday. They do incredible work helping disadvantaged parents—please make sure your donation is generous.'

She turned away from him and walked quickly towards the station, the low heels of her summer sandals clipping on the footpath, her loose blonde hair shimmering in the sudden burst of sunshine that broke free of the cloud mass.

For a brief moment he felt elation.

And then he remembered what it was he was facing this weekend.

Isabella asleep in his arms, Max stared out of the jet's window, his thoughts clearly far, far away, which Carly supposed was a welcome change from how he had longingly been eyeballing his phone, which was lying on the coffee table sitting between them. After Isabella had fallen asleep, he had asked her to pass it to him but she had whispered, 'No, it will disturb Isabella. Use this time to enjoy holding her; giving her the comfort she wants.' He had thrown her an exasperated look but she had just shrugged and returned to pretending to read the magazine the jet's hostess had passed to her along with the best Americano Carly had ever tasted.

The implications of Max's words yesterday that his plane had a slot at five for take-off hadn't fully registered with Carly until she had seen his private jet sitting on the runaway. He owned a plane. Max Lovato was even wealthier than she had first guessed and that wealth made her uncomfortable and extra cautious around him. It made her want to push him to prove that he was a good father to Isabella. To figure out what his real priorities in life were—wealth or family?

Soon after take-off Carly had suggested that Isabella should have a nap; from her eye rubbing and yawns it was clear she was tired. Max had questioned whether they should instead keep her awake in the hope she would sleep through the night but had accepted Carly's explanation that they needed to avoid Isabella being overtired and taken her into the jet's bedroom. But Isabella had refused to settle and had clung to Max instead. Guessing that Isabella was picking up on her father's stress, lying down in the middle of the day clearly not being his thing, Carly suggested that they come back out into the lounge and cuddle. Within five minutes Isabella had fallen fast asleep.

Now, Carly tried to focus on an article about the benefits of superfoods and whether they were superfoods or not, but her attention kept being drawn back to father and daughter.

Isabella had her father's mouth, the soft wave now relaxed in sleep from its earlier unhappy jutting out. When Carly had boarded the plane, Isabella had eyed her warily before burying her face into her father's chest, her little hands bunching the light blue material of his polo shirt. Isabella's complexion was lighter than Max's—her skin was the colour of golden honey, her hair adorable chestnut curls. Her eyes were molten chocolate brown and could easily break your heart with the defiance that sparked in their depths and spoke of a toddler struggling to understand her world.

Alongside his polo shirt, Max was wearing navy chinos, his sockless feet in loosely laced navy boating shoes. Carly's gaze time and time again was drawn to his bare ankles, the smoothness of his dark tanned skin over the ankle bone oddly compelling.

He had started off sitting upright, his reluctance to relax, to spend downtime with his daughter obvious. What was holding him back from fully engaging with his daughter? Was his job that pressurised? Was it the need for success and even more wealth and power? Or was he simply struggling like so many other parents? She thought back to that torment she had witnessed the first time she had seen him and winced. She wanted to help him in his grief for his wife, in his struggle with understanding and connecting fully with his daughter. That was why she had agreed to this weekend. Even after he had shamelessly turned up at her meeting Wednesday afternoon in a bid to persuade her to go with them to Lake Como. But to give him his due, he had listened attentively to her talk, which she had delivered in a more faltering than usual style, thanks to his unnerving concentration that had his gaze follow her every movement. After, out in the street, she had heard the sincerity in his voice when he said he needed her help.

But, despite all his well-meaning pledges, she wasn't yet convinced he really was prepared to put the effort into what needed to be done.

As Isabella had relaxed in her sleep, as though by osmosis, Max too had visibly unwound. He had shifted forward in his seat, his legs moving outwards, his shoulders dropping, his right hand relaxing to gently rub against his little girl's bare leg where her pink denim dungarees had ridden up from her bare feet.

Isabella's earlier hot cheeks from fighting both sleep and her father had now cooled and Carly smiled at the little girl, already taken by her strong spirit.

Her gaze shifted back up to Max. His eyes were

closed. Was he asleep too? Carly sank further into her chair and tried to ignore just how attracted she was to him. He was a client. She was here to do a job.

Carly knew only too well how workplace romances derailed life. Her parents had once owned an accountancy practice...until her mother had fallen for one of their clients. Carly, then aged eleven, could still remember to this day the elation that had shone in her mum's eyes when she had spoken every evening at the dinner table about her new client. She had relayed with awe the details of his holiday home in Sardinia, his corporate jaunts to sports events and conferences in exotic locations. How devoted to and proud he was of his three high-achieving and beautiful daughters. How miserable his ex-wife had made him.

All this her mum would recount with great animation, her voice bright, which only emphasised the dislike that settled on her features when Carly's father would interrupt with some story of his own.

Carly had been devastated when her parents split but she had held out hope—after all, her dad promised that she could stay with him at weekends and she was gaining three sisters. Carly had always wanted siblings. But with the business collapsing amidst a bitter divorce, her dad had left England for a new life in New Zealand where his sister lived. And Carly's three new sisters, all much older than her, showed little interest in her on their visits home from university other than to make it clear that they considered her nothing other than a nuisance who would never be welcomed into their tight circle. They idolised their father and jealously guarded their relationship with him.

Carly shivered. The air temperature in the cabin had dropped. She smiled as Isabella snuffled, turned her cheek into her father's chest and sighed. Carly's throat tightened at the sight of Max's strong forearm lying so protectively around Isabella's tiny waist.

Then Max stirred, his head shifting to the left. But he continued to sleep, his chest rising and falling regularly. Even sitting four feet away, Carly could see the long dark length of his eyelashes. His eyebrows were thick and expressive; his nose was at a perfect angle to complement his high cheekbones; his chiselled jawline travelled down in a perfectly defined curve from his ears to end in a cleft chin that gave his face a devastating beauty.

Standing, she tiptoed across the cabin and picked up a lemon-coloured wool throw from the lounge sofa. Tucking the blanket around Isabella, she pulled back, lifted her eyes and looked straight into Max's gaze.

'You think of everything.' His voice was low, croaky from tiredness. And so, so sexy. Her feet curled in her trainers. Her stomach did a little flip.

She was not going to blush. She was going to brazen this out.

She inhaled a scent that reminded her of the summer she had gone Interrailing as a student and camped in a Croatian forest next to the Adriatic—sea mist and earthy pine combining to produce a potent sense of vitality and adventure. 'All part of the service.'

He raised an eyebrow.

She stepped back. 'Can I get you anything else?'

His lips twitched. He nodded to the table behind her. 'My phone.'

'Not until Isabella wakes.'

Carly sat back in her chair. Aware of his gaze on her, she picked up the magazine and tried to develop an interest in a berry favoured by sub-Saharan goat herders.

'Are you sure that sleeping like this won't teach her bad habits?'

She dropped the magazine. 'Isabella needs to feel secure with you. This will teach her that you will spend time holding her, comforting her when she needs it. Being with her, responding to her needs—this is the starting basis of developing good sleeping technique. In the next few days hopefully you will start to appreciate that.' She leant towards him, determined that he understood the main message of her sleeping technique—that parents learn to allow themselves to be tender with their children and themselves. 'We all need physical touch. We all need to have someone hug us and tell us that everything is going to be okay.'

His expression hardened. A tense silence settled between them.

Confused, Carly stared at him, slowly realising what she had said. 'I'm sorry—that was insensitive of me. With your wife—'

He interrupted her with a quick shake of his head. 'It's okay.'

Carly's gaze shifted down to Isabella, her arms suddenly aching with the desire to hold her. 'Trust me on this, Isabella won't want your cuddles in a few years' time…and when she's a teenager she won't even want to know you. So you should enjoy it while you can.'

His gaze dropped down to consider Isabella for a moment before he asked in a low voice, 'Were you like that with your dad when you were a teenager?'

'My dad moved to New Zealand when I was twelve. I didn't get the chance to…'

'You miss him?'

Carly's heart fell. She spoke to her dad occasionally but there was so much time and distance between them now that their relationship just consisted of the polite conversation of assuring one another that all was well in their lives, and a hollowness when she ended the call that would stay with her for hours. 'Sometimes.'

'Have you other family?'

There was a gentleness to his tone that stirred unexpected emotion in her—a loneliness, a longing for a family of her own that she was usually so good at burying. 'No—my mum remarried. It was messy.' She gave a shrug, trying to dredge up her usual acceptance of her situation but there was something about Max's intelligent gaze that was stopping her doing so. 'I'm not close to my mum and her new family, but I have good friends, people I trained with. We all live close to one another in London.'

'Were you going away with them this weekend?' He paused for a moment. 'With a boyfriend perhaps?'

'Six of us were heading away together…all friends.'

He nodded to her answer and shifted the arm that was resting on Isabella. 'Thank you for agreeing to come with us this weekend. I realise it was a lot to ask of you.'

She studied him for a moment, thrown by the sincerity of his tone, the restrained pride in his expression. Maybe he was different from her stepfather, who would always somehow twist everything he did for people, whether they wanted it or not, into the fact that he was doing that person a favour. He had insisted that Carly attend boarding school and signed her up for endless residential courses during half-terms and summer holidays. He had claimed that he wanted her to be more adventurous, more ambitious, more accomplished, just like his daughters. The unspoken truth was that he hadn't wanted Carly around.

She nodded in acknowledgement to his thanks and said, 'Most of the parents who come to me find it difficult to talk about their child not sleeping. They think they should instinctively know how to get their child to sleep, that they are somehow failing as a parent. Which of course is not true. The parents I meet are doing their best in their individual circumstances. I try to help them see and understand that…to learn to be tender with themselves.'

Carly laughed when Max's smooth forehead creased at her last sentence. 'You don't like that expression "be tender with themselves"?' she asked.

'I can't see any man buying into it.'

'You'd be surprised.'

He shifted in his seat, his expression sceptical. 'Is this going to work?'

'If you allow it to—if you give it the time and patience needed.'

'You think I'm impatient?'

'I get the feeling that you like to be on the move a lot. With children you need to slow down, to connect with them.'

He looked down at Isabella and shook his head.

'With this firecracker I've no option the way she clings to me.'

There was such weariness to his voice. Understanding the positives in Isabella's personality might help him in dealing with his daughter. 'At least you know that Isabella will fight for what she wants—she's determined. It will stand her in good stead in life, having that strength of character.'

For a long while he stared at her, considering what she had said. 'I hadn't thought of it that way... I guess you could be right. Do you want children of your own some day?'

Carly smiled at his question, while inside it felt like a soft swift pinch to her heart. She had envisioned herself and Robert having children quickly; they had even spoken about trying to have a baby soon after they married. 'Some day hopefully I will. I love being with children. Before I set up my sleep consultancy business I was a Montessori teacher, but I have to meet the right person first.'

'That hasn't happened yet?'

Carly paused, a heavy weight lodging in her chest. 'I thought it had. A few years back I was due to marry. But three weeks before the wedding my ex broke it off.'

Emotion continuing to whirl in her chest, Carly grabbed the magazine and again pretended to read it.

'I'm sorry.'

Carly nodded but refused to look up from the magazine, hating how exposed, how humiliated she felt having told him. She flicked through the pages of the magazine, trying to understand why the publishers thought their readers would be interested in the weight gain of a soap-opera actress. Hadn't they heard about emotional eating? Carly might have binned her wedding cake but that hadn't stopped her from eating her own body weight in ice cream and her favourite comfort food, Brazil nuts, in the weeks that followed. It had taken her months to return to her normal weight. A weight that wasn't particularly impressive in the first place. But Carly had long ago accepted that her body would never be lean, no matter how much she dieted or exercised.

'Tell me about your ex—what happened?'

'I'd prefer not to.'

'It clearly upsets you.'

Carly raised her eyes. She knew she should change the subject. Not answer even. But there was a genuineness to his expression, as though he really wanted to understand what had happened to her that had her blurt out, 'He told me he was still in love with his ex-girlfriend.'

Max's eyes softened. 'That must have been heartbreaking for you.'

Something popped in Carly's heart. She had expected pity, perhaps even outrage from him. Just as her friends had been outraged on her behalf, calling Robert every name under the sun, telling her she needed to be positive, that there were plenty of other guys out there. Her mother meanwhile had fretted over what people would think while her stepfather had simply asked why she could never get things right in life. Nobody had got just how sad it all had been. Until now. Carly's throat closed over; she felt undone by the understanding in his eyes. She shrugged.

'I'm sorry you had to go through that,' he said gently.

Carly nodded, not trusting herself to talk.

Max considered her for a while and then, with a gentle smile, he added, 'I bet he's regretting it now, letting someone like you slip away.'

Carly grimaced. 'Not really. He's married his ex since.'

He tilted his head. 'But I bet he's not on the way to taste the best chocolate ice cream in the world.'

Carly laughed, something lightening in her. 'That's true.'

They smiled at each other for the longest while. Carly felt the heat grow on her cheeks. Max's smile disappeared to be replaced by a tension in his expression that reflected the heavy beat of disquiet that was drumming in her heart.

She tore her gaze away, picked up her magazine.

\* \* \*

The sun had set when Max turned his car into the driveway of Villa Isa with the beginnings of a throbbing headache about to take hold.

The narrow road cut into the hillside and, surrounded by woodland, hid well the exquisite beauty about to be revealed.

'Wow, oh, wow—now that's what I call a view.' He winced at Carly's excited exclamation as Lake Como in all its magnetic night-time beauty of shadowy mountains and fairy-tale villages with twinkling lights opened up to them.

He pulled the car to a stop in the carport and looked towards the brightly lit villa with a heavy heart. His housekeeper, Luciana, had turned on the lights in many of the downstairs rooms to welcome them before she left for her home in nearby Bellagio. He knew he should be feeling pride in the renovations he had commissioned to restore the mid-twentieth-century villa to its former glory. So many would have knocked it down, but Max had loved its quirkiness, its tall ceilings, exposed stonework and vast open-plan living spaces. But instead of pride he just felt a numbness, a detachment from the villa that was once supposed to be his primary home.

'Papa, out!' Isabella's call was accompanied by her feet banging against the sides of her car seat. Since they had landed Isabella had been truculent, running away on the tarmac, refusing to sit in the car that had been waiting beside the runway on their arrival. And once in the car she had immediately begun to grumble, unhappy at being restrained in her car seat.

Carly's pert nose had wrinkled when he had admitted that he didn't have any nursery rhyme CDs he could play for Isabella. So they had spent the journey from the airport with Carly leading a sing-along and insisting he join in. Unfortunately Isabella became fixated on 'Three Blind Mice' and insisted they sing it time and time again.

He had known it was a bad idea to allow Isabella to sleep on board the plane.

'Out!' Isabella shouted again, her foot furiously hammering her car seat.

He had work to do. It was going to take him for ever to get Isabella to settle.

He turned and regarded Carly. 'Are you so certain of the benefit of allowing her to nap now?'

Carly glanced back at Isabella, gave her a smile. 'You just want to run around, don't you, Isabella? Why don't you play with Papa?'

'It's beyond her bedtime. She should be asleep by now, not bouncing off the walls.'

Carly shrugged and got out of the car. She went to unlock Isabella's belt but Isabella shook her head and then buried it into the side of her car seat, refusing to allow Carly to lift her out.

The headache gripping his temples ever tighter, Max pushed open the driver door and lifted Isabella out of her seat. His phone, in his trouser pocket, buzzed once again.

'I'll say it again, the views from here are spectacular. And it's so warm, even at this time of the night. I've missed the heat so much. What's the nearby town called? It looks so cute.'

Distracted by an email from a client in Taiwan, he glanced over to see Carly at the edge of the driveway, looking beyond the brightly lit terraced garden that sloped down to the waterfront and his private jetty, and vaguely answered, 'The town is Bellagio…' This was unbelievable—how did the client expect the new train terminal to open in time if at this late stage they wanted to make changes to the roof design?

'I have a call to make.' He attempted to pass Isabella to Carly but Isabella clung to his shirt, her legs wrapping even more tightly around his waist.

Carly folded her arms. 'No calls. You must settle Isabella first.'

'This is important.'

'I'll sort out the luggage. Isabella needs some exercise to wind down. I suggest you take her down to the garden, let her explore for a while. In the meantime, I'll prepare her a small snack.'

He was about to argue that she should take Isabella down to the gardens instead but before he could do so, Carly had popped open the boot of his car and was walking towards the front door, carrying two heavy suitcases with ease. There went his excuse that it made sense for him to look after the heavy luggage instead of playing with his little girl.

He glanced down at Isabella. She frowned back at him. His daughter might not have many words but she sure seemed to understand every word spoken around her.

How did a twenty-two-month-old possess the capacity to make him feel like a completely lousy dad?

He was still standing by the car when Carly returned to retrieve more luggage.

She steadily ignored him but gave Isabella a smile.

Isabella tucked her head into his shoulder.

He yelped when her fingers pinched his skin as she gripped onto his shirt sleeves.

Carly ducked her head, laughter threatening on her lips.

He stared after her once again retreating back as she carried more suitcases into the hallway, before he climbed down the steps and headed in the direction of the playground that had been constructed to the side of the terrace. He went to place Isabella onto the swing but she clung to him. He tried not to sigh and instead sat on one side of the sprung see-saw. He bounced up and down, feeling ridiculous. He was about to climb back off but then he heard Isabella chuckle. He bounced again, his heart lifting to hear her chortle again. His serious-minded daughter rarely laughed.

He bounced and bounced, feeling an unexpected happiness. And he remembered some of the things Carly had said during the past few days—that it was natural for children to wake, that Isabella wasn't alone in doing so.

A movement inside the villa caught his attention.

Carly was inside the open-plan kitchen searching through the cupboards, taking out some items, pausing to stretch her back, roll her head side to side as she studied the contents of the fridge. She had tied up her hair into a loose ponytail and rolled up the sleeves of her blue blouse that was tucked into slim-fitting, navy, ankle-length trousers. Her body was curvy. He supposed some men would say sensual.

He slowed in his bouncing and winced at the realisation that it felt good to have her around. Yes, he had employed nannies, had some support. But Carly was different. She had the strength of conviction to tell him things he didn't want to hear but with an empathy that had him struggling to argue back. He admired her for that. As much as he hated to admit it, he was enjoying her company.

And earlier, in the tight confines of the plane,

when Carly had placed the blanket on his lap, when he had woken to see her staring at him, as they had spoken in low voices to one another, he'd known he could no longer ignore the kernel of attraction for her growing inside him.

This was not supposed to be happening.

Isabella squirmed in his arms, began to protest at the lack of movement.

Her once again serious eyes glared up at him.

Fresh guilt slammed into Max. He had no right to enjoy the company of another woman.

# CHAPTER THREE

AFTER PREPARING A snack for Isabella, Carly had
unpacked both her own and Isabella's suitcases,
carried out a recce of Isabella's room and returned
to the kitchen to find Isabella sitting in her high
chair, munching on a banana, her gaze firmly fixed
on her father, who was typing on the keyboard of
his phone.

Carly came to a stop beside him and waited until
he finally looked up. 'I chose a bedroom for myself
close to Isabella's so that I can help you during the
night when she wakes.' She pushed on in the hope
that if she spoke quickly there was less chance of
her giving away just how disturbed she felt to be
in the intimacy of his home. 'I left your suitcases
in your bedroom.' She didn't add that she knew
it was his bedroom because a quick look into the
attached dressing room had revealed a row of bespoke suits and expensive casual wear. His whole
bedroom, with its accent blue wall behind a white
supersized headboard filled with dramatic modern art and pale wooden floor boards, was mas-
culine. Him.

Her own room, next to his, decorated in soft

greens, had the same breathtaking views of Lake Como and shared the same terrace that led down to the floodlit outdoor pool. She just hoped that they never bumped into each other out there. The image of Max dressed only in swimwear strolling down to the pool made her pause; she'd happily bet the entire annual income of her business on the guess that he had a seriously impressive body.

'I...' She paused as the image of Max's powerful broad shoulders, narrowing to a slim waist, swam unwanted into her mind. 'I... I...yes, what I was trying to say was that I had a look at Isabella's bedroom to ensure that it's the right environment to promote sleep. I suggest you install blackout blinds in addition to the curtains that are already there.'

Max considered her for a moment, his raised eyebrow the only hint of mischief in his otherwise deadpan expression. 'I take it that you're wanting some company in bed tonight?'

Carly stared at him; only after a long few seconds did it dawn on her that her mouth was gaping open. She snapped it closed. 'What? Certainly not!'

Max's lips curled upwards before he nodded towards the toys in her arms. 'I meant the soft toys... are you taking them to bed with you?'

Carly shook her head, trying to rein in her embarrassment. She hit him with an unimpressed glare and went and placed the three stuffed toys on the long sleek white kitchen table that complemented the steel and pale wood of the supermodern kitchen.

Turning, she moved back to him, held out her hand. 'Okay, for the next hour we're having a phone-free zone.'

He pulled his phone out of her reach. 'Please tell me that you're joking.'

She shook her head. 'Phone on the kitchen counter, where I can see it.' Then she wiped Isabella's hands free of banana mush and cleaned the tray of her high chair with some wipes. She placed all three toys onto the high-chair table—Sami the white long-eared rabbit, Skye the blue bear and Sunny the grey elephant. Isabella eyed the three toys dubiously but then lurched and grabbed hold of Sunny, squashing his long trunk in under her armpit.

Carly smiled at Isabella and touched her fingertips against Sunny's grey velvety fur. 'This is Sleepy Sunny, Isabella. He and his friends here, Sami and Skye, live together in Sleep World. They love nothing more than lying in bed, being all snugly and warm and falling asleep.'

Isabella looked at her doubtfully and held onto the heavy-eyed and tiredly smiling Sunny even closer.

Carly turned to Max. He was propped against

the kitchen's central island thick slab of white marble countertop, arms crossed with a bemused expression on his face. 'And tonight your papa will read to you a story about Sunny in Sleep World, won't you, Papa?'

He eyed Sunny and the other animals. 'Will I?'

Carly decided to ignore his dubious expression. 'You mentioned at the parent talk on Wednesday that Isabella has no particular toy she uses as a comforter.' She had shown the group the story book she had written and published to encourage sleep, *Sleepy Heads in Sleep World*, and the three main characters that were available as soft toys, Sami, Skye and Sunny. 'As Isabella clearly has taken a shine to Sunny, for the next few days we're going to include him in all of Isabella's activities until she identifies with it as being something of comfort and reassurance.' Max's sceptical frown only intensified when she added, 'Starting now. I found a toy teapot and teacups in Isabella's room. I've left them on the rug there—I want you to take Isabella and Sunny to her room and for all three of you to have a tea party.'

'I don't have—'

Carly interrupted Max, choosing to ignore his horror at her suggestion. 'Give the tea party ten minutes. I want Isabella to associate her bedroom with comfort, that it's a nice safe place for her to be in.' Moving to the door that led to the main hall and stairs, Carly added, 'In the meantime I'll run a bath for Isabella. You can bathe her after your tea party—make sure to bring Sunny along to take part. Then it's into bed and you can read *Sleepy Heads in Sleep World* to her. After that it's lights out. If Isabella is still restless I have a lavender massage cream that you can use with her.'

'I've calls—'

With a bright smile Carly interrupted him. 'Let's go. Think of this as the new, exciting beginning of you and Isabella spending some fun time together.'

Max's expression grew incredulous.

And as though to make her position clear, with one mighty throw, Isabella threw Sunny towards her father, the drowsy elephant hitting Max square on the shoulder.

Carly fled the room, her initial amusement at Isabella's amazing aim giving way to disquiet as she climbed the polished concrete stairs. Would she ever manage to get Max and Isabella in tune with one another? And more to the point, would she manage to get through this weekend without embarrassing herself by revealing that, rather foolishly, she was attracted to him?

An hour later, Carly stood at Isabella's door, hearing Max speaking in low whispers to his daughter as he sat on the side of her bed. Isabella's room was in darkness, the only light coming from the faint moonlight twinkling through the roof lights that ran along the corridor.

Max was whispering in a mixture of English and Italian, his voice deep, gentle.

Carly closed her eyes, suddenly tired after such a long day, her shoulder dropping against the door-frame.

Max's whispers continued.

Carly inhaled the lavender massage cream Max had at first reluctantly massaged into an equally reluctant Isabella. Max had used unsure strokes on Isabella, who had slapped his hand away when he had first begun to massage her forearm as Carly had suggested. But slowly and rather miraculously father and daughter had eventually given in to the soothing pleasure of the massage.

'You're tired.'

Carly jumped. Her eyes shot open to find Max standing directly in front of her. Unnerved at having him stand so close, unnerved by his height, the force of the bone-melting energy that oozed from him, the darkness enclosing them, she edged back into the corridor.

Max followed slowly closing Isabella's door, but leaving it slightly ajar.

He nodded when she asked if Isabella was asleep.

She gave him a smile, trying to focus on being

professional. 'You did a really good job tonight. Well done.'

In the faint light of the corridor she saw a gleam of amusement light in his eyes. 'Apart from bath time, you mean.'

Carly laughed softly. 'I'm sure Isabella didn't mean to soak you.'

'You reckon?'

Carly tried not to react to the lightness, the teasing in his eyes, all the while doing her best not to recall how gorgeous he had looked as he knelt beside the bath earlier, his damp hair slicked back, his tee shirt soaked through, his exasperation towards Isabella's splashing giving way to amusement and shared laughter.

'I've an office downstairs—I must go and make some calls. My housekeeper, Luciana, has left food in the fridge. Please help yourself.' He went to walk away but, pausing, he added, 'Thank you for your help tonight. It was calmer than usual.' He rubbed a hand tiredly at the base of his neck. 'It took for ever, though. I won't be able to spend so much time settling her every night.'

For a moment Carly considered Max. He was so loath to relax, to allow himself to enjoy being a parent. Sometimes, a lightness broke through his intensity. She needed to help him appreciate the joy of being a father. 'You know, with time, you might grow to enjoy spending your evenings with Isabella.'

He shook his head, clearly unconvinced. 'Why did no one warn me just how exhausting and time-consuming being a parent is?'

'But it's rewarding too.' Carly waited for a response from Max but when none came she asked, 'Don't you agree?'

Rewarding. That was not the term Max would use for being a parent. Bewildering. Frustrating. Exhausting. Those were better words. But what parent could admit to those feelings?

He winced at Carly's calm gaze.

And then her hand was reaching out, touching his bare forearm. 'Things will get better, Max... you've been coping for far too long on your own.'

He swallowed at the gentleness of her tone. He should step away, tell Carly that he would see her in the morning. But for the first time since Marta's death he wanted company, he wanted to be able to sit down and eat a meal with another human being. Apart from work dinners, he ate alone, mostly snacks taken at his desk.

He wasn't sure what madness was taking him over, and quickly he rationalised to himself that, as it was at his insistence she was here this weekend, the least he could do was be hospitable. And after this weekend he would rarely see Carly Knight again, so what was the harm in sitting down and sharing a meal with her?

'You know, I'm hungry. Let's go and have dinner. We can sit outside on the terrace, where you can take in the view—you haven't seen much of Lake Como since you arrived.'

Carly edged away from him. 'I…' She wrapped her arms tightly around her waist, her fists bunching against the red wool of the jumper she had earlier pulled on. He could tell she wanted to say no. Was she this wary of all men thanks to her ex? A desire to somehow make it up to her in some small way saw him offer her his arm. 'Luciana makes the best pasta in the whole of Italy…she'll have left some in the fridge for us to have tonight.'

Carly eyed his arm warily but then with a disbelieving eye-roll she placed her hand on his arm.

In the kitchen he told her to take a seat on one of the stools at the kitchen island.

He caught her gazing about the room, taking in the artwork and the furniture.

'I'm guessing the villa was recently renovated?' she asked as he swung open the fridge door.

He rifled through the contents of the fridge, reading the labels of the containers Luciana had left, finally settling on one lidded bowl, which he laid on the countertop. 'It was renovated last year…' Pointing to the bowl, he asked, 'I've chosen *ravioli di zucca e ricotta*, pumpkin and ricotta ravioli, for us to eat—is that okay?'

Carly nodded, her gaze once again shifting around the room. She tilted her head back to gaze up at the modern chandelier he had commissioned a local artist to make, the almost translucent ceramic pieces engraved with images of the villa at different stages of the renovations. 'It's such a beautiful villa. Were you in charge of the renovation designs?'

Max busied himself filling a large pasta saucepan with water, pleased with her words, but unsettled at the truth that despite all his best efforts to make this villa a home—the endless hours he had put into the designs, the daily calls to the renovation team, the meticulous sourcing of just the right furniture and artwork—he felt nothing for it.

'I wanted to keep the uniqueness of the existing villa intact so most of the original features were retained but some new windows were added to take advantage of the views, internally the walls of some of the smaller rooms were knocked through to create larger spaces. We also built a new boathouse down by the waterfront and the pool was made bigger.'

Carly stood from her seat and wandered around the open-plan dining room, taking in the décor and the nooks and crannies of this unconventional villa.

'The renovations are beautiful—you're seriously talented. What's the history of the villa—has it been in your family for many years?'

Putting the saucepan on the hob to boil, he inhaled a deep breath before admitting, 'No, we only bought it two years ago. When Marta became pregnant she decided that she wanted to move back here to Lake Como to be close to her parents. She found the villa when she was six months pregnant with Isabella.'

He waited for Carly to smile awkwardly at what he had said, to change the subject, but instead she nodded and said, 'Marta clearly had good taste.'

He could not help but smile at that. 'Well, she did agree to marry me.'

His heart lifted to hear Carly's laughter. Shaking her head, she asked gently, 'What was Marta like?'

Taken aback, he turned away from Carly, busied himself with taking oils and condiments from the pull-out drawer next to the hob. For so long he had pushed all thoughts of Marta away, the grief of recalling her too intense. But now, for some reason he found himself wanting to tell Carly about her. 'She was smart...really smart—she was the only student in her law-degree year to be awarded maximum marks on a difficult course. And she was ambitious; she was specialising in intellectual property law. She loved being pregnant, being a mother.'

Emotion tightening his chest, Max took a tray from a cupboard and started to load it with glasses.

Carly stood and moved next to him. 'You take care of the cooking, I'll set the table out on the terrace. I know where everything is from preparing Isabella's snack earlier.'

With the water boiling in the saucepan, Max turned the temperature down. When the water was simmering he carefully placed the handmade ravioli into it. He turned as Carly lifted the tray now loaded with cutlery and glassware. She smiled at him, a smile full of warmth and kindness. 'You know, it sounds like Marta was an incredible person. And she was right to want the support of her family. Have you considered moving back here to Lake Como to get that support yourself?'

Max considered for a moment shrugging off Carly's question with some vague answer but there was something about her open gaze that had him admit, 'It's Marta's family who live here. I grew up in Rome. I've no family of my own since my mother died when I was nineteen. Marta's family…they have never approved of me.'

'Why?'

Trying to focus on keeping the cynicism from his voice, aware that he was speaking about Isabella's grandparents, he answered, 'My in-laws, the Ghiraldini family, own one of the biggest pharmaceutical companies in Italy. They've always been suspicious of my reasoning for marrying Marta.'

'But you're wealthy in your own right.'

'Now I am. Not when we met at university. Back then I was nothing but a kid from the wrong side of the tracks with a mother who worked as a chambermaid and a deadbeat father who had disappeared from my life when I was three.'

Carly lifted the wooden tray closer to herself. 'But now, with your success and having got to know you, Marta's parents must approve of you.'

Max turned away to check on the pasta. He waited with his back to her, expecting to hear her footsteps as she went out to set the table, but after a while he realised she wasn't going to leave until he answered her. Swinging around, he stared at her, his arms folded on his chest. Inside, he was on fire with emotion, but his answer came out in an icy tone. 'Their daughter died when married to me. Why on earth would they approve of me now?'

'But it was a car accident.'

The guilt inside him exploded in the quietness of the villa, in his jet-lagged exhaustion, in reaction to Carly's softly spoken words, at the compassion in her eyes. Without meaning to, for the first time since Marta died he spoke out loud some of the torment living inside him. 'I should have taken better care of Marta, made sure she wasn't out driving late at night.'

He whipped around, grabbed the saucepan… but the handle was too hot. It scorched his palm. But he bit against the pain and continued on to the sink where he drained the pasta.

He tried to ignore Carly, who had come to stand beside him. 'What happened on the night Marta died?'

He lowered his head, wanting to keep that night inside himself. But he was so tired of hiding it. He turned around, placed his back against the sink. The act of turning to face the villa for which he and Marta had cherished such dreams caused him almost to back out of speaking. But Carly's steady blue gaze, the softness of her expression, brought him to say, 'Isabella had woken just after midnight. Marta had fed her but Isabella wouldn't settle. I took her downstairs, walked her in my arms. She would fall asleep but the moment I took her back upstairs and laid her down she started crying again. Marta got up and told me to go back to bed. I had an early flight to Munich later that morning. Marta left a note on the hall table saying that she was taking Isabella out in her car for a drive in the hope that she would settle. It was three in the morning. I was asleep. An hour later our intercom rang. It was the police. A taxi had driven through a red light and smashed into Marta's car. Isabella was uninjured…but Marta…'

For long moments Carly closed her eyes. 'I'm so

sorry.' She stepped even closer, her hand reaching against the countertop, inches from him. 'It must have been such a horrible shock. You can't blame yourself for it though.'

Carly was wrong. He was to blame. If he and Marta hadn't argued that evening then everything would be different. He struggled to breathe against the shame filling his chest. No one knew of their argument. No one knew that Marta had died when they weren't speaking to one another. Max hadn't had the opportunity to say he was sorry, to hug her, to ask for forgiveness for not being there enough for her and Isabella. 'If I had managed to get Isabella back to sleep, Marta wouldn't have been out driving.'

'If your roles were reversed, if it had been you who had gone out and been in an accident, would you blame Marta?'

'Of course not.'

She tilted her head and gave him a sad smile full of care. 'Why are you any different?'

Heat burnt on his cheeks. Her question, that until now he had never considered, hit at the core of his guilt. He had seen his mother struggle his entire childhood after his father had abandoned them and had sworn he would always protect his family. 'It's a husband's job to care for and protect his wife, the mother of his child.'

Carly considered him for a moment. 'Would Marta have agreed with that?'

He could not help but smile. 'No. She would have yelled that she was a strong woman perfectly capable of taking care of herself.'

Carly smiled back. He knew he should end this conversation now. Already he had divulged too much personal information. But Carly's compassion, her humour and intelligence in the midst of all he was telling her, was proving hard to walk away from.

'I'm sure your in-laws will appreciate how well you're caring for Isabella.'

At the mention of the Ghiraldini family again, he realised just how badly he needed a drink. 'Yes, I'm caring for Isabella so well that I've been forced to employ a sleep consultant.'

Carly pushed the sleeves of her blouse further up her arms, clearly unamused at his attempt at dark humour. 'There's no shame in asking for help.'

She was wrong. He should be able to father Isabella without help. Frustrated with his own incompetency, frustrated at the thought of facing his in-laws tomorrow, at having to sit through Tomaso's wedding which would bring back so many memories of his own wedding day, he turned and studied the pasta, which was now dried out and cold. He grimaced and looked towards Carly, who was scrutinising the pasta too.

A grin broke on her mouth. 'I don't think we're going to be able to rescue our dinner. I saw some sourdough bread in the cupboard—how does a cheese and pepperoni toasted sandwich sound to you?'

She had to be kidding. 'In a word, horrible. I'm Italian, we love our food…proper food.'

She popped a hand on her hip. 'You haven't tasted my toasted sandwiches. They were legendary with my friends when I was at college.'

He raised his hands in surrender to the playful indignation sparkling in her eyes. Grabbing hold of a corkscrew, he said, 'I'll open some wine.'

In the midst of raiding the fridge, Carly popped her head out. 'Not wine, you need beer with toasted sandwiches.'

'This is sacrilege—your first night here in Lake Como and you want toasted sandwiches and beer.'

'I can't think of anything better.' Now armed with a selection of cheeses and cold cut meats, Carly added, 'You go and set up the table outside, I'll make the sandwiches.'

Ten minutes later, Carly popped the already toasted sourdough bread, now loaded with pepperoni, mozzarella and goat's cheese, under the grill and then began to clear the counter top.

Her hands were trembling. She pulled in some deep breaths, trying to relax, but the heartbreaking emotion in Max's voice when he had spoken about Marta, how he blamed himself for her accident, continued to upset her. He had clearly loved Marta greatly.

Carly felt a deep need to reach out and help him. He had been trying to manage on his own for far too long. But to help him properly, she knew she had to put aside any feelings, any attraction, she had towards him.

The food ready, Carly took it out onto the terrace. Max soon returned from checking up on Isabella, nodded that she was still asleep and popped the baby monitor on the terrace table.

Once they were both seated at the table, Max bit into his sandwich and chewed slowly, his forehead bunched sceptically. Carly pretended to ignore him but could not help but smile in relief when he said, 'These aren't too bad.'

Carly lifted her beer glass. 'Especially when washed down with a good cool beer.'

Max toasted his glass against hers, amusement dancing in his eyes, 'Tomorrow, I'll introduce you to proper Italian food.'

'Don't forget about the ice cream.' Taking a bite of her own sandwich, the melted cheese tasting sensational, Carly sat back in her chair, trying to focus on keeping the conversation light, trying to ignore how disturbingly good it felt to be sitting across the table from Max in the peace of the Italian countryside. The night was balmy and overhead stars and the faint moon, the lights of the villages in the distance, all contributed to a gorgeous setting. *Romantic, you mean?* Carly pushed that thought away.

'It's so peaceful here, you must enjoy visiting the villa with Isabella.' Pointing towards the playground with its swings and slides and sunken trampoline to the side of the terrace, she added, 'That playground is most kids' idea of paradise.'

'This is Isabella's third time in Villa Isa.'

'Really? It's so perfect here—I thought you'd visit regularly.'

In the shadows of the night, Carly saw Max's chest rise and fall heavily, his expression tighten. 'It's not easy coming here. Marta had so many dreams for this villa…and then there's Marta's parents…' He paused. Carly's heart flipped to hear the emotion in his voice he clearly was trying to disguise. 'They're still deeply upset by her death.'

So many dreams cut short, no wonder he found it hard to come here, and if he wrongly blamed himself for Marta's death then facing her parents must be incredibly difficult and something he would be keen to avoid. But in doing so he was isolating himself and potentially cutting off a source of support in raising Isabella.

'With time, the more you visit here, you and Isabella can create wonderful memories and dreams of your own for summers on the lake. And I appreciate that things haven't always been easy between you and Marta's parents but you've been through a lot. Maybe Isabella's grandparents could support you, especially as you have no family of your own—'

With a shake of his head, Max interrupted her, clearly not wanting to discuss Isabella's grandparents and his need for support. 'Why did you decide to be a sleep consultant?'

Carly considered for a moment pushing the point about Isabella's grandparents but decided that was a conversation for another day. So instead she answered, 'I trained originally to be a Montessori teacher. In that work, I heard from many parents who struggled to cope when their children didn't sleep.'

Taking a sip of her beer, Carly waited for Max to say something, but he didn't. Instead he considered her with his head tilted, an intelligence in his eyes that told her that he had picked up on the emotion in her voice as she remembered the catalyst that led her to training as a sleep consultant. She knew she shouldn't get into explaining her decision any further, she knew she should keep this conversation impersonal, but there was something about Max's gaze, the silence of their surrounds, knowing just how much Max was struggling to understand Isabella's disturbed sleep, that had her admit, 'One of my pupils in particular got to me—Mikey. He was gorgeous.' Carly smiled in remembrance of Mikey's wild blond curls and how he used to suck his thumb, his huge baby-blue eyes staring into hers when he used to sit on her lap for a cuddle. 'His sleep became very disturbed when his parents split up. I guess he reminded me of myself when my parents divorced. Even though I was eleven, I found it really hard to sleep. I used to stay awake worrying about my dad. Worrying about everything, in fact. If somebody had stopped to reassure me, to spend time with me, I think I wouldn't have been so confused.'

Max considered her words for a while. 'Do you really think that's key to Isabella's sleep, for me to spend time with her?'

'Yes. It doesn't have to be twenty-four hours a day. Just some good quality time and a regular bedtime routine should really help her sleep better. It will help you too.'

'What do you mean?'

'You should be enjoying being a father—I sense there's a reluctance in you to do so.'

Max shrugged at that, nudging his now empty plate away from the edge of the table. 'I grew up without a father—sometimes I'm not sure what my role should be.'

Carly's heart tightened to hear the quiet pride

mixed with confusion in Max's voice. 'Just love her with all your heart. Give her your time—there's nothing more precious.'

Max's green gaze held hers. He leaned further into the table, his hand reaching into the centre to play with the base of one of the two white ceramic candlesticks there. 'You said earlier that you're not close to your mum—why's that?'

Carly swallowed. 'My stepfather Alan and I have a difficult relationship. It's easier to keep my distance.'

'Do you miss having a close family?'

Carly swallowed again, her heart feeling undone by the understanding in his voice. He had lost people from his life. His mother. His wife. 'Sometimes I do.'

'What happened between you and them?'

'My mum had an affair with my stepfather. My parents divorced and their business collapsed. Soon after, my father moved to New Zealand. I struggled to integrate with my step-family—my step-sisters didn't want me around, the same as their father. He wanted my mother, not an angry and confused teenager.'

'And things haven't improved since then?'

'I decided a few years back to step away for my own peace of mind. It was killing me constantly trying to gain their approval, the disappointment of being excluded. I've learned to have no expectations of them. Life is easier that way.'

Max nodded. He arched his back, considering her for a moment. 'Come to my father-in-law's party tomorrow with me and Isabella.'

Taken aback by his invitation, Carly asked, 'Is that appropriate?'

'It would be nice to have a friendly face there.'

'I thought you considered me a thorn in your side.'

His eyes were green pools of amusement. 'Yes, but so far your methods appear to be working.'

'Does that mean less resistance to what I say?'

A mischievous glint grew in his eye. 'If you come to the party.'

'But I have nothing to wear.'

'There are boutiques in Bellagio.'

Carly shifted her plate to the side of the table, pulled her beer glass towards her. She took a drink. She was here to do a job, not accompany her client to a party. Especially not a client to whom she was futilely attracted. A man still in love with his late wife. 'I don't think I should.'

'My in-laws know how to throw a great party and you get to be in my company for a while.'

Carly laughed at the cheeky glint in his eye. 'I think you need to sell the idea of me going with you a little bit harder.'

Max laughed too and something light danced

between them as they held each other's gaze. Their laughter faded into the night. Carly looked away from Max, hating just how hard her heart was beating in her chest.

And then she jumped when a cry rang out from the baby monitor.

Max sighed. 'I guess I spoke too soon about your technique working.'

Carly stood and began to clear the table. 'I told you it would take time. I'll tidy up here. Go to Isabella and talk to her. Reassure her, rub her back, maybe sing her a lullaby.' Seeing Max's doubtful expression, Carly gave him a smile of encouragement. 'Experiment—you'll eventually find a way that settles her. And most important of all, you should consider Isabella waking as being a precious time for you to bond.'

The kitchen cleaned, Carly switched off all the downstairs lights and climbed the stairs in time to see Max leave Isabella's room.

When they met in the corridor she asked in a whisper, 'All settled?'

He grimaced. 'Eventually.'

It felt good to be standing so close to him. To hear his low voice. To see his hand rub against the taut bicep of his opposite arm. He had changed earlier, after Isabella's soaking, into a dark navy tee shirt that pulled tight against his frame. 'You've done well today. Go have a shower…' She paused, disturbed by the image of him in the shower, and added quickly, 'Take some time to relax. I'll listen out for Isabella.'

Max shook his head. 'No, I'll take care of her— as you pointed out yourself, you're not a nanny.'

That was before Carly had learned just how alone he was. Now she wanted to give him some support, even if it was only for a few days. 'Let me do it for you…you need to look after yourself as well as Isabella. Do you have time away by yourself, time for hobbies and your own interests?'

'*Dio!* What do you think? I've multibillion-euro projects to run and a strong-willed toddler who doesn't sleep.'

Carly winced at the tiredness in his voice. She should let things be, tell him to go for his shower, but instead she said, 'Life is a series of choices. Choose well both for Isabella's sake but for your own too. You deserve to be happy.'

Max's mouth tightened for a moment but then his green eyes searched hers softly. 'Are you happy, Carly?'

Carly swallowed hard. She thought she was happy. But looking into Max's eyes, remembering the loneliness she felt when she had gazed at Max and Isabella asleep earlier on the plane, she realised she wasn't quite so certain any more. 'I try to be.'

He blinked at her answer…or more to the point the croakiness of her voice. What was it about Max Lovato that left her feeling so exposed?

His hand reached for her arm. She tried not to react, not to give away just how much pleasure soared through her at his touch. She breathed in, in the vain hope of steadying her pulse.

He tilted his head, shifted in closer. His expression was hard to read. His eyes held hers for much too long. She held her breath, her pulse pounding in her ears. Then lightly, tenderly, he whispered, '*Buonanotte*, Carly,' and turned for his bedroom door.

# CHAPTER FOUR

MORNINGS AND CARLY had never seen eye to eye…
and after the previous night's broken sleep they
most definitely weren't on speaking terms. With a
heavy groan she flung her forearm across her eyes
wanting to block the day out. Was it seriously time
to get up already? Groggily she wondered what it
was that had woken her. Her alarm? But why was it
no longer beeping? She was pretty sure she hadn't
touched the snooze button.

Eventually she dragged up enough energy to
locate her phone on the bedside table, in the vain
hope that she might be able to squeeze an extra few
minutes in bed. She squinted at the time display.
And squinted again, but this time even harder. It
wasn't seven as she had set her alarm for but an
insane five-forty. Five-forty! The last time she'd
been awake at five-forty in the morning was during her college days when her gang used to head
to a late-night café near Billingsgate after a night
out clubbing.

Her gaze moved around the darkened bedroom.
Her alarm was set for seven. So what had woken
her? She listened hard, but there wasn't a sound to

be heard throughout the villa—unlike during the night when twice Isabella's loud cries had pulled her out of a deep sleep.

On both occasions she had found Max already in Isabella's bedroom, holding her in his arms, pacing the floor. She had guided him to tuck Isabella back into her bed alongside Sunny, to rub her back and chat to her quietly.

He had whispered for Carly to go back to bed, but Carly had shaken her head and whispered back that she wanted to observe how Isabella reacted. Which admittedly was only part of the reason why she had stayed—the other being just how wrong it would have felt to have walked away from them both; she had wanted to stay and support them through Isabella's upset…no matter how befuddled her brain had felt at being woken in the middle of the night.

The first time round it had taken Isabella over twenty minutes to drift back to sleep. And three times she had reawakened just as they were about to creep out of her bedroom door. Carly had understood Max's soft sighs of frustration but had assured him that things would improve.

The second time Isabella had stayed awake for less than ten minutes and thankfully hadn't reawakened when they left the room.

Both times outside the bedroom, they had awkwardly said goodnight, the act of whispering in a moonlit corridor, them both dressed in night clothes, oddly intimate and disorientating.

Now, the disappearance of a faint light at the corners of the bedroom curtains had her wonder if a light coming on outside on the terrace had woken her.

Was it a security sensor light?

She eyed the curtains. Should she go and see what might have triggered the light in the first place?

She closed her eyes and sank her head further into her pillow, too tired to move.

But what if there was someone or something out there?

With a groan she clambered out of bed, knowing she wouldn't settle until she was certain that the alien creature who had terrified her dreams during her teenage years, thanks to watching a horror movie late one night in boarding school, wasn't outside the window.

Tentatively she parted the curtains, her already unsteady heart banging even harder against her chest.

Outside, the sky was a deep purple, the stars fading diamonds in the sunrise that was soon to come. The terrace was in near darkness but she could just about make out the faint outline of the terrace furniture and the path down to the pool.

She moved closer to the window, her gaze shifting across to the street and house lights of the villages on the opposite side of the lake. Would she get to visit those villages during her stay? See what secrets lay beyond those lights? She smiled, imagining picturesque villages with houses tumbling down to the lake, magnificent and elegant villas with terraced gardens.

And then she yelled.

Not a quiet yelp.

But a full-on howl.

A hand clasped to her mouth, she stared out of the window, her legs about to give way.

Outside, in full sight of her now that he had triggered the sensor light, was Max, staring back at her wearing nothing but a pair of navy swimming trunks, a towel slung over his tanned shoulder.

He mouthed, 'Are you okay?'

She nodded. But in truth her heart felt as if it were about to launch right out of her chest and fling itself down into the pool.

Max's head tilted. He gave her a smile. An apologetic smile that was rather cute. Then with a pointed finger he motioned towards her bed.

She glanced at it and then she looked back at him and raised a cautious eyebrow; not wanting to give away the wicked thoughts running through her mind thanks to the combination of seeing in quick succession a near naked Max and a rumpled bed.

He laughed, pointed to her and then cradled both

hands under his tilted head to indicate sleep. He was telling her to go back to sleep!

She had known that. Of course she had.

With a nod she went to close the curtains and laughed when he gave a wave goodbye that was full of mischief.

She waved back.

They both laughed and reluctantly but with a playful flourish she shut the curtains to his glinting green eyes.

Stumbling back to bed, she collapsed down onto the mattress.

Light-headed, she willed her heart to stop gallivanting around her chest with such merry abandon.

And then she giggled, crazy happiness bubbling in her chest.

It was ridiculous.

But it had felt so good to share that moment with Max. To see his light-hearted amusement. The silent communication they had so effortlessly slipped into.

Her laughter petered out but a smile persisted on her lips. He had looked good—all bronzed skin and gorgeously pumped muscle. She closed her eyes and wriggled in the bed. Her shock shifted to a euphoria she couldn't rationalise away.

She could not help smiling and giggling in remembrance of how his swimming trunks had clung to his thick and powerful thighs. And then there was his chest, broad with a generous smattering of dark hair that screamed abundant testosterone. Yep, she had been right about happily betting her yearly income on his body being particularly delicious.

She groaned.

Then she yanked the pillow over her head, fear slowly threading its way along her veins. She didn't want to fall for a man again. She couldn't take any more heartache.

*She must not ogle Max.* Time and time again she chanted that to herself, in the vain hope it would eventually have her drift off into an untroubled sleep. But of course it didn't work.

What did have her drift off, as she curled up onto her side and snuggled into her pillow, was the memory of Max's eyes dancing with laughter. How incredible it was. How incredible it was to cause such delight.

*'Buongiorno.'* Max waited for Carly to look up from breaking an egg into a bowl before adding, 'Again.'

Her cornflower-blue eyes held his for a split second, the charge that ran between them all the more intense because of the brevity of their exchange, before her attention shifted to Isabella, who was in his arms. Reaching her hand across the kitchen counter, Carly touched her fingertips lightly against Isabella's bare leg. 'Good morning, gorgeous, how are you today?'

Isabella shifted her leg away from Carly's touch and buried her head into his shoulder.

For the briefest of moments, Max saw hurt flash in Carly's eyes at Isabella's reaction. Then laying her hand on the counter, the other on her hip, Carly tried to eye him crossly, but the smile threatening on her lips ruined her attempt to appear to be irate. 'What on earth were you doing up so early anyway?'

'Swimming.'

She picked up a fork and attacked the eggs in the bowl with energetic whisking. 'That I know, but why so early?'

'I always get up at five.'

'But that's insane when your sleep is interrupted so much.'

'Hence the need to start the day with a swim.'

Carly shook her head as though he was a lost cause and diverted her interest once again towards Isabella. 'You were fast asleep when I checked in on you a little while ago.'

Once again Isabella turned away from Carly's attention. Max curled his hand around Isabella's head and stroked her hair. Sometimes Isabella's dependence on him didn't scare him but instead sent a warm flush of love through his entire body. And this morning, to his surprise, this tenderness for his daughter was so strong that he felt the compulsion to comfort Carly as well—he actually was tempted to reach out and touch her hair too, soothe the hurt in her eyes at Isabella's rebuff. He walked around to the other side of the counter, and propped himself up next to Carly. He ran his hand along the tiny curve of Isabella's back, inhaling her sleepy scent.

'She just woke. I heard her crying on the baby monitor in my office.' He shifted Isabella in his arms, smiling when she looked up at him with her serious-minded gaze. 'You're not a morning person are you?'

Carly regarded Isabella affectionately, the hurt of Isabella's rebuff easily forgotten. 'Well, that makes two of us, Isabella, I hate mornings too.' Her gaze shifted up to his. 'Have you been working?'

'For the past two hours. I needed to catch up on the calls and emails I missed last evening.'

She shook her head at that, clearly not impressed. 'I'm making scrambled eggs for breakfast. Will you both join me?'

He nodded and went to place Isabella in her high chair. But before he could do so, Carly ran to the high chair, which sat next to the kitchen island, and said, 'Rather than have Isabella sitting out here on her own, let's move her chair in next to the kitchen table.' She removed the chair that sat at the top of the table and had the best view of the lake and placed Isabella's chair there instead.

He cleared his throat, trying his best to sound annoyed. 'That's where I usually sit.'

She did nothing to disguise her glee. 'Yeah, I thought it would be. But now we can both sit comfortably at either side of Isabella and help her eat.' With that she disappeared out of the kitchen, calling out from the hallway, 'I'll be back in a minute.'

Max sat Isabella in her chair and she thumped the plastic tray with her fist and gave a squeal of what sounded like delight.

Max shook his head, sure the two females in this house were starting to gang up on him.

When Carly bounded back into the kitchen he tried to glare at her but, dressed in a thigh-skimming white denim skirt and blue tie-dye tee shirt, holding onto a heavy eyed Sunny, she looked so pretty he had to turn away and busy himself by first popping some of Luciana's frozen pastries into the oven and then switching on the coffee machine.

For a while they worked in silence, Carly at the hob stirring the eggs, him making coffee. Isabella meanwhile eyed Sunny, whom Carly had propped on a chair at the table too, as though Sunny were waiting for breakfast also, and thrashed the rattle that was set into the table of her chair.

Above the noise of the spinning rattle, as she spooned the eggs onto plates for them and into a plastic bowl for Isabella, Carly asked, 'So what are your plans for today?'

He gestured to the now brewing coffee. 'Will you have a cup?'

She grimaced. 'Do you have tea?'

'I'm afraid not.'

She rolled her eyes but then good-naturedly said, pointing to the apple-juice carton he had already used to fill Isabella's drinking beaker, 'I'll join Isabella and have some apple juice. I'm sure it's much better for me anyway.'

'You'll be glad to hear that I've taken on board your advice that I spend more time with Isabella. So the three of us are going cycling this morning,' he said, pouring their drinks.

In the midst of placing cutlery at the seats either side of Isabella, who was busy sipping her juice, Carly said, 'Cycling...the three of us? Don't you want to spend one-to-one time with Isabella?'

He caught the hesitancy in Carly's voice—a hesitancy he understood. Their conversation last night, the closeness that had come from tending to Isabella together in the silent intimacy of the late hours when it had felt as though only they had existed in this world, their laughter this morning when he had woken her...they all added up to an ease, a familiarity arising in their relationship that Max wasn't comfortable with. But he had made promises to Carly, ones he wasn't about to back out of. 'I seem to remember offering to show you Lake Como.'

'You also promised me ice cream…but I'm happy to look around the lake myself.' Carly paused and considered him for a moment. 'Perhaps you should take Isabella to see her grandparents this morning instead?'

Placing Carly's glass and a basket of breads and pastries onto the table, he took one of the seats next to Isabella. He tore off a piece of *cornetto* and handed it to Isabella. He watched her chew on the soft dough, wondering how she was going to behave in the company of her grandparents. He wanted them to see that he was coping, a good father to their only grandchild. 'My plan for the day is that we first visit the Ghiraldinis and afterwards we can cycle around some of the local attractions. I would like you to meet them before the party this evening.'

Bending down to pick up Isabella's beaker, which had fallen to the ground, Carly said, 'About the party… I'm really not sure.'

'We want Carly there, don't we, Isabella?' As he said those words, Max realised just how keenly he meant them. And it was a realisation that was deeply uncomfortable. He shouldn't want Carly there. He was becoming too attracted, too distracted, by her. He could try to pretend to himself that he wanted her there as support in case Isabella became irritable, but in truth, last night when Isabella had woken, he had been blown away by just how calmly encouraging and supportive Carly had been. It had been a welcome reassurance after months of pacing the floor on his own, wondering what it was he was doing wrong. He had long abandoned the practice of having the nanny do night duty when he was at home as it only ever intensified Isabella's upset. It was that aloneness that he struggled most with as a single parent, the responsibility of every single decision you took, the lack of another person's reassurance that you were doing the right thing; the moments when you could laugh together even in exhaustion over something your child did or said.

This morning it had felt so liberating to laugh with and tease Carly over her terror when he had triggered the sensor light. She had stood beyond the window staring at him so wide-eyed that it had made her mussed-up bedhead hair look as though it were standing on end from shock. During the night, in Isabella's room, she had worn a long white cotton robe, but when she had stared out at him, she had been wearing only bed shorts and a skimpy vest top. Despite himself, his gaze had wandered down over her frame, taking in the high swell of her breasts, the voluptuous curve of her hips. *Dio*, he loved her shape. It was so feminine, soft, inviting.

'You can charm the Ghiraldinis if at any point Isabella and I need some time out. It might be overwhelming for Isabella—we have not met them in months. I'm not sure how things will go.'

'Are you kidding me? How exactly am *I* going to charm them?'

He laughed at her incredulous tone. 'You're witty and engaging. The Ghiraldinis will enjoy your company.'

'Really?' She paused and sipped her apple juice, her eyes over the rim holding his with a dubious gaze. 'I wonder who's doing the charming now.'

He could not help but grin. 'Is it working?'

'You're trying to charm the wrong person.' The laughter in her voice trailed away. 'I'm immune to anyone's charm. Remember that I'm cynical and jaded thanks to my past.'

He shook his head. 'I can understand why you think you are, it's your armour against being hurt, but you're not cynical, Carly. That's not who you are.'

'Trust me, Max, I'm cynical.'

'There's too much kindness and goodness in you. Look at how you are with Isabella, with the advice you give.'

She rose from the table and began to clear away some plates. She smiled at Isabella, who had eaten most of her scrambled eggs by herself, only a little falling to the tray and onto her bib. 'Children are different.' She directed her gaze back to him. All hints of humour had disappeared. 'I reserve my scepticism for adults.'

* * *

White sails out on the lake, villas overgrown with ancient vines and secluded terraces, wildflowers tumbling over the pathway, which was a patchwork quilt of light and shade, Carly pedalled furiously past them all, trying not to laugh because it would only slow her down.

She knew he was teasing her. Allowing her to be in the lead.

Daring a quick glance behind her, she saw that Max was gaining on her.

Her calves were yelling in protest; there was no way she could pedal any faster.

Why on earth had she suggested they race in the first place?

*Because you wanted to break the delightful pace that you had been cycling at—a pace of easy chatter, warm sun, a soft breeze carrying the perfumes of pine and sweet jasmine, spontaneous smiles at Isabella, who stared back at you with that sharp and perceptive gaze that turned your heart over, smiles at her father who cycled one-handed while pointing out local places of interest, his voice melting every bone in your body. You wanted to put distance between you. In every sense of that word.*

Enormous black-and-gold-painted wrought-iron gates appeared on the opposite side of the road that ran parallel to the pathway.

High up in the hill beyond the gate, a villa stood

watch over the lake, like a mother looking down on her child at play.

Villa Fiori. Her pedalling slowed. She was intimidated by the size and grandeur of the Ghiraldini home—a three-storey neoclassical villa with an imposing colonnade to the front.

Max and Isabella sailed by her, Max with a look of quiet amusement, Isabella with Sunny tucked in beside her in the bike carrier, frowning as though she was disappointed in Carly for allowing her father to win.

She pushed down on the pedals, suddenly really wanting to win. Wanting Isabella's approval for reasons she couldn't even begin to understand.

She gained on Max and together they crossed their finish line—the entrance gates to the villa. They both drew to a stop just beyond the entrance, the high structure of the gates towering over them.

She leant on her handlebars and studied him. 'You could have won.'

Those misty green eyes of his held hers for a moment. 'I guess I could.'

Her heart jigged at the smile that followed. She tore her gaze away from him to stare instead towards the villa, thrown by the pleasure she felt at the fact that he had deliberately ended the race with them both crossing the winning line together.

'What a gorgeous villa… Does one family really live here, all alone? It's bigger than most hotels.'

Max stared towards the villa and then with a resigned shrug began to walk up the steep driveway. Carly followed, grateful he wasn't going to attempt to cycle any further, as there was no way she'd be able to cycle up the steep gradient.

They passed terraces of olive groves and lemon orchards, and as they neared the villa abundant rhododendrons and azaleas bordered rock gardens and valleys full of ferns, century-old cedars standing guard beyond them. All the while they walked in silence, tension radiating off Max.

Which wasn't surprising given the heartbreaking history of their shared loss of Marta, the often complex and fraught relationship that had to be negotiated when a grandchild became part of a family that was not fully united—and then, beyond all of that, the history of how Max had been received when Marta had introduced him to the family. How must he have felt the first time he came here as a young student? When he'd had nothing to his name, when he'd had no family of his own. How intimidating it must have been for him. Had he longed to be accepted by them, to belong to this family?

A few steps ahead of her, Carly stared at the hard muscle of Max's back visible beneath the bright white polo shirt he was wearing today. Had he longed to belong to Marta's family just as she had with her new step-family all those years ago? Carly sighed at the memory of how she had turned herself inside out in her attempts to be accepted by her stepfather and stepsisters. But instead of being welcomed into their fold she had faced an indifference from her stepsisters that had seen her confidence eroded and her aloneness in the world magnified. She had even home-dyed her hair to be the same shade of brown as her stepsisters and slavishly copied their clothes. All to no avail.

It felt horrible to be an outsider.

She called out to him, 'Max…' and when he slowed and waited for her to catch up she added, 'Why did the chicken cross the road?'

Perplexed, he stared at her.

'Because it was free range.'

His expression went from perplexed to bewildered. But then he began to chuckle.

And together they climbed the last of the ascent, both of them lightly teasing one another until the driveway ended in a vast cobbled semi-circular entranceway with a fountain at the centre. A member of staff rushed out of the ivy-clad main entrance and took their bikes while another member of staff welcomed them to Villa Fiori and led them through a marble and columned hallway, along a corridor lined with paintings and tapestries, through a light-filled living room adorned with gilded furniture sitting on oriental rugs on marble floors and out towards a terrace with spectacular views of the lake.

A woman sitting at an outdoor table with a silver-haired man cried out when she saw them. Jumping up from her seat, the petite woman, dressed in white palazzo pants and a white silk shirt, heavy gold jewellery on her neck, rushed towards Max and Isabella. 'Isabella! *Vita mia!*'

The woman held her arms out, wanting to take hold of Isabella but Isabella buried her head into Max's chest.

The woman looked at Max, her expression crestfallen. *'Non mi riconosce.'*

Max tensed. 'No, of course she remembers you…she's like this with everyone at the moment.'

The silver-haired man approached the woman and placed a hand protectively on her waist. Then he nodded to Max with a guarded expression. *'E bello vederti.'*

Max answered, 'It's good to see you too, Giulio.'

Though Giulio Ghiraldini was much shorter than Max, he bridged the height gap with an aura of self-confidence. Both men eyed each other suspiciously, their chins raised in proud defiance.

But then Giulio's stare shifted to her.

His eyes narrowed before he shot his glance back to Max.

Max stepped back towards her, his arm reaching around her waist to guide her forwards. 'This is Carly Knight. She's…'

Carly smiled at Giulio, trying not to show her

shock at how good, but yet so wrong, it felt for Max to touch her, but also trying to hide her unease at how Max was struggling to explain who she was. Was he still resenting having to seek out her services? Did he still dislike having to seek support from others? Had she made no inroads in having him accept that to seek support was a strength?

Max cleared his throat but there was still a catch in his voice when he said, 'Carly is a sleep consultant who is working with Isabella at the moment to help her sleep. Carly doesn't speak Italian so we must speak in English. Carly, let me introduce you to Giulio and Valentina Ghiraldini.'

Carly shook hands with both, who looked at her and then at Isabella with concern.

The heavy tension bouncing between the four of them thankfully disappeared when a man in his early twenties bounded out onto the terrace and with a shout of delight pulled Max and Isabella into a hug.

Lifting off his sunglasses, the dark-haired man, dressed in red shorts and a white and navy polo shirt, spoke rapidly in Italian, his hand affectionately touching against Isabella's cheek and then lingering for a while on Max's arm, his pleasure in seeing them both clear.

Max managed to break through the man's constant stream of happy chatter to introduce him to Carly. 'Giovanni, let me introduce you to Carly

Knight. Carly is helping me with Isabella for the weekend.' While Giovanni shook her hand warmly, Max explained, 'Carly, Giovanni is Marta's...' Max paused. A rush of pain, the same anguish she had witnessed in him that first time she saw him outside her office, flashed on Max's expression. Giovanni winced while Valentina bowed her head. For a brief moment Carly saw bottomless grief in Giulio's dark eyes before he pushed on the sunglasses he had been carrying in his hand.

Max cleared his throat and said quietly, 'Giovanni... Giovanni is my brother-in-law.'

Giovanni gave a bittersweet smile and once again embraced Max and Isabella, saying, 'It's been too long, Max. We need to see you more often.'

With that, Giovanni enthusiastically led them all inside the villa, insisting that they immediately see the surprise Valentina had organised for Isabella, promising that refreshments would soon follow.

Valentina smiled in anticipation at Isabella as she slowly opened the door to the room where her surprise was. Isabella frowned and turned her head away from her grandmother. Disappointment flashed in Valentina's eyes. Carly called, 'Isn't this exciting, Isabella?' Isabella looked at her dubiously but then, her curiosity piqued by Carly's enthusiasm, she tilted her body away from Max to gaze into the room.

The room was a child's paradise. An indoor miniature old-fashioned corkscrew fairground slide sat in one corner of the playroom, an array of soft toys in another, an exquisite doll's pram sat alongside a more robust push-along trolley filled with building bricks. One wall held a vast library of children's books, another arts and crafts supplies and various games.

Isabella eyed the room suspiciously.

Valentina looked at her again expectantly, waiting for a reaction. When none came, for a moment Valentina looked dejected but then went and reached up to select some wooden jigsaw puzzles stored high up on a shelf. When she couldn't reach them she turned and asked Max, the tallest in the room, if he could reach them for her.

Max lowered Isabella to the ground and went and helped Valentina, who took the puzzles and, removing her high heels, went and sat on a pink rug imprinted with silver stars by the already open French doors that led back out onto the terrace. Once seated she began to remove the pieces of a wooden car puzzle.

Carly smiled, immediately warming to Valentina and her quiet determination to connect with her grandchild.

Her smile faded however when she spotted Giulio eying her suspiciously, which only worsened when Isabella toddled over to her and, grasping the light cotton of her trousers, hid behind her legs. Carly wanted to clap her hands and give a little shout of triumph. Isabella had come to her! Voluntarily. It shouldn't matter that she did but it made Carly's heart waltz with delight. She reached her hand down and tentatively stroked Isabella's curls, not daring to say anything in case she frightened her away.

'So, how long do you and Max know one another?' There was an accusation to Giulio's tone that had Carly will herself not to blush.

Max, who had come to stand beside her, frowned at his father-in-law. He went to speak but Carly managed to get there before him. 'Only a matter of days. Max contacted me earlier this week when his paediatrician recommended me. Isabella's sleep is increasingly becoming disturbed.' She deliberately paused and shrugged before adding, 'It's very common with children Isabella's age and not a major issue. I must commend Max, however, on being proactive and seeking outside help. Being a lone parent is difficult and he should seek as much support as he can.'

Carly pretended not to see Max's annoyance at her words and she bowed down to gently chat to Isabella, pointing in the direction of Valentina, encouraging her to go and see what she was doing.

Isabella, always her own person, decided to remain clinging to her leg.

When she straightened, Giulio considered her for a moment and asked quietly, 'And do you usually travel with your clients?'

Carly decided to ignore the censure in his tone and answered brightly, 'No. But when Max explained that Isabella is to be a flower girl at the wedding and how keen he was that she be well rested for such a special occasion, I decided I would travel with them.'

Giovanni, who was kneeling on the floor trying to coax Isabella out from behind Carly's leg by holding a rag doll and waving her hand, broke from making playful noises to look towards Max. 'Tomaso and Bianca are arriving later this morning. They'll be so excited to see you,' Giovanni paused, a cloud of sorrow passing in his eyes. 'It really has been too long since we last saw you.'

With Max standing close beside her, Carly could feel his body tense. 'I've been busy with work.'

Giulio shook his head and waved his hands in the air with a disgruntled grumble. 'You must always make time for family.'

Across the room, Valentina looked up at her husband's angry tone and winced. And then her gaze shifted towards Max. She looked at him with such sadness that Carly had to look away.

Isabella cautiously started to move about the room. She paused for a moment by the toy kitchen and picked up a yellow saucepan, before moving on to stand a distance away from her grandmother, who had gone back to playing with the jigsaws, her heavy curtain of jet-black hair cut into an elegant bob, hiding her expression. Carly's heart pulled painfully hard for Valentina—how were you supposed to cope when you lost the most precious thing in the world?

Isabella leant forward to see better what Valentina was doing, losing her balance in the process so that she stumbled forward. Righting herself, she moved closer. Valentina gave no reaction. Isabella landed on her bottom with a bump opposite her grandmother. She stared warily at Valentina when Valentina edged the almost complete puzzle towards her. But when Valentina began another puzzle, Isabella dropped the yellow saucepan and picked up the one remaining puzzle piece and easily slotted it into the awaiting space.

'Those puzzles…'

Valentina looked at her husband and finished his sentence, her tone sad but determined. 'Yes, they were Marta's. I thought Isabella would enjoy them. They're so alike.'

Max moved across the room. Kneeling down, he spoke directly to Valentina. 'Thank you for creating this room for Isabella.'

'In the future…perhaps she could visit us more often? I can go to London and collect her.'

Max tensed. 'At the moment she wants to be with me all the time.'

'But if she spent time with us alone then—'

Standing, Max interrupted Valentina. 'I've promised Carly that Isabella and I would show her Lake Como.'

Valentina looked up at Max with dismay. 'You have to leave? But you've just arrived.'

Max's expression softened at Valentina's upset. 'We'll be back this evening for the party.' Then glancing towards her, he added, 'Carly will be joining us this evening.'

Carly smiled wanly in Giulio's direction and saw he wasn't looking too happy at the news she was coming to his party. 'I hope that is okay with you?'

Giulio blinked at her question and with an abrupt nod of his head said gruffly, 'Of course.'

Passing another jigsaw puzzle to Isabella, Valentina stood and reached out and touched her hand against Max's bare forearm. In a low voice she asked, 'Can Isabella stay here with us? It would be so nice to spend time with her.'

Max shook his head. 'She doesn't stay with others—she gets upset when I leave.'

Carly moved across the room. She knew that Giulio was suspicious of her relationship with Max and what she was about to say might add fuel to that particular fire, but she knew she should encourage Max to leave Isabella in Valentina's care.

Standing next to Max, she said in a low voice, 'Isabella looks content here. Explain to her she'll be staying here for a few hours but you'll be back later. See how she reacts.'

Max spoke to Isabella, who nodded. Max stood, explained again to Isabella he would be back soon. Again, Isabella gave a bare nod, her attention fixated on the wooden pieces of a rainbow puzzle.

Max gave Valentina a detailed run-through of all the items in Isabella's changing bag. At one point Valentina caught Carly's eye; both women smiled secretly at Max's anxiety at leaving Isabella.

He stood at the playroom door, watched Giovanni join Valentina on the floor, Giulio sit on a nearby chair, the three of them laughing at something Giovanni said to Isabella, who smiled faintly at her uncle. Max called out to them, 'We'll collect Isabella at three in time for her to have an afternoon nap.'

The foursome on the rug looked briefly in his direction and then away.

Max's mouth tightened. He glanced in her direction, the initial uncertainty shifting to a proud tilt of his head before he walked away.

# CHAPTER FIVE

MAX STRODE THROUGH Villa Fiori until he reached the entrance courtyard, where despite wanting to punch something instead he smiled when Hilda, the Ghiraldinis' ancient Labrador, trundled towards him with heavy pants of delight.

Crouching down, he patted Hilda, who offered him a paw by way of welcome. They had always been friends...even when he had been decidedly persona non grata in this household.

A rush of footsteps behind him had him turn to find Carly running towards him. Bending over, she scratched Hilda behind her ears. 'I see someone else is also delighted to see you.'

'They're delighted to see Isabella.'

Her hand came to a stop on Hilda's fur. 'You as well, Max.'

Standing, he gestured towards the gardens of the villa. 'We can walk to Bellagio through the gardens. There's a private entrance that leads out into the town.'

They walked up a flight of steps, the ancient stone mottled and worn with time, and along a pebbled path filled with tall palms and Italian cypresses, towards the sound of a classical piece of music. Carly gave a laugh of pleasure when they came upon musicians out in the internal courtyard of the villa, their playing just about drowning out the sound of the vast catering team also there, busy setting up the tables for tonight's party.

Carly paused to watch the team place gleaming silverware and vast urns of fresh flowers onto the snowy white linen tablecloths. 'Are the tables for this evening's party or the wedding?'

'Tonight's party.'

Carly's gaze widened. 'I hadn't realised it was going to be such a big party—there must be seating for at least three hundred.'

'The great and the good of Italian society will be here tonight. Giulio likes to do things in style. Tomaso and Bianca's wedding reception will take place here too—the ceremony will be in the gardens as the villa's chapel is too small to accommodate all of their guests.'

As they continued along the path, Carly asked quietly, 'Did you and Marta marry here also?'

It was strange—if anyone had asked him about Marta before he would have shut them down. But with Carly it didn't feel wrong; instead it felt natural, respectful. Was it that time had passed or was it more to do with Carly's empathy that seemed completely authentic? 'We married in Milan. Just the two of us and two friends who were witnesses.'

'Because of her family?'

'Yes.'

At the wrought-iron gate that led into the villa's orchards, Carly stopped at his side when he held the gate open for her. 'Did you or Marta mind marrying without your families?'

His heart turned over to see her concern. For a moment he considered not answering her, but something inside him wanted to be always truthful with Carly Knight. 'We were in love…at the time that was all that mattered. But I know it's not the wedding Marta had dreamed of.'

'I'm sure it was still a magical day.'

Surprising himself, he smiled gratefully at Carly. It felt good to remember the happy times he'd had with Marta—up until now it had been too painful to recall those times. 'It was a special day.' Then, remembering her planned wedding, he asked, 'Would your family have been at your wedding— if it had gone ahead?'

'They said they would…'

Max regarded her curiously, 'You don't sound certain.'

Years ago Carly had built a wall around herself when it came to her family. A wall that was easier to maintain when she didn't have to think or speak about them, about how disappointed, how let down, how rejected, how lonely she felt amidst them. She considered changing the subject but she could tell by Max's expression he wasn't going to let her. 'My stepfather Alan has a habit of finding excuses when it comes to anything to do with me. No doubt some urgent business would have cropped up and as my mother is the chief financial officer in his company, he would have insisted she accompany him.'

Max's eyebrows shot up. 'On your wedding day?'

Carly shrugged, desperate to keep up an act of nonchalance, while inside it hurt like hell to talk about all of this. 'It happened on my graduation day, my birthdays. My stepfather's focus in life is his company and my mother. His daughters come after that. Then I'm somewhere down the list.'

With that she walked away, along the path between the blossoming trees. Max soon caught up with her, a hand gently touching against her elbow. 'What about your mother—are you close?'

Her feet threading against the grass at the edge of the clay path, Carly answered, 'My mother tries to smooth things over between us. But she's deeply in love with Alan.'

'Why, when he doesn't sound like a nice guy?'

Carly paused as, not for the first time, she tried to fathom her mother's complex relationship with Alan. 'She was happy with my father but with Alan it's as though he freed something in her. She loves his drive, his ambition, his energy.'

'Wasn't your father like that?'

Carly smiled. 'No, he was soft and gentle. He used to take me fishing to the river that ran through our hometown, and we would go camping.' She came to a stop. Her eyes flickered away from Max's intent gaze, the sadness inside her overwhelming, before she added, 'But sometimes he was distant. It was only when I was a teenager that my mum told me of his depression. How he had struggled at work. My mum ran the business mostly by herself—in the end she grew tired of all that responsibility.'

Max inhaled deeply. 'That must have been very difficult for them both.'

'When I was younger I couldn't forgive my mum. I told her she was selfish for leaving him for Alan.'

'And now?'

'I guess I realise that life isn't as black and white as I thought it was when I was a teenager. We argued a lot back them. Alan used to intervene, which of course only made matters worse.'

'Maybe he was trying to protect your mum?'

Carly blinked at Max's words. She was about to angrily tell him that no, Alan had only been looking to find reasons to create a wedge between her and her mum, but then she paused and admitted,

'At the time, when they sent me away to boarding school, and constantly found me courses to attend during term breaks, I assumed Alan in particular was rejecting me. But maybe you're right, maybe part of his reasoning was that he was trying to protect my mother from our arguments.'

'Would you like to be close to your mum now?'

All the sadness inside her suddenly centred in her throat. It was beyond painful when she swallowed against what felt like a boulder of emotion stuck there. 'I don't know—it's hard to trust after being let down so often.'

Max nodded, his green gaze swallowing her up with gentle understanding. 'Have you told her how you feel?'

Carly smiled, her sadness dissipating a little in the face of his attention, his empathy. 'About her leaving my dad, yes. But about how Alan treated me, how upset I was when they didn't attend events, no—in truth I was embarrassed at how excluded I was. Somehow it felt as though it was all my fault, as though it defined me as a person— that I was the type of person who deserved to be excluded.'

'You should talk to your mum.'

Carly nodded. Max was right. She *should* talk to her mum. But what if it only led to more disappointment, more times when she was let down?

She raised an eyebrow, happy to change the

subject back to Max. 'As you should speak to the
Ghiraldinis. They seem very fond of you now,
Max. Whatever happened in the past, however
hurtful it was, maybe you should embrace this
family. You need and deserve their support.'

An unripe fig lay on the path before them. Max
picked it up and tossed it into the dense foliage of
the grove. 'If Isabella wasn't part of the equation
I've no doubt I'd no longer be welcome in their life.'

'I don't agree.'

'You saw how Giulio was—he still has issues
with me. And who can blame him after everything
that has happened?'

At the wooden bridge that ran over a stream and
led to the pine forest, Carly looked down into the
lightly flowing water. 'I think right now I'm to
blame for Giulio's unhappiness.'

'You?'

'He's worried that there's something between
us.'

'Why would he think that? I've visited with a
nanny before.' Even as he said those words, Max
felt his pulse quicken. There was an ease between
him and Carly that had not been there in his formal
and distant relationship with the nannies he had
previously employed. An ease Giulio must have
picked up on. Guilt caught him by the throat. 'Giulio should trust me better than that.'

Carly's head jerked back. He hadn't meant to speak so loudly, so harshly.

He let out a sigh. 'I'm sorry...'

She gestured towards the path leading through the woods. 'I'll visit Bellagio by myself. There's no need for you to come. It would be...less complicated.'

He cursed himself for her hurt expression. 'I've many faults but the one thing I never do is break my promise. And I promised to show you Lake Como.'

Carly backed away from him, her hand trailing along the wooden handrail of the bridge. 'Well, I absolve you of that promise.'

He followed her. 'I *want* to show you around.' His words were out before he had really thought about them. But they were the truth. He did want to show Carly Como, spend some time with her. Especially after everything she had just revealed. How on earth did this beautiful, intelligent and compassionate woman think for a moment that she deserved to be excluded from anyone's life? And for the first time in years, he was finding it possible to speak to someone, even have some fun. He shoved the guilt that came with that thought deep down inside him and said, 'And I'll even laugh at your jokes.'

After a moment's hesitation Carly turned in the direction of the woods. They walked in silence, their footsteps crunching on fallen pine needles, the warm air thick with the scent of earth and pine, their arms brushing against branches of rhododendrons spilling out over the path.

'Knock, knock.'

He laughed and asked, 'Who's there?'

'Owls say.'

'Owls say who?'

Her eyes twinkling, Carly answered, 'Yes, they do.'

He opened the pedestrian gate from the villa chuckling, a lightness, a feeling of freedom causing him to pause on the narrow road that led into the centre of Bellagio. 'I must remember these jokes for when Isabella is old enough to understand them.'

They moved down the cobbled road, passing ancient ochre and umber-coloured town houses, villas covered in ancient vines. Carly's blue eyes glittered with amusement. 'I used to tell jokes to my Montessori pupils—there's honestly nothing better in this world than to hear a young child laugh.'

Dressed in a white cotton tee shirt tucked into green and navy floral trousers, her hair tied back into a ponytail, Carly smiled at him with such brightness and optimism that for a moment he felt a peace, a belief that life would be okay. A peace that allowed him to admit, 'It feels odd to be without Isabella. Usually I'm either with her or at work.'

The cobbles dipped downwards, and Carly, taking small steps against the steep gradient, said 'You've forgotten what it is to have free time.'

He laughed at that. 'I don't think I ever knew what it was to have free time in the first place.'

Carly paused outside a store selling leather goods and asked, 'Why do you work so hard?'

Her tone was concerned but there also was a hint of misgiving. He had never spoken of his childhood with anyone other than Marta before…and even with Marta he had glossed over some of the detail, ashamed of the poverty and struggle he came from in comparison to her family's vast wealth. But with Carly, knowing of her own childhood, it felt easier to be open.

He gestured for them to move down towards the main square of the town and said as they walked, 'I grew up seeing my mother struggle financially. Even when she was sick she had to work.' Wincing at the memory of his ill mother, thin and frail, but with defiance flashing in her eyes when she came home from work, he admitted, 'She developed cancer when I was in my late teens. Her employer had no sickness scheme. She worked when she could throughout her chemotherapy to support us. I wanted to leave school and then university but she refused to allow me. I had part-time jobs but not enough to support us. She said that I was her future. I guess I never want to go back to that poverty, or let her down.'

Under a plane tree in the square, Carly stopped and considered him, her long slim neck stretching up for her to hold his gaze. 'Your success is for her?'

He swallowed at the gentleness of her tone, the shine of tears in her eyes. 'Yes, and Isabella now too.'

'Know when enough is enough though, Max… These are precious years with Isabella. Enjoy them when you can. I'm sure your mother would want that too.'

He rolled his head side to side, easing out a kink at the base of his neck, remembering the hours he had spent with his mother in the hospital the day she died. She had been unable to speak, had been drifting in and out of sleep but when she'd woken her eyes had immediately searched for his, silently communicating her love. He had stayed holding her hand long after she had slipped away. Later he had gone home to their empty apartment and howled in pain.

He had to protect Isabella from that pain by making her more tenacious and independent than even he had been as a child. Life was unpredictable and unfair and he had to arm her against its cruelty. But now was not the time to point that out to Carly Knight. He was supposed to be showing her Lake Como after all. He nodded to one of the store windows behind her. 'That dress in the window would be ideal for the party later.'

Carly walked over to the window. 'It is beautiful.'

He joined her there in the shade of the store awning. 'It matches the colour of your eyes.'

She shrugged at that and wrinkled her nose. 'It's…a bit daring though, isn't it?'

Max stared at the dress trying to figure out what she meant. The sapphire-coloured knee-length dress with diamantés subtly applied to the flared skirt and fitted bodice was to him elegant. But then he looked at the neckline and realised it was scooped rather low. He swallowed at the tantalising image of running a finger down Carly's sternum, skimming between the valley of her high breasts.

He spoke to her reflection in the store window. 'It will look fantastic on you.'

Carly ran a hand against her neck, touched the lobe of her ear, her gaze in the reflection shifting from him to the dress and back again. 'Maybe I should try it on.'

'Do you want my opinion? Will I go in with you?'

She turned and looked at him. 'I… I'm not sure that it's appropriate that a client helps me shop.'

Max drank in the fluttering of her thick eyelashes cloaking her amazing eyes, the pink in her high and curved cheekbones, the plumpness of her lips. He dropped his head, a delicious burn of attraction humming through him, and spoke against her ear. 'I think we've moved beyond the normal client relationship, don't you?'

Carly arched her back, breathed out a low sigh. 'Have we?'

Max had to fight the urge not to fix the soft blonde hair that had fallen loose from her ponytail behind her ear. And worse still, he wanted to kiss Carly Knight. He wanted to feel her plump red lips under his. He wanted her soft body with all its curves pressed into his. Carly shifted even more to face him square on. A heavy intoxicating charge ran between them. His breathing hitched. His hand reached out, lightly fell on her waist just above the band of her trousers. His pulse upped another notch at the heat of her skin. She smelt of vanilla and citrus; he wanted to kiss her, taste her, explore her body…make love to her.

Thrown, he stepped away. That was *not* going to happen. He wasn't going to open up the potential of Carly being hurt again after all the hurt and rejection she'd experienced in the past. And he certainly didn't need added guilt and complications in his life. He could see the confusion in her expression at his abrupt movement. He nodded towards the boutique window again. 'Can I buy the dress for you?'

Carly's eyebrows slammed together. 'Absolutely not.'

'Why?'

'Because…because…' She stopped and asked angrily, 'Why would you want to buy it for me?'

Why was she so angry? Because he had almost kissed her or because he wanted to buy her the dress? 'As a thank you for coming to Lake Como, of course.' They eyed each other unhappily for a few seconds. But then once again he was drawn in by her soft mouth, by the constant chemistry swirling between them. He stepped back towards her and said, 'As a thank you for agreeing to come to the party later.' His voice dropped another notch as fire slowly licked along his veins. 'For being a good listener. For staying up so late last night with Isabella. As an apology for scaring you this morning. For making me laugh for the first time in years.'

Her eyes widened, she touched a hand to her neck again, her skin now the colour of a cream rose brushed lightly with pink. 'I'm glad I came, Max… I'm enjoying getting to know you and Isabella. There's no need to thank me or want to buy me things.' Pausing, she gave him a tentative smile. 'Seeing you relax and connect with Isabella is enough reward.' Turning, she opened the door to the store. He called out to her the name of the restaurant he would meet her at after she was finished shopping.

Max swung around and closed his eyes, taken aback by just how much he wanted Carly Knight in his arms…in his bed. For a moment he looked about the square, disorientated, but then the colourful summertime dresses in the window of a children's clothes store across the square reminded him that it was his daughter he should be thinking of, not his attraction to her sleep consultant.

Carly moved across the restaurant terrace, trying to act nonchalant, which wasn't easy when Max Lovato's gorgeous gaze followed your every step. It was a gaze so disturbing that it took her a while to realise he was on his phone, yet again. Carly's heart skipped a beat when she recalled how intoxicating it had been when they had stood close together outside the boutique earlier, his scent, the heat from his body, the low timbre of his voice all making her light-headed…and forgetful of her pledges to keep her distance, protect herself from him. They had almost kissed, for crying out loud.

He ended his call and stood as she approached the table. Their table was directly in front of the lake with unrestricted views of the glistening water. Overhead, heavy vines on a pergola gave them shade from the intensity of the early afternoon sun.

Max held out a chair for her, and nodded to the pink suit bag she was carrying. 'Did you buy the dress in the window?'

Carly nodded yes. The dress had fitted her perfectly. She was still a little unsure about how low cut it was but the store assistant had assured her it was entirely appropriate for Giulio's flamboyant birthday party, which apparently was the talk of the town with so many Italian politicians and high-profile screen and sporting stars about to descend on the town later today.

Max called a waiter and asked that special care be taken of the suit bag.

It was only then that Carly spotted a white package wrapped in a blue ribbon sitting on the plate before her. She lifted it up. 'Is this for me?'

When Max nodded she opened the present, hoping that there was nothing expensive inside. All the memories of her stepfather's presents that were bought to impress but with little thought for what the receiver actually wanted made her stomach churn.

Her hand went to her mouth. She giggled—with relief and delight. Without stopping to think what she was doing, she leant across the table and kissed Max on the cheek. Flustered, she sat back down, trying not to react to his surprised expression and then the quiet smile that grew on his lips. 'A box of English tea! Exactly what I needed. Thank you.'

Softly Max muttered, *'Prego.'*

Around them people chattered in an international blend of languages and accents.

The water gently lapped against the quayside.

Carly shifted in her seat, searching for something to say, but touching Max's skin had dulled her brain.

'I called Valentina. Isabella is out happily exploring the gardens with her grandfather and Hilda, apparently.'

Carly smiled to know that Isabella was happy but also at the bewilderment in Max's voice. 'How fantastic for her to spend time with them. And as she grows older that bond will become stronger and stronger.'

Max shrugged at that and the arrival of the waiter meant they had to focus for a while on deciding what they would order.

Once they had ordered and the waiter had poured them the white wine they had both agreed upon, Carly sipped the crisp lemon-scented wine and asked, 'Why are you so reluctant to accept any support from the Ghiraldinis?'

Max picked up a bread roll from the basket the waiter had left on the table and broke it in two. For a long while he said nothing but then he quietly said, 'Growing up, the area where I lived, you had to be strong, determined. Many of my friends got involved in crime, became addicted to alcohol and drugs. I knew I had to get away. My mother was of the same mind. She wanted more for me. I spent my weekends and holidays working in the hotel where she worked. After school she expected me to study and would test me for hours when she came home from work. She constantly told me that I would only ever be able to rely on myself in life, that only I had the power to better my life.'

Carly watched Max's long fingers tear at the soft dough as he broke the still-uneaten roll into ever smaller pieces. 'Your mum obviously was a very strong and determined woman. But the downside of that is not accepting how sometimes we do need support. We need to be part of a wider community. We can't live in isolation.'

'Maybe it would be easier if we did.'

'Meaning?'

His gaze shifted away to look over her shoulder at something out on the lake. 'Losing someone…losing someone you trusted, someone you had mapped out your life with…'

His gaze moved back to hers. Carly's heart missed a beat to see the pain etched on his face. 'You miss Marta terribly.'

His jaw worked but then he dropped heavily back into his chair and said softly, 'It's not as awful as it was. But… I worry about Isabella.'

'You are doing a good job, Max…yes, I think there are areas you could improve on, like asking for more support. But you are only human. Don't put unrealistic expectations on yourself.'

His mouth curved upwards. 'You really aren't the cynic you like to think you are, are you?'

Carly's heart kicked at the sight of him smiling. 'I try to be tough, not as easily taken in or hurt as I once was.'

Finally eating some of his roll, which he first dipped into some olive oil, Max said, 'Working hard at being a cynic—is that your motto?'

Carly laughed at the playfulness twinkling in his eyes. 'I guess.'

'Be true to yourself. Don't change or try to be something other than yourself because others have hurt you. Trust in yourself, in how incredible you are.'

Carly was about to argue that she was being true to herself but doubt had her pause.

Max picked up a fresh roll from the basket and, breaking it in two, dipped one piece in the olive oil and handed it to her. 'You should try this. The oil is incredible.'

She took a bite, the oil smooth at first, kicking hard against her throat when she swallowed. Her eyes watered.

'Buona?'

Her answer was to dip her remaining roll in the oil. She bit into the roll with relish, licking her fingers as the golden oil dripped down. Patting her

lips with her napkin, she paused when she saw Max staring at her, his darkened eyes sending a delicious wave of warmth through her body.

'Were you in love with your ex?'

She blinked at his question, at the tightness in his jaw. 'Robert—yes, I did love him. I loved him but I don't think I was in love with him. We were really compatible—it was an easy relationship: we liked the same food, the same TV programmes, we both dreamt of living near the sea one day. He was kind and gentle. But deep down I think I knew he was holding part of himself back. I never really knew the true him. I patched things over, which was wrong.'

'What do you mean?'

Carly really didn't want to get into any of this. 'I shouldn't be dumping this on you.'

Max held off until the waiter who had arrived with their starters had left before speaking. 'You said earlier that you like getting to know me better. Well, the same goes for me wanting to know you.'

Carly's insides melted at his softly spoken words. 'Is that wise…is any of this wise?'

'Maybe this is a weekend we both need…to process the past.' Max paused, his misty green eyes holding a tender hopefulness. 'To enable us to move on.'

Carly speared one of her ravioli pieces blindly trying to force her heart to calm down. She made

an attempt to raise her fork to her mouth but knew there was no way she was capable of eating right now. She dropped the fork. 'Do you want to move on?'

Max shrugged and ate some of his raviolini before asking, 'What did you mean when you said that patching things over with your ex was wrong?'

Carly picked up her fork again, dipped the ravioli into the oil and pepper at the bottom of her bowl, trying to ignore how defeated she felt by Max not answering her question about moving on. 'I patched things over for selfish reasons. I wanted love, my own family. I kidded myself that all was well with Robert, ignoring the feeling of disconnect.' Carly paused and, reddening, she admitted, 'That passion that should be there when you're in love.'

'Do you still want love, a family?'

Carly ate some of her pasta, the sweetness of the pumpkin popping in her mouth. 'Maybe…if I ever manage to find the right person.' She speared another piece of pasta, moved it about her bowl, before staring straight into Max's gaze. 'But this time I'm going to make sure that it is an absolute and mutual true love, for us both.'

Something ticced at the side of Max's cheek. He shifted his gaze away, took a drink of his wine. 'Your parents' marriage hasn't put you off?'

'I was oblivious to the problems in their marriage. They protected me from it all. I grew up happy and adored by them both. When they divorced that all fell apart. I guess I'm looking for that again. Being part of a family, knowing you belong and that they will be there for you regardless—my friends have that with their families, so I know it exists. I just have to find it—but not at any cost.' Carly paused as the waiter cleared their plates before adding, 'I'm tired of being second best. I was second best to Robert, second best to my stepfather.' She held Max's gaze and said with a defiance that came from deep inside herself, 'It's not going to happen again. When we first met, my stepfather said to me, in front of my mother and his daughters, that he wasn't sure if he had room in his life for yet another female. He pretended it was a joke, but even as an eleven-year-old I knew he was being serious.'

Looking horrified, Max asked, 'What did your mother say?'

'She laughed it off...which made it all the harder to deal with. I felt I couldn't say anything.'

'You were a child—how could he be so callous?'

'Alan likes to have the upper hand in any situation, for people to defer to him. I tried to indulge him, I so wanted to fit into my new family, but I was also angry and confused and sometimes I stood up to him. He didn't like that.'

Max shook his head. 'In my experience people like Alan, bullies, people with misplaced egos, often are hiding some deep feeling of inadequacy within themselves.'

Carly wrinkled her nose. 'I don't know.' But then pausing, she admitted, 'His first marriage was deeply unhappy. He's infatuated with my mother—even I have to admit how much he loves her. Looking back, I think my relationship with my mum threatened him.'

'And how is his relationship with his own daughters?'

'I used to think my stepsisters had everything but now I can see how Alan plays one off against the other. It has created this weird insecurity in all three. They are outwardly super-confident but are constantly vying for their father's attention. Adding me to that mix only added to their competition so they never welcomed me into their lives. When I was younger I was sometimes left in their care—they were all at university at that stage. The house would become party central. I thought it would be cool to hang out with them, but in reality I was pretty daunted by the amount of alcohol being consumed. And they weren't too impressed with having their geeky stepsister follow them around everywhere.'

Even though the waiter had returned with their main courses, Max didn't wait to respond to what

Carly had said. His voice incredulous, he said, 'You were never geeky—you're way too beautiful.'

The waiter looked from Max to Carly. And nodded in agreement. '*Sì*, you are truly a beautiful woman.'

Carly rolled her eyes, feeling herself blush from her toes to the tip of her head as Max and the handsome waiter shared a wicked grin.

When the waiter had left, Carly eyed him across the table. 'So you do possess the Italian charm your countrymen are fabled for.' Her stomach flipped to hear Max's low throaty laugh. 'Trust me—with glasses, braces, a bad home dye and no clue how to dress... I really did look terrible as a teenager.'

Max took a bite of his swordfish and then sat back in his chair, his gaze not leaving her. Carly cut into her sea bass and forced herself to eat a few mouthfuls, unnerved by the intensity of his gaze. She jumped when he eventually spoke, his voice like a low caress. '*Sei irresistibile*...you're irresistible...you do know that?'

For a moment she considered telling him the truth. Of how she had always felt like the ugly duckling next to her gorgeous stepsisters, how Robert's love for his ex had further eroded her self-confidence. She shrugged off his question with a laugh. 'I'm no supermodel so I try to focus on my inner beauty instead.'

His eyes burnt into hers. 'Most men aren't looking for supermodels.'

Her throat tightened. 'What are they looking for?'

'A woman who's clever, one that radiates beauty through her kindness.' His voice dropped a note. 'A woman who knows how to love.'

Carly's heart spluttered to a stop. She searched for something to say and eventually she blurted out, 'I reckon you should have a conversation with my stepfather. He still grumbles about the money he spent straightening my teeth.'

'Perhaps one day I will.'

Carly dropped her fork at the menace in his voice. And then she laughed, laughed until her sides ached. She could see Max squaring up to Alan, dragging him down a peg or two with his quick intelligence.

Max raised an eyebrow at her laughter, a quiet smile on his lips.

After a while Max pushed his plate away and rested an elbow onto the table, his hand cupping his chin. His eyes held understanding, respect. He didn't say anything for a while, just quietly considered her. Carly knew she should look away but something too powerful, too amazing was passing between them. She couldn't name it but it felt as though something was shifting between them.

'You can always call on me and Isabella when we go back to London. It would be nice to see you.'

Her heart lifted at his softly spoken words. With a shake of her head she asked, 'Are you looking for some free professional advice?'

He gave her a look that said she was incorrigible. 'Obviously,' he said, rolling his eyes. Then after a pause he added, 'We get on...we have things in common.' His voice dipped. 'I find it easy to talk to you.'

Disappointment threaded its way through her at the implication of his words that he wanted to meet as friends. She forced herself to make light of it all. 'You forgot to add that we have the same taste in terrible jokes.'

His eyes danced at that. 'True.'

Carly tried to look away from the fondness shining in his eyes. It would be so easy to fall for him, to believe that there was something more than an odd friendship between her and a billionaire single father still grieving his late wife. Perhaps Max was right when he argued that she wasn't cynical, but she was a realist and resilient. Both traits drove her to say, 'Let's not make any promises we can't keep.' Looking around for the waiter, she added, 'I think we should ask for the bill. It will be Isabella's nap time soon.'

Max nodded, but then he reached down to the side of his chair. Lifting a bag, he removed first a toddler's white full-skirted dress embroidered with silver butterflies and then a pair of matching silver shoes with clipped-on silver butterflies. Carly exclaimed at the cuteness of both. Max smiled in delight, pausing to ask if she thought they were the right size for Isabella. And in his uncertainty, in his keen concern that Isabella would like her new clothes, Carly felt any last vestiges of cynicism ebb away like ice melting beneath a seductively warm sun.

# CHAPTER SIX

ISABELLA'S FEET TAPPED proudly on the wooden floor of her bedroom and then, stopping, she once again inspected her new silver shoes, lifting her right foot up, waiting for Carly's approval.

'Oh, Isabella, they're the most beautiful shoes ever.'

Isabella gave a nod of agreement. Carly bit back a smile; Max was going to have serious shoe bills when Isabella was a teenager.

'Now come here and let me do the buttons on your dress,' Carly said from her seat on the side of Isabella's bed, opening her arms out wide in invitation.

Isabella eyed her, seriously at first but then something glittered in her eyes. Carly laughed. Isabella had inherited her father's mischievousness after all.

Backing away, Isabella ran to the other side of the room, an impish angel in her new white shimmering dress.

Carly liked to play fair so, throwing off her shoes, she climbed down onto her knees. Crawling across the room, she took care not to kneel on the heavy skirt of her dress. A quick check told her all was well in the décolletage area—the bra cups of the dress were thankfully holding everything in place, just as the sales assistant had assured her.

Isabella squeaked in delight as Carly neared her. 'I'm going to catch you.'

Flapping her arms, Isabella dashed off giving Carly a wide berth.

Carly swung around. Chased after her.

By the time Carly caught Isabella, her arm wrapping affectionately around her waist and lifting her up, her knees were starting to ache and with a sigh she plopped them both down onto Isabella's bed. Singing a nursery rhyme, jigging her legs playfully, she did up the zip of the dress and then the tiny buttons that ran along the zip seam.

Her heart gave a little quiver when Isabella started to hum along to the tune.

And when Carly set an all-buttoned-up Isabella down onto the floor and Isabella turned and placed both of her hands on Carly's cheeks and playfully squeezed them it felt as if fireworks had exploded in her soul.

Carly let out a playful gasp, pretending to be surprised. And crossed her eyes.

Isabella chuckled.

Carly lifted her back up onto her lap and began to lightly tickle her. Isabella squirmed and laughed. When the game was over they were both a little breathless and happy to sit for a while to gather themselves.

It was only then that Carly saw Max leaning against the doorframe watching them, a hand in one pocket suggesting that he had been standing there for some time. Carly swallowed, her already unsteady heart doing a few flips. He was dressed in a black tuxedo that emphasised the dark tones of his skin, the broadness of his shoulders, the long length of his legs, his curls tamed by some hair product; his gaze caught hers and something potent whipped between them. 'You two look amazing in your new dresses,' he said in a low husky tone that sent a jolt of pure attraction through her body.

Isabella climbed off her lap and toddled over to him. Carly stood and fixed her dress. Max lifted Isabella into his arms and Carly tried to ignore the burning heat from his gaze, which was still on her. She touched her hair, making certain it was still in the bun she had pushed it into when dressing earlier.

Max, with Isabella in his arms, walked towards her, his gaze once again sweeping over her. Carly waited for him to speak. There was a hum of attraction…and, okay, she would admit it, sexual tension, in the room. Carly inhaled deeply wishing Max would talk, break the connection that had somehow left her incapable of speech.

Too late Carly realised she was fiddling with the front of her dress, adjusting the neckline a few centimetres. She dropped her hand, blushed when Max's gaze remained there.

She cleared her throat. Scrabbled her brain for something to say. 'Luciana told me you were working so, after her nap, I gave Isabella an early dinner and bathed her for the party. She slept really well.' Carly paused and touched her hand against Isabella's new shoes. 'Didn't you, sweetheart? And you just love the new dress and shoes Papa bought for you, don't you?'

Carly laughed at the delighted squeal Isabella gave.

Max considered Isabella with surprised amusement. 'I'll have to buy you more dresses if this is the reaction I'll get.'

As if to say yes, Isabella buried her head into his shoulder. Max's large hand gently capped Isabella's head. Then his gaze travelled down the length of Carly's body, a low, slow deliberate gaze. 'You're looking very beautiful.' He paused, his eyes darkening. *'Potrei guardarti tutta la notte...* I could watch you all night.'

Startled and with way too many parts of her body about to go into meltdown, Carly grabbed her phone and, calling to Isabella, said, 'Time for a father and daughter photo, I reckon.'

Isabella thankfully turned and, though she was

once again serious eyed, she co-operatively stared into the camera as Carly made cooing noises to keep her attention.

Max laughed out loud, his head falling back.

'Isabella is being the perfect subject but you're making it impossible to take a photo,' Carly chided Max.

'It's those noises you make...you sound like a pigeon.'

Carly threw him an indignant look. Max made a valiant attempt to sober but his eyes were still heavily creased in laughter lines in each of the photos.

When Carly declared the job done, Max said, 'Thanks.'

'For what?'

'I can't remember the last time I've had my photo taken with Isabella... It's something I need to do more of.'

'I promise I won't make the pigeon noises the next time.'

'Do, they're cute.' Then, shifting backwards, he asked, 'Are you ready to go?'

'I just have to grab my purse from my bedroom.'

'Meet us outside—on the terrace.'

Uncertain why they were heading to the terrace when they should be heading for the carport, after a quick check on her make-up, Carly joined Max and Isabella out there. In the brilliant evening sunshine, Max was crouched down next to Isabella, chatting to her while Isabella had her nose firmly pressed against a large candyfloss-like white and pink-tipped peony.

When Max heard her approach he lifted Isabella into his arms, and, pulling his phone out of his tux jacket, said, 'I reckon we need a group photo.'

Self-consciously, Carly stood next to Max, her spine stiff. Her unease soon ended, however, when Isabella lunged towards her and, wrapping an arm around her neck, pulled her in tight against Max. Max laughed and Carly tried to smile but it was rather disturbing to have her breast held prisoner against Max's arm, to have her belly pressed against his hip. She tried to pull away but Isabella held on tight.

Max gazed down at her. Her breath held at the dark awareness in his eyes.

He glanced down at his imprisoned arm and her body pressed against it. 'I hate to break this up, but I can't take a photo now.'

His tone was way too deep and throaty.

She nodded wildly in agreement but Isabella still refused to let go. In the end Max managed to wrap his arm around Carly, pulling her more or less centre of his body in doing so, and Carly smiled into the camera, knowing her cheeks were glowing as Isabella's hold pulled the entire length of her body against the hard muscle of Max's.

\* \* \*

Night had fallen and now that the birthday celebration meal was over, couples were out on the dance floor, twirling and twisting under the hundreds of fairy lights strewn across the courtyard.

Beside him, on Valentina's lap, Isabella giggled at Giovanni's disappearing act behind his napkin. Max had been taken aback when Tomaso had told him they were to be seated at the top table along with the rest of the Ghiraldini family. Giulio had stared unhappily at Carly when she had taken her seat beside him. Given Valentina's whispered words in Giulio's ear and his shrug after, Max guessed it was at Valentina's insistence that Carly got to sit with him and Isabella for the meal. If Giulio had had his way, Max reckoned Carly would have been seated in the further reaches of the courtyard…if not in the kitchen itself.

Giulio's mood hadn't improved when Tomaso and Bianca, clearly taken with Isabella's insistence on squeezing Carly's cheeks tight at every available opportunity, chortling in delight when Carly crossed her eyes, had invited Carly to attend their wedding on Sunday.

Max hadn't thought that far ahead. It was the polite thing to do—he could hardly leave Carly at home while he and Isabella attended the wedding. But…this weekend with Carly was getting too intense. He was feeling things for her that he had no right to be feeling. Earlier when he had spotted her and Isabella playing on Isabella's bed he had been torn between joy at Isabella's happiness and guilt that it had taken an outsider to unleash the playful child in his daughter.

When Carly had stood up his pulse had hit the roof. Her dress fitted her like a glove, the deep slash in the neckline revealing a tantalising glimpse of her breasts. He closed his eyes for a moment recalling how good it had felt to have her body pushed against his when he had taken their photo. How her hair had tickled his chin, her light floral perfume doing crazy things to his brain.

Throughout the meal she had chatted to Giovanni about his life in Athens, where he headed up the family's Greek subsidiary, and then excitedly with Tomaso and Bianca about their planned honeymoon trip to Croatia, giving them tips on little-known places to visit. Once or twice she had tried to engage with Giulio but he had shut down her attempts. Each time Carly would tense beside him, growing silent for a while as she absorbed Giulio's rebuttal. Each time Max had glared in Giulio's direction before chatting himself with Carly, wanting to ease her discomfort.

Which made Carly's invitation to Giulio to dance with her all the more puzzling. They were now out on the dance floor, Giulio leading Carly. At first they had danced together stiffly, barely a word passing between them, but now they were talking animatedly. What were they talking about? Max had the uncomfortable feeling it had something to do with him.

When the song ended, Carly returned to the table but Giulio moved to the stage.

Loud applause and whoops of encouragement followed his words of welcome to all of the guests. Max forced himself not to do an eye roll when Giulio gave a long name-check of all the politicians and celebrities present, often adding anecdotes of humorous encounters and experiences he had previously enjoyed with them.

But then he looked towards their table and with deep emotion expressed his love for Valentina and his sons. He tried to continue but his voice caught. He cleared his throat, attempted to continue but it sounded as if a vice were gripping Giulio's throat. Panic stirred in Max. *Please don't mention her.*

Giulio puffed out his chest, gripped the microphone even tighter. 'Great sadness has visited our family in recent years.' Beside him Valentina stiffened. Isabella, sitting on her lap, looked curiously at Valentina as though sensing her upset.

Up on the stage Giulio continued, his gaze not leaving their table. 'At times my wife and I didn't know how we would manage to carry on. But we will, for our beautiful boys, Tomaso, Giovanni…' Pausing, Giulio shifted his attention towards Max.

Max's heart came to a standstill. 'And Max.' Giulio cleared his throat. Max felt as if he had been hit by a sledgehammer.

'I'm ashamed to admit that it has taken losing my beloved Marta to fully realise that the only important thing in life is those whom you love.' Once again Giulio's gaze moved back to him. Max shifted in his seat, confounded by what he was hearing.

'We all need to cherish our families, to be there for one another. Support one another. Not hide away, not be too proud to ask for help, to ask for what we need in life.' There was an edge to Giulio's voice now. Max rolled his shoulders, anger stirring in his belly. Was that what Giulio thought…that he was too proud and hiding away?

'And it's important to remember that, however dark the present is, there is always a future.' Giulio's tone lightened. 'A future of weddings and new members in our family. Bianca… Isabella, our gorgeous granddaughter who gives us hope and purpose. Two years ago I didn't think I would be able to stand here and talk to you as I celebrate my sixtieth birthday, but losing Marta has taught me that we should cherish life and each other, to embrace the future.'

Around him, people stood to applaud Giulio, who stepped down from the stage with an extravagant bow of acknowledgement.

'Are you okay?'

He turned at Carly's question, stared at her blankly for a few moments before saying, 'We should head back to the villa… It's beyond Isabella's bedtime.'

For a moment it looked as though Carly was going to argue with him but something shifted in her gaze and she nodded.

After saying their goodbyes to all the family, including a terse thank you and nod towards Giulio, they drove home in silence. A silence that continued apart from forced chatter with Isabella as they gave her a drink before bed.

He attempted settling Isabella himself, but Isabella insisted on Carly being in the room too. Which did nothing for Max's bad humour. What the heck was he going to do if Isabella wanted Carly when they got back to London?

He read Isabella *Sleepy Heads in Sleep World* distractedly, but thankfully she was exhausted by her day and fell asleep quickly.

He and Carly crept out of her room. Outside the door, Carly asked, 'Will you join me in having a drink?'

He wanted to say no. He wanted to clam up.

No, actually, he wanted to say yes so that he could let loose on all of his frustrations with Giulio.

He didn't know what he wanted. So with a

curt nod, he led the way downstairs and into the kitchen.

He pulled two beers out of the fridge and passed one to Carly.

Outside on the terrace, they sat on the L-shaped sofa overlooking the pool.

Sitting at an angle from him, Carly pushed off her high heels, swung her body in his direction and, folding her legs under her, asked, 'Do you want to talk about it?'

He shrugged. 'Not particularly.'

Carly took a sip of her beer. 'I'm guessing Giulio's speech upset you. It must be hard hearing Marta's name mentioned.'

'It's not that.'

'What is it so?'

'*Dio*, Carly, you heard Giulio yourself, do you need to ask that question?' He stopped and tried to swallow the impatience in his voice. Carly, after all, had nothing to do with the frustration coursing through him. But years of being looked down on, the guilt of Marta's death, spilled out regardless. 'The assertion that I've been hiding away. Not caring about them. I stayed away because I didn't want to cause them even more upset. They never approved of me. I allowed their daughter to die... why would they want to see me? I invited them to visit us in London soon after Marta died but they never came.'

'But Giulio is concerned for you, Max—he cares for you.'

'How do you know that?'

'His speech…'

He shook his head. 'That was nothing but a veiled condemnation of me.'

'I disagree…' Carly paused and shifted closer to him. 'When we were dancing Giulio asked about you. How you are coping.'

About to take a drink of his beer, Max paused, the bottle hovering in the air, a sinking feeling in his stomach. Quietly he asked, 'Why did you ask Giulio to dance with you?'

'I wanted…' Carly paused, gave him an uncertain look before admitting, 'I wanted to tell him that you need his support.'

'You did what?'

'But you do.'

Max slapped his beer bottle down onto the glass-topped table in front of the sofa. 'If I wanted Giulio's support I would ask for it.'

Carly unfolded her legs, sat upright and shook her head. 'No, you wouldn't, and Giulio and Valentina are too nervous to ask for your support.'

'*My* support?'

Carly looked at him as though she couldn't believe he wasn't following her train of logic. 'Being closer to you and Isabella would help them in dealing with Marta's death.'

'Why haven't they visited us in London if that's the case?'

'Have you invited them recently? Straight after Marta's death would have been too painful for them.'

He gritted his teeth. 'I do have my pride, Carly.'

Carly frowned. And then after a moment's consideration nodded and said, 'I can understand that, but I think the Ghiraldinis are nervous about getting things wrong in their relationship with you.'

Max threw his head back and stared at the overhead stars. He tried to temper his frustration when he said, 'I'm really not following this.'

'Don't you see, you hold all the power in your relationship. They want to be with Isabella but know that you could stop them seeing her at any point.'

Affronted that anyone would think he was capable of that, he bit out, 'I would never stop them seeing her.'

'I understand why it must be hard for you but perhaps you need to let everything go that happened between you and the Ghiraldinis in the past and focus on where you are now. You need to start talking to them, Max. For all your sakes. I honestly don't believe the Ghiraldini family hold you responsible for Marta's death. Giulio told me tonight that you were a wonderful husband to Marta.' Stopping, Carly cleared her throat, but her voice was still cracked with emotion when she added, 'He said you made her very happy. He's very proud of all that you have achieved.'

Max narrowed his gaze, not buying it. 'You're making this up.'

Her mouth dropped open before she made a disbelieving squeak. 'I most certainly am not.' She gave a little huff, folded her arms and eyed him crossly.

Max swallowed a smile at Carly's outrage; sparks were practically firing from her eyes. 'So are you saying that I should invite Giulio and Valentina to come and visit us in London?'

The sparks in her eyes disappeared to be replaced with shining enthusiasm. 'Yes, and you should visit Como more frequently.'

He picked up his beer bottle. Eyed her over its rim. 'If the Ghiraldinis come to London, I'm going to insist that you visit and you can be the one who has to listen to Giulio's tall tales.'

She threw her head back and laughed. Then, with a satisfied smile, she countered, 'But you'll have no need for me to visit. Isabella will be sleeping perfectly. My work with you will be done.'

Max took a long gulp of his beer. He tried to imagine never seeing Carly again. He took another gulp, thrown by how his heart dipped low in his chest at that thought. He placed his bottle onto the table top again. 'Did you enjoy the party?'

Carly rubbed her hands against her bare arms. 'Of course.' She gave a light laugh that travelled through his body like warming brandy. 'I'd defy anyone not to enjoy such a lavish party.' She wrinkled her nose. 'I was looking forward to dancing more though. You dragged us off home before I got a chance to dance with Isabella as I had promised her.'

Before he knew what he was doing, Max found himself standing and holding his hand out to her. 'Will you dance with me instead?'

For a split second her mouth widened in a brilliant smile but instantly it faded. 'There's no need.'

He kept his hand reaching out, refusing to listen to the voices telling him he was acting crazily, and said quietly, 'How about we forget about reality for a few minutes and pretend we have just seen each other across a room?'

Her head tilted. 'Like in an old movie?'

'Exactly.'

She considered him for a moment. 'Are you the hero or the villain of the movie though?'

Good question. Max stepped closer. Suddenly realising that with Carly he wanted to be a hero as corny as that sounded. He wanted to treat her right, protect her, earn her respect. 'The hero of course.'

Her eyes danced with merriment. 'I like the idea of suspending reality for a while.'

'How about we pretend it's a Viennese ball?'

She stood and playfully bowed. 'I would be honoured to dance with you, Count Lovato.'

'And I with you, Princess Carly.'

He held her at a distance, humming lowly. They danced around the terrace, the stars shining down on them, the still night air whispering against their skin. He felt Carly shiver. He stopped and removed his jacket. Helped her pull it on. Instead of waltzing this time, his hands went to her waist, hers to his shoulders. He pulled her closer, she came willingly. Her thigh bumped against his. He tightened his hold. Her hip touched against his upper thigh. His hand roamed upwards. His thumb ran along the outer side of her breast. She exhaled shakily. Fire raged through his veins.

Her eyes were heavy, mirroring his own need. He lowered his head. Her eyes fluttered closed, her soft plump mouth parted. With a groan his mouth found hers. His arm around her waist, he arched her body against his and she whimpered, her fingers reaching up to press against his scalp. All the while they tasted and nibbled and inhaled each other. One hot mouth on the other, their bodies twisting and bumping against each other. He longed to push back the deep neckline of her dress. To thumb the soft flesh of her breasts.

But then with a shaky breath, he pulled away, knowing it all was about to get out of control. He ran a hand along his jaw. 'Forgive me.' She went to protest but he shut her down. It would be easier if they both pretended that this was something he had got wrong, that he was the only one who wanted this kiss, this fire. He pressed on. 'That was inappropriate. I would like to apologise.'

He stepped back, gestured to the villa. 'I'll walk you to your room.'

Carly removed his jacket and passed it to him. Tilting her chin, she said, 'There's no need.'

She swooped down and picked up her heels.

Max watched her walk away. And closed his eyes when she went inside, a wave of frustration washing over him.

A kiss that was so wrong shouldn't have felt so perfect.

# CHAPTER SEVEN

'*UNO...UNO...UNO.*' Her peach shorts covered in a heavy dusting of sand, Isabella picked up one creamy white stone after another from the beach and dropped them into her rapidly overflowing red sand bucket.

Her brown curls peeking out from beneath her white sunhat, she looked adorable sitting on the pebbled section of Max's private beach.

Closer to the water, the beach was made of a bank of fine sand and for the past hour the three of them had played there building sandcastles. Of course, building sandcastles with an architect was never going to be straightforward and they had ended up creating an impressive fort complete with moat, battlements and drawbridge.

Now, as Max sauntered down the steps of the boathouse heading in their direction carrying a laden tray, she lowered her sunglasses from where she had earlier perched them onto her head and bit back a groan. Why were men blessed with such good legs?

Beneath his white shorts, Max's were bronzed and muscular, no doubt as a result of his morning swims. The outside light had triggered again this morning when he had gone down to the pool. She had forced herself not to peek out, which had called for an iron will, given how tempting the prospect of seeing a half-naked Max had been.

Instead she had lain in her bed and confronted some home truths she'd have much rather preferred to ignore.

Number one being the most obvious: her behaviour last night in kissing Max had been totally unprofessional. He hadn't fooled her in his apology—they both knew that they had equally wanted it, but she should have known better.

Two, hadn't she learned anything from the Robert debacle? Max was still in love with Marta. Falling for a guy whose heart lay elsewhere was plain insanity.

Three, Max was a struggling dad trying to negotiate his relationship with his in-laws over an emotionally charged weekend. Was her proximity, the fact that they got on, that there was an attraction between them, nothing more than a welcome diversion for him?

Fourth, and the most crucial truth of all, was Isabella. Carly knew her focus should be in helping develop a stronger bond between Isabella and her dad. Which was why, this morning, Carly had breezed into the kitchen, determined that last night was a temporary blip in the weekend, and suggested they all spend some time together on the beach.

The tray casually hoisted onto one shoulder, Max strolled across the sand in his bare feet. Carly led Isabella by the hand down to their picnic blanket on the sand and, when Max joined them, Carly nodded in the direction of the tray balancing on his shoulder. 'Neat trick.'

Max laid the tray down at the centre of the rug with a flourish and grinned. 'I was a waiter when I was studying.'

Max sat on the turquoise blanket and Carly, sitting across from him, patted a spot between them for Isabella to sit on. But Isabella, as ever, had her own idea and plonked herself firmly down on Carly's lap.

Laughing, Carly glanced in delight towards Max, who looked from her to Isabella with a frown.

Carly placed her hand on Isabella's knee, her forearm lightly preventing her from toppling over. In truth she wanted to wrap her arms tightly around her waist, hug her tiny body in close, but given Max's disquiet she decided not to make a bigger deal out of Isabella's ever growing acceptance of her than was necessary.

All morning Max had been relaxed and courteous towards her. A little too courteous for her liking...he was treating her as you would a colleague you were fond of.

Despite herself she wanted to scream. She wanted to ask if he had felt the same surge of hot hormones, the thrill of something new and wonderful, that same rightness of their kiss. The rightness of two bodies, two mouths and the perfect blend of pheromones all colliding in one incredible explosion of perfection.

But that laid-back vibe he had been projecting all morning was now history. He looked rattled. Why did he have a problem with Isabella sitting with her? Wanting the awkwardness to disappear, she pointed to the tray filled with juices and fresh fruit and delicious-smelling pastries. 'Look, Isabella, at all the wonderful things Papa has brought for our picnic.'

Isabella clapping her hands excitedly seemed to snap Max out of whatever was bothering him. He placed a napkin on his forearm with a flourish and, picking up a plastic beaker of orange juice, presented it to Isabella as though she were royalty. *'Signorina Isabella, succo d'arancia per te.'*

To Carly he passed a tall narrow glass filled to the brim with iced coffee. 'And for you, Signorina Carly, iced coffee hand-blended by myself.'

Did he really have to talk in such a low sexy voice, which sounded like an invitation to do something naughty?

Isabella drank her juice and munched happily

on a piece of a cookie Luciana had baked earlier that morning.

Max's boathouse was a contemporary, two-storey flat-roofed structure. Storerooms were located on the ground floor while upstairs there was a large kitchen and living space with spectacular views out onto the lake and a balcony suspended over the water. A wooden jetty to the side of the boathouse led to Max's powerboat.

Her cookie finished, Isabella began to swing in Carly's lap as she softly hummed a tune to herself. She and Max exchanged a humorous look at Isabella's tuneless humming. Their gazes held. A charge of attraction crowded the air space between them. A shiver ran through her.

Disconcerted by the intensity of the chemistry playing out between them, Carly bowed her head and ran her hand over Isabella's sun hat, wishing she could touch her soft curls instead.

'Isabella is growing very fond of you.'

Carly blinked at the concern in his voice. 'You're worried about it?'

Unease flickered in his expression. 'With Marta…all the nannies who've come and gone… I worry about the amount of loss she's had in her life.'

Her heart almost snapped in two to see the worry etched on his face, the sadness in his voice. Isabella shifted in her arms, her head lolling back against her chest. 'Children are resilient. As long as she knows she can rely on you then she will be able to handle other people coming and going in her life.'

Max's gaze stayed fixed on hers as he considered her words, the intensity of his reflection and deliberation of what she said lifting her heart—he really wanted to do right by his daughter. But it was also his respect for her opinion that got to her. Her stepfather had always disregarded her views. For a long time it had dented her self-confidence and had made her question her abilities and even her right to express her opinions. Dropping her cheek to rest gently against Isabella's head, Carly closed her eyes. Drew in a long breath. Sighed it out silently as her heart took another tumble forwards in falling for Max.

'You're very good with Isabella.'

Carly opened her eyes in surprise at Max's softly spoken voice. Looking down, she smiled fondly when she spotted that Isabella had fallen asleep in her arms. Carly leant back so that Isabella was in a less upright position, a wave of warmth spreading through her as she watched Isabella's long dark eyelashes flicker in her sleep.

She floundered for a moment, knowing she needed to say something, to look in Max's direction, but she didn't want him to see just how emotional she felt. She searched her brain for something suitable to say and eventually managed to ask, 'Has your nanny agency found any suitable candidates for you?'

'They've emailed some profiles through. On paper they look good—' he shrugged '—but so did all of the others that I recruited.'

'If you want a second opinion, I'll happily interview the candidates with you.'

Max looked at her curiously. 'Is that part of your service?'

It wasn't. But without realising it until she'd offered, Carly felt invested in Isabella's future. She wanted to make sure she was well cared for. 'It's not something I usually do...' Carly grimaced down at Isabella, who was leaning heavily against her chest. She leant even further back on her arm that was keeping them both upright. Her bicep and wrist protested with a sharp ache. 'Gosh, she's heavier than I thought.'

Max shuffled over on the picnic blanket to sit next to Carly. His thigh touching hers, he reached over towards Isabella. 'Let me take her from you.'

Their hands met as they passed Isabella between them, their bowed heads almost touching. It was such an intimate act, gently passing a sleeping child, so full of innocence, so defenceless, between them.

Carly's heart missed a beat. And another beat

when she saw Max's tender gaze down onto his daughter as he settled her into his arms.

'You really love her, don't you?' Carly asked softly.

Max's green gaze shifted up to her. Emotion filled his eyes. 'Sometimes...sometimes I'm afraid...' Max trailed off. Carly held her breath, waiting for him to continue.

They both jumped at the sound of shifting pebbles behind them. When they turned they found Valentina staring in their direction, her expression unreadable.

She and Max jerked away from one another, Isabella waking in the process. She gave a little whinge, but then as she grumpily sat up in Max's lap her scowl morphed into a shy toothy smile when she spotted Valentina.

Valentina bent down and held her arms out wide to Isabella. Isabella clambered off Max's lap and tottered towards her grandmother.

Valentina hugged Isabella, pressing tiny kisses against her cheek before taking her hand and leading her down towards the picnic blanket. Carly and Max had already sprung up from the blanket and were standing far apart from one another.

Max stepped towards Valentina, who eyed him cautiously.

Footsteps on the path down from the villa had them all turn to see Giulio making his way towards them.

Max looked at his watch. 'I wasn't expecting you until lunchtime. If I had known you were coming earlier I would have made sure to have been up at the villa.'

Giulio's gaze flicked towards his wife and then upwards, his head shaking as though to say, *I told you so*, but then his expression softened and he crouched down next to Isabella. 'Valentina couldn't wait to see Isabella again. We tried calling you to say we were coming early but you didn't answer,' Giulio said, poking Isabella affectionately on the belly with his index finger. *'Cuore mio, come va?'*

Isabella giggled and held onto Giulio's finger. Giulio made a big act of struggling to get his finger back out of Isabella's grip, much to Isabella's amusement.

Carly stepped back from the group, feeling wrong-footed that Max had not mentioned the Ghiraldinis were calling. Valentina frowned at her movement. Carly bent down and began to tidy their picnic tray.

'The renovations, your new boathouse, all very impressive, Max,' Giulio said a little gruffly.

Max's only response was a quick nod of his head in acknowledgement.

Carly cringed at the awkward silence that followed and only ended when Max said a little unenthusiastically, 'Luciana won't have lunch ready for another hour—would you like to join us in our picnic?'

Giulio eyed the blanket as though it were an alien concept to sit on the hard surface of a beach to eat.

'Thank you for your lunch invitation, Max,' Valentina said in a low voice, 'but if it's okay with you we would like to bring Isabella back to Villa Fiori for the afternoon. The rest of the family would love to spend some time with her...' Valentina paused and her gaze ran between Carly and Max '...and I'm sure you both could do with a break.'

Giulio looked at his wife in puzzlement, obviously only hearing now this change in plans, but his expression soon changed to one of pleasure at the prospect of having Isabella for the afternoon.

Carly willed herself not to blush. Valentina's gaze was a knowing one, giving a whole different meaning to her words. A meaning that had Max work his jaw. 'I'm sure you're busy preparing for the wedding tomorrow. There's really no need.'

Valentina, still holding Isabella's hand, moved closer to Max. She gave him a gentle smile. 'It might be a long time since my children were this age, but I remember how exhausting it is, especially when they aren't sleeping through the night.' Her voice dropped low. 'Let me help you, Max. Please. It's important to me.'

Max's head bowed at Valentina's words but then he slowly nodded his head.

Valentina reached out and held his forearm for a moment. 'Thank you. I will drop her home about seven.' Valentina's gaze shifted towards Carly. 'Has Max taken you to see any of the other lakeside villages yet?'

Carly hesitated for a moment, not sure how to answer. 'No…not yet.'

Valentina looked at Max. 'You should take Carly on a tour of the lake this afternoon.'

Giulio cleared his throat. 'I'm sure Max has work to do.'

Carly added, 'I need to buy a dress for the wedding tomorrow. I'm going to cycle into Bellagio.'

Max picked up Isabella's changing bag from the blanket, clearly wanting to change the subject. 'Why don't we go back up to the villa? I'll need to give you some of Isabella's things and run through her routine with you. She'll need to nap around three.' The four of them walked towards the path back up to the villa. When Max realised Carly wasn't following he turned and looked at her with a questioning frown.

Carly gestured to the blanket and tray. 'I'll stay here and tidy up.'

Giulio gave a nod of approval but Valentina called out, 'Have a wonderful afternoon, Carly…

and make sure Max relaxes. He works much too hard.'

She watched them climb the path and sighed when they went out of sight. Carly turned to the lake, stretched her arms out wide, opened her mouth and gave a silent scream. This was all getting too complicated. Valentina obviously thought there was something going on between her and Max. And seemed to be encouraging it. Which was so at odds with Giulio's constant suspicion of her. Admittedly, he wasn't as hostile now that they had spoken last night, but he was still wary of her.

Picking up the tray and folding the blanket over her arm, Carly walked to the boathouse. At least Max was reaching out to his in-laws. Maybe everything would work out for the best this weekend… At the top of the steps to the boathouse, Carly's gaze shifted over the lake and then up to Villa Isa. She doddered on the threshold of the boathouse for a moment, wondering how this afternoon was going to pan out. Then she realised she needed to take control of it. Make the most of her time here in Lake Como. She would go for a swim, cool down, and then cycle into Bellagio. Max no doubt would spend the afternoon working. Which suited her perfectly.

Was he really seeing Carly wearing nothing but a black bikini walking along the jetty? Max edged to the side of the terrace, annoyed at his lack of will-power. Of course, he should turn around and head for his office. But the sight of Carly in a skimpy bikini was way too tantalising.

As she came alongside *Alighieri*, she stopped to give his powerboat a quick once-over. He could see her ponytail swinging from side to side as she ducked down in her appraisal of the forty-five-foot boat.

Then she moved on further down the jetty, walking close to the edge. At the end of the jetty she came to a stop and peered into the water. He waited for her to turn around. When he saw that she was back in the safety of the boathouse or even on the beach then he would go to his office.

Her body swayed. *Dio!* She was going to fall in if she wasn't careful.

She lifted her arms. Max was already running before she dived cleanly into the water.

She surfaced with a yell that echoed up the hill, her arms thrashing the water.

He vaulted over a cluster of terracotta pots and then a low wall, grunting when he hit the path far down on the other side.

He raced down to the beach, all concerns about Isabella becoming too attached to Carly, his discomfort over Valentina's misguided approval of their relationship, his frustration over how keenly he wanted her physically, vanishing.

Nothing mattered.

Other than saving her.

He cursed when the beach house blocked his view of her. He ran past it, his heart tightening in panic.

He bolted down the jetty.

Carly, lying on her back, was motionless in the water.

He dived in beside her, surfaced and grabbed hold of her, pulling her towards the shore.

With a shriek Carly shouted, 'Max, what the hell are you doing? You've almost scared me to death.'

His ears ringing, he stopped and shook his head. Carly pushed his hands away from where he was holding her around her waist.

'You were drowning.'

Sparks flew from her eyes. 'No, I wasn't.'

'Why did you scream and then lie in the water motionless?'

'I screamed because it's freezing…' she flicked some water towards him, splashing him deliberately on the face '…and it's advised that you float when you hit cold water to allow your breathing to adjust. People often drown because they panic and inhale water while hyperventilating.'

'I thought…'

The anger in her eyes disappeared. 'Were you trying to rescue me?'

When he nodded yes she tilted her head, a smile

of gratitude lighting up her face. And then she was laughing, and shaking her head, her gaze on his saturated tee shirt. 'You're soaked through.'

Beads of water threaded her long eyelashes, her cornflower eyes even more vivid with her hair sleeked back, the delicate lift of her cheekbones more pronounced. Her lips were plump and ruby red from the cold.

He cursed silently his lack of willpower. He breathed in time and time again, trying not to speak the words that eventually broke free of him. '*Vorrei darti un bacio*… I want to kiss you…again.'

Her eyes widened. It took a long while before she asked, 'Are you asking for my permission?'

Her voice was husky and filled with promises that made his head spin. He touched his thumb against her cheek, and then lightly over her lips. 'I can't promise—'

Her hand landed on his, stilling his progress. 'Don't. I know, I don't want to hear…' She trailed off and then her mouth was on his.

It was a lustful kiss. Hot and passionate. Her hands clasped his neck, deepening the kiss. He pulled her in closer, pressing her body against his. Her pebbled nipples pressed against his chest, her legs threaded in between his. He deepened the kiss, began to edge them both towards the shore, using his free arm to pull against the water.

Even in his testosterone-overloaded state he knew he had to get her to safety.

Her body was trembling and as soon as his feet reached the lake bottom, he lifted her into his arms, ignoring her protests as he carried her to the beach.

There he walked directly to the beach house, where he grabbed a towel from the stack of them in the utility room and, wrapping her in it, laid her down on the sofa.

She jumped off the sofa the moment he took a step backwards.

A silence full of questions, uncertainty, desire stretched between them.

An angry sigh came from her mouth. 'I didn't need rescuing.'

He should leave, say he had work to do. He shouldn't be so drawn to Carly Knight. He had nothing to offer this woman who'd had her heart broken by another man and needed to learn to trust again. He knew all that but yet he heard himself say, forcing a lightness into his voice even though his heart was laden down with emotion, his body alive with a physical connection to her, and gesturing to his dripping clothes, 'You don't deserve it, but after we shower and change, I'm taking you for an ice cream.'

Carly wrinkled her nose. 'I have to go and buy a dress for tomorrow.'

'I'm taking you over to Mantovana. There's a good selection of boutiques you can visit there.'

Her gaze narrowed. 'I'm buying the dress myself, Max… There are going to be no arguments today.'

'Accepted.' He waited a pause. 'Now, can I suggest that we strip?'

Her eyebrows shot up. *Dio*, even though it was wrong of him, he loved seeing her riled, seeing her blush, seeing the flicker of anticipation in her eyes.

'Strip?'

He went into the utility and gathered up some more towels. He tossed one to her. 'Strip out of our wet things, of course. We can then go up to the villa to change. I'll strip in the bathroom—that is unless you need some help?'

She held the towel tight against herself. 'I'm sure I'll manage by myself.'

He laughed at her sarcastic tone.

He was about to go into the bathroom, when he stopped and said, 'By the way, I've transferred additional funds into your bank account to cover all of the extra expenses you've encountered this weekend.'

She dropped her towel, sighed. 'There was no need.'

He tried to keep his eyes averted from the heavy swell of her breasts beneath the black bikini top. But in the end he gave up and stared at them, desire pounding through his veins. Carly inhaled a shaky breath. 'Are we doing the right thing?'

Her voice was low, gravelly. The burn inside him for her upped another notch. He fisted his hands. No, they weren't doing the right thing, but he could contain this, not allow it all to go too far. He wanted to spend time with Carly. For once forget about all his responsibilities. 'Do you want to stop?'

She shook her head.

'Me neither,' he said.

Taking a lick of her ice cream, Carly threw her head back in pleasure as the intense but oh-so-smooth dark chocolate hit her palette. She closed her eyes to the vivid blue sky, her bones melting under the afternoon sun.

The heat, the ice cream, the lap of the water against the stone wall she and Max were sitting on, their legs trailing over the side, had her thinking of the childhood summers she had spent on the Kent coast with her parents.

'*È buono*…is it good?'

Carly eyed her double-scoop ice cream and shrugged. 'I'm not sure…you really can't beat a Mr Whippy.'

Max looked at her aghast. 'Mr Whippys are nothing but fluff.'

'They most certainly are not! They're creamy heaven on a wafer.'

Max laughed, throwing his eyes skywards. Lake Como suited him. He looked incredible in a suit, but the casual clothes of the lake suited him even better. She could imagine him taking long hikes into the hills, thriving in the outdoor lifestyle. 'Do you think you'll ever come back here, to Lake Como, permanently?'

Max lowered his pistachio single-scoop. 'Perhaps.' His gaze moved across the boats moored in the harbour, out across the simmering lake towards Villa Isa. 'I like London. The culture, the opportunities there.'

Carly squinted against the glare of the sun. 'I want to move to the coast. We spent all my childhood summers in Whitstable on the Kent coast. In a few years I want to move there…perhaps commute to London for work when necessary.'

'What type of house would you live in?'

Carly had imagined herself living in a Victorian redbrick house with tall ceilings and views of the sea from its bay windows. But now she knew differently. 'Your boathouse transported to Whitstable.' In response to Max's surprised look she added, 'It's perfect. Full of light and clever designs that means it has everything you need in a compact space—perfect for cleaning.'

Max laughed. 'You don't like cleaning?'

'Or any type of housework, I'd much prefer to be out surfing.'

'If you find a plot, I'll design it for you.'

Carly laughed, knowing this was all fantasy but enjoying allowing her imagination to run free. 'Have you surfed before?'

Max took a bite of his waffle cone and shook his head.

'You design a house for me and I'll teach you and Isabella how to surf. Does that sound like a fair exchange?'

She was teasing him, of course—a few surfing lessons weren't exactly a fair barter for the designs from an award-winning architect.

Max pondered her proposal for a few moments as though seriously considering it. 'The boathouse has no bedrooms though…are you going for loft-style living?'

'You can add in a bedroom for me.'

Having finished his own ice cream, Max reached for hers and before she could protest he had taken it from her and was happily licking it. Carly went to grab it but he shifted away. His eyes twinkling in mischief, Max asked, 'Won't you want more bedrooms for a family?'

Carly made another lunge for her ice cream but Max held it away from her. 'If that happens I can extend. Now can I please have my ice cream back?'

Max took another bite, his eyes daring her to stop him. Only then did he pass the ice cream back to her with a satisfied grin. Carly's insides warmed at the light fun dancing between them and she had the crazy urge to kiss his lips, to taste the ice cream on his breath.

'Why not simply add the bedrooms when you're building? It would be more cost-effective and avoids future disruption'

'Because I might jinx it.' Seeing Max's confusion, she added, 'I've stopped hoping for things to happen for me relationship-wise. What will be, will be.'

'You don't believe in a proactive approach?'

'Hah…look where that got me with Robert.' She paused, and, not sure how Max would respond, mumbled, 'We met on an Internet dating site.'

When he didn't respond, she glanced in his direction. 'There are other people out there, you know,' he said softly.

Her stomach suddenly jittery, she handed her cone to Max, who took it and bit into it. 'Maybe.' She shook her head when Max handed her back the cone. 'You finish it.'

He ate it all up in four bites. Carly smiled at his enjoyment. She was going to miss him. That thought slammed into her. 'What about you? What are your dreams for yourself and Isabella?'

Max stood and tossed their paper napkins from the *gelateria* into a nearby bin. 'For now, it's about getting through each day.'

'What about dating, a new relationship?' Carly asked, trying to keep her tone light as he sat back down beside her.

'Not for me.'

Her smile wavered at the certainty of his tone. 'Never?'

'Never.'

Carly wanted to tell him that that would be such a waste. He would make some woman really happy. But she was *not* going there. 'You must have other dreams though.'

He stood again and, picking up her shopping bags, gestured that they walk towards the launch that would bring them back to his boat moored out on the lake. The village was winding down after a busy lunchtime, the locals heading home for siesta. Beside her, Max seemed deep in thought and oblivious to the appreciative looks of the women they passed by. 'Do you think I should move here with Isabella?'

Carly allowed her gaze to move over the ancient terracotta-tiled houses of the village. She could imagine Max and Isabella here, the lake becoming their playground, Isabella exploring the countryside when older with her friends. 'Having family support would be good. The Ghiraldinis obviously would like you to move here.'

The launch was already out on the water so they waited on the platform for it to return. Carly could tell Max was trying to build himself up to say something by his restlessness. Eventually he said quietly, 'Leaving London would feel like I'm leaving Marta behind.'

Would a man ever love her the way Max obviously had loved Marta? 'She'll be with you wherever you go.'

He turned and touched her arm, a gentle smile on his lips. 'Has anyone ever told you just how incredible you are?'

Carly laughed. 'Yes, but usually they're drunk.'

Max eyeballed her. 'You *are* incredible.'

Carly playfully gave him a little push on his arm. 'Stop. You're making me blush now.'

'You deserve happiness. Someone who will treasure you.'

Carly gulped, her stomach doing cartwheels at the sincerity in his eyes. Some of the self-doubts that clung to her from Robert's rejection loosened their grip in the pit of her stomach. 'And you deserve that too, Max.'

'*Dio!* I don't have the energy,' Max said, running a hand tiredly through his hair.

'Valentina was right earlier—you do work too hard. You should have some fun in your life.'

Those misty green eyes, already shimmering in the brightness of the day, flashed with a hint of wickedness. 'Maybe I should take you up on your offer to teach me to surf.'

'You'd really enjoy it.'

'If you promise to wear a bikini like you did earlier then I'd definitely say yes.'

Warmth rippled through her body at the heat in his voice. She arched an eyebrow. 'Sorry, but I wear a wetsuit when surfing in England.'

He shrugged. 'In that case...' Pausing, he inched closer, his voice dipping low, 'Although I'd bet you look gorgeous in one.' His head dropped close to her ear. 'I do know how to have fun, Carly.'

Her breath caught at his near growl. She turned her head, answered back, 'Prove it so.'

His gaze darkened. 'Is that a dare?'

A slow sultry smile formed on her lips. 'Yip.'

Max waved to the launch owner, who was nearing the platform, and, turning with a devilish smile that sent shivers of excitement through her bones, said, 'You might live to regret that dare.'

# CHAPTER EIGHT

ADRENALINE WAS STILL pumping through Carly as she helped Max tie up the boat to the jetty.

Job done, she high-fived him. '*That*, without doubt, was the best experience I've ever had in my life!'

Clearly entertained by her enthusiasm, Max smiled broadly before jumping back on board *Alighieri*, his bullet-shaped powerboat, with its long extravagant nose.

'What does *Alighieri* mean?'

Grabbing hold of the gold-embossed shopping bag containing the dress she had purchased over in Mantovana, Max answered, 'It's the surname of one of Italy's most famous poets, Dante Alighieri.'

'Did *you* name the boat?'

Lifting his mirrored sunglasses off, he eyed her indignantly. 'There's no need to sound so surprised. I do have a romantic side, you know.'

Carly gave a snort at that, which only doubled Max's look of indignation.

Back on the jetty Max shook his head when she gestured she'd carry the bag and then, reaching up his hand to rub against the corded muscle of his neck, he admitted ruefully, 'Admittedly, I'm a little out of practice romance wise...'

'Well, that makes two of us.'

He gave her one of those heart-melting smiles that spoke of understanding, before nodding back to *Alighieri*. 'You certainly don't scare easily.'

After Carly had taken a turn at driving the boat—and she was pretty proud about how well she had handled the boat given that it was her first time in a powerboat—pushing it hard through the calm waters of Como, Max had taken over, and showed her just what the boat was capable of. She had clung to the hand rail at the side of her seat as the boat had soared through the water, screaming with delight, much to Max's amusement.

Now they sauntered down the jetty towards his boathouse, neither of them seeming to want to end their afternoon yet. 'I have to admit to being a bit of an adrenaline junkie—the higher the roller coaster, the better for me. Anyway, I knew you were in control.'

Max laughed. 'Such trust.' But then drawing to a halt, he asked, 'Do you trust me, Carly?'

Carly's stomach flipped at the heat in his voice. 'That's a big question to answer. I'm... I'm...' She paused, struggling how to articulate the innate caution and scepticism that were still inside her. And then Max's words yesterday that she needed to trust herself echoed in her mind and with them came dawning realisation that it wasn't Max she didn't trust, but herself. She didn't trust herself not to fall for the wrong guy again. Which had nothing to do with Max, who was staring at her with an intensity that was threatening to set her aflame at any moment.

'Yes, I do trust you.' How could she not after he had been so candid over the past few days, telling her things, opening himself up to her in ways she knew were a first for him? In his care for Isabella, in how he was reaching out to the Ghiraldinis despite the hurts of the past.

Something shifted in the air between them. Max's fingers gently landed on her forearm. Sudden and unexpected desire bubbled through her veins. 'Will you join me for a drink in the boathouse?'

The chemistry shimmering between them gave his invitation a meaning beyond the words alone. In going with him she knew she was about to step into the unknown.

Of course, she should say no. But being an adrenaline junkie—albeit suppressed in recent years thanks to her experience with Robert—was pushing her to say yes. That, combined with the delicious intoxicating warmth from his fingers tantalisingly stroking her skin, from the dark promises in his eyes, had her nod yes.

Inside the boathouse, Max folded back the glass

doors to the balcony before taking a bottle of prosecco from the fridge.

'I'm more used to having a cup of tea at four in the afternoon,' Carly said, amused when he passed her a glass of the bubbling liquid.

Max casually leant against the kitchen countertop. 'This weekend has been good for me…thanks again for coming with us.'

Carly tapped her shallow champagne glass against his and sipped the deliciously cool wine, the bubbles exploding in her mouth. Her heart was racing like crazy, her insides melting with a slow-burning heat. 'I'm glad I agreed to come.'

'I like you, Carly…'

She swallowed. Finished what he was trying to say. 'But you're not in the right place—I get it, Max. I'm not looking for anything from you.'

'I don't want to hurt you.'

'I'm a grown woman. I know what I'm getting into.'

'You've been hurt before. I don't want to add to that.'

Carly understood why he felt that way but she was tougher than he gave her credit for. 'And I'm equally concerned that you might get hurt, Max… I hope you don't think that I might be using you?'

'Using *me*?'

'As a way of easing myself back into the whole dating scene.'

Max threw his head back and laughed. 'That's the worst excuse for sex that I've ever heard.'

Carly blushed at the sensual way he said sex. Max edged closer to her, his hips mere inches from hers. She inhaled his scent, felt the warmth from his body. 'How about we sleep together because you find me irresistible and because you are everything I look for in a woman—intelligent, sexy, and adorable?'

'I wouldn't use the word irresistible...' Laughing at his knitted brow, she admitted, 'But there's something about your voice... It's pretty hot.'

He gave a nod of satisfaction. 'And you have the best legs ever.'

'I hit you with your most excellent eyes.'

Those misty green eyes twinkled like dew on a blade of grass before he said, 'And right back at you with your mouth—it should be made illegal...' his index finger lifted and for a brief second ran gently across her bottom lip '...your mouth is so sensual.'

Carly let out a shaky breath, hot desire swirling in her belly.

Max's hand landed on the cotton of her tee shirt, the warmth seeping down to her ribs. The age-old story of God creating Eve from Adam's rib sprang to her mind—man and woman were part of the same one. Was that all-powerful need inside her to find someone, to connect with them, to give her heart and soul to them, was that because she wouldn't feel whole until she did?

Of course, she wouldn't give her heart to Max. Her heart she would protect from this man who didn't want a relationship. She would feel fondness, affection, respect for him, but that was all. The road she was on with him was about seeking physical pleasure, and allowing herself some fun for the first time in years.

Her gaze shifted over his face. His features were like a roadmap to his personality: the soft waves of his lips that at times could be as demanding as any churning sea, but at other times soft and gentle like waves lapping smoothly onto shore; his broad and prominent cheekbones telling of his strength to deal with what life had thrown at him; his long and chiselled nose, his pride, which saw him achieve so much in business but which cost him in seeking out the support he needed.

'You accused me of not being romantic earlier.'

A shiver ran the length of her at the heat in his eyes. 'I wouldn't say accused…'

Taking her hand in his, he whispered in a low growl, 'Let me show you just how romantic Italian men can be,' before leading her out of the boathouse and down the steps to the jetty.

Five minutes later she eyed the long length of the jetty dubiously…anything to distract her from the sight of Max standing next to her wearing nothing but his black form-fitting boxer shorts radiating testosterone and vitality. 'I thought you were going to show me how romantic you are.'

'You're the one who said you were an adrenaline junkie.'

'But the lake is freezing…jumping into it once today was enough.'

'But this time you'll be doing it with me…come on, it will be fun.' His smile fading, Max added, 'This weekend… I'm finally starting to feel alive again. I want to do something stupid, something irresponsible.'

Carly shook her head but she could not help smiling at him wildly. She knew what he meant, understood what it was like to live under a cloud of memories and broken dreams and mistrust. It was a cloud she was starting to burst through, thanks in part to the man she was standing next to, and she wanted to shatter that cloud even further with an act of defiance.

She pushed off her flip-flops and then her shorts. Pulling her tee shirt over her head, she caught Max's glance down over her body as he took in her white panties and bra… Her sensible everyday underwear did not appear to disappoint him given the flare of heat in his eyes.

Taking hold of her hand, he asked, 'Ready?'

Then they were racing down the jetty, their footsteps echoing lightly against the wood. Carly giggled wildly, revelling in the freedom of running hard and the kiss of the sun on her skin.

Her adrenaline soared as the jetty ran out and the vast expanse of the lake began. She considered slowing, backing out of this altogether, but Max's hand held hers even tighter, giving her the encouragement to keep going.

They sailed through the air and Carly's heart sailed up into her mouth.

Max's hand broke away from hers.

She hit the cool water, sank low into the darkness of the lake. She inhaled some water. Panic rushed through her body. Her legs flailed. Her arms reached out, searching, searching…after a few seconds she realised it was Max she was searching for. She wanted him. Needed him.

And then he was there, taking her hand, wrapping his arm tight about her waist.

They surfaced together.

Carly spluttered, gasping for some air. Her body was anchored against his, his arm about her waist. She shoved him in the chest. 'That was the worst idea ever. As for being romantic, Max Lovato, you've a lot to learn.'

Max laughed. Carly tried to remain angry but his laughter was too infectious. They laughed together, their joined bodies reverberating with the song of happiness and release coming from deep inside them both.

And when their laughter eventually died, Max gently smoothed her dripping hair back from her face, and whispered, 'Maybe you'll consider this romantic.'

His mouth touched the tender skin by her ear before running a slow path down along her jawline. She arched her neck, groaned at the deliciousness of his warm lips on her skin. And then his mouth was on hers. She practically whimpered at the beautiful heat of his kiss, his initial gentleness intensifying to an all-consuming, electrifying kiss that had them clinging to one another, her legs threading around his.

But soon the cold of the water forced them apart to swim back into shore.

On the shore, he lifted her up into his arms and headed back to the boathouse. Carly considered saying she could walk but realised that she didn't want to—she was going to embrace this afternoon wholeheartedly, allow herself a few hours of insanity. She knew it wasn't going to lead anywhere, or happen again, so why not for once in a very long time be hedonistic and forget about all the rules?

In the boathouse Max brought her to the bathroom. Perching her onto the side of the bath, he asked, 'So how am I doing on being romantic?'

She gestured around her, grimaced. 'A bathroom…what can I say? Currently I'd give you four out of ten.'

He shook his head. 'I obviously need to up my game.' He went and switched on the shower. Then leading her in, he placed her under the heavy flow of warm water. She closed her eyes, goose bumps popping onto her skin despite the heat, when he began to wash her body with a lemon-scented wash. His hands ran over her arms, along her shoulders, down her back. She arched into him, unable to open her eyes because of the heavy drunken desire flowing through her. Her skin, so cold only a few minutes ago, was now flushed. Every cell of her body felt aroused, her mouth heavy and sensual against the flow of water pushing against it. Her hands reached out and blindly she ran her fingertips over the hard muscle of his chest, down over the taut skin of his abs.

Her legs were shaking and almost gave way when he twisted her around. His hand ran down her back, skimming over her bra, dipping and staying for a while just above her panty line. She arched her back once more. Max ran kisses along her neck.

And then he was washing her hair. The smell of coconut filled the walk-in shower. Carly placed her hands on the wall tiles for support. His hands slowly massaged her scalp. She groaned in pleasure.

'What would you rate me now?'

'Oh…oh, a very impressive seven.'

He rinsed the shampoo from her hair. He stepped closer, pulled her body to his. The hard plains of his body pushed into hers. His arm encircled her waist. 'I love how narrow your waist is...' His other hand landed on her hip bone. 'How your hips flair...everything about you is beautiful.'

She swallowed at the intensity of his voice.

She twisted around. 'My turn to wash you.'

He shook his head, washed himself quickly, his large hands sensually running over the taut muscles and sinew of his body.

Switching off the shower, he stepped out and wrapped a towel around his waist, before passing her one. 'I'll see you out in the living room.' His head dipped down so that his mouth was next to her ear. 'By the way, I'm not going to stop until you give me a ten out of ten.'

Carly drew back. 'I have very high standards.'

His mouth curled upwards devilishly, his eyes darkened. 'Prepare to have your standards blown right out of the water.'

Five minutes later, Max turned to the sound of Carly clearing her throat. Wrapped in a towel, her skin flushed, her eyes bright, she bit her lip. 'My clothes are still out on the jetty.'

He shifted away from the kitchen counter and watched a droplet of water run from her damp hair down along the creamy skin of her collarbone and disappear beneath the towel into the valley of her breasts.

Heat and desire and temptation swirled between them.

He rolled his neck back at the doubts silently but persistently sitting at the base of his skull, pushing them away.

'I promise to fetch them...but only when you give me a ten out of ten.'

She rolled her eyes. 'Don't tell me you're going to hold me hostage.'

He grinned. 'Don't be putting ideas in my head.' He was joking, of course...but the thought of holding Carly Knight captive was rather enticing.

Taking her by the hand, he led her down the steps to the sitting area of the boathouse. Popping open a fresh bottle of prosecco, he filled two glasses and passed one to Carly who was sitting propped against the thick pillows of the sofa, her legs curled up.

Kneeling down before her, he tipped his glass against hers. 'Here's to romance.'

Carly sipped her drink, and then holding up her glass, she eyed it critically. 'It's nice...but isn't the whole prosecco, champagne, whatever you like to call it, a little clichéd when it comes to romance?'

Placing his glass down, he lowered his hands onto the sofa, leant in good and close to her and began to recite one of his favourite Dante Aligh-ieri poems in Italian.

After the first line, Carly's skin had flushed even more.

With the second line, a heaviness had invaded her gaze.

By the third line she whispered, 'What…what does it all mean?'

He broke off from reciting the poem, touched his hand against her bare leg and said, 'Listen to the sounds, the cadence, it will tell you all you need to know.'

By the tenth line she had slipped down against the pillows, and he had propped himself beside her, lying on his side, his hand running along the delicate skin of the inside of her arm.

When he finished the poem, she inhaled a deep breath. 'Tell me at least what the last line means… you said it so quietly.'

He hesitated for a moment, but then decided to translate it, his head dipping close to hers. Into her soft gaze he whispered, '"Tis such a new and gra-cious miracle."'

'Max.' She spoke with wistfulness, wonder, want.

His mouth sought hers out, the emotion burn-ing inside him for her, playing out in a kiss that contained his soul.

Her body arched into his.

He twisted onto his back, rolling her with him until she lay on top of him.

Her hands captured his head pressed into the vast mountain of pillows behind them. Her fingers raked through his hair, while her mouth, now in control, explored his with unrestrained passion.

Her hips rolled against his, her breasts lifting and dipping, sending his pulse into dangerous territories.

He groaned when her legs shifted to either side of his, her kiss deepening even more. He broke away, breathed heavily, 'Before we go any further…are you sure this is what you want?'

She nodded her head, her eyes bright. 'Yes.'

Flipping them both over so that he was now on top, his pulse was drumming in his ears, his body was demanding that he stop talking but, touching his fingers against her cheek, he said, 'You've been hurt in the past, Carly. I don't want to add to that.'

Indignant resolve sparked in her eyes. 'That doesn't mean that I'm going to be celibate for the rest of my life.' Her voice dropped to a bare whisper. 'What about you—why do you want this, Max?'

Looking down at Carly, her cheeks blushed, her eyes a mixture of passion and expectancy, he answered from his heart. 'Because I want some joy, some comfort… I want to give you those things too.'

Carly's answer to that was to wrap her arms around his neck and lower his mouth to hers.

Soon their towels had disappeared. He touched her breasts, kissed them, worshipped them, his hand trailing over her curves, his body thrilling to feel her tremble.

The breeze from the lake whispered over their naked flesh when they became one. They both grew silent, stared into one another's eyes, the far-off sound of birdsong reaching them as they blinked and considered each other with wonder.

# CHAPTER NINE

Tomaso kissed Bianca, one hand cupping her neck, the other wrapping protectively around her waist. The wedding guests clapped and whooped. With a flourish, Tomaso leant Bianca backwards, her veil tumbling down across the ground like a light snowfall, deepening the kiss before swooping back up. With a raised fist Tomaso signalled his delight to the crowd, his wide proud smile springing unexpected tears into Carly's eyes.

She blinked. She was *not* going to cry.

Tomaso turned to Bianca, touched his fingers against her cheek. A look of raw emotion passed between bride and groom. Carly ducked her head and swiped at the tears spilling onto her cheeks.

She angled her body even further away from Max, who was sitting at her side. Her gaze wandered beyond the wedding couple and the garden to the frothy wisps of clouds hugging the mountain tops. Anything but dare look in Max's direction.

The wedding ceremony was taking place on the lawn below Villa Fiori. The air was filled with the scent of nearby lavender and pine. The late afternoon sun was gently bathing the wedding party, the beaded full skirt of Bianca's gown sparkling in its mellow rays.

Max's upper arm came to rest against Carly's.

She waited for him to shift away. When it remained there, the warmth of his tuxedo jacket against her bare arm startlingly intimate, she glanced in his direction.

His gaze was on Tomaso and Bianca, strain etched on his face.

She wanted to reach out to him, place her hand on his leg and ask if everything was okay. But with the Ghiraldini family seated directly in front of them, she couldn't dare to show any level of intimacy towards Max in their presence. Carly wasn't going to make what must be a difficult day even harder by intimating that there might be something between Max and herself.

She leant a hair's breadth closer, waited to see if he pulled away, if his initial touch was unintentional. His arm shifted against hers, applying a minuscule amount of extra pressure, but enough to communicate a silent connection.

The priest performing the marriage ceremony invited Tomaso and Bianca to kneel before him and he began a blessing for them and their marriage.

Carly swallowed. Her heart was heavy. Heavy with joy for Tomaso and Bianca's happiness and love for one another. Heavy with concern for Max—it must be so difficult for him to sit through this wedding, to be reminded of his and Marta's day.

In front of them, sitting on her own chair in between her grandparents, Isabella giggled at something Giulio whispered to her. Valentina shot him a warning look, a reminder that the priest was still saying his blessings, but then Valentina smiled ruefully when she saw the laughter in her husband's eyes. Giovanni, the best man today, shifted forward in his seat next to Giulio and made a silly face at Isabella, who giggled even more.

Carly blinked again, fresh tears stinging the backs of her eyes. It was so wonderful to see Isabella being embraced by the Ghiraldinis, to see the wealth of love in their family.

She adjusted the straps of her gown, shifted in her seat, and trailed her eyes along the pastel tea roses and peonies that had been threaded into the long rows of Italian cypress trees flanking the lawn. She tried to ignore the yearning inside her for a family of her own.

Last night, after Valentina had dropped Isabella home and they had settled her, Max and she had had dinner together. It had been a confusing evening of a thousand different emotions—they had managed to maintain a degree of their previous amiable chatter but every now and again the fire between them would spill out and they would touch one another before springing away. When it had come to saying goodnight to one another, Max had kissed her with a gentleness that had nearly broken her apart and asked if she would spend the night with him.

She had been so tempted. Her knees had practically buckled with the desire to experience making love with him again. Never had it been so intense, so physically mind-blowing. Unfortunately it had also scared her. After, when she had lain in his arms in the boathouse, his hand stroking her hair, a deep storm of unexpected and unwanted emotion had risen within her. She had vaulted off the day bed and disappeared outside, a towel wrapped around herself, to collect her clothes. She had dressed on the jetty, not willing to face the likely consequences of going back into the boathouse—even more hot but damaging sex. Sleeping with Max had made her vulnerable. She had so desperately wanted it to be nothing more than fun but instead it had cracked open her heart. She had to protect herself better. Which was why she had said no to his invitation to spend last night with him. And why today she was working really hard at keeping everything light between them.

Isabella turned in her chair. She eyed Max seriously and then, with an angelic smile, her tiny teeth showing, she waved at him. Max waved back. Isabella's gaze then shifted to her. Carly waved at her. Isabella's smile died.

Carly inhaled a shaky breath. She tried not to take it personally but her heart was on the floor. Isabella turned away and shuffled off her seat. Valentina fumbled to catch hold of her, casting a nervous glance towards the altar, but Isabella moved out of her reach, dropped to her knees and crawled under her chair. Popping up in front of Carly, the skirt of her pale pink flower-girl dress streaked with a knee-shaped grass stain, her headpiece of tiny rosebuds askew, she lifted her arms up, and gave Carly a heart-piercing smile.

Settling Isabella onto her lap, Carly buried her head for a moment into her curls. Her senses swam at her floral scent, at the weight of her body. Heat flooded her cheeks and those damn tears threatened again. But then, gathering herself, she drew back, rubbed the grass stain and adjusted Isabella's head piece. Only then did she look up to see Giulio and Valentina staring back at her. She exhaled in relief when they smiled and nodded as though they accepted and welcomed Isabella's fondness for her. But her relief was short-lived when she saw the deep disquiet marring Max's face.

Max clinked his shot glass against Giovanni's and then Tomaso's. *'Mille congratulazioni.'*

Tomaso nodded his acceptance of Max's congratulations and then all three of them swigged back their shot of ouzo.

Max coughed, while Tomaso gulped for air, before hitting his brother lightly on the arm with a closed fist. 'You are learning some bad habits in Athens, Giovanni,' Tomaso admonished his brother.

Giovanni's eyes flashed. 'You have a long night ahead of you. A little ouzo will give you energy.'

Max stepped away from the easy banter between the brothers, still thrown that they had insisted he join them in their private celebration of the wedding under the boughs of the huge eucalyptus tree that sat in the gardens overlooking the dance floor in front of the villa's courtyard. 'It's close to Isabella's bedtime. I should take her home,' Max said, shifting further away.

Giovanni held up the ouzo bottle in his hand. 'Have another drink with us.'

Before he could argue Giovanni poured another shot into the glasses. Tomaso raised his in toast. 'Here's to family.'

Max clinked his glass against theirs. Shook his head when Tomaso nearly choked on his drink again. He left his drink untouched.

His coughing fit over, Tomaso said, 'It's good to see you back in Villa Fiori, Max.' Tomaso cleared his throat, rolled his shoulders. 'We weren't sure if you would come.'

Max frowned. 'Isabella and I were always coming to your wedding. There was never any doubt about that.'

Tomaso and Giovanni looked unconvinced.

Then Giovanni's gaze shifted towards the dance floor. Couples were dancing beneath the gold chandeliers, streamers and globes of fresh flowers the florists had hung from invisible wires over the courtyard. And in the middle of the dance floor, her head thrown back in laughter as she swung a giggling Isabella around and around, was Carly, one hand bunching up the length of her rose-pink gown to avoid tripping over it.

Her dress was perfect—its delicate colour highlighted the creamy perfection of her skin, the cut showcasing all her curves, her toned arms, the delicate strength of her collarbone, her hair twisted into a tight bun. Max considered his shot glass, wondering if the ouzo would somehow douse the heat burning inside him. In their lovemaking Carly had been sensual and fearless. She'd given but also had taken what she needed from him. It had been hot and fiery lovemaking that had left him wanting more. Much more.

But Carly obviously thought differently.

He tossed the ouzo onto the ground. *Accidenti!* Her rejection last night stung like hell. And her cool indifference today wasn't much better. It was as if yesterday afternoon hadn't happened. At times today he wondered if he had actually dreamt it. Dreamt of that passion, that connection of skin against skin, gaze upon gaze. It wasn't as though she was avoiding him—the opposite, in fact, she had stuck by his side all day. Before the ceremony she had teasingly given him the thumbs up in approval of his tuxedo; smiled banally when he complimented her on her dress. It had only been during the wedding ceremony that he saw her drop her guard. He had seen her tears. That brief connection of arm against arm had exploded a whole pile of emotion in his heart. He had realised just how much he wanted her company, wanted her attention and awareness, how he wanted to be there for her.

Could they be friends?

On the dance floor Carly slowed her spinning.

Her hands wrapping around Carly's neck, Isabella planted a huge wet kiss on Carly's cheek. Max closed his eyes. He was allowing Isabella to grow too close to Carly.

'Carly *è stupendo*. Is there something between you—?'

Before Giovanni could say any more, Max interrupted, 'No, there isn't.'

Giovanni flashed him a smile and, walking away from them, did a little quickstep dance move and twirl on the lawn before calling back, 'I'm suddenly in the mood for dancing.'

Tomaso laughed. 'I reckon you might need to

rescue Carly in a little while—the last thing you need is for your nanny to have a broken heart.'

Max was about to point out that Carly wasn't a nanny, but Tomaso waved in response to Bianca's beckoning to him from the dance floor—Giovanni having pointed her to where they were hiding out—and said with a chuckle, 'It looks like I can't avoid dancing any longer.'

Giovanni paid all his attention to Isabella at first, twirling her around, but then he edged in closer to Carly, his hip bumping against hers. Giovanni could dance. And he had a cheeky charm that women seemed to find irresistible.

Max squared his shoulders, stalked across the lawn and onto the dance floor. Isabella squealed in delight when she saw him. Max picked her up, tickled her on the belly. And held out his hand to Carly. He twirled her under his arm, moved her away from Giovanni.

Giovanni began to weave over, his hips gyrating much too suggestively. Max considered standing in Giovanni's way, perhaps stepping on his toes, but the arrival of Valentina and Giulio into their dancing group diverted all their attention.

Valentina shuffled her shoulders, her feet making small movements on the dance floor. Giulio grimaced and swayed his hips a fraction. A clearly bemused Tomaso and Bianca joined their ever-increasing circle. Giovanni clapped his hands in delight and then, grabbing his father's hand, pulled him into the centre of the group. Giulio attempted to copy Giovanni's moves, wriggling down towards the floor, his body loosening up with the beat of the music. Max laughed, taken aback but tickled by this more playful side of Giulio. In his arms Isabella chortled. Giulio smiled fondly at her delight and then gestured to Max for them to come and join him and Giovanni. Max shook his head. Giulio wiggled his way over to him. He held out his hand, gesturing with a nod to the centre of the group. Max hesitated. Giulio stopped dancing. Without looking, Max knew that everyone was waiting to see what was about to happen. The proud appeal in Giulio's eyes caught him right in the chest.

Max, shaking his head in disbelief, stepped forward.

A cheer went up from the rest of the family.

Isabella chuckled when he began to dance. Valentina after a while came and took Isabella from him. No doubt she was worried that she might get injured in the dance off that had sprouted up between him and Giovanni. Max tugged off his suit jacket, threw it in Carly's direction. She threw her head back in laughter when she caught it. And Max, already dizzy from his spinning and cavorting, swayed on his feet at how his heart splintered to see her infectious joy.

\* \* \*

The wedding was still in full swing when it was time for them to take Isabella home. Kneeling down in the driveway, Carly removed Isabella's headpiece as Max said his goodbyes to Tomaso and Bianca, who had walked out with them. Giovanni then joined them and, smiling down at her, said, 'I never got to dance with you, Carly.' Raising an eyebrow in Max's direction, he added, 'I know when I'm beaten by a better man.'

Pulling an exhausted Isabella up into her arms, confused by what Giovanni meant, Carly was about to ask him, but Giulio and Valentina arriving to say goodbye stopped her. With tears in her eyes, Valentina leant in and hugged Isabella. Then Giulio joined in, his arm, like Valentina's, wrapping around Carly. Though she was thrown to be part of this unexpected group hug, Carly's heart danced with pleasure. Eventually Giulio pulled back and then eased a reluctant Valentina away, his arms wrapping around her shoulders protectively. His gaze shifted from Isabella to Carly. Quietly he said, 'Isabella is fond of you. It would be nice to see you again with Max and Isabella.'

Carly nodded, knowing she was blushing especially given the surprised expression of all the others who had heard Giulio. Her gaze moved over to Max. His expression was bewildered but then, with a quick nod, he led her and Isabella away to their awaiting car.

* * *

'Now, that's a wicked laugh if ever I heard one.'

An hour later Carly gasped and sat back in her chair, clasping a hand to her breastbone. 'Crikey, Max, don't creep up on me like that.'

*Especially wearing a tuxedo, the bow tie undone, looking ever so sexily ruffled after a long day.*

Placing the baby monitor on the terrace's coffee table, Max dropped down beside her. Carly edged into her side of the sofa. Max, a silent moonlit night, the bittersweet euphoria of having spent the day at a spectacular wedding filled with love and joy…they all spelt danger.

Max gestured to her phone. 'So what's so amusing?'

Carly swiped her phone screen before holding it out to Max. In the picture on her screen, Max and Giovanni were attempting to outdo themselves in a move that was akin to a Cossack dance.

Max groaned.

Carly flicked through some others photos. 'There are other photos I want to show you…'

'No, thanks.'

'These are gorgeous, honestly.' Carly frowned as she scrolled through the endless photos, wondering just how many photos she had managed to take today. 'Did you enjoy the day?'

Max ran his hand along his jawline as he considered her question. She squirmed in her seat to hear his skin pull against his bristle, imagining what it would feel like to have it pressed against her own skin…on her belly, on her breasts, between her legs.

Max's mouth tightened. Heat blasted in her chest. Had he guessed what she was thinking?

'Giovanni is interested in you…but I would advise you to stay clear of him.'

Carly dropped her phone. Stared at him. For a moment she felt a flash of vain pleasure— Giovanni was a good-looking guy after all, funny and a fantastic uncle to Isabella. But that soon dissipated to annoyance. Did Max actually think she would sleep with him one day and consider dating his brother-in-law the next? Anger bubbled in her stomach.

'I don't know, he's handsome, rich and available, there's a lot to be said for all three things,' she said in a breezy tone when in truth she wanted to fling her phone at him.

Max frowned but then a slow shrewd smile formed on his lips. 'I thought you said money doesn't matter to you.'

'It doesn't.' She threw her hands up into the air. 'For crying out loud, Max…we slept together yesterday.' She paused, trying to contain her anger. 'Do you actually think it meant so little to me that I would date *your* brother-in-law?'

Unperturbed by her anger, Max shifted forward

in his seat. Placing a hand on the sofa between them, he leant in, those green eyes searching hers. 'What did it mean to you?'

Goosebumps jumped to attention along her body, domino style—up her arms, chasing around her neck, then down her spine. Did he really have to speak so low…as low and tenderly as he had whispered her name yesterday when his back had arched and his body at a precipice had stilled?

She tried to dredge up the laid-back front she had worked so hard to maintain all day, but it was nowhere to be found. She was too exhausted, she was too damned aware of Max, to keep up the pretence. 'It was very special.'

He nodded to her whisper, placed his hand lightly on her knee. Her heart sank in fear while her body did a hula-hula dance. She picked up her phone, needing a diversion before things got out of control. And given the sparks of desire flashing between them, one wrong move could prove fatal. She was *not* going to sleep with Max again. No way.

'Here! I found it! The photo I wanted to show you.'

Max reluctantly took the phone from her, his calculating gaze studying her first. He looked at the photo. Didn't say anything. Thrown, Carly asked, 'Isn't it the most adorable photo ever?'

* * *

Max stared at the photo, his throat closing over. He gripped the phone tighter, something twanging in his heart. Unbeknownst to him, Carly had taken a photo of him and Isabella when he had been talking to Valentina's sister and her family. His back was to the camera, his focus on the family, but Isabella, who was in full view of Carly, was staring up at him with love and adoration in her eyes.

He blinked, dazed by the rush of love for his daughter pounding through him.

He nodded blankly when Carly asked, 'Are you okay?'

Heat beat through his body. He yanked off his already open bow tie, which Isabella had undone when he had read her book to her earlier. He had pretended not to notice and when he had acted all confused when he pretended to spot it, Isabella had giggled in delight.

'She adores you.'

Max nodded. He bit the inside of his cheek, knowing it was crazy that he was struggling so much to talk, but what he was about to say came from the very depths of him, words that he had said before but without the intensity of emotion now coursing through him. 'I…and I love her.' He looked up and into Carly's cornflower gaze and heard himself say things he'd never thought he'd dare say to anyone. 'When Marta died… I was afraid to love Isabella.' He ran a hand through his hair. 'Losing Marta tore me apart. To lose Isabella would be incomprehensible.' He stopped, pain and shame sweeping over him.

'You wanted to protect yourself against further pain…that's understandable.'

'But not excusable. *Dio*, she was a three-month-old baby—what was I thinking?'

'You were in shock, in pain. You're not a robot, Max, you're human. These feelings happen.'

'I thought it would be best if she was independent, not reliant on me…in case anything ever happened to me.'

With a sigh Carly shifted in her seat. She laid her hand on top of his. 'You're a good dad, Max. Isabella has always been well cared for.'

The disquiet churning inside him stilled at her touch, at the sincerity of her tone. 'Will you send me a copy of this photo?'

'Of course.' She picked up her phone, swiped to some other photos. 'I'll make sure to send you the ones of you dancing too.'

He groaned. 'Those you can delete.'

Carly chuckled. 'No way! A hot Italian guy dancing… I can't wait to show them to my friends.'

He lunged for the phone. Carly shifted it out of his grasp, holding it high above her head. He leant into her. She fell against the back of the couch. He followed. His body was on hers, his mouth hovering over hers. 'Give me the phone, Carly.'

Her eyes twinkled, daring him. 'And what exactly are you going to do if I don't?'

He bit back the urge to growl. 'I'm going to kiss you and a whole lot more.'

Carly's eyes darkened. She breathed out a faint gasp. 'In that case I guess I won't be giving you the phone.'

Later that night, lying in Max's bed, her fingertips digging into his shoulders, her body taut with desire, Carly stared into Max's eyes, her heart splitting open at the desire, at the tenderness there, and in that moment, as his body arched and hers bowed up to meet him, she gave up all pretence of toughness and cynicism, all pretence that she was capable of protecting her heart against this incredible man.

She was in love with him.

# CHAPTER TEN

THE FOLLOWING MORNING, Carly sank her nose into Isabella's cotton candy-striped pyjamas, inhaling lavender with an undertone of mashed bananas. Carly called out to Isabella, who had tucked Sunny into her bed and was attempting to read him *Sleepy Heads in Sleep World* even though she was holding the book upside down. 'Sweetheart, you have to learn to eat your bananas properly.'

In response, Isabella gave her a beam of a smile.

Carly ignored the painful tug on her heart and focused on packing Isabella's suitcase.

The job almost complete, the sound of familiar footsteps out in the corridor had her grabbing hold of the final few items from around the room and packing like a ninja suitcase packer. The sooner they got back to London, the better.

'I was wondering where the two of you had got to.'

Carly forced herself to smile breezily, to contort her face into what she hoped was a chilled-out expression. 'Isabella and I were playing with her toys.' She paused and gestured to all the toys strewn around the room. 'We got a little carried

away in a name-and-find-it game. I'll tidy up once
I have her case packed.'

She went and scooped up a bunch of Isabella's
tiny socks from the top drawer of her wardrobe.

'You don't have to pack Isabella's suitcase,' Max
said, coming closer.

She tried not to wince, wishing he would keep
his distance from her. 'Luciana said that you had
some urgent business to attend to. Why don't you
go back to that?'

Max stilled. Carly grabbed Isabella's hairbrush
and hairclips from her dressing table and packed
them into the vanity bag that came with her suitcase.

'What's going on, Carly?'

Carly considered Max for a moment, seriously
tempted to tell him that she was hacked off because she had woken this morning in *his* bed only
to find that he had long vacated it, given how cool
the sheets were on his side of the bed. She was
hacked off she had slept with him last night. She
was hacked off because she dreaded saying goodbye to Isabella. She was hacked off because last
night, as Giulio and Valentina had hugged her and
Isabella goodbye she had realised that she didn't
want to say goodbye for ever to the Ghiraldini family. She was hacked off because last night, when
Max had laid her down on his bed and with infi-
nite care and tenderness brought her to climax time

and time again, every defence in her had melted away. She was in love with him. So yes, she was majorly hacked off…and embarrassed.

But she wasn't going to let Max know any of that. Instead she said, 'I hate the thought of going back to work tomorrow. I have a meeting with my accountant. That's never fun.'

Max eyed her dubiously.

Carly kept his gaze, trying to remember everything she was hacked off about, but with his nearness, the inhaling of his freshly showered scent, she felt her anger, her defensiveness crumble so she pirouetted around and went and flung open Isabella's bedroom window, desperate for some fresh air.

'I've rearranged some meetings that I was due to attend later today in London. We can delay our flight until this evening. Let's take the boat out again, go for lunch in Argegno,' Max said.

Carly flipped the lid of the suitcase over and, zipping it shut, dropped it down to the floor. 'I said I would meet a friend this afternoon.' Which was kind of the truth—she had told Agata, a friend from her college days, she would meet up with her some day this week. Given Max's suspicious look, he obviously wasn't buying it. But there was no way she was staying here a moment longer than she needed to.

She was holding onto her sanity with the thinnest of threads. She needed to get back to London, have some space and time to try to process just how much she had fallen in love with Max and Isabella.

And the worst part of it all was that in seeing Tomaso and Bianca's love for one another yesterday, the way the Ghiraldini family had each other's backs, she knew now more than ever that she wanted a family, love, a marriage of her own.

And what had she done? Only gone and fallen in love with a man who wanted none of that.

'Cancel your meeting with your friend.'

Carly startled at the soft plea in Max's words. He looked as though he really wanted to spend the day with her. Images of the three of them out on the lake, eating a lazy lunch in a waterside restaurant, had her wavering. But no. She *was* going to stay strong.

She shrugged, said, 'I don't want to,' before dropping to her knees to pick up the army of soft toys Isabella had scattered around the room.

She ignored Max when he said Luciana would take care of the tidying.

About to crawl behind the toy kitchen to rescue a dejected-looking toy pig, she came to a halt when Max's feet stepped in to block her way.

Sorely tempted to push him out of the way, she had enough sense to know that she would have little hope of budging him. This was the man who had effortlessly pinned her to the bed with his legs last night as his mouth wreaked havoc on her never-before-so-sensitive breasts. The pain had been delicious.

Now, she rocked back onto her haunches and glared up at him.

He didn't move an inch.

'I'd like to see you again in London.'

For a moment elation steamed through her. She was going to see him again! But then cold reality slammed into her. She nodded, smoothed her hands over her blue trousers. 'In a professional capacity, I assume.'

Glaring up at him, her cheeks flushed, a toy silver tiara on her head, Carly looked like an angry princess from one of Isabella's story books.

Max couldn't decide whether to crouch down and pull her into his arms or to back right off. This conversation wasn't going the way he had anticipated. This morning when he had woken at his usual time of five, for the first time in years he hadn't felt the need to jump right out of bed in a bid to ignore the loneliness that had been slowly eating him away.

Instead he had wanted to stay with Carly's body pushed against his. To make love with her again. But it was that thought, that…inevitability that had seen him reluctantly climb out of the bed and dive into the pool.

Last night, their lovemaking had been hot and wild at first, a crazy, lustful, head-spinning, time-stopping exploration of each other's bodies. But when he had carried her to his bedroom, Carly's giggles had faded, and when he had laid her down on his bed, everything had shifted between them. He had seen in her eyes the same tenderness, vulnerability, uncertainty grabbing his heart. They both knew that making love in the intimacy of his bedroom would change things. It would shift their relationship up a gear.

He had offered to take her back to her bedroom but she had said no, said that she wanted to spend the night with him.

Their lovemaking had been slow, tentative, achingly delicate…as though it had been the first time for them both.

He had made love to Carly with his heart jammed with emotion, his skin tingling with the connection, the consuming need burning between them.

When he had ploughed through the pool earlier this morning he had had to stop and pull himself out of the water, disorientated, breathless at just how close he felt to her, at the speed of what was happening between them. He needed to slow everything down, to back off from making love together for a while. Instead he wanted to get to know Carly fully without the emotional minefield of sex.

He knew it would be torture to see her and not act on the chemistry that detonated between them whenever they were in the same room. But they had both been hurt in the past, they needed to take things more slowly. He wanted to show Carly just how much he wanted her in his life but he didn't want to scare her away. So he had cleared his appointments for later today, intent on spending time with her. But Carly obviously had other ideas.

He backed up two steps, creating enough distance to ensure he couldn't touch her, and crouched down.

He picked up a purple plastic mirror and tossed it into the apple-green toy box Carly had been dragging behind her in her clean-up, trying not to let his nervousness and doubts show. 'I want to see you outside work—maybe we could go on a date?'

Carly sat back on her heels. 'Why?'

Taken aback by the coolness of her tone, the defensiveness in her eyes, Max wondered if he had read this all wrong. He certainly was out of practice with everything to do with dating. Panic rolled like waves in his stomach. He stood and went to the bedroom windows and breathed in some fresh air. From the lake he could hear a father on an outboard calling out instructions to the child who was alongside him sailing a dinghy and failing to catch the wind.

He turned, trying to ignore his male pride, trying to ignore the fear, the dread, the apprehension of inviting someone into his life. 'I enjoy your company. You're fun…even if your jokes aren't great.'

Given Carly's unimpressed scowl, he reckoned his attempt at humour had died.

Building bricks and trains and dolls were all gathered up and thrown into the toy box, which was then tidied away beside the bedroom's bookcase, before Carly stood and regarded him with her hands on her hips. 'So we'll meet as friends?'

'Yes.'

Her eyes narrowed, her lips pursed. 'I've enough friends, Max.'

He flinched at the coldness of her voice. He studied her for a moment, trying to figure out how to make all of this okay. 'We can be friends at first… then we can see how things work out.'

'What do you mean?'

'Let's date for a while, see how we get on. I want you in our life.'

Her nose flared and she tossed her head back. 'Why?'

Her tone was blunt, hacked off. He rolled his neck against the stiffness there. 'We're good together.'

Carly folded her arms, clearly unimpressed. He

stumbled on. 'Maybe things can become more permanent between us after a while…it's too early to say if they will, of course. There's no point in rushing things, is there?'

Glancing back at Isabella, who was busy baking and cooking at the toy kitchen, Sunny sitting in the tiny sink, watching the proceedings, Carly stepped closer to him and whispered, 'Permanent?'

He hesitated for a moment… *Dio!* Why was she looking for so many answers? This was all getting out of control. He fought the urge to walk away, a primal fear gripping his heart, a fear of loving again and losing that person. But the need to keep Carly in their lives had him say, 'Maybe you'll move in with us.'

Carly shook her head. 'Look, Max, it was a good weekend. Let's not overcomplicate this.'

'Isabella will miss you.' Carly's furious expression had him rush on, gesturing to the villa, to the lake outside. 'I can give you a good life—we'll travel, come here to Lake Como.'

Carly stepped even closer, her blue eyes sparking. 'I don't want your money, your lifestyle. My job is in London. I don't have the time to be travelling or coming here with you.'

Thrown by her outright rejection, Max asked, 'So is this it? You don't want to meet me again?'

Carly bit her lip. 'Outside of you being my client, no. It's for the best.'

Max inhaled a breath before pointing towards the door. 'You go and pack. I'll finish up here.'

'I'm almost done and I've promised Isabella that I'll take her out to the swings once we're packed.'

Max went and picked up Isabella. If Carly did not want to be part of their lives, then he wasn't going to beg her…or prolong this goodbye. Anger, disbelief, hurt pride welled up inside him with a crushing intensity. 'I'll take care of Isabella. Go and pack. We'll leave for the airport immediately.'

Max's car passed a signpost for Regent's Park and London Zoo. For a moment Carly was about to turn around to Isabella and ask if she'd like to go there, to visit a real-life Sunny in the elephant enclosure. When she'd been writing *Sleepy Heads in Sleep World* she had often visited the zoo to observe the animals for inspiration. But she caught herself in time, the sensation of Max's gaze on her having her sitting ramrod straight in the passenger seat next to Max's driver, Thomas.

At the airport, she had been about to sit in the rear seat next to Isabella but Max had asked her to sit in the front seat instead. He had asked her in the same detached tone he had been using all day since their conversation in Isabella's bedroom. If you could call it a conversation. It had been more like a dance between two different viewpoints of reality—hers that their relationship had to end,

Max's that they could just amble on, see where life would take them. Didn't he anticipate at all the hurt, the pain that would come as a result of his *laissez-faire* approach?

He was shielding Isabella from her. On the plane back to London, he had taken Isabella into the bedroom, saying he would try to get her to nap. But Carly had heard their voices and laughter. She had felt physically sick with the feeling of being excluded, an outsider once again. She had spent the journey alone, trying to focus on the sleeping plan for Isabella she had typed on her laptop and printed out using the plane's on-board printer.

Max had taken it from her when he and Isabella had come out for the landing, silently nodding when she had talked him through the key aspects of the plan. He'd been courteous, attentive but completely detached from her.

She squeezed the soft leather of the car seat, cursing the early afternoon traffic they were now snarled up in. She wanted to get home to her apartment. Sitting here, having Max sitting behind her, hearing him and Isabella quietly chat to one another, was torture. She needed air, space to think. She needed to cry. Which annoyed her beyond belief. She had got herself into this mess. Once again, she had got a relationship all wrong—falling for Max was nothing but a rerun of her relationship with Robert.

She should have seen the signs with Robert, how he would never speak about his ex, but when her name was mentioned Carly saw the memories, the wistfulness in his eyes that took him away from her. It had been strange, an odd sensation, to be next to someone and know that in those moments, emotionally, they were with someone else.

Max was still in love with Marta. Why then did he want to see her again, even talk about things possibly becoming more permanent?

There were only two obvious conclusions. Because they were so good together in bed, or he was looking for a mother substitute for Isabella.

The car edged its way through the traffic lights close to Baker Street underground station.

When the car eventually pulled up outside her apartment block, Max told Thomas to remain in the car as he would see to Carly's luggage himself.

Carly ignored Max's look of displeasure when she stopped by Isabella's door and, opening it, leant in and gave her a cuddle. She wanted to say that she'd see her soon, she wanted to say that she loved her but instead she dragged in some air, inhaling her baby sweetness and playfully tickling Isabella on the belly, smiled brightly and said, 'Make sure to put Sunny to sleep early tonight. He'll be tired after his long trip on the aeroplane today.'

Isabella hugged Sunny closer to her. Nodded

seriously. But as Carly pulled away her bottom lip dropped.

Emotion strangling her throat, Carly walked around the car to join Max at the top of the steps to her apartment.

She searched her bags for her keys, trying not to show how her hands were trembling. 'Call Nina during the week to arrange a follow-up appointment. If you have any questions in the meantime, feel free to call me.'

Max nodded, his jaw tight.

Carly wanted him to just go. To not prolong this goodbye. She found her keys and, lifting them up, attempted a smile. 'Found them. I can see myself in from here.'

'I'll carry your luggage in for you.'

No! The thought of Max coming into her apartment was too much. That was to be her sanctuary. She didn't want to have memories of him standing inside there saying goodbye every time she left or came home. She shook her head, 'I can take care of the luggage. You go. Isabella needs you.'

'How can I make this right?'

Her heart dropped, fresh tears flooding her eyes at his softly spoken question. She inhaled a shaky breath to see the confusion clouding his eyes. 'That first day outside my office, you stopped and looked like you were saying something…to someone.'

Wincing, Max dropped his head and then softly said, 'Marta.'

Max went to say something else but a cry from Isabella rang through the air. 'Car…ee. Car…ee.'

Carly stared towards the rear door that Max had left open when he had climbed out of the car. Isabella was calling her name. She wanted to run to her. Pick her up and hold her for ever. Emotion clumped in her throat.

She grabbed hold of her suitcase even though she was not sure her legs would carry her anywhere, took a weak step backwards. 'Go. Isabella needs you.'

# CHAPTER ELEVEN

'WHO ARE YOU?'

Carly crouched down at the doorstep of the small terraced house to the little boy whose gaze was as curious as his question. 'I'm Carly and you must be Jacob.'

Jacob's amber eyes narrowed. 'Are you here to see my sister?' He shook his head before Carly could answer and said in an unimpressed tone, 'She's asleep. We have to be very quiet.' He paused to stare unhappily up at his mother, who had answered the door with him, and then in a poor attempt at a whisper added, 'Mummy says so.'

Carly swallowed down a smile at Jacob's disgruntled tone. 'I'm here to chat with your mum but I promise to be quiet. I'd like to chat with you too.'

Jacob's eyes brightened. 'Will you come and play with me?'

Carly clapped her hands softly and said, 'I'd love to.' Standing up, she said her hellos to Jacob's mum, Marsha, who had called her earlier in the week. Jacob, who was three, had in recent weeks being waking during the nights complaining of a monster in his bedroom wardrobe. Carly guessed that the arrival of his baby sister, Naomi, might have something to do with his waking.

An hour later, Carly stood on the doorstep saying her goodbyes. After playing with Jacob, which had involved her dressing up as a fire chief and pretending to drive the fire truck while wedged into his climbing frame in the garden, Carly had talked through a plan of action with Marsha, which included her spending some one-to-one time with Jacob, and for her to encourage visitors to spend time with him as well, thereby showing that he was just as important as ever in the household and not being displaced by his baby sister.

Crouching down, she high-fived Jacob. 'See you later, alligator.'

Jacob giggled and rushed in for a quick hug, almost sending Carly toppling backwards.

Carly and Marsha shared a smile and when Carly stood, Marsha, who was holding Naomi in her arms, let out a sigh. 'It was good to talk things through.' She paused and rolled her eyes. 'I was starting to stress myself out, which of course wasn't helping the situation, but now I feel more in control.'

Carly gave Marsha a quick hug and was about to leave when Jacob called up to her, 'You can cuddle Naomi too.'

Carly smiled down at Jacob. 'That's okay. I got so many cuddles from you today I think I'm full.'

Jacob giggled at how Carly patted her tummy but then shook his head seriously. 'No. You must… she's nice.'

Marsha's eyes shone with light tears. Taking Naomi into her arms, Carly crouched back down next to Jacob. 'When she's older, Naomi will be able to play with you.'

'Will she like my sandpit? I've a blue bucket she can use.'

'I bet she'll love your sandpit.'

'She can't have my special spade though.' Jacob leaned into her and whispered, 'That spade is magic—a pirate gave it to my daddy.'

'Wow!'

Jacob gave a nod, satisfied at Carly's amazement.

Standing, Carly gazed for a moment down at Naomi, her heart splitting open at her perfection.

Much too reluctantly she handed her back to Marsha and said, 'I'll call you next week to check how things are with you all. Have a nice weekend.'

As the door closed behind her Carly winced. It was Friday evening. The weekend stretched out in front of her. Friends had invited her out for drinks tonight but she had made up an excuse that she had paperwork to catch up on. Work she could handle right now, social conversation she couldn't.

She had waited all week to hear from Max. At

the start of the week a knot of dread had sat in her stomach at the prospect of him calling or Nina telling her that he had made an appointment to see her. But as the week had dragged on the knot had disappeared to be replaced with a restlessness that willed him to call. She wanted to know how Isabella was doing. If she was sleeping okay. Had she learned new words? Was she still refusing to eat her yogurts? Was she still insistent on having *Sleepy Heads in Sleep World* read to her every night? Had she recovered from the light head cold she had developed in Lake Como?

She missed Isabella with her heart.

She missed Max with all her soul.

She missed his physical presence, his touch, how his eyes followed her as she moved around a room. She missed the passion, the disbelief in his eyes when they made love. She missed his wry sense of humour, his intelligence, his kindness. She missed seeing him hold Isabella. She missed seeing him blossom in expressing his love for his daughter that he had supressed for so long, believing he was doing right by her in making her independent and strong.

She missed the feeling of belonging, of family that had been there when they had breakfast together each morning, when they drove in the car. She missed his life-affirming kisses that infused her with hope and anticipation.

She walked past Hampstead underground station, deciding to walk home instead. She guessed the walk would take over ninety minutes, but it was preferable to facing the quietness of her apartment. She might stop off for a coffee on the way. Or browse some bookstores.

Her fingers itched with the urge to pull out her phone. To check if there were any missed calls. Maybe even call him.

She walked even faster. Past pavement-side cafés with laughing couples, couples holding hands, couples chatting seriously. Past fathers holding hands with their toddlers. Past mothers pushing strollers. Forcing herself to become breathless.

She was not going to rerun her relationship with Robert again.

She was not going to become involved with a man whose heart belonged to another.

Tomorrow she was meeting with her mum. Carly had called her earlier in the week. Seeing Max reach out to his in-laws, talking to him about her own relationships, she had realised that she wanted to try to connect with her mum again. Max was right. She wasn't a cynic. She was an optimist who wanted to believe in new beginnings. Maybe she and her mum could forge a new relationship, based on who they were now rather than on the past. Maybe with time, she could even forge one with her stepfamily.

* * *

There were some sights in life Max had never dreamt he would see. Giulio Ghiraldini sitting at the top of a red corkscrew slide, Isabella between his legs, was one of those sights.

'*Sbrigati, Giulio!* There's a queue forming behind you,' Valentina, standing on the soft play tiles beneath the slide, called up to Giulio.

Giulio raised both hands in a gesture that said Valentina should stop fussing, but then pushed off down the slide. Isabella's eyes and mouth popping open in wonder, Valentina clapped her hands in delight, while Max videoed the entire event on his phone. Tomaso and Giovanni would no doubt tease their father about it in the months ahead when Max shared it on the new online sharing group he had created for the family earlier in the week.

Giulio and Valentina had flown to London for the weekend. The day after he had returned from Tomaso's wedding, he had called them, suggesting that he and Isabella would video call them a few times each week.

The suggestion had been received with great enthusiasm and now he and Isabella called them before bath time most nights, Isabella insisting that she call her *nonna e nonno*, loving the funny faces her grandfather pulled unbeknownst to her *nonna*.

Leaving the playground, they walked towards

the park's bamboo garden, Isabella tottering in the centre of the group, refusing to hold hands with anyone, determined to act all grown up. Carly had been right. By showering her with his attention and love, he had helped Isabella find a new confidence and desire to be independent. So many times over the past two weeks he had been tempted to call Carly to tell her of Isabella's progress. To hear her voice. To know how she was. But what was the point? She had made it clear she didn't want to see him again. Time and time again over the past couple of weeks he had asked himself why. Was she still in love with her ex?

He smiled down at his daughter as she weaved an unsteady but determined path on the concrete pavement. Carly had opened his heart fully to Isabella, allowed him to realise that he shouldn't fear loving her with all his being. His gaze shifted over to Giulio and Valentina. Carly had opened his heart to them too. She had shown him that it was not a weakness to ask for support. Isabella was blossoming in their company. And for him their support brought reassurance, a peace to know that there were others out there who cared for Isabella, who cared for him. Now, thanks to Carly, he could fully see that allowing others into his life gave it more colour and meaning.

The other three carried on for a few steps before turning around. He waved them on, telling them he wanted to take a photograph of them walking with Isabella.

He took out his phone and snapped them, his throat tight at the sight of Isabella's yellow polka-dot dress blowing in the wind against her bare legs, her curls dancing with each step, Sunny tucked under her arm.

He stopped dead on the footpath.

Carly had thought him to be open, to be vulnerable. Not just with Isabella. But with his in-laws. She had given him the gift of tenderness, of being capable of stopping and understanding his own fears and need.

He had feared being hurt again, of losing someone. He had feared opening himself up to another person, showing his fragility.

But in all of that he had lost sight of Carly's fears and needs.

He cursed under his breath. Disbelieving just how thoughtless he had been. Carly feared trusting others. He had done nothing to prove to her that he would always be there for her, that he understood her. He had done nothing to make her feel secure, wanted, treasured. Instead he had reverted to his old ways of keeping others at a distance, of showing no vulnerability. He had tried to keep her in his life using logic when he should have spoken from his heart.

He hadn't told her he loved her.

He loved her.

Only now could he admit that to himself.

But in truth he had known he loved her the day he'd thought she was drowning. He would have given his life to save her.

But fear and the lifelong habit of distancing himself had stopped him admitting it to himself.

He opened up the gallery of photos on his phone, to the pictures they had taken of the three of them on the terrace of his villa before Giulio's sixtieth party.

They all looked goofy but incredibly happy in the photo. Even Isabella, who so often frowned at the sight of a camera, had a grin on her face as she tugged on Carly's neck.

*Dio!* They were meant to be together. But had he left it too late? Messed up too much?

# CHAPTER TWELVE

As she turned the corner onto her street, Carly's footsteps faltered. Somebody was sitting on the steps outside her apartment block. She glanced around her. The street was empty. Lights and the shadow of flickering TV screens shone from some of the nearby houses. Would they hear her if she screamed?

The person on the steps stood. All six feet four of him.

Carly's heart missed a beat and then it raged in her chest.

Her footsteps clipped on the pavement. Within a few seconds she was standing in front of him.

'Max.' She tightened the belt of her jacket before clasping the strap of her handbag, eying him with hot anger.

'How are you?'

No! He was not doing this to her. Using those weapons of his soft green gaze and gentle tone on her. She was impervious to all of that now. 'What are you doing here?'

He blinked at her question before dropping down to join her on the pavement. Now that he was closer, out of the shadow of the steps and under a nearby street light, she could see the strain in his expression.

Her heart splintered.

*Walk to him, Carly. Lay your head against his chest. Inhale his scent, his warmth that melts into your bones, wrap yourself in his strength.*

Another, wiser voice popped into her head.

*Don't you dare. You're enough of a mess as it is. Do you really want to make it worse?*

'Can we go up to your apartment and talk?'

Carly shook her head.

'You were out?'

For a moment she toyed with the idea of pretending she'd been out on a date. She wanted to hurt him, just as she was hurting. Not a particularly noble sentiment, but there was nothing noble about her mood right now. 'Why are you here, Max? You scared me sitting there.'

'I'm sorry.'

Carly eyed him. Was he sorry for frightening her or was it a more general apology?

'How long have you been sitting here?' she asked.

He looked at his watch. 'About three hours.'

'Three hours! Are you crazy?'

'We need to talk and I knew you'd have to come out or go in eventually.'

'And if I didn't?'

'I'd have stayed here until you did.' And he

would have—Carly could see it in the calm resolve of his gaze.

She waited for him to explain why he was here but instead he ran a hand tiredly against his neck, tilting his head. His jaw line was heavy with evening shadow, the lines at the corners of his eyes more pronounced than usual. He looked tired.

She gave a little gasp, raw panic coursing through her. 'Isabella—is everything okay?'

'She's fine.'

His voice held a tender certainty but Carly needed to know more. 'Who's minding her?'

'Giulio and Valentina.'

Carly paused, trying to make sense of his answer. 'Isabella is in Lake Como? Why are you here, then? Why aren't you with her?'

'Giulio and Valentina are here in London. They're staying with us.'

Thrown, Carly cleared her throat. 'Isabella must be delighted to have them stay.'

'As much as Giulio and Valentina are about spending time with her. They're spoiling her.'

Her head spun with how good it felt to hear the affection in his voice. She gritted her teeth. 'I hope they're keeping to her sleeping plan.'

'I'm insisting upon it.'

'Did you find a new nanny?'

'No. We've agreed that between the three of us we'll take care of Isabella for a while. Giulio and

Valentina are staying in London for a few months. They're renting an apartment close to us and we'll all go to Lake Como for the month of August.'

Thrown by this news, missing Isabella even more than ever now that they were talking about her, Carly asked, 'How is she?'

'She's still waking at night, but usually only once. Bedtimes are easier, and she's still addicted to reading *Sleepy Heads in Sleep World.*'

Faced with his tender voice, her anger was slipping away from her. She needed to get away. She moved onto the steps. 'It's late.'

'She misses you.'

She somehow managed not to trip on the steps at his words and made it as far as the door before she turned and admitted, 'And I miss her.'

He moved onto the first step. 'Come and see us.'

Carly winced. Did he have no understanding of just how impossible all of this was for her? Her anger surged back and, walking towards him, she demanded, 'Why haven't you called? It's been two weeks. I'd have liked to have known sooner how she was.'

'I needed some space to think.'

'About *what*?'

He hesitated for a moment before answering, 'About us.' He shrugged and added, 'You could have called us, you know.'

There was disappointment, hurt in his voice that

made her feel as if she had failed him somehow. 'I was going to call next week.'

He nodded at that but she could tell that he didn't believe her. 'There are things I need to say to you.'

Carly fumbled with her handbag, trying to locate her keys, knowing that talking would resolve nothing. 'Is there any point?'

'I've been sitting here for the past three hours so I sure hope there is.'

The hope, the solemnity etched in Max's face had her open the door and silently wait for him to follow her into the hallway, her heart pounding at the pride in his gaze as he passed her by.

Carly's apartment was on the second floor of a redbrick Georgian town house. The interior had been renovated in recent years but still retained the original ornate cornicing and fireplace in the living room. The walls were painted a soft green, an eastern-inspired rug on the varnished floorboards. The walls either side of the fireplace were covered in an array of paintings in various sizes and subjects.

He inspected them as Carly threw her handbag onto the grey linen sofa opposite the fireplace and removed her jacket.

'A family collection?' he asked, nodding to the pictures.

'No, just an addiction to car-boot sales and flea markets.'

Max smiled but inside his stomach was twisted into a hundred different nasty knots. He had been nervous outside on the street, but standing here, seeing Carly's home for the first time, his doubts were off the scale. She had a whole life without him—a job she thrived in, a beautiful home, a busy social life. What if she said no again? Was he doing the right thing? The right thing by Isabella? What if Carly said yes but six months, a year, two years down the line wanted out? Isabella would be three, four by then. How would she cope? How would he cope losing someone else he loved?

He loved Carly.

That thought galvanised him.

Carly had moved into her adjoining kitchen, filling the kettle, taking cups and glasses out of cupboards with a frenetic energy.

He held out his hand to her.

She stared at it as though it were a dangerous animal.

'Let's go and talk.'

For a moment it looked as if she was going to refuse, preferring to stay in the kitchen for the night boiling endless kettles of water instead of hearing what he wanted to say. But then with an impatient toss of her head she stalked back into the living room, where she sat on a primrose-yellow corded art deco chair and pointed him towards the sofa.

He sat as close as he could to her. Carly in response swung her knees away, while pushing herself into the furthest reaches of her chair.

*Dio!* He hadn't realised just how hard this was going to be. He rolled his shoulders, tried to release the tight tension in his throat that was making speech near impossible. His stomach was a bag of angry cats.

'When Marta died…' He paused as his voice cracked.

Carly inhaled deeply, her expression haunted. 'Max, please…'

'I want you to know everything about me. When Marta died I shut down. We had argued the night she died over Isabella not sleeping. She died when we were still angry with one another. I couldn't bear the guilt or the pain so I shut myself down to life, to the people around me. Even to my own daughter. And I was scared for Isabella, I wanted to protect her from life's unpredictability and cruelty by making her independent. But I was wrong. Being with you, all the lessons you have taught me in caring for Isabella—being open, being tender with her, the importance of reaching out to others—has taught me that isolating ourselves is not the answer. My mother wanted me to be fiercely independent but she was wrong.'

He took a deep breath to fight the lifelong certainty that to love others was to make you weak and vulnerable, a belief that he had tossed away when he met Marta only to later feel the full force of the devastation of losing her. Finally, he admitted, 'My mother was distraught when my father left us—she blamed her family for causing him to leave because they never liked him. She refused to ever speak to them again and closed us both off to the world. It was her way of coping with the pain of him leaving. I don't want to make her mistakes, to shut myself away from people who care. I want people in my life. I want you in my life.' He cleared his throat. 'I love you, Carly.'

Carly shot out of her seat. He was not going to do this to her. To tell her he loved her. To tell her lies just as Robert had.

She stood with her back to the fireplace and faced him down. 'You want a mother for Isabella.'

His expression shifted from dumbstruck to incredulous. He stood. '*Che cavolo!* Rubbish! Is that what you really think?'

He paced the room, his big body too large for her tiny living room, raking a hand through his hair. He yanked off the sports jacket he was wearing over faded jeans and flung it onto the back of the sofa. 'I… I…' He threw his hands up in disbelief. 'You don't trust me at all, do you?'

Carly shrugged, taken aback by the sadness in his voice, the disappointment in his eyes.

'Can't you see the risk I'm taking inviting

you into our lives? Isabella has already lost her mother… I've lost someone I loved.' His voice cracked; he looked away in pain, in exasperation. '*Dio*, Carly, it would be so much easier not to love you, not to run the risk of you leaving us some day. Isabella says your name all the time. Last week she mistook a woman on the street for you. She tried to climb out of her stroller to get to you. She loves you, but I am *not* looking for a mother for her, that's not why I want you in our lives.'

'Is it because you're lonely?'

Her question was received with a disbelieving bark of laughter. 'Seriously? I've fallen in love with you because I'm lonely? I'm in love with you because you're intelligent, empathetic, beautiful. You bring out the best in me, you lighten my life. *Mi fai sognare*…you make me dream. I love you because we want the same things in life…we can have a good life together.'

She was unable to make sense of everything he was saying; memories of Robert's false promises had her saying tersely, 'Your lifestyle, your money isn't important to me.'

'That's not what I meant. I want to create a family with you. You, me and Isabella. Hopefully in the future there will be more *bambini* for us to love. You're the person I want by my side through life.'

Carly closed her eyes, but she couldn't stop the tear that slid down her cheek. She liked to think she was stoic by nature, a long way from being a drama queen, so she winced when she dropped to her knees, knowing just how over the top it was, but what she had to say literally chopped her off at her knees. She flinched, trying to find the right words, her insides one mass of tumbling emotion. She was aware of Max sitting back onto the sofa, his arms resting on his legs as he leant down to watch her. She stared at the tiny circular holes punched into the soft brown leather of his shoes.

His head inched down, trying to catch her gaze. 'Carly?'

She raised her head to be embraced by a look as tender as his quietly spoken question.

'What about Marta?'

His expression fell. 'What about her?'

'Are we doing the right thing by her?' Carly paused, her heart breaking in two. 'I don't want to dishonour her, Max. It's all so sad that she died so young. It feels so wrong to take her place.'

Max joined her on the floor. His eyes were awash with tears. 'This is why I love you, Carly. You are so incredibly kind and sensitive. You constantly think of others. Marta would have really liked you.'

Carly rubbed her hand over her eyes. They felt so tired and strained from holding back the tsunami of unshed tears clogging her head.

Max reached and gently wiped at the tears that

had managed to break free. She hiccupped a little cry at his touch, the warmth of his fingertips like a warm blanket wrapping around her.

'I blamed myself for Marta's death but talking to you helped me see that I couldn't hold onto that guilt—it was serving no purpose other than to drive away those around me. That wasn't a way to honour Marta. It doesn't reflect the generous and outgoing person she was who embraced family and friends and would want me to do the same for Isabella. I've spoken to Giulio and Valentina about the night Marta died, how we had argued earlier that night. I needed them to know everything before I invited them to London.'

'How did they react?'

'Not well initially. They ended the call soon after. I didn't hear from them for two days. But then Giulio called me. He said that all couples argue, especially when trying to cope with a newborn, that it's not the fairy tale of contentment the advertisers and movies would have us believe. He said that I had been a good husband to Marta, that he was proud to call me his son-in-law.' He stopped and once again brushed his thumb lightly against her cheek. His eyes shone brightly with tenderness, with gentle understanding, with love. 'They know that I'm here tonight.'

'They do?'

He smiled at her hiccupped question. 'I told

them that I love you. They like you, Carly. They think you're good for me and Isabella.'

Startled, Carly sat back on her haunches. What must it have taken Max to tell his in-laws that he loved her. She stared into his eyes, a wonderful, glorious dawning slowly taking hold. He did love her. He really meant it.

'I loved Marta, but I love you now with all my heart. Marta will always be part of who I am, Isabella will be her legacy, but now I want to give you my heart...if you want it.'

A bubble of laughter erupted from Carly's throat. 'Of course I want your heart. That day when you arrived at my office, outside, you were upset. Something drew me to you. I wanted to know you better, to try to help. And then when we met, I just put what we had down to physical attraction. But it was deeper than that. It was an emotional connection that's hard to put into words.' Looking down, she frowned as she tried to find the right words, wanting him to know what was in her heart. 'It's like an incredible thrill yet a comfort, an ease in meeting the right person; but everything around us was so complicated. I thought I'd end up being hurt again so I tried resisting you so hard. It still feels unreal, and in truth it still scares me. Can we slow things down like you suggested in Italy?'

His hand ran against her arm, sending a thrilling warmth through her. 'Let's date for a while. I like the thought of walking you home at night, kissing you goodnight on the steps outside.'

She giggled at the mischief in his eyes. 'Will you come surfing with me?'

'Only if you promise to come and visit some of the buildings I've designed.'

Her smile widened. 'I'd love to see them. And I want to introduce you to all my friends.'

He pulled back a fraction from her, his expression sobering. 'Are you willing to become part of the Ghiraldini family?'

Carly edged away from him, the reality of entering into a relationship with Max starting to dawn on her. 'Does that mean you want to move back to Lake Como?'

His hand reached for hers. 'I'll go wherever you want to live.'

Did he really mean that? Did he see her needs as being equal to his? Was he willing to adapt to her way of life? 'So you'll stay here in London?'

He shrugged. 'If that's what you want.'

'And if I want to move to the Kent coast?'

He smiled. 'Then we'll go there and I'll design you the house of your dreams.'

Carly folded her arms, suddenly wanting to test him. 'I won't put up with you working crazy hours.'

His eyes glinted with self-satisfaction. 'Not a problem. I've been home by seven every night since we returned from Como.'

'And travel?'

'I've curtailed my business travel for now. But I do want to travel with you. I want to explore the world, live life to the full with you and Isabella at my side. And other children if they come along.'

Carly laughed at the excitement in his voice. 'But we're only dating for now.'

'You can't blame a guy for dreaming.'

Carly's heart flipped over and over again at the hope and love glittering in his green eyes. He loved her. She inhaled, trying to make sense of it all, needing him to understand the fears deep inside her, how much it hurt to be away from him. 'I've been miserable for the past two weeks. And as the days went by, I got more and more furious when you didn't call. But my anger really wasn't about you not calling, it was because I was so scared I'd never see you again. I pushed you away in Como because I couldn't face being second best in your life.'

His expression grew incredulous. 'Never! You will *never* be that. You'll always be the centre of my life.'

Carly smiled at his certainty, at the love, at the astonishing joy and security swelling inside her. 'In telling the Ghiraldinis, by everything you have said tonight, I know that I can trust you.' She paused as tears welled in her eyes again. 'I've missed you.' Her voice cracked but she continued on. 'I can be myself with you. You're supportive, you listen to me. You're never dismissive. You get me.' She paused and softly whispered, her heart aching with love, *'Ti amo.'*

*'Veramente?'*

*'Sì!'*

*'Quanto?'*

*'Mucho.'*

He threw his head back at that, his deep laughter reverberating around the room. 'That's Spanish. I think you mean *molto*…at least, I hope you are trying to say that you love me a lot.'

Carly's answer to that was to lean into him, her eyes swallowing up the happiness in his, her mouth landing on his smiling lips. He gave a moan and deepened their kiss. It was a kiss full of love and tenderness and laughter and wonder.

It was a kiss that ended with them both lying on the living-room floor, wrapped in each other's arms, smiling into each other's eyes in happiness.

'Knock! Knock!'

Max shook his head ruefully. 'Who's there?'

'Olive,' Carly replied, laughter bubbling in her throat.

'Olive who?'

'Olive you and I don't care who knows it!'

Max groaned but within seconds his mouth was on hers again. And they kissed and chatted late into the night, fighting the urge to move into Carly's bedroom, preferring instead to wait, to spend time opening their hearts ever more to one another.

# EPILOGUE

THE FOLLOWING YEAR, on a hot August day, Carly walked through the rose gardens of Villa Fiori, the heavy floral scent and view of Lake Como bright and dazzling in the fierce heat, making her head spin with even more disbelieving happiness.

Her smile grew even wider and with a laugh she picked up the long skirt of her bridal gown and began to run towards the villa's private chapel. Which wasn't easy to do in four-inch heels and thirty-degree heat.

Waiting at the door of the chapel, dressed in a tuxedo, his wide smile glorious, Max lifted Isabella up and pointed towards Carly.

'Car-lee! Car-lee!' Isabella shouted, waving her bouquet of roses she had personally selected from the rose garden before breakfast this morning, aided by a local florist.

Inside the chapel, heads turned at Isabella's call. The chapel could seat thirty. The perfect number for their wedding. The Ghiraldinis and Vittoria and her family, along with some other of Max's friends from London sat on the right-hand side of the aisle. On the left-hand side were Carly's friends and family. Her dad had even travelled from New Zealand for the occasion. Carly had been torn about whether to ask him to walk her down the aisle, but in the end had decided she wanted Max, Isabella and herself to walk together, to signify that they were about to become a family.

Her relationship with her mother and stepfamily was growing stronger. Aided by the confidence Max's love and encouragement had given her, she had spoken frankly with her mum and later with Alan about the past. It had healed some wounds and allowed them to focus on the future. And her stepsisters were seeing beyond the child who had arrived into their lives at a time when they too were struggling with all the changes in their home.

She slowed as she neared the chapel.

Suddenly she felt shy.

Max lowered Isabella, who ran and hugged Carly fiercely around her knees before running into the shadowed light of the chapel in response to her uncle Giovanni's teasing call.

Max took Carly's hand and drew her away from the chapel door and from the view of everyone inside.

'Come sei bella.'

Carly shivered at the intensity of his gaze. 'And you look very handsome.'

His fingers tracing against her cheek, he lowered

his head and whispered against her ear, 'Thank you for agreeing to be my wife.'

Her head swam at the sensual tone of his voice, at the love swirling in her heart. 'There's something you need to know.'

He reared back, worry darkening his gaze. 'What?'

She smiled. And smiled even more. Eventually she managed to say, 'I'm pregnant.'

'*Fai sul serio?*'

'Yes, seriously.'

He shook his head and smiled, his eyes alight with joy. But then his smile disappeared with a shake of his head. 'You shouldn't be running!'

'I couldn't help it, not when you were waiting for me.'

His frown shifted into a tender gaze. '*Il mio cuore è solo tua*—my heart is yours.'

Carly laid her hand on his cheek, as his hand touched against her stomach. Her heart fluttered out of her chest into the wonder and beauty of the day and she said, '*E tu mi hai rubato il cuore…* and you have stolen my heart.'

\* \* \* \* \*